The LAST
LOST GIRL

The LAST LOST GIRL

MARIA HOEY

POOLBEG
CRIMSON

Published 2017 by Crimson
an imprint of Poolbeg Press Ltd

123 Grange Hill, Baldoyle,
Dublin 13, Ireland
Email: poolbeg@poolbeg.com

1

A catalogue record for this book is available from the British Library.

ISBN 978-1-78199-8311

Printed by
CPI Cox & Wyman, UK

 www.facebook.com/poolbeg
 @PoolbegBooks

www.poolbeg.com

About the Author

Maria Hoey has been writing since she was eight years old. Her poetry has appeared in Ireland's foremost poetry publication, *Poetry Ireland*, and her poems and short stories have also appeared in various magazines. In 1999, Maria won first prize in the Swords Festival Short Story Competition. In 2010, she was runner-up in the Mslexia International Short Story Competition and was also shortlisted for the Michael McLaverty Short Story Award.

Maria was raised in Swords, Co Dublin, and has one daughter, Rebecca. She lives in Portmarnock with her husband, Dr Garrett O'Boyle.

The Last Lost Girl is her first novel.

Acknowledgements

My thanks to all the lovely people at Poolbeg, in particular Paula Campbell and my superb editor Gaye Shortland. My gratitude and love to all my family, especially my mother Mary and my father Noel who long ago taught me a love of books. My thanks also to my extended family, my friends and colleagues, all of whom have cheered me on to finish this book.

And finally, my thanks and indebtedness to my wonderfully patient and earliest readers: my husband Garrett O'Boyle, my daughter Rebecca D'Arcy and my sister Caroline Hoey-Edwards.

For Rebecca, who always believed

Chapter 1

1976

Lilly's radio is playing "Young Hearts Run Free".

Lilly is lying face down on the brown blanket. Her green bikini has a tiny frilled white skirt that flutters when the wind blows, but there isn't any wind today. Lilly's toes almost touch the glass bottle that glitters in the grass. Jacqueline can just make out the words on the bottle's greasy label – Red Lemonade – but there isn't any lemonade now, only oil mixed with vinegar to make Lilly's skin turn brown in the sun. Jacqueline closes her eyes, but the light seems to seep under her eyelids and there is no escaping the heat. Even the tar on the road is sweating – it clings to the soles of Jacqueline's white summer sandals like black chewing gum. Daddy says this is the hottest month of the hottest summer in living memory. Jacqueline supposes he means that only dead people can remember a hotter summer, but that doesn't make any sense. So many things don't make sense, like why Goretti Quinn gets to lie next to Lilly on the brown blanket when Jacqueline does not. But Lilly is my sister, Jacqueline thinks, not Goretti Quinn's. She opens her eyes. Goretti Quinn has rolled over onto her stomach. The waistband of her skirt is folded so far down that Jacqueline can almost see Goretti's bottom. Mrs Quinn won't let Goretti wear a bikini. "Big girls should wear big skirts," she says – and, looking at Goretti Quinn's thick pink thighs, Jacqueline thinks that she agrees with Mrs Quinn.

"Get us some water, Jacks, please? I'm parched."

Jacqueline is so surprised that for a moment she does not move. Lilly is smiling at her, calling her 'Jacks' and saying please. Then she jumps to her feet and runs all the way to the house.

Daddy and Gayle are at the kitchen table – Daddy is teaching Gayle how to gut fish. He looks up and smiles when Jacqueline comes in.

"What are you up to, pet?"

"Lilly needs some water – she's parched."

"Why can't she get her own water?" says Daddy. "You'd think she'd be glad to get out of the sun for five minutes. The pair of them must be roasted alive out there by now."

"Lilly is just trying to get a bit of colour – what's wrong with that?" says Jacqueline's mother, coming into the kitchen with Granny's vase full of red and white roses. She carries it the way she always does, as though, Jacqueline thinks, it were made of gold instead of glass. "Out of the way, Jacqueline. You've no idea how heavy this thing is when it's full of water."

She puts the vase on the dresser and steps back to look at the flowers, her head dipping from side to side.

"What's wrong with the colour she was born with?" Daddy gives Jacqueline a wink. "And do they have to stretch themselves out like that for the whole world to see?

That Quinn girl looks like a Mullingar heifer."

Jacqueline laughs as loudly as if she has never heard the joke before. Through the open window, she can hear Lilly's radio playing "Let Your Love Flow" and remembers why she has come in. She takes the big jug from the press, and carries it to the sink.

"That's not fair," says Jacqueline's mother. "Goretti is a perfectly nice girl."

"All the same, she's no Liz Taylor," says Daddy.

"Everyone can't be Liz Taylor, Frank. And will you stop running that tap, Jacqueline Brennan. In case you haven't noticed, there's a water shortage. When are you going to be finished with that mess, Frank? You're stinking the house out."

"We're nearly there," says Daddy. "Now, are you watching this, Gayle?"

"Yes, Daddy," says Gayle.

Jacqueline turns off the tap and carries the jug carefully across the room. She stands next to her sister. Gayle's pale-blue eyes are staring at the fish lined up on the table. Her body is stiff – exactly, Jacqueline thinks, as though she has died standing up. Her long fair plait reaches almost to her bottom. Lilly says Gayle is too old at fourteen-going-on-fifteen to be wearing her hair in a plait all the time, but Gayle says who cares, it keeps it out of her way for running.

Jacqueline looks down at the blue-bellied mackerel – they stare back from dead eyes. The Irish Times is spread across the yellow oilcloth – fish scales have fallen between the headlines like silver confetti.

BANK STRIKE TALKS TO GO AHEAD BUT SHUTDOWN LOOKS LIKELY

THREE SHOT DEAD IN PUB OUTSIDE BELFAST

"Are you watching, Gayle?" Daddy's knife slides along the length of the fish's belly. "You want to make your cut here, at the gills. Then you stick your finger in and pull gently, just a little tug, like this, to detach the gut. Now, you see that little dark vein running along the backbone? Do you see it, Gayle?"

"Yes, Daddy."

"Well, you need to scrape that right out. There you are."

Daddy holds up the knife and Jacqueline sees what looks like a thin dark worm on the glinting silver blade. Gayle's hands go to her mouth and Jacqueline wonders if she will throw up all over the table. She kind of hopes she will.

"Why do you want to learn how to gut fish, Gayle?" she asks.

Gayle does not answer and Jacqueline remembers something Lilly once said: "You're such a lick, Gayle – always trying to make Daddy notice you."

Jacqueline had not understood what Lilly meant, because Daddy notices Gayle – he notices her all the time. The china cabinet in the sitting room is full of trophies and medals that Gayle brings home from running: "Look, Daddy, look at what I won today!"

Gayle is the one he wakes first in the mornings, to go collecting mushrooms. Gayle is the one he asked to hold the ladder when he mended the roof and it is Gayle he takes with him to gather sticks for the fire. Daddy taught Gayle how to repair a bicycle puncture and how to oil the lawnmower and how to pluck a turkey. Looking at Gayle's face now, Jacqueline wonders if Gayle really likes mending punctures or plucking turkeys either.

4

Daddy slides the fish onto a plate. "There we are, all done. Give those a rinse under the tap, Gayle love. Gently does it now, don't damage the flesh."

Gayle carries the plate to the sink with outstretched arms, as though she wants to keep the fish as far away from her as possible. Daddy gathers up the newspaper, folding it over the fish heads and guts.

Jacqueline carries the jug to the back door.

"Tell Lilly her dinner won't be long," says Daddy, "and maybe she'd like to put some clothes on."

Jacqueline turns in the doorway. "What's Lilly having for her dinner?"

"She's having fish like everyone else – what do you think she's having?"

"But Lilly doesn't eat fish, Daddy."

"Of course she does. Lilly loves a bit of mackerel."

"Not any more, she doesn't," says Jacqueline. "She's a vegetarian now. She says she's never going to eat anything with a face ever again."

Daddy laughs. "Lilly a vegetarian? I'll believe it when I see it. Lilly likes her meat too much." He walks to the sink and moves Gayle aside. "Here, let me do that – you'll be there all day."

Outside in the garden it feels hotter than ever. Lilly has turned over onto her back and Jacqueline puts the jug down carefully next to her head.

"I got your water, Lilly."

"Thanks." Lilly doesn't open her eyes and Jacqueline sits down at the edge of the blanket. Lilly prods her in the back with her toes. "You can't sit there – get your own blanket."

When Jacqueline doesn't move, Goretti Quinn raises her head and says, "You heard Lilly – now, go on, scoot!"

Jacqueline feels her face going red. She gets up as slowly as she can and takes a few steps away from the blanket. Then she sits down on the grass, folds her arms, and watches them. She wishes now that she had told Lilly to get her own water. She tries to think of something clever to say that will make Lilly and Goretti Quinn sorry.

"Daddy says you have to eat a big fat mackerel for your dinner, Lilly Brennan!"

Goretti and Lilly turn their heads and look at one another, then they burst out laughing.

"Top up my back, will you, Goretti?" says Lilly.

Goretti Quinn groans, but she gets to her knees and reaches for the bottle. She pulls out the paper stopper and pours the oil and vinegar mixture into the palm of her hand. Jacqueline watches as she rubs her hands together then begins rubbing the oil into Lilly's back.

Goretti looks up and sees Jacqueline watching her. "What do you think you're looking at?" she says.

"'I'm looking at you, your eyes are blue, your face is like a kangaroo!'" says Jacqueline.

Lilly and Goretti start laughing again.

"You smell like a chip shop, Lilly Brennan," says Jacqueline.

"Do I look like I care?" says Lilly.

Jacqueline sticks out her tongue at them but nobody sees.

Lilly has stretched out her hand and is turning up the radio. "Oh, I love this song!"

"Oh, me too!" Goretti Quinn pushes the stopper into the bottle and stands it in the grass. "I hope they play it at *the festival dances. I can't wait, can you, Lilly? Did you ask your da yet?"*

"Not yet," says Lilly and begins singing along to the radio.

Goretti Quinn rubs her oily hands against her thighs, then she lies down next to Lilly again, closes her eyes and begins to sing too. Jacqueline is the only one who sees Daddy coming. His shadow falls across Lilly's back.

"For God's sake, turn that racket down, Lilly!"

Jacqueline smiles. Daddy thinks all music is a racket, unless it's Frank Sinatra or Jim Reeves.

Lilly stops singing but she does not move.

Goretti Quinn jumps up. "Hiya, Mr Brennan!" She tries to pull her skirt down but it won't go.

"Hello, Goretti," says Daddy but he does not smile.

Jacqueline knows why. Daddy wishes Lilly wouldn't hang around with Goretti Quinn so much. Daddy thinks Goretti is as thick as two short planks. She heard him say so.

"What if she is?" Jacqueline's mother said. "Not everyone can be intelligent. And Lilly likes Goretti so that's all that matters."

But Daddy said, "That's all very well, but I like to think that Lilly is just that little bit above." Daddy is always saying that the Brennans are "just that little bit above". When he says it, he puts one hand above the other like shelves. Jacqueline supposes he means that they, the Brennans, are the top shelf.

"Lilly, I asked you to turn that music down," says Daddy.

Lilly slowly reaches out and turns the silver dial. "There, are you happy now? And can you get out of the way, please, Daddy? You're blocking the sun."

"Do you not think you've had enough sun for one day?"

"I could never have too much sun," says Lilly.

Daddy, looking down at her stretched out on the blanket, scratches his head. "Well, anyway, your dinner will be ready in half an hour. I got us a nice bit of mackerel."

Jacqueline looks at Goretti Quinn as though to say: I told you so. Goretti Quinn starts to giggle.

"I don't eat fish anymore," says Lilly. "I'm a vegetarian. Daddy – please – the sun – do you mind?"

"Told you," says Jacqueline to Daddy.

Daddy opens his mouth as if he is going to say something else, but then he just turns and walks away.

Goretti watches him go. "Bye, Mr Quinn!" she calls.

Daddy does not answer.

"I think your da is lovely," says Goretti. "You should have asked him about the dances, Lilly."

"I'll ask him when the time is right," says Lilly.

"Do you think he'll let you go?" says Goretti.

"He has to let me go," says Lilly and she reaches out and turns up the radio again, just in time to hear the man say, "That was Dr Hook, and 'I'm Gonna Love You a Little Bit More'."

Chapter 2

Afterwards

He had the front door open before the car came to a stop. Jacqueline watched through the windscreen as he carefully negotiated the two shallow steps. His hair was too long and he was wearing a shabby old grey cardigan, too heavy for a fine July evening. Jacqueline was almost certain it was the same one he had worn the last time she saw him. As he came closer, Jacqueline could see that the third button down had been sewn on with bright-blue thread. She imagined him holding a needle up to the light as he struggled to thread it. She told herself that Gayle would see to it when she came home.

She got out of the car and they embraced clumsily, their lips missing one another's cheeks so that he ended up kissing her right ear. It made her smile that, like her, he had never quite got the hang of this hugging and kissing lark, every single time you saw someone. Then again, it had been a long time since she had seen him.

"You're as welcome as the flowers in May," he said, and Jacqueline smiled again.

She wondered how she could forget, every time, how

effortlessly he disarmed her. This close, she could scent the whiskey on his breath, but he smelled clean too, and under the terrible cardigan he had on a fresh shirt and cream slacks with sharp creases. His green eyes seemed cloudier than she remembered, like bloomy grapes. She noticed how the wattle under his chin wobbled when he moved, how the light shone through the pink tips of his ears like sunshine flooding through a stained-glass window. She turned away from him and went to the car. She pulled out her bag and her laptop.

"Is this all you have?" he said and took them from her, ignoring her protests. "Gayle said you'd be staying the three weeks. Gayle always stays for three weeks in July. Right up until . . . well, you know. But I suppose with your work and all . . ."

"I can work anywhere as long as I have broadband, Dad," said Jacqueline, "but that's neither here nor there. I'm here for three weeks." She saw the anxiety leave his face.

"Oh, we have the broadband alright," he said. "Gayle got it for me. Broadband, isn't that a marvellous thing?"

"Marvellous," Jacqueline agreed.

She walked behind him to the house, thinking that he looked like he might snap under the weight of her bags.

"Poor old Gayle, always trying to teach me how to use the email, but sure I can't get the hang of it at all. She's an awful woman to be spending her money on computers and the likes for me."

"She likes to keep in touch," said Jacqueline.

"She's a good girl. The things she does for me when she's home, you'd hardly believe it."

"Oh, I'd believe it," said Jacqueline, remembering the

last in a series of telephone conversations with her sister.

It had begun with an assurance: "Please don't think of this as a to-do list, Jacqueline, and I'm not suggesting for a minute that you have to do everything. I'm just telling you what I do. Are you with me?"

Jacqueline said she was with her, and Gayle began. "Well, I always like to give the place a good going-over when I'm there. To be fair, Dad does his best but it's *man*-clean if you know what I mean. He'd never think of washing the paintwork now, or a wall or anything like that. And you'll need to take down the nets – it wouldn't occur to Dad to wash a net curtain."

Listening to her sister it occurred to Jacqueline, not for the first time in her life, that she had inherited her mother's woeful housekeeping gene. It was probably just as well that her own rented house in Donegal did not have nets. She promised Gayle that she would wash the nets.

"And the heavy curtains in the sitting room need cleaning too, but they can wait until my next visit. I'll be over as soon as the baby is out of Intensive Care and Alison doesn't need me so much. I just can't leave her right now while she's still so anxious."

"How are they both?"

"They're fine. Alison is doing well and the baby is the most adorable little scrap you've ever seen. I think she looks like ... well, never mind, I know you're not a baby person, Jacqueline. So anyway, you'll need to do a good shop. Frozen vegetables – fill up the freezer with frozen vegetables – Dad would live on onions and tinned peas if you let him. Oh, and this time of the year I always check to see if he needs new underpants and vests for the winter."

"Do you really?" Jacqueline mentally baulked at the

idea of rootling through her father's underwear drawer.

"I have to," said Gayle. "He'd wear them until they fell apart if I didn't. And make sure to check the towels. There's a stack of new ones in the airing cupboard but Dad just goes on using the same old worn-out rags."

Jacqueline promised to check the towels.

"And you'll stay for the three weeks, won't you, Jacqueline? Dad will expect you to, the same as I always do, at least until after ..." Her voice trailed into silence.

"You can say it, Gayle: at least until after the anniversary. I already told you there's no problem."

"I know you did – it's just that I've always come home in July – I've never missed a year before."

"Well, except when Alison was born."

"Right, of course, except that year ... sorry, I've lost my train of thought. So you'll be able stay for three weeks ... that's great, Jacqueline."

"No problem," said Jacqueline. "I'm long overdue a trip home. I didn't make it this Christmas after all."

"Nor the Christmas before that ..."

"Well, yes, but that was because of the snow, Gayle."

"It's three years since the snow now, Jacqueline."

"It can't be."

"It is. I remember because that was my year to stay in England for Christmas, so when you couldn't make it down Dad had to go and have his Christmas dinner with Auntie Carol at the last minute. And the year after that, I came home and you were supposed to come too, but you didn't. But never mind all that!" Gayle's tone lifted a couple of notches as though to indicate that she, for one, was determined not to mind all that. "The important thing is that you'll be with him until after the ... anniversary."

Jacqueline agreed that that was the important thing.

The hall smelled of roasting meat and cabbage. "You must be starving," he said. "I got you a bit of lamb."

"A sandwich would have done, Dad."

"You'll need more than a sandwich after travelling from the wilds of Donegal, but it's probably cremated by now anyway. I was expecting you earlier."

"I'm sorry, Dad. I hope you had your own dinner?"

"Don't you worry about me." He started up the stairs. "How long did it take you anyway? Best part of four hours, I'd say."

"You can do it in three now, Dad."

"Isn't that marvellous? I must take a spin up there one of these days."

It was a time-honoured routine and Jacqueline played her part as she always did. "You should, Dad, I think you'd really like it."

On the landing, he pushed open the door ahead of them and stood aside. "There you are, I made up the bed for you."

Jacqueline blinked at the bright-green walls, the duvet with its enormous lime flowers, the green velveteen curtains. "You've had it done up," she said.

"Just a lick of paint and some new curtains. Is it a bit green?"

Jacqueline thought of her mother saying, *"Your father can only see two colours, red and green."*

She smiled. "No, it's lovely, Dad. And you took up the carpet."

"That's been done these two years now – that oul' carpet held the dirt. Right, well, get yourself settled and I'll go and get your dinner on the table."

"Thanks, Dad, I won't be long."

Jacqueline waited until she could no longer hear his footsteps on the stairs. She went out of the room again and looked at the door at the farthest end of the landing. For a brief moment, it was as though the sign was there again, written in her sister's bold hand: *STOP THE WORLD, I WANNA GET OFF!*

Jacqueline walked to the door and turned the handle. Here, too, the carpet had been taken up and the floorboards stained. Otherwise, everything was as it had been the last time she had looked: a double bed, a chest of drawers, a wardrobe, a chair. Just a room.

"It doesn't make sense to have two growing girls stuck in there together, Stella, not now when there's a room lying empty."

"Empty? How can you say it's empty when it's full of Lilly's things? All her clothes, the bed where she slept? It's Lilly's room, do you hear me, Frank? It's Lilly's room and it will be Lilly's room until the day I die."

Jacqueline's eyes went to the ceiling. Gayle had mentioned that the roof had leaked during the last heavy rainfall of winter. Jacqueline thought of all those things bundled into bags and boxes: cheesecloth tops, T-shirts and flared jeans, the shoes and the posters, the bundles of *Jackie* magazines, the schoolbooks in their flowered-wallpaper covering – all of them mildewed now, as likely as not, and smelling of damp. She shuddered and shut the door.

He was waiting for her in the kitchen, his sleeves rolled up, a tea towel over one shoulder. He had a glass of wine in his hand and he knocked it back when she came in. Behind him on the windowsill there was a whiskey glass, its bottom thinly lined with amber liquid; Jacqueline wondered where he had stashed the bottle of Jemmy. He pulled out a chair for her and she sat down; the table had been laid for one.

He poured some wine into a glass. "See what you think of this stuff – it's made in the Vatican – they say the Pope drinks it. It's not a bad drop in my opinion."

Jacqueline sat down, sipped her wine and nodded her approval. "That's grand, Dad."

"Good stuff," he said, smiling. He pulled the tea towel from his shoulder then bent down and took a plate from the oven. It was covered with a saucepan lid. "Mind now, it's red hot," he said as he set it on the table before her.

Jacqueline lifted the lid and they surveyed the ruin of lamb, cabbage and mash.

"Cremated," he said cheerfully, "and that was a grand bit of lamb. You always liked a bit of lamb."

For no reason she could clearly identify, Jacqueline felt like crying. "I'm sorry I haven't made it down for so long, Dad," she said.

"Not at all, love – sure you have your own life."

"Even so, I should make more of an effort ..."

"Don't be silly," he said. "You're here now, aren't you? Eat up your bit of dinner, or is it too dried up?"

"No, it's fine, Dad." Jacqueline smiled fiercely and picked up her knife and fork. "You went to so much trouble. And tomorrow it's my turn to make you a lovely dinner."

"No need for that." He pulled out his chair at the top of the table, next to the cooker. "But maybe one of the days we'll pop over to your mammy's grave."

"Of course, Dad," said Jacqueline.

He sat with her while she ate, topping up her glass and

his own, talking a little ramblingly, his eyes straying from time to time to the window and the garden beyond.

Afterwards, they sat in the sitting room. He opened another bottle of wine and spent a long time flicking from channel to channel until he found a film he thought she would enjoy. Before it was half over, he fell asleep in his chair by the window. Jacqueline smiled when he began to snore. It's like I never left, she thought. She looked around her, at the dull gleam of Gayle's plaques from the china cabinet in the corner of the room where the sun never reached. At the row of brass elephants marching along the mantelpiece; she was sure that Gayle would say they needed a polish. Her eyes went to the curtains – they looked fine to her, but maybe they were only "man-clean". She really must wash the nets.

When she got up to go to bed, he jolted awake.

"There you are, pet, sound as a trout."

He locked up while she went to get some water.

Starting up the stairs, she saw him standing on the wide landing, gazing through the window. He looked down at her and smiled. "Your mother always said it was bad luck to pass someone on the stairs."

Jacqueline came up and stood next to him.

"There's a moon for you now," he said, "whole as a host."

"Isn't it bad luck to look at a full moon through the glass?"

"Ah, that bad luck will get you every way you turn," he said.

"Goodnight, Dad," said Jacqueline and kissed his crinkled-paper cheek.

"Goodnight, pet," he said.

Chapter 3

1976

The Quinn kitchen smells of gravy. Regina Quinn's mother is at the cooker stirring a saucepan with a wooden spoon. Jacqueline wonders if it is the same spoon she uses for slapping the Quinns. The Quinn baby will not stop crying; it has lost its soother and is waving its short fat arms above the top of the pram. Regina says her baby brother is pop-eyed but Jacqueline cannot see its face to make sure.

Suddenly, Mrs Quinn puts down the wooden spoon, spins around three times and says: "'Please, Saint Anthony, look around – something's lost that can't be found.'" Then she goes back to stirring the gravy.

Jacqueline can hardly remember when she last tasted gravy – her mother says it is too hot to cook these days. They have "tea dinners" instead of real dinners, which means no potatoes, just cold ham, hard-boiled eggs, bread and salad. Jacqueline does not like salad and Daddy says cucumber is not even a proper food. He says he agrees with Samuel Johnson: "Cucumber should be well sliced, and dressed with pepper and vinegar, and then thrown out as good for nothing."

He says the same thing every time they have a tea dinner. The last time he said it, Jacqueline's mother told him she was sick to death of Samuel Johnson. "If I want to know what Samuel Johnson has to say, I'll read it for myself," she said.

Jacqueline has only come home with Regina so she can read The Lives of the Saints, *because Regina says it is "full of sex and stuff and people gettin' their diddies chopped off".*

"It's not 'diddies', Regina," Jacqueline told her for the millionth time. "It's 'chests'." Jacqueline is not interested in sex and stuff but Lilly and Goretti whisper and giggle about it so much she thinks she might as well find out what she can.

"Yeah, but diddies grow on your chests when you get big," Regina said. "Oh, God, Jacklean, imagine if your diddies didn't grow! Some girls' don't. I'd just die if my diddies didn't grow!"

Jacqueline decided to move away from the subject of diddies. "Can't you just borrow The Lives of the Saints *and we can read it in the orchard?"*

"No way – my ma won't let it out of the house," Regina told her. "She makes us wash our hands before we can even hold it. She'll make you wash your hands too, wait and see."

"Why do I have to wash my hands?"

"Because my ma says it's a sacred book and all about God's holy saints."

"If it's all about God's holy saints then how come there's stuff in it about sex and didd– chests?"

"I don't know, there just is," Regina told her.

The Quinn baby is getting louder and louder. Jacqueline

peeps into the pram, but his face is all scrunched up and purple with anger and his eyes are shut tight so she cannot see if they are popping or not.

"Shouldn't we try looking for the soother?" she whispers to Regina.

"No need," says Mrs Quinn. "Saint Anthony will find it, he always does."

Regina says her mother has bionic ears and Jacqueline thinks it might be true. She watches as Mrs Quinn goes over to the pram and gives it a shake.

"Hush now, Pius! Saint Anthony is looking for your soother." Pius's roars grow louder and angrier.

"How long does St Anthony usually take?" Jacqueline whispers, quieter this time.

"It depends," says Regina. "Sometimes a few minutes, sometimes hours."

"Then how do you know it's Saint Anthony at all?"

Regina shrugs. "Because my ma says so."

"That's right," says Mrs Quinn. "Saint Anthony never lets you down. Praise the Lord!"

"Praise the Lord" is one of Mrs Quinn's favourite sayings, and she has a lot of them: "The Lord is mighty" – "A whistling woman makes the Virgin Mary cry" – "When you think you're flying, it's then you're only fluttering."

Jacqueline watches Mrs Quinn sprinkle pepper into the bubbling gravy then cover it with a lid.

"Now you two wash your hands and keep an eye on the baby," she says, "and I'll go and get The Saints." She smiles at Jacqueline. "I suppose you want to read about your namesake? Though I have to admit I don't think I've ever come across a Saint Jacqueline."

She pronounces it Jack-a-lean, and Jacqueline thinks

that it would be nice if just one person would get her name right.

"I'm not called after a saint, Mrs Quinn," she says. "I'm called after Jacqueline Kennedy and my second name is Caroline, after Princess Caroline of Monaco."

"Princess Caroline of Monaco!" Mrs Quinn rolls her eyes. "Janey Mack, you're very swanky! But your mammy is all into the fashion, isn't she? I saw her the other day, all out in her figure. What I'd like to know is how she manages to keep herself looking so nice and still get her housework done."

Jacqueline opens her mouth but closes it again. How to explain to Mrs Quinn that her mother is more interested in practising her flower-arranging and listening to Glen Campbell records than doing her housework? Harder still, how to explain that housework is not something Jacqueline's mother thinks of as belonging to herself especially? In her head, Jacqueline can hear her mother's voice saying: "Five people dirty the house so five people can clean it." Somehow, Jacqueline is sure that Mrs Quinn would not understand. Mrs Quinn wears overalls and slippers and ties her hair up in scarves. She has a row of safety pins on her chest that looks to Jacqueline like some kind of badge and she smells of milk and casseroles. Jacqueline's mother wears flowery dresses and white patent-leather sandals and her skin smells of Imperial Leather soap and Tweed perfume. Something about the way that Mrs Quinn is looking at Jacqueline stops her from even trying to explain all of this.

"Make sure you two girls wash your hands properly," says Mrs Quinn. "I'll be checking them carefully."

"Yes, Ma," says Regina.

"Yes, Mrs Quinn," says Jacqueline.

"Told you," whispers Regina.

"Next time I'll bring gloves," says Jacqueline.

The Quinns' kitchen sink is so shiny that Jacqueline can almost see her face in it. The soap is smelly and yellow and it slithers from her hands under the running water, bounces off the edge of the sink and falls to the floor. Bending down to pick it up, she sees something blue under the table.

"I think I found the baby's soother!"

"Well, would you look at that!" says Mrs Quinn, coming back with a book in her hands.

She bends down and picks up the soother. She sticks it in her mouth then pulls it out and jabs it in a jar of honey that is standing open on the kitchen table. Then she shoves the soother into the baby's mouth. There is silence in the kitchen.

"Praise God," says Mrs Quinn. "Saint Anthony never fails."

That's not fair, Jacqueline thinks, Saint Anthony didn't find it, I did.

They move into the sitting room and the girls sit side by side on the sofa. Mrs Quinn leaves The Lives of the Saints open on the table before them.

The Quinns' sitting room is very neat and tidy and smells of lavender polish. In the winter, it smells of the nappies that Mrs Quinn dries on the fireguard. It is also very small – the very first time Regina brought her home, Jacqueline wondered how all fourteen Quinns could fit in it at the same time. But somehow they do, along with the baby's pram, and somehow everyone finds a place to sit. They even manage to make room for Jacqueline.

The Quinns live in a house in Beechlawns Estate.

Jacqueline thinks that maybe there was a time when beech trees grew here, but there aren't any now. The only green things to be seen are the tiny front gardens and the single cherry tree in every fifth garden. All the houses look exactly the same except for the different-coloured front doors and Jacqueline is almost certain that nobody has an orchard. Children play chase and Red Rover in the road, the girls chalk hopscotch squares on the paths and the boys go speeding past on go-carts they've made themselves from old bits of wood and rope. Lilly says she wishes she lived in Beechlawns because there is always someone to hang around with there. Jacqueline thinks she means boys.

"Will we start with Saint Dympna?" Regina leans over the book.

But Jacqueline is not thinking about Saint Dympna now. "What did your mother mean when she said my mam was all out in her figure?"

"Don't ask me." Regina is turning the pages of the book. "Here – I found it. Saint Dympna is the one that had her head cut off by her da because she wouldn't have sex with him."

"Your mother doesn't like my mother, does she?" says Jacqueline.

Regina looks up and shrugs her shoulders. "No, I don't think she does – she thinks your ma is stuck up."

Jacqueline is angry. She is angry with herself for having asked the question when she already knew the answer. She is angry with Mrs Quinn, but mostly she is angry with Regina Quinn, who never seems to understand that there are times when lying is the only thing to do. Lying comes naturally to Jacqueline, like reading or breathing, and she can never understand why Regina should be any different.

"Well, at least she's not a religious nut," she says. "That's what she calls your ma. She says only a religious nut would have twelve kids and call them all after stupid saints!"

Regina does not look annoyed at all. "Only the girls are saints – the boys are popes." She rhymes them off on her fingertips: "Peter and Stephen and John and Paul and Leo and Baby Pius. Dympna and Catherine and Veronica and Goretti and me. See, six popes and six saints."

"Well, it's still stupid," says Jacqueline. "So what else did she say about my mam?"

Regina closes The Lives of the Saints. "That she thinks she's something she's not and that she wouldn't be going around with her nose in the air if it wasn't for Maisie Day. That she –"

"What about Maisie Day?"

"My ma said if it wasn't for Maisie Day your ma and all the rest of you would be living in Beechlawns the same as we are."

"Why would we be living in Beechlawns?"

"My ma says you would, if Maisie Day hadn't left your ma and da the house in Blackberry Lane."

Jacqueline stares at Regina. She knows the story of Maisie Day. Even though nobody has ever told it to her from beginning to end, she has fitted together the pieces she has heard.

The beginning of the story she heard from Daddy, how he and her mother had met in London. Jacqueline doesn't even need to imagine this part because there are photos of her parents in the sitting room. Daddy is in a funny checked jacket and her mother is wearing a swing skirt and

23

white shoes with silver buckles. There is another photograph of them on their wedding day: Jacqueline's mother in a white dress with a wide skirt and white high-heeled shoes and Daddy in a suit with a white flower in his buttonhole.

The next part of the story Jacqueline heard from Lilly.

Lilly told her: "I was born in London but Mam didn't want me to grow up in England so we came home. At first, we lived with Nanny and Auntie Carol, but Mam and Nanny didn't get on and one day they had a big fight over the dishes and a tea towel got torn in two ..."

Jacqueline had trouble imagining her mother fighting anyone over a tea towel.

"So then Mam told Daddy that he'd better find them a place of their own or she'd pack her bags and take me and get on a plane back to London. So the next day Daddy went off on his bike. He was gone all day and when he came back in the evening, he told Mam to hop up on the crossbar because he had something to show her."

This part of the story is Daddy's again and Jacqueline has heard it so often it feels just like a memory, as though she had been there with them that day. She can almost hear the sound of the wheels on Daddy's bicycle going round and round, imagine them crushing the daisies that grow in the thin strip of grass that runs up the middle of Blackberry Lane. She can see her mother sitting on the crossbar, legs swinging, her feet in the shoes with the shining silver buckles. She can see the two of them moving slowly under the tunnel of trees, passing the gap in the hedge where in summer the yellow light spills out from the buttercup field.

The next part is Lilly's again: "And when Daddy knocked on the door and Maisie Day opened it, Mam got a fright because Maisie Day looked like an old witch with a pointy nose and chin and no teeth."

"And was she a witch, Lilly?" Jacqueline wanted to know.

"No, of course she wasn't a witch," said Lilly. "She was very kind and she gave me sweets and she kept a goat in the garden and she used to tell me that the droppings were the goat's currants."

"And then what happened, Lilly?" asked Jacqueline.

"We came here to live and we had only one room and there was no running water and no electricity."

"But we do have running water and electricity, Lilly."

"We do now, but we didn't back then. We had to use oil lamps and get water from the well in the garden, but Mam said it was better than living with Nanny and, anyway, Daddy told her it was only for a while until the Council gave us a house. But it was years before that happened and Gayle was born ..."

Jacqueline thought, I'm not in the story yet – everyone else is there except me, and she felt suddenly jealous of Lilly and Gayle who got there first and remembered the time of wells and oil lamps.

"Then Daddy got a letter from the Council, telling him we had a new house. He and Mam went to get the key, and when Mam saw the new house she burst into tears. Daddy thought it was because she was so happy – the new house had running water, an inside bathroom, three bedrooms and shiny black-and-white tiles in the hall. But Mam wasn't crying because she was happy, she was crying because she didn't want to leave the house in Blackberry Lane. Daddy said, 'But what about the bathroom and the running water?' But Mam said she would rather live in one room with no bathroom and no running water for the rest of her

life than live somewhere where there were no trees. Maisie Day heard Mam crying and that was when she said we could all stay with her if we liked. She said we could have another room and Mam could use the kitchen. And then, when Maisie Day died, Mam and Dad found out she had left the house to us, because she had no family of her own."

"What happened to the goat?" Jacqueline wanted to know.

Lilly said she didn't know what happened to the goat, Daddy didn't know either and Jacqueline's mother said she didn't remember any goat. Jacqueline could not help thinking it was a pity it was not a story in a book, because then she'd have been able to find out what had happened to the goat.

Jacqueline can hear the ticking of the clock on the Quinns' mantelpiece and, from outside, the sound of the boys and girls yelling to one another. She thinks about the house in Blackberry Lane, the sloping garden and the orchard that she loves. She wonders why it has taken her until now to realise that the place with no trees was Beechlawns. She supposes that if her mother, instead of crying, had loved the bathroom and the black-and-white tiles, she herself would probably have been quite happy living here in Beechlawns. Lilly certainly would, and the children playing outside in the street sounded very happy. She tries to imagine living here or anywhere that is not Blackberry Lane but she cannot do it. In a way she cannot explain even to herself, the place in which she lives makes her who she is. Daddy, her mother, Lilly and Gayle: they are the Brennans who live on Blackberry Lane. If they did not live there, they would be other people with other lives.

Jacqueline realises Regina is staring at her.

"I suppose you don't want to read my ma's stupid book now, do you? Is it because my ma doesn't like yours?"

Something in the sound of her voice makes Jacqueline think she might be about to cry.

"Because what does it matter?" says Regina. "Your da doesn't like my da so we're even now."

Jacqueline would like to argue, but Regina is right – Daddy says Slinky Quinn is a weasel. Jacqueline has never seen a weasel but she thinks Slinky Quinn's eyes are too small. He never remembers Jacqueline's name and once, when she met him up the river by herself, Slinky looked her up and down in a way that made her feel funny.

"If you keep this up, young Brennan," he said, "you'll be nearly as good-looking as your sister."

He did not say Lilly, but he didn't have to: everyone always meant Lilly.

"Let's start with Saint Goretti?" says Jacqueline and Regina smiles and opens The Lives of the Saints *again.*

"Yeah, that's a good one," says Regina. "She was stabbed to death by her brother because she wouldn't have sex with him."

Why, Jacqueline wonders, does everyone want to have sex with their daughters and their sisters? She smiles at the idea of Goretti Quinn with a knife stuck in her heart.

"I'm glad," she says.

"Glad that Saint Goretti wouldn't have sex with her brother?"

"Glad that she was stabbed to death," says Jacqueline.

Chapter 4

Afterwards

"You need a good haircut, Dad."

He was standing at the kitchen window and turned as she came in. The unkind morning light made the changes in him more starkly obvious, the brown patches on his face and hands, as though someone had tried to mend him with the wrong coloured wool. In the loose cardigan his body looked like bones in a grey bag.

"Is that your breakfast?" she asked.

He looked down at the whisky glass in his hand, raised it in a mute toast to Jacqueline and drank. "Can't you cut it for me?" he side-tracked her. "Gayle always does it when she's home."

"I'm not Gayle, Dad, I can't cut hair. But I'll take you into the town and you can have it done properly there. I'll ring and make an appointment somewhere."

"The barber's on the main street will do fine," he said. "But it's not that bad, is it? Can't it wait until Gayle comes home?"

"Yes, it is that bad and, no, it can't wait until Gayle comes home. She won't be here for another month at least, not until Alison's baby is out of Intensive Care and home."

"Alison's baby …" His eyes turned hazy. "Gayle tells me the poor creature is no bigger than a bag of sugar."

"So I believe," said Jacqueline. "But Alison was premature too and look how she's turned out."

"So she was, so she was," he turned his back on Jacqueline again, "but that was a long time ago. Gayle tells me she's not getting married either – Alison."

"So I gather, but I don't think she's been with the father very long."

He shook his head a little mournfully. "Sure I don't suppose it matters these days, as long as she's happy."

"No, it doesn't matter, Dad." Was Alison happy? Jacqueline had no idea. She pictured her niece as she had last seen her. She was certainly a smiler, with dark eyes and sallow skin and black curling hair.

"Little Alison, it's hard to believe."

"Not so little anymore, Dad," said Jacqueline. "She must be thirty now."

He appeared not to have heard her and raised the whisky glass again.

Jacqueline left him to his contemplation of the garden and, as she walked away, she wondered how many hours of every day he spent that way.

She drove him into the town for his haircut.

"You've changed your car," he said. "You're a great one for changing your car."

"Am I?" Off the top of her head, Jacqueline counted seven. *Four more cars than I've had men, Dad*, she thought of saying, but didn't. "That old Ford Fiesta of yours doesn't owe you anything. We should look into getting you another one."

"Don't be silly, love," he said. "I think that one will see me down."

"Now you're being silly," she said, but as they drove into the town she found herself wondering what would happen when he could no longer drive, no longer look after himself. She had never really thought of him as old before now.

She knew she had made a mistake as soon as they walked into the salon. The music was raucous and the black-clad stylists all looked like adolescents.

He looked around him with clear dismay. "Are you planning to get me a makeover or what? I told you the barber's would do me grand."

Jacqueline avoided his eye. "It's a bit trendier than I expected alright, not the way I remembered it at all. But we're here now so we might as well stay."

But she didn't stay; she waited until he had been draped in a fluorescent pink gown and bent backwards over a basin and slipped away. She told herself that this was as good a time as any to buy that underwear Gayle had gone on about, so she left the car and walked to the shopping centre on the outskirts of the town.

But there, too, the music seemed too loud and, faced with the array of men's underclothing available to her, she realised that she had not done her homework. She knew neither his size nor style. Perhaps she should have asked him: *What do you fancy when it comes to knickers, Dad?* She thought about texting Gayle but Gayle didn't really do texts – Gayle did long involved phone calls. Jacqueline's courage failed her at the thought and she abandoned the project in favour of a cup of coffee and an Apple Danish. Halfway through the pastry, her conscience pricked her: just how long did a man's haircut take? He was probably sitting there now in that awful disco salon, waiting for her. She quickly finished eating and hurried back into the town. At least she could deliver on her promise of a nice dinner. Gayle was right: a cursory inspection of the cupboards had confirmed that her father's idea of vegetables was limited to onions and tinned peas. She picked up some green beans and carrots and then headed for the butcher's.

While the steaks were being cut, an elderly man came through from the back of the shop. He was whistling but stopped abruptly when he saw Jacqueline.

"Hello, Mr Sweeney," said Jacqueline.

Everything about the man had changed, she thought, everything but those big sombre eyes. She half expected him to ask the question she had, in the past, come to dread: *Is there any word of your poor sister?*

"Back with us for a while then?" said Mr Sweeney.

Jacqueline nodded. "Just for a while, Mr Sweeney."

"Well, I see you're looking after him well." He nodded at the steaks as the young butcher bagged them.

"Doing my best, Mr Sweeney." Jacqueline paid for the meat, picked up the bag and hurried from the shop.

This, she thought, imagining the butcher's eyes on her back, this was why she stayed away.

"It's Jacqueline Brennan, isn't it?"

About to push open the bakery door, Jacqueline turned and looked into a stranger's face. The man was tall and handsome, probably somewhere in his mid-thirties, and he was smiling down at her. Jacqueline tried to place him but failed.

"You haven't a clue who I am, have you? Pius, Pius Quinn."

31

Popeye, thought Jacqueline, and she smiled involuntarily at the memory of a screaming infant waving his legs above the top of a pram. "Of course," she said, "Pius."

"Wait till I tell Regina I saw you, Jacqueline! You're looking great."

"I doubt that," said Jacqueline, but Pius was smiling at her as though he really meant it. There was no doubt, she thought, that he for his part really was looking great, and she smiled again at the miracle of one of the Quinns having turned out good-looking.

"Always thought the world of you, Regina did," said Pius. "How's the family anyway – your da keeping well?"

Jacqueline said her da was keeping well. She should, she knew, return the courtesy by asking after Pius's family, but Agnes was dead and she didn't care how Slinky was.

"Actually, my dad is waiting for me right this minute," she said, "so I'd better run. But it was nice seeing you, Pius. Bye."

In the doorway of the bakery, she looked back. Pius Quinn was standing where she had left him, smiling after her. She waved to him, then hurried into the shop and picked up the first apple tart she saw.

As she came through the salon doorway, she met her father's accusing eyes in the mirror. He shook his head and the wattle under his chin waggled from side to side.

"Are you happy now?" he said. "They've scalped me."

After she had put the food away, she went upstairs to change her shoes. She caught her reflection in the mirror on the wardrobe door and thought about Pius Quinn saying she looked well. But people said that all the time, even when it wasn't true – particularly when it wasn't true. She did it herself and she had no idea why. But overall, she decided, she didn't look too bad for forty-eight. She was neither fat nor thin, her hair was thick and healthy – the same ash-brown shade it had always been, more or less, if you ignored a little grey coming through at the temples and in the parting. She should have done her colour before coming down to Dublin. But then again, why should she? On the off-chance of running into Pius Quinn? She leaned in closer: there was a wrinkle on the bridge of her nose she was almost certain had not been there yesterday. Nose wrinkles – you didn't really expect that – around the eyes, yes, she had a few of those, but nose wrinkles? Oh well, never mind, best to focus on her good points. She had nice eyes – everyone always said she had nice eyes. She stared into her own eyes: they were bright and green as ever. There was a hair on her chin and she brushed at it but it did not move. She frowned and touched it with the tip of her finger. It felt coarse and it was dark, much darker than the hair on her head, almost black in fact, and it was growing out of her chin. It was only short now, but no doubt it would grow. Should she pluck it? She had read somewhere that after the age of forty, if you plucked your eyebrows they never grew back. But they also said that if you pulled out a grey hair from your head, two more would spring up in its place. Was that a universal law that applied to chin hair too? Jacqueline frowned. Was this how it would be from now on: wrinkles and facial hair springing up like mushrooms overnight? Another thought struck her: Pius Quinn had probably been looking at the hair on her chin when he told her she was looking well. He hadn't been admiring her, he had been trying to cover up his fascination with her chin hair. She looked at her reflection in disgust and conceded for the first and only time in her life that Mrs Quinn was right about one thing: the Brennans did care too much about their looks.

She served him his dinner in his chair by the sitting-room window. There were bald patches where his head and arms had rested over the years and he had bottomed his shape into the seat. Gayle had said: "I'm sure he never sits down at the table for his meals anymore. I've found peas down the back of that chair of his in the sitting-room, so when I'm home I make him sit at the table to eat. Make sure you do the same."

When he saw Jacqueline coming with the tray, he flung his paper aside and snatched off his reading glasses. "I'll come into the kitchen, love," he said, "and eat at the table."

"No, stay where you are, Dad – I'll bring mine in here too."

He sat back down and let her settle the tray on his knees.

"Look at that," he said when he had finished. "The sea couldn't have done a better job of cleaning that plate."

His eyes lit up when Jacqueline brought him apple tart and custard.

"I found the custard at the back of the press," she said. "I hope it's edible. I'll do a proper shop tomorrow – I promised Gayle I would."

"It's only lovely," he said, and Jacqueline found herself watching him as he devoured it. His face was intent and, after every mouthful, the slack lips closed over the spoon making a soft sucking sound, like a feasting child. His bony fingers scraped the spoon round and round the bowl, scooping up the last of the crumbs.

"That was a grand bit of apple tart," he said and Jacqueline felt her heart swell with an uncommon emotion: gratification.

Three days later, in that sagging chair that bore the shape of him, he died. The bone of his lamb cutlet was picked clean. His plate, knife and fork were on the tray in his lap. On the floor by his feet lay the TV guide, his evening viewing plan marked in red circles:

7.55 Wildlife on 2
8.55 Garden Challenge
9.35 Who Wants to Be a Millionaire?

So many times over the years, Jacqueline had come upon him in just that way, the sleep-slack face folded on the chin, the chin caved into the chest, the beer-domed belly rising and falling. So many times she had switched on the lamp at his elbow, drawn the curtains and quietly removed the dishes. But there was no doubt in her mind that this time there would be no waking for him. She knew that if she shook him, he would not blink, widen his eyes and nod at his plate, as though he had not been asleep at all, smile and say: "That was a grand bit of dinner, pet, sound as a trout."

Even so, Jacqueline bent over him, patted his arm and felt the bobbling of his grey cardigan. She shook him gently. "Daddy, wake up, Daddy."

But he did not move and the thought came to her: I'm nobody's pet now.

"But he can't be," said Gayle. "I'm only after talking to him last night."

At any other time Jacqueline would have thought it an

35

inane and foolish thing to say. But the thing she was telling herself inside her head was almost identical: I was only talking to him two hours ago, he can't be dead.

"I know it's hard to believe, Gayle," she said.

"But I can't believe it, Jacqueline. Where is he?"

"He's in the sitting room, in his chair."

"Are you with him?"

Jacqueline looked at her reflection in the hall mirror. "Yes, I'm with him."

"Stay with him, won't you, Jacqueline? I don't want him there on his own."

"Okay."

"Oh, poor Daddy, poor Daddy! Are you sure, Jacqueline? Could he not just be asleep?"

"I'm sure, Gayle," said Jacqueline even as it struck her that they had both reverted to the childish use of 'Daddy'.

"I should have been with him," said Gayle. "I should be there now. Oh God, I don't know which is worse, you there on your own with him or me stuck here and not able to see him or do anything." She began to sob.

Jacqueline sat down on the bottom stair and was quiet until the worst of the tears had abated. "Are you alright, Gayle?" she said.

"Yeah, I'm alright. Jacqueline, you know there are things that have to be done, don't you?"

"I know, Gayle, I'm just not very sure what they are."

"Don't worry," said Gayle. "I'll help you, sweetheart. Have you called anyone yet?"

"Only you," said Jacqueline.

"Right, well, you need to call Dr May – his number is in the little book beside the phone. And after that, the priest."

"Why a priest? Dad isn't religious."

"No, but he's still a Catholic – it's what you do. You should be able to find the number for the sacristy from the parish magazine. There's always one lying around."

Jacqueline found herself thinking about a passage in *Brideshead Revisited*: Lord Marchmain *in extremis*, making the Sign of the Cross. She wondered why, at all the really important moments of her life, she found herself thinking about something she had read. Surely the idea was that books should reflect the human experience and not the other way around – so why was it that what she had read always seemed more concrete to her than anything in the real world, while life seemed like a pale imitation?

"Are you listening to me, Jacqueline?"

"Yes, Gayle, you said you'll try to get a flight tonight and I'm to ring the doctor and the priest."

"And Auntie Carol, don't forget Auntie Carol. See if she can stay over with you tonight so you won't be on your own if I can't get a flight until the morning."

"Okay. Don't worry about me, Gayle."

"You're a good girl, Jacqueline," said Gayle.

It should have sounded condescending, the older sister talking to a child, but Jacqueline found it comforting.

For a while there was silence.

"Are you still there, Gayle?"

"I'm still here, Jacqueline. I know you need me to hang up now so you can do what you have to do, but I don't want to. I know it doesn't make any sense, but it feels like, as long as I stay on the phone, this isn't really happening. Like we're only talking about things, you know, phoning the doctor and where to find the number for the priest and all that stuff? But as soon as I put the phone down, I know

37

it will be real. And I don't want it to be real."

"I don't either, Gayle."

"But I'm being stupid and I know I am. I'll hang up now. Will you be alright? I'll ring you back as soon as I've organised my flight home."

"I'll be fine, Gayle, don't worry about me."

After she had phoned Dr May, Jacqueline went into the kitchen to search for the parish magazine. She found it stuffed into the vegetable rack. It had been rolled up tightly and, unfurling it, she stared at the black smudge in one corner, remembering how he had used it to swat a fly. That had been only this morning, and now he was dead. Her mind wrestled with the incomprehensible nature of things while her eye found the number of the sacristy.

The woman who answered the phone promised to send Father Tom straight away. "God grant him rest," she said.

Jacqueline wondered if she meant Father Tom or her father.

And then there was nothing else to do but wait. She went back to the room where he was and was not, and looked at him in his chair by the window. He did look like he was sleeping. She slid to the floor next to his chair and let her head fall against the armrest. She thought that it would not have surprised her if his hand had reached out and touched her hair as it used to do when she sat this way as a child – nor would it have frightened her. But his hand was quite still and impervious to her will, and Jacqueline stayed that way until they came.

Chapter 5

1976

"Wake up, Jacqueline! There's a boy in the garden with a guitar."

At first, Jacqueline cannot be sure where the voice is coming from. Then her eyes grow accustomed to the dim room and she can make out Gayle in her white nightdress, standing at the far window next to the wardrobe, looking out on the front garden.

"A boy with a guitar?" she says. "Are you sure you're not sleepwalking again, Gayle?"

"Don't be stupid, Jacqueline. If I was sleepwalking I wouldn't exactly know it, would I? And I'm telling you there's a boy in the garden."

"With a guitar. You said he had a guitar. It's the middle of the night, Gayle. What would a boy be doing in the garden with a guitar?"

"I don't know, but he's there and I should know because I'm looking straight at him."

"Okay, then tell me what he's doing."

"He's playing a guitar and singing. Can you not hear him?"

Jacqueline listens. She knows the sounds of the night-time house by heart. She hears them when she is reading her book by the light of her torch, long after everyone is asleep. She knows every creak and whine by heart – they do not frighten her. All day long, the house has to listen to the sounds of the Brennans, so Jacqueline thinks it is only fair that at night the house has its turn.

Gayle is right. There's a new sound now and it's enough to make the sleepiness dissolve. Jacqueline jumps onto her knees. Her bed is against the wall and right under the window. She pulls the curtains apart.

"Don't let him see you!" whispers Gayle, so loud that Jacqueline wonders why she bothers to whisper.

"There really is a boy with a guitar," says Jacqueline.

"I told you there was."

"But what's he doing here?"

"I think he's singing to Lilly," says Gayle.

"But why?"

"Maybe he likes her."

"Do you think Lilly knows he's there?"

"How do I know?"

"Well, I'm going to find out." Jacqueline unlatches the window and pushes it up.

The boy's voice rises from the garden.

"Don't forget to remember me ..."

Gayle giggles and hurls herself onto the bed behind Jacqueline. She is so close that Jacqueline can feel her breathing in her ear. "Can you see him, can you see him?"

"Get off me!" Jacqueline wriggles away from her sister, pushing her body further out across the windowsill. The problem with Gayle is that she does not seem to understand how much space she takes up in the world.

"*Be careful!*" hisses Gayle. "*You'll fall out!*"

"*Well, keep a hold of me then.*" Jacqueline gives a little squeal as Gayle's hands encircle the bare skin of her waist where her pyjama top has ridden up. "*Don't tickle me, Gayle! Oh, I can see Lilly – she's at her window.* Lilly! Lilly!"

"*Shut up!*" Lilly's voice is both a whisper and the crack of a whip and Jacqueline draws her head back as though she has been struck.

Maybe the boy has heard too, because he loses his place in the song and begins singing the chorus again.

"*Oh, I think it's the boy from the bus stop,*" says Gayle.

"*What boy from the bus stop?*"

"*I saw him talking to Lilly when we got off the bus from school.*"

Daddy says Jacqueline is "*the eyes and ears of the house*" but this is the first she has heard of the boy at the bus stop. If only she didn't have to wait another whole year before she can go with Lilly and Gayle to St. Teresa's Convent School.

"*How does he know where Lilly lives?*" asks Jacqueline.

"*Maybe he followed her,*" says Gayle, "*or maybe Lilly told him. Oh no, he's getting louder!*"

"*I hope Daddy doesn't hear him.*"

"*He won't hear anything in the front garden unless he comes out on the landing,*" says Gayle.

"*He might, it's very loud.*"

"*Why doesn't Lilly make him go away?*"

Jacqueline wriggles herself out a little more. "*Lilly!*" she calls, as quietly as she can. "*Gayle thinks you should make the boy go away before Daddy hears him.*"

"*I thought I told you to shut up!*" hisses Lilly. "*Go back to bed, both of you!*"

41

Jacqueline pulls her head in again and Gayle lets go of her waist.

They can hear Lilly's voice calling softly, "Luca, you'd better go away now before you wake my dad!"

"Luca," says Jacqueline. "Lilly called him Luca. How does she know his name?"

"How would I know? Oh God, I wish he'd just go! Oh no, I think Daddy's up. Quick, Jacqueline, tell Lilly that Daddy is up. I think he's going to the bathroom – he'll hear the boy."

"Lilly, Daddy's up!" Jacqueline makes her whisper as loud as a whisper can be. "He's going to the bathroom and Gayle says he's going to hear the boy."

Lilly's head disappears and Jacqueline hears the sound of her window rumbling down.

The boy has stopped singing and for a while the only sounds are the ones from the bathroom – the flushing of the toilet, the gurgling of the cistern and Gayle muttering under her breath, "Please God, please God …"

Jacqueline knows what Gayle is praying for – for the boy not to sing, for Daddy to go back to bed, for nobody to get into trouble – and she knows she should want the same things. But what she wants, what she really wants, is for SOMETHING TO HAPPEN.

"He's washing his hands," says Gayle and for no reason Jacqueline starts to giggle.

The boy begins to sing again.

"He must only know one song," says Jacqueline.

In the bathroom, the water stops running and Jacqueline hears the door open. She holds her breath and closes her eyes.

"What's going on in there – is somebody singing? Go to sleep now, girls."

Jacqueline opens her eyes and lets her breath out in a loud burst of laughing.

"Shut up, Jacqueline," says Gayle.

"Is that you, Jacqueline?" says Daddy.

The door opens and Daddy's head comes round.

"Do you know what time it is?"

The boy's voice rises from the garden.

"What in the name of ..." Daddy pushes the door wide open. He strides over to the window and pulls back the curtain. "I'll give that little blackguard something to remember alright," he says. "I'll shoot him, I'll bloody shoot him!"

"No, Daddy, don't shoot him!" Gayle jumps down from the bed and runs after him as he rushes from the room. "You'll go to jail!"

"Don't be so stupid, Gayle!" Jacqueline calls after her sister. "Daddy hasn't got a gun."

She follows them out onto the landing.

Lilly's door is shut. Jacqueline's mother comes out of her room. She is wearing a white nightdress and it barely comes down to her knees. Her hair is hanging around her shoulders and she has no make-up on her face. Jacqueline thinks it makes her look like someone else, a young girl, a stranger.

"Will everyone please stop shouting?" she says.

She goes downstairs. Jacqueline looks again at Lilly's door and then she hurries after her mother.

Jacqueline has only been to one play in her life. It was at St Teresa's Christmas concert. She remembers how, when the curtains came up, all the actors were already on the stage but nobody was moving. It is like that in the garden now.

Jacqueline's mother is standing next to Gayle. Gayle has her arm out and her hand on Daddy's shoulder. Daddy is standing looking at the boy. The boy is standing next to the magnolia tree. In the daytime, the buds of the tree remind Jacqueline of stumpy pink-white candles, but now in the darkness they give no light. The boy is holding his guitar over his head like a tennis racket or a weapon he might use to hit someone. Then the play begins.

"I said get out of here – I won't tell you again." Daddy takes a step forward and Gayle moves with him.

The boy takes a step backward and almost falls into the hedge. Jacqueline hears the sound of laughing, and when she looks up Lilly is leaning out of her bedroom window. Jacqueline thinks: Lilly is enjoying the play.

Daddy takes another step and the boy moves quickly along the hedge and makes a dart for the gate.

"He's going, Frank," says Jacqueline's mother. "Now come back inside."

"If you come back again I'll skin you alive!" Daddy yells. "Do you understand me?"

"He understands you," says Jacqueline's mother. "Now leave him and come inside."

The boy runs through the gate and disappears into the lane and Daddy runs to the gate after him. Gayle screams.

"For God's sake," says Jacqueline's mother. She follows them slowly across the garden and into the lane.

Left alone, Jacqueline looks down at her bare feet. The grass is cool and damp, and she wonders if anyone else remembered to put on shoes. She turns and looks up at the house but Lilly's window is shut and the curtains are drawn.

Daddy comes back with his arm around Gayle's

shoulders. Jacqueline can see now that he is wearing his mustard-coloured slippers. Her mother comes next and she is wearing her white fluffy mules. Only Gayle has bare feet like Jacqueline. When they are all inside, Daddy shuts the door and bolts it, top and bottom.

Jacqueline follows Gayle slowly up the stairs. The soles of her sister's feet are stained brown and Gayle is shivering, almost, Jacqueline thinks, as though she hasn't enjoyed the play one little bit.

On the landing, Daddy stops at Lilly's door and knocks. "You awake, Lilly?"

There is no answer, but Jacqueline can hear Lilly's radio playing "Midnight Train to Georgia".

Chapter 6

Afterwards

Father Tom was tall, lean, black, and very young. His movements and speech were slow and circumspect and he was deadly earnest. He explained in the gentlest of terms that, under the circumstances, there could be no administering of the Last Rites to Frank. Jacqueline sensed that she was expected to protest and, the priest's distress on the subject being clearly greater than her own, she shook her head sympathetically. Father Tom then quickly assured her that he could still pray for the forgiveness of her father's sins. "And I will ask God to graciously receive Frank into His Kingdom." Jacqueline wanted very much to tell him she thought it was all nonsense, but somehow the priest's patent sincerity made her hold her peace and she found herself thanking him instead. Things, it seemed, were a whole lot simpler for Dr May, who, once he had satisfied himself with a quick examination, quietly and without fuss signed the death certificate.

"Why did he die?" said Jacqueline. Spoken aloud the question sounded childish, even to her.

"He was old," said Dr May. "His heart just gave out."

Jacqueline nodded. She knew Dr May of old. He was short and portly and pushing seventy now; she had always liked his brusque kindness. And why should he make any bones about it? Life ends; there is no mystery.

"What happens now?" said Jacqueline. "Do I have to do something, phone someone? Mam died in the hospital and things just happened …"

"When you're good and ready," said Dr May, "I can call the undertakers for you. They will take it from there. But what about you, who do you have?"

Who did she have? "I'm alright," she said. "My sister will be here first thing in the morning. It was too late for her to catch a flight tonight."

"Poor Gayle," said Dr May. "She'll take it hard."

Of course, thought Jacqueline – he knows Gayle so much better than me.

Dr May called the undertakers on her behalf and stayed with her until they came. She found his quiet presence comforting. Father Tom stayed too, but, kind and earnest as he was, she found herself wishing he would go. Twice he said the words "mortal remains" and each time it made her flinch. He kept asking her questions too, about "Frank", his life and tastes and habits. Getting his facts straight for the funeral, thought Jacqueline, because he had never known her father in life.

But in the end she was glad of him.

"Daddy's going now, Gayle. You said to let you know when the time came."

On the other end of the phone, Gayle made a sound Jacqueline imagined might qualify as keening.

"*No, don't let him go, Jacqueline!*" she wailed. "*I don't want him to go – please don't let him go!*"

47

Glancing up, Jacqueline found the priest watching her, "My sister Gayle," she said, "she's very upset. Could you ..."

Father Tom nodded and Jacqueline got up, handed him the phone and left him to it. Outside she stood and looked at the sky. The moon was only just less than the perfect whole they had admired together a few days ago. The air was sweet with the scent of his roses and she thought of how carefully he had tended them. All those years of pruning and spraying and feeding, and now he had gone and the roses went on being beautiful without him.

When she went back inside, Father Tom was still on the phone, his head bent forward. His voice was so low and gentle that it was impossible to overhear what he was saying to Gayle. His legs were crossed at the knees and his trousers had rucked up so that Jacqueline could see his black socks. She wondered if that thing from *Father Ted* were true, that priests' socks were blacker than ordinary socks, and then she wondered if there was something wrong with the way her mind worked.

"Gayle would like to speak to you now, Jacqueline," said Father Tom and Jacqueline took the phone from him.

"I'm sorry, Jacqueline." Gayle's voice was calm and steady. "I lost control of myself for a while but I understand now that Daddy has to go. Father Tom made me feel so much better."

Jacqueline met the priest's eye. What secret did he possess to have given Gayle such comfort? And why didn't it work on her?

"Is Carol there yet?" said Gayle.

"Not yet."

"That's a pity. I think she'd have liked to see Daddy before he ... but the traffic is probably bad. But don't worry, Jacqueline, Father Tom promised me he'll stay with you until Carol comes, so you won't be on your own. And Carol will just have to go and see Daddy at the funeral home when – when he's ready."

As the tears threatened once more, Jacqueline finished the call as quickly and gently as was possible.

They carried him from the house to the hearse. It moved away so slowly that Jacqueline was able to walk behind it halfway down Blackberry Lane. She stood at the gap for the yellow field and watched until it disappeared from sight. He came on his bicycle, she thought, and he's leaving in a box. Her vision blurred and she wiped her tears with the back of her hand. When she turned, the priest was behind her. She had not heard him coming; perhaps priests had special shoes too. He walked back with her to the house but she stopped him on the steps.

"There's no need for you to stay, Father Tom. I appreciate you offering, but I want to be on my own. Please don't phone my sister – it will only worry her and I won't change my mind."

He argued gently as he followed her into the house and collected his things. He was still arguing when she closed the door on his earnest and troubled face.

Jacqueline went straight to the kitchen and took the half-full bottle of Jemmy from the cupboard under the sink. She poured a large measure into a glass and raised it: "Here's to you, Dad!" She drank it back and it caught at her throat – she had never liked the smell of whiskey, let alone the taste. She poured another glass. "And here's to me."

When the bottle was empty, she hunted until she found another full one, pushed in behind the jugs and cups on the kitchen dresser. She took it into the sitting room and drank herself into oblivion, woke with vomit in her throat and only just made it to the bathroom.

Afterwards she rinsed her mouth and staggered to her room and lay on the bed. She intended to stay only a minute, rest her eyes. When she opened them again, a blonde-haired giant was standing over her, watching her from gentle blue eyes.

He smiled at her. "Hello, Auntie Jacqueline."

"How could you, Jacqueline? Auntie Carol, for God's sake! I asked you to phone her and you let me think you had."

"I'm sorry, Gayle, I meant to, but I fell asleep."

"You mean you got blind drunk," said Gayle. "How could you forget something like that? Poor Auntie Carol – when I called her, she didn't have a clue what I was talking about. Daddy's only living sister and you didn't even bother to tell her! Can you imagine how I felt?"

Jacqueline thought she could imagine if she really tried, but her head was too painful for trying. "I said I'm sorry, don't keep going on about it."

"Fine," said Gayle. "Then tell me again what happened with Daddy."

"Ah Gayle, how many times have I told you!"

"Tell me again!" Gayle's voice was shrill and rising.

Behind her, the blonde giant who was her son Roy looked up from his phone. Jacqueline was not sure exactly how old he was – twenty or twenty-one, she thought. He had been born so many years after Alison – blonde and quiet and grave, as unlike his sister as it was possible to imagine – that Jacqueline could not remember having paid any particular attention to him. But, according to Gayle, he was very fond of his Auntie Jacqueline. Jacqueline had no idea why. When he was very small, she remembered harbouring a vague notion that Roy was a little slow. Perhaps it had something to do with her father, who had never been able to see the boy without remarking on the size of his head: "That's not natural, there's something wrong with that child. Mark my words, there's something wrong there somewhere."

At any rate, Roy's head matched his body now and for some reason Jacqueline found his silent presence comforting.

"Alright, Gayle," she said, "I'll tell you again. I made Daddy his dinner and I gave it to him in the sitting room. I wasn't very hungry so I went out for a walk."

"What time did you go out?"

"About six o'clock, I think."

"And there was no sign, nothing at all?"

"I told you there wasn't – I wouldn't have left him if there had been. He was fine, he was eating his dinner and I was only gone for about an hour. And I told you what Dr May said: Daddy's heart just gave up, Gayle, and he died, he just died."

Gayle began to cry and Roy looked up from his phone again and patted his mother's arm.

Later Jacqueline stood with him in the doorway of her father's bedroom while Gayle agonised over the choice of burial clothes. Should they go for a blazer and slacks or should they just buy him a new suit? What did Jacqueline think?

"Whatever you think, Gayle."

"I don't know." Gayle laid the dark suit out on the bed and examined it minutely. "I bought him new socks. I got them at the airport."

"That's nice," said Jacqueline. She could not think of anything else to say.

Later, in the funeral parlour, Gayle began to wail. "Oh Daddy, what have they done to your beautiful hair?"

Jacqueline looked at her father laid out against the white satin, looking like himself, but in the new suit that Gayle had finally decided must be had, and with lipstick on. His hair did look shorn.

"He needed a haircut, Gayle," she said.

Gayle put her face in her hands. "I should have been here – if only I'd come home!"

Roy said, "Don't, Mam," and Auntie Carol looked at Jacqueline and tightened her lips.

They all think it's my fault, thought Jacqueline.

In the evening Roy sat in the chair where his granddad had died, playing games on his phone.

Gayle fretted aloud about the condition of the house. "There's no way we can bring everyone back here after the funeral – we'll just have to organise food in The Shilling. They do a nice hot meal. Daddy would prefer a hot meal."

He would if he was around to enjoy it, thought Jacqueline, but she held her tongue. Levity had no place in the face of Gayle's visible grief and she wished now that she had washed the nets.

Later, when the doorbell went and Gayle hurried to answer the door, Jacqueline slipped out to the kitchen. There was an opened bottle of white wine in the fridge and she took it and a glass up to her bedroom. It was still light outside and she sat on her bed with the curtains open and finished the wine and then fell asleep.

When she woke the room was dark and the house was quiet. She checked her phone: it was just after midnight. She switched on the bedside lamp, drew the curtains and carried the empty bottle and the glass downstairs to the kitchen. She rinsed the glass and left it on the draining board and disposed of the bottle. Her head was thumping so she poured herself a glass of water and sat at the table to drink it.

"Is it alright if I get some water, Auntie Jacqueline?"

Jacqueline turned. Roy was standing in the doorway. His hair was tousled from sleep and he was dressed in a short-sleeved black T-shirt and green-and-black shorts that came down to just below his knees. His legs were pink and very hairy.

"Work away," said Jacqueline.

He came into the room and lumbered about looking for a glass. When he turned on the tap, the water spat and sprayed his clothes. He jumped back, "*Shit!*" He turned and smiled. "Sorry, Auntie Jacqueline."

The smile transformed his humdrum features into something else completely and Jacqueline smiled too.

"No worries," she said, and watched as he carried the glass carefully to the door. "Goodnight, Roy."

Roy turned. "Auntie Jacqueline, do you really live in a cave?"

Jacqueline put her glass down on the table. Perhaps her father had been right after all. "No, Roy, of course I don't live in a cave. What gave you that idea?"

"Granda told me you did, when I was little. He said you lived in Donegal, in a cave, in the middle of nowhere. He said you were a hermit crab."

"Did he now?" Jacqueline smiled, but it hurt, so she took another drink of her water. "Well, I don't. I live in a cottage. In the middle of nowhere."

"Aren't you ever afraid, living all on your own?"

Jacqueline thought about the small shut-up house with the curtains drawn. The small bedraggled garden with the grass growing too high, the wild roses and the currant bushes, and behind it all the hulking hills – and the Donegal sky. Right now it was probably raining or it had rained or was about to rain and the letterbox was probably flapping in the wind. Perhaps it had been one of those rare days when the sun shone, the sort of day when if she had been there, she'd have worked with the windows open wide, the day flooding in, yellow and smelling of warm grass. And no-one to call and disturb her, all the livelong day. Was she afraid? When she had first moved in, she had lain awake at night listening, starting at every leaf fall, every gust of wind.

"I've grown used to it," she said and thought that what she meant was that now her fears were rational, no different than those she would have in a town or a city. "There's another house just down the road and it's not a long drive to the nearest village."

"I knew you didn't really live in a cave," said Roy. "Only, you know, when you really believe something it stays with you, doesn't it, even when you know it isn't true?"

Jacqueline took another sip of water. "Yes, Roy, sometimes it does."

"And anyway, Mum explained to us that you went there on your holidays years ago and then you decided to stay because you were thinking of writing a book. Are you still writing a book, Auntie Jacqueline?"

Jacqueline looked down at her hands. Was she? "I'm still thinking about writing it," she said.

He nodded. "Goodnight, Auntie Jacqueline."

"Goodnight, Roy."

Chapter 7

1976

Lilly's radio is playing "Shake Your Booty". Jacqueline can hear them in Lilly's room laughing and singing along to the music. Jacqueline has no idea what booty is, but she wishes she could be in there with Lilly and Goretti Quinn. Instead she is outside, staring at the sign on Lilly's door: STOP THE WORLD, I WANNA GET OFF!

When Lilly first put it up Jacqueline asked her what it meant.

"It means mind your own business!" said Lilly.

But Jacqueline thinks it is her business – as long as she can remember, she has been allowed to go into Lilly's room when she likes. While Lilly read or did her homework, Jacqueline used to lie for hours on Lilly's bed, stroking the silky eiderdown and staring at the little blue flowers that grew up Lilly's walls. And sometimes Lilly let her take down the dolls that sat in a row on the windowsill and dress and undress them. But that was before Lilly started calling Jacqueline names, like Little Big Ears, Creep, Spy, Little Freak. That was before Lilly stopped caring about anything except washing her hair and whispering to

Goretti Quinn about stupid boys. Now Jacqueline has to keep out of Lilly's room while Goretti Quinn goes in to laugh and sing with Lilly, and dance and play stupid records.

Sometimes, when Lilly goes out, she forgets to lock her door. Then Jacqueline goes in and lies on the bed. The eiderdown still feels just as smooth and silky but the dolls have gone from the windowsill. The little blue flowers have gone too. The walls are painted red now and covered with posters from Jackie *magazine. Most of the posters are of the same boy. His name is David Cassidy and Lilly says she's going to marry him. Jacqueline thinks he has hair like a girl. She cannot understand why Lilly likes* Jackie – *it never has good stories like the ones in* Bunty, *just stuff about boys and hairstyles and beauty tips.*

"How to make the most of your figure! If you don't like your arms, wear bright long-sleeved tops! Choose a slimming skirt if you love your legs!"

Jacqueline does not understand why anyone would love their legs or not like their own arms. The only good things about Jackie *are the free gifts: the stickers and badges and combs and once a bracelet with a pretty blue stone.*

The song comes to an end, and Jacqueline can hear Lilly squealing, "Oh no, I've got another conker!"

"Where, where is it?" *says Goretti Quinn.* "I can't see it – you're imagining things, Lilly."

"I am not. Look, there it is, right in the middle of my chin. Don't pretend you can't see it – you can't miss it!"

Jacqueline imagines Lilly standing at her dressing table and staring at her face in the mirror. Daddy says Lilly thinks far too much about the way she looks and pride comes before a fall. Daddy says they need two bathrooms in the house, one for Lilly and one for everyone else.

"God, I look like Eddie Sexton."

Goretti Quinn squeals, "Oh God, Lilly, imagine having as many spots as Sexy Sexton!"

Lilly laughs. "Did you see that carbuncle on his forehead the other day? It looked like a third eye. And what was that white stuff he had all over it?"

"Toothpaste. I think he uses it to suck out the pus or something."

"That's disgusting," says Lilly. "And anyway it doesn't work – even his spots have spots."

They squeal with laughter.

"Did he ask you to go with him again, Lilly?"

"Yeah, he did."

"Did you say no?"

"Of course I said no! As if I'd let that long streak of paralysed piss near me!"

"Yeah – which would you rather – run a mile, suck a boil, eat a bowl of snot or kiss Sexy Sexton?"

And they burst out laughing again.

Jacqueline can hear someone thumping up the stairs and she jumps away from Lilly's door and pretends to be just going down the stairs. She knows she will be in big trouble if she's caught listening at doors again. Gayle pushes past, her face pink, her plait flying out behind her, and Jacqueline thinks that only Gayle would run in this heat. Gayle never walks when she can run.

Downstairs in the kitchen, Jacqueline picks up her book. She is reading The Riddle of the Sands. *It has a lot of fog in it and people who say things like "The dinner is execrable, and the ventilation is a farce". They spend a lot of time dredging and kedging off, and half the time*

Jacqueline cannot understand what is happening but she doesn't mind. The two things she loves doing most in the whole world are reading and cycling her bike. It is too hot to cycle now, but books are always ready and waiting. Sometimes she reads two at a time, one in the morning and the other at night and the stories jumble themselves together in her dreams.

She takes her book to the orchard and reads for a while.

She hears her mother calling her now, but does not answer. It is too hot to answer – it is too hot for anything, even reading. The air feels fat and puffy with heat and Jacqueline closes her book and puts it down. She lies back and stares up at the leaves of the twisted crab-apple tree. It is the oldest tree in the orchard and her favourite one. The leaves are green on top but pale and creamy underneath and the apples are very, very sour and quite small. But the tree does not smell sour, it smells of sugar. In the spring, the pink-and-white petals fall to the ground like crashed butterflies. Today the leaves are quite still because there is no wind at all. Jacqueline likes windy days in the orchard best of all. Then, the leaves shiver and the wind sweeps the light across the grass like a giant invisible broom. Jacqueline used to believe that the wind was a living creature, that when it wasn't blowing everything about, it slept in a cave by the sea, curled about the rocks like a grey cat's tail. That was when she was very small and believed impossible things.

From the garden, she can hear Goretti Quinn laughing and then the sound of music: Lilly's radio. It is too far away to tell what the song is, but Jacqueline imagines them spreading the blanket on the grass and lying down together. They are probably still giggling about Sexy Sexton's spots.

"I won't call you again, Jacqueline!" *her mother yells.*

Jacqueline closes her eyes. If they want her, let them come find her – everyone knows where she will be. Lilly says the orchard is too full of wasps and only uses it as a shortcut to the river and Gayle never has time for sitting down, but the orchard is Jacqueline's favourite place in the whole world. Where else can you always find something to eat, no matter what time of the year it is? First there are the Peach Melba – not peaches at all, but crisp sweet little red-and-yellow apples – then the orangey-yellow Widow's Friend and later in the year the Ardcairn Russets that Daddy says taste better when they get a bit of frost on them. Jacqueline knows exactly how far it is from the orchard to the house: she and Daddy worked it out. They used their feet and, for every step Daddy took, Jacqueline had to take three. Then, Daddy did a sum in his head and said, "Forty yards."

"Right, that's it, Jacqueline Brennan. You've missed your lunch so you can do without it now. And I'm sending Regina Quinn down to you."

Jacqueline opens her eyes. She really hopes her mother is joking. But before long she hears the sound of someone coming closer and closer – the grass is so dry it rustles like paper underfoot. Jacqueline sits up quickly and picks up her book.

"Howya, Jacklean," says Regina. "Are you coming out to play?"

"In case you're blind," says Jacqueline, "I'm already out and I'm reading."

Regina sniffs loudly. She is always catching cold and she never has a hanky so she wipes her nose with the back of her hand, leaving silver tracks like snail trails that glitter when the light catches them.

"That's alright," she says. She comes and sits down on the grass beside Jacqueline. "I'll wait for you. Oh, and your ma said I was to tell you that you're not getting any lunch today."

"I don't care," says Jacqueline.

"I'm starvin' – will I pick us some apples?"

"If you can find any," says Jacqueline. She does not want apples. Now that she has been told that she won't get any, she wants her lunch. "But if you're starving, I suppose I'd better go and get you something from the kitchen."

"Thanks, Jacklean." Regina smiles, flashing her buck teeth.

As Jacqueline walks away she can hear her sniffing.

Lilly's radio is playing "Let's Stick Together".

Jacqueline hears them before she can see them. Her mother is there too. They are sitting on the brown blanket with empty plates and glasses on the grass next to them.

Lilly is telling Goretti Quinn about the boy with the guitar. "I wouldn't mind if he could even sing – he was completely out of tune. I thought Daddy was going to kill him."

Everyone laughs, even her mother, and Jacqueline thinks about what Daddy would say if he could hear them.

"How did he know where your room was?" asks Goretti Quinn.

"I heard him, so I got up and opened the window," says Lilly, "and he saw me."

"I hope you're not encouraging him, Lilly," says her mother.

"I don't have to encourage him," says Lilly. "I saw him in the town once and he talked to me, and another day he asked me if he could walk me home. I didn't say yes and I

60

didn't say no, but he walked with me as far as the turn for Blackberry Lane. I made him go home then. What am I supposed to do? It's not my fault if he likes me."

Her mother nods her head as though she can understand that. "I remember I used to be like that."

"In the olden days," says Lilly, and Goretti Quinn bursts out laughing.

"Don't you be so cheeky, Lilly Brennan," said her mother.

"I wish I was like that," says Goretti Quinn.

"I mean it, Lilly," says her mother. "Make sure you're not encouraging that young lad or your daddy really will buy a gun." She looks up and sees Jacqueline standing there. Shading her eyes with her hand, she says, "It's too late to come looking for your lunch now, Jacqueline – the sandwiches are all gone."

"Oh, I hope I didn't eat yours, Jacqueline," Goretti says with a smile and puts a hand to her mouth quickly to hide it.

Lilly laughs out loud.

"You've no one to blame but yourself, Jacqueline," says her mother. "If I called you once, I called you six times."

"You called me three times," says Jacqueline," and you didn't tell me you were having a picnic."

"So you did hear me," says her mother. "Well, let this be a lesson to you. Maybe next time you'll come when you're called. It wasn't meant to be a picnic – Lilly said it was too hot to eat inside so we brought our sandwiches out. Now go and get yourself a glass of milk and a couple of biscuits if you're hungry."

"I'm not hungry." Jacqueline walks past them with her head in the air.

In the kitchen she stares at the greasy wrapper lying on

the table. There is a tiny scrap of meat stuck to it. Jacqueline pins it with the tip of one finger and puts it on her tongue: corned beef, her favourite. She is even more starving now. She goes to the fridge and takes the milk and fills herself a tall glass. She drinks it standing at the window, staring out at the three of them, then she puts the glass in the sink and opens the cupboard. There is half a packet of Marietta biscuits and she takes the pack and shoves it under her T-shirt.

Outside, nobody even looks up when she passes. Lilly and Goretti Quinn are stretched out on the blanket with their eyes closed. Jacqueline's mother is lying between them, her head fallen to one side and her eyes hidden beneath her sunglasses. Lilly's radio is playing "You Just Might See Me Cry".

In the orchard, Regina Quinn is crunching on an apple and she has two more in her lap. She grabs the biscuits from Jacqueline's hand and eats them two by two. Jacqueline's biscuits stick somewhere in the middle of her chest. My own mother, she thinks, my own mother let Goretti Quinn eat my corned-beef sandwiches and Lilly only laughed. I hate them, I hate them all – my mother and Goretti Quinn and I hate Lilly Brennan too.

Chapter 8

Afterwards

The last wishes of Francis Anthony Brennan took up less than a single sheet of A4 paper. Jacqueline wondered why she felt surprised that there was a will at all. Perhaps it was because her mother, who had at least had some notice, did not make one. While the solicitor talked, Jacqueline sat next to Gayle, her eyes on the square of office window that framed the sky, watching as the day turned from fair to foul. It had rained on the morning they buried him too. Auntie Carol's stilettos pierced the wet earth and left a track of dainty holes behind her. Watching her father lowered into the ground, something he had said came back to Jacqueline, "Maybe one of the days we'll take a spin up to your mother's grave." She doubted this was what he'd had in mind.

Gayle apparently saw it differently. "At least they're together again," she said, "after all this time."

Looking at her sister's face, features deformed by grief, Jacqueline could see that the notion gave her comfort. Her own mind strayed back to their mother's funeral. It had been a bright but bitterly cold day in March. The sunshine only intensified the awful yellow of the daffodils that nodded on a nearby grave and, as they had walked away, a flock of Brent geese flew overhead, the sound they made like the creaking of a thousand tree branches. Her father stood still for a moment and gazed up at them. "There they go now, away home," he said. The memory moved Jacqueline to tears, the first she had shed that day.

As she drove them from the solicitor's office to the airport, rain, relentless as Gayle's sniffing, streaked the windscreen in parallel lines. In all her life, Jacqueline had never known anyone with such an ability to cry as Gayle had; she wondered if it was a blessing or a curse. In sight of the airport, Gayle began to wail in earnest and Roy's large hand reached through from the rear seat to pat his mother on the shoulder. In the rear-view mirror, Jacqueline could see his blond head bent over his phone. Multi-tasking, she thought.

"Don't upset yourself like this, Gayle," she said.

"I can't help it," said Gayle. "It's bad enough that Dad is gone, but now I have to go and leave him behind. It's not like I can go and visit his grave tomorrow the way you can, Jacqueline."

Would she visit his grave tomorrow, Jacqueline wondered.

"And I'm leaving you too, Jacqueline, with everything to do all by yourself."

"I've told you a hundred times that I'll be fine, Gayle. Don't worry about me."

"But it isn't just the house, there's the legal stuff. And all Dad's things. I wish you had let me make a start on his clothes when I wanted to."

64

"We agreed it was too soon for that."

"I know, but there are so many other things, memorial cards to be ordered …"

"I can do that too."

"Everyone who sent a Mass card has to get one. I've made a start on a list, it's on the kitchen table, but you'll need to add on any more that arrive after I've gone. You won't forget, will you?"

"You've already told me all this. I won't forget."

"You'll need to pick a verse, and a photograph of Dad for the memorial card. Remember we had a lovely one for Mam, with the words from 'Lead, Kindly Light'? That was her favourite hymn. Dad didn't have a favourite hymn really, had he?"

"No," said Jacqueline, "but we'll think of something."

"We should have a poem. Dad liked poetry."

"Good idea," said Jacqueline.

"Jacqueline, about the house, I don't suppose you'd want to come back?"

"And live there?" Jacqueline shook her head. "I don't think so."

"No, I didn't think you would."

"You?"

"Us? Oh, God no, I could never …" Gayle turned and met Jacqueline's surprised eyes. "I mean, I don't think we could, not now. The kids' lives are in England, and there's Alison's baby now. But, all the same, I don't think I can bear to think of strangers there."

"Then don't think about it," said Jacqueline. Her voice must have sounded harsher than she intended because Roy's head jerked up suddenly. She met his eyes in the mirror and gave him a reassuring smile. She was thinking:

we won't be the Brennans of Blackberry Lane anymore.

Jacqueline hung her damp jacket on a hook behind the door. The house was silent and she realised that it was the first time she had been alone there since they took his body away. She wondered if the fact of his having died here meant the house would always be inextricably linked to his death in her mind. It had been different with her mother who had died in the hospital. Perhaps that accounted for Gayle's response to the idea of coming to live here herself. Surprising all the same – there had been something almost visceral to her reaction. Turning, she caught her reflection in the mirror. The day had changed and sunshine streaming through the stained-glass pane above the door threw a spangling of false colour across her pale face.

In the kitchen, the first thing she saw was his grey cardigan draped over the back of his chair. Jacqueline went to stand behind the chair and rested her hands on the shaggy old wool. If she closed her eyes, she could imagine she was touching his bony old shoulders. She raised the cardigan to her face, it was rich with the smell of him. Her vision blurred and she swiped at her eyes, then she put the cardigan on, pulling the bobbly wool tightly around her. She filled the kettle and, while she waited for the water to boil, twiddled the button with the blue thread. It felt loose and she wished she had taken the little time it would have needed to sew it on properly.

The water boiled and she picked up a mug and reached for a teabag. *"Them oul' teabags don't taste the same."*

Jacqueline heard him as clearly as if he were standing behind her.

"Fair enough, Dad," she said. "I'll do it the proper way

so." She put the teabag back in the box and carefully warmed the fat blue teapot; its inside was stained a rich dark brown. Jacqueline reached for the tin canister. It had been badly scratched, the lid had a small dent, but the colours seemed as rich and true as they had when she was a child. Red and gold glinted in the folds of the slender girls' kimonos in their unmoving graceful procession toward the fat ponytailed man sprawled on a mountain of cushions. When she lifted the lid and smelled the sweet pungent perfume of the tea, for no reason she could comprehend and just for a nanosecond she felt bleakly happy. She spooned the tea into the pot, poured on the water, replaced the lid and picked up the tea cosy. It was grimy and had a rent in one side and a large singe mark on the other. She wriggled it carefully over the spout of the teapot and pulled it down tight, like a mother dressing a child to go out on a frosty morning. She looked at the pot and smiled.

"How's that, Dad?" she said. "Does that meet with your approval?"

She drank the tea, sitting in his chair at the kitchen table. It was much too strong for her liking but she drank cup after cup.

The letterbox flapped, and something fell onto the hall floor. Post continued to come, addressed to him – there was a stash of it shoved in between the phone and the mirror in the hall. It would have to be opened, action taken. Things needed to be cancelled, as his life had been cancelled. She had to stop putting things off, and she would. But not just yet.

She moved into the sitting room where she picked up his reading glasses from the coffee table. She moved her fingers gently across the thick shiny frames then replaced them and picked up the book from the table next to his chair – *Daniel Deronda*. She flipped the dog-eared pages. The thought came into her head: Where are you, Dad?

She carried the book upstairs to his bedroom. The dark-stained boards creaked as she moved about in her stockinged feet. She stared around the stark room that had been his for the greater part of his adult life: at the jaded rug, the bookshelf and the bed. The bed had been stripped and the things he had left lying about had been put away, but the room still smelled of him. His bedside locker held a rolled-up tube of haemorrhoid ointment, a bottle of Syrup of Figs and the glass, that, had he died in his bed, would have held his teeth. She went to his dresser and opened a drawer. She remembered how she had baulked at the idea, yet here she was after all, rifling through his collection of underpants and long johns, his socks, his stash of cotton handkerchiefs, not ironed but folded in neat, slightly crumpled squares. Underneath, she found a tiny notebook, its shabby black covers falling apart. In it he had scribbled some telephone numbers and addresses, but mostly it was quotes written in his neat and distinctive hand, extracts from plays, Shakespearian sonnets and other poems.

The stag at eve had drunk his fill,
Where danced the moon on Monan's rill,
And deep his midnight lair had made
In lone Glenartney's hazel shade . . .

Jacqueline thought about him keeping the notebook next to him as he read, jotting down something that he liked or wanted to remember, a word he wanted to look up in a dictionary. It satisfied her in a way that nothing else had so far, as though at last, just for a moment, she might be holding a part of him in her hands. She read it through from cover to cover and then put it in the pocket of his cardigan. In the shelf in his wardrobe, she found unopened birthday and Christmas gifts: soap on a rope, aftershave, gift sets still in their unopened packages, unused ties, pyjamas, DVDs in cellophane wrappers. She thought of how he had always said to his daughters: "*You shouldn't have, love.*"

And as it turned out, perhaps they really shouldn't have.

His sagging bookshelves held the weight of Shakespeare, Walter Scott, Henry Fielding, Gerard Manley Hopkins, Anthony Trollope, Dickens, Hardy, George Elliot, Robert Frost, *The Letters of Samuel Johnson* and a couple of John le Carré's: "*I don't like that modern stuff much.*"

By modern stuff, he had meant anything later than the 19th century. Jacqueline looked about her. This was his room and these were his things but, apart from his books and some jottings in his notebook, of her father's inner life, the world uniquely fashioned by his consciousness, she had found little trace.

Chapter 9

1976

Daddy is making his dinner. The kitchen smells of fish and turnip.

The door opens and Lilly comes in. She is wearing her denim flares and a white smock top and she is in her bare feet. "Good morning, Daddy," she says. "Good morning, Jacqueline."

Jacqueline and Daddy look at one another, then Daddy looks at the clock.

"It hasn't been morning for over an hour now. And what's that muck on your face?"

Jacqueline looks at Lilly's face: she is wearing purple eye shadow and bright-pink lipstick.

"It's just a bit of make-up, Daddy."

"'Tis unnecessary and silly to gild a lily'," says Daddy.

Jacqueline waits for Lilly to roll her eyes, but Lilly is pouring cornflakes into a bowl.

"Poor Daddy," Lilly says, "I bet you wish you didn't have to go to work on such a gorgeous day."

Daddy winks at Jacqueline. "How would you know if it's a gorgeous day? You've slept the best part of it away."

Lilly smiles. "I know, I'm such a lazybones." She pulls out a chair and sits down next to Daddy at the table.

Jacqueline decides to make herself comfortable. She has only come in to get her cool pops from the fridge, but Lilly is up to something, Jacqueline just knows she is. Lilly never stays in the kitchen when Daddy is cooking. Jacqueline cannot blame her. Anything might come out of the pot when Daddy makes his own dinner: nettles, pig's trotters, sheep's brains, something's head or tongue or heart. Jacqueline's mother says Daddy has the stomach of an ox.

Jacqueline slides to the floor, feeling the delicious coolness of the fridge door through her T-shirt. She watches Daddy lifting the fish from the pan. He puts it carefully on his plate, then gets the pot and piles turnip in to a steaming mountain next to the fish. Lastly he pours the grease from the pan over the turnip. Lilly's nose wrinkles but she keeps on eating her cornflakes.

"What's the war paint in aid of anyway?" says Daddy.

"Me and Goretti are going in to the Dandelion Market to buy records."

"Goretti and I," says Daddy.

"Goretti and I." Lilly smiles again.

"How you can listen to that rubbish you call music is beyond me," says Daddy. "Which reminds me, Frankie will be on soon. Stick on the radio, Jacqueline, love."

Jacqueline looks at Lilly. Lilly hates Frankie Byrne because she plays nothing but Frank Sinatra records, but Lilly is eating her cornflakes and she is still smiling. Jacqueline gets up and turns on the radio then goes back to her place by the fridge. She bites through the plastic cover on her cool pop and sucks: strawberry ice melts on her tongue.

71

Daddy puts the pot of boiled potatoes on the table, then sits down and begins peeling them, letting the skins drop into the pot. For a while there is no sound in the kitchen except the man on the radio talking about mange and white scour and tuberculosis.

"Daddy?" *says Lilly.*

"Yes, love?"

"You know the festival is starting soon?"

"Which festival is that, Lilly?"

"You know which festival, Daddy – it's on every year."

And Jacqueline thinks: Of course Daddy knows which festival, everyone knows. The posters have been up all over town for days now. There is one on the telegraph pole at the turn for Blackberry Lane. Soon the big white marquee tent will rise up like a giant mushroom in the field behind the GAA clubhouse, and best of all the carnival will soon be there too.

"Well, what about it?" *says Daddy.*

"Is it okay if I go to some of the dances?" *says Lilly.* "Mam said I can, if you say I can."

"What dances are these now?"

Lilly puts her spoon down. "The festival dances, Daddy, the ones in the marquee. Goretti Quinn is going, everyone is going. I don't have to go to all of them, just three or maybe four ..."

"Four," *says Daddy.* "Are you sure that will be enough now? Here, love, have a bit of ray. I've far too much here." *He holds out his fork with a lump of fish on it.*

"No, thanks, Daddy." *Lilly pulls her chin back and closes her eyes.* "I'm alright – I'm having cereal."

"A bit of fish would be better for you. What about you, Jacqueline? Will you have a bit of fish, love?"

"No, thanks, Daddy, I'm having my cool pops." Jacqueline does not take her eyes from Lilly's face.

"So can I go, Daddy?"

"Why would you want to go to a carnival tent full of drunks?"

Lilly stops smiling. "It's not a carnival tent, Daddy. The carnival is separate from the dances."

"All the same it's no place for a young girl. You're best to stay clear." Daddy has picked the top side of his fish clean and Jacqueline watches him slide his knife under the big flat bone to loosen it, then lift it and drop it into the pot of potato skins.

Lilly is watching him too. "But lots of girls my age are going, Daddy," she says, "and they don't sell alcohol in the marquee."

"Maybe not," says Daddy, "but as soon as the pubs close, every drunken Tom, Dick and Harry falls into those dances. This is a grand bit of ray – are you sure you won't have some, love?"

Lilly pushes her bowl away. "I don't want any fish, Daddy. Please, can I go? Everyone else is going!"

"Not everyone," says Daddy. "You don't hear Gayle asking to go to dances in tents."

"Yeah, well, Gayle is weird – all she cares about is running," says Lilly, "and, anyway, Gayle is only fourteen and I'll be sixteen in August."

"Be that as it may," says Daddy, "there'll be plenty of time for dances when you finish school."

"But I don't finish school for another two years! What are you saying? That I'm not allowed to go to a dance for two whole years?"

"Don't be so dramatic," says Daddy. "You go to those

discos, what more do you want? And, come September, you'll be studying for your Leaving Certificate. You need to forget about dances and concentrate on your books."

"School discos!" Lilly stands up and her chair scrapes against the lino. "It's because of what that old crow Sister Agatha said, isn't it? Stupid old mickey-dodger!"

Jacqueline starts to laugh. When Daddy looks at her, she pretends she is choking on her cool pop. She knows exactly what Sister Agatha said because she overheard her mother telling Daddy. Daddy never goes to parent-teacher meetings because he cannot stand nuns. Sister Agatha said, "I'm afraid, Mrs Brennan, that Lilly has an eye for the boys. And it's a great pity because Lilly has great potential and a good head on her shoulders if she'd only use it."

"That's lovely language in front of your little sister," says Daddy, "and it has nothing to do with Sister Agatha." He stops chewing and puts down his knife and fork. He sticks his finger in his mouth, wiggles it around and pulls something out, examines it and puts it down carefully on the side of his plate. "That's a grand bit of fish," he says, "but it's very bony."

"Then why won't you let me go to the dances?" says Lilly. "All the girls in my class are allowed to go!"

Daddy picks up his fork again. "I'm not concerned with all the girls in your class, I'm concerned with you, Lilly. Now can you let me have some peace, please? I have to go to work in half an hour and I won't get out again until ten o'clock tonight."

"But, if you let me go, I'll study really hard when I go back to school in September."

"Time was," says Daddy, "when you didn't wait until you went back to school to pick up a book. What's *happened to you, Lilly? You used to be the best reader I ever met in my life."*

Jacqueline wants to shout: No, Daddy, that's not Lilly, that's me! I'm the best reader, I'm the one who loves books – Lilly only likes boys.

She sucks hard on her cool pop but her tongue tastes only water, and when she looks down all the colour has drained away and all that is left is a colourless bag of ice. Maybe, Jacqueline thinks, it's not so hard after all to understand why Gayle wants to learn how to gut fish and mend punctures.

"Please, Daddy, please can I go?"

"I said no, Lilly. I'm not having a daughter of mine hanging round in a tent full of drunks."

"But it's not fair! Everyone is allowed to go! Why not me? Why won't you let me go?"

"I've told you why, Lilly. Now can I have my dinner in peace?"

"Please, Daddy!"

"I said no, Lilly, and that's final."

Lilly rushes out and bangs the kitchen door so hard it shakes.

The woman on the radio says: "Dear Frankie, I've been keeping company with this man for ten years …"

"Why me?" says Jacqueline. "Why do I have to wash the dishes?"

"Because I said so, that's why." Jacqueline's mother is sitting at the kitchen table with both hands wrapped round her cup.

"But five people had lunch, so five people should do the washing up – that's what you always say, so –"

"Just do the dishes, Jacqueline, and don't give me any of your lip."

Lilly comes down the stairs and into the kitchen, in her green-and-white bikini and her new white flip-flops. Goretti Quinn is trailing behind her, carrying the brown blanket, two cushions and the bottle of oil and vinegar. Lilly has her transistor radio under her arm. It is switched on and a man is singing "I Love to Boogie".

Every time Jacqueline sees Lilly's radio she wants it more, but there isn't any point in asking. Her mother will say what she always does: "Lilly is fifteen – you can have one when you're a teenager."

But Jacqueline sees no reason why she shouldn't have one now. She is eleven years and eight months old and why should she have to wait until she is thirteen to have the thing she wants most in the whole wide world? If she ruled the world, anyone could have a radio the minute they wanted one.

Goretti Quinn's flip-flops are exactly the same as Lilly's. You big copycat, Jacqueline thinks, as she watches them flip-flopping across the kitchen.

At the back door, Lilly stands back to let Goretti Quinn go first. "The dirt before the brush," she says.

They go out into the sunshine laughing and Jacqueline watches them go.

Jacqueline's mother is watching them too. "Mind you don't get sunburnt!" she calls.

She gets up and goes to look at herself in the mirror on the wall. She puts her head to one side and her hand to her right cheek. Her fingers move slowly down to her chin, then up again to the corner of her eye. Then she does something to make the skin of her face tighten and the corners of her eyes tilt upwards. Jacqueline wants to look away but she cannot.

Ever since THAT night, she just can't stop watching her mother. Until THAT night, her mother was just her mother, always there, but you never really looked at her, not really. Now it is as though Jacqueline has only just realised that her mother has a body. Now she is noticing things about her mother that she never did before. Like the slow way she moves and how the shiny material of her flowery dresses sticks to her bottom. How hot she always seems to be, the sweat frizzing the short hairs round her face and neck. How she uses bits of paper and old envelopes as fans, cooling herself with quick flicking movements of her wrists.

If she could, Jacqueline would forget THAT night. She only came down for a drink of water but the sitting-room door was open. The television was on – The High Chaparral. *Jacqueline could not see it but she could hear Big John and Victoria arguing. Through the banisters she could see her mother's legs. The green basin was on the floor and she was soaking her feet in it. Her tights lay next to it like a little brown puddle on the floor. There was a hand on her mother's thigh, very brown against the white skin, with dark hairs on the wrist. The fingers were spread wide and, as Jacqueline watched, they moved as though they had a life of their own. It took her a few minutes to realise that the hand belonged to Daddy. Suddenly she wasn't thirsty anymore and she crept back upstairs very quietly. It was a long time before she could go to sleep.*

Just remembering is enough to set Jacqueline's face on fire. She runs the tap and clatters the plates together noisily in the sink.

"Mrs Quinn hasn't got a mirror in the kitchen," she says. "Mrs Quinn has a giant-sized picture of *The Last Supper.*"

"Good for Mrs Quinn," says Jacqueline's mother. "Now, can you try not to break every dish in the house, please?"

Jacqueline sticks out her tongue at the window. It makes her feel a little bit better. She tells herself that maybe her mother isn't her mother at all, that maybe she is adopted and that makes her feel even better. As long as Daddy is really her daddy, she doesn't care.

She finishes the dishes as fast as she can, then dries her hands and picks up her book from the table. The cover shows a photograph of a young girl with big dark eyes and dark ringlets. Jacqueline stares at it and wonders if maybe it is too sunny to read about a girl who had to spend summer days, just like this one, locked away in an attic. And who, after all that, still had her life stolen from her. But it wasn't only that. Reading the words of Anne Frank made Jacqueline think about her own diary and wish she could think of something clever and interesting to write. Somehow, she cannot imagine anyone ever wanting to read the stuff in her diary, which is mostly about her mother and Lilly, and Goretti Quinn and how much she hates them all. Anne Frank had a terrible life but at least she is famous – nobody will ever forget her. The thought makes Jacqueline feel guilty and, to punish herself and make it up to Anne Frank, she decides to go and sit in the orchard and read the book for at least an hour.

Lilly's radio is playing "Fool to Cry".

They are sitting on the blanket, their heads close together. Jacqueline, crouching behind a bush, is so close she can hear every word they are saying.

"It's not fair!" says Lilly. "You're allowed to go. Everyone in the world is allowed to go, except me!"

"Can't you just ask your ma?" says Goretti Quinn.

"Don't be so stupid, Goretti! What's the point? I told you what she said: I can go if my father says I can go."

"Ask him again then."

"I'm not asking him again. He'll just say no and start quoting Shakespeare at me again."

"What's Shakespeare got to do with it?"

"Ask him," says Lilly. "He's always quoting Shakespeare at me, ever since he bought me the complete works for my fourteenth birthday. I don't even like Shakespeare. I hate Shakespeare. He bought it for himself, if you ask me. The Complete Works of William Shakespeare for my birthday. Imagine!"

"Imagine!" says Goretti Quinn. "God, what are you going to do about the marquee dances, Lilly?"

"I'm going, of course," says Lilly.

"But how can you go if your da won't let you?"

"I don't know but I'll think of something – there's no way I'm missing them."

"And are you going to enter the Festival Queen Competition, Lilly?"

"I don't know, I might." Lilly shakes her head back. "Do you think I –"

"Shhhh, Lilly," says Goretti Quinn, turning around suddenly.

"Don't tell me to shhhh, Goretti Quinn! You just asked me if I was going to enter –"

"I know that," says Goretti Quinn, "but Little Big Ears is listening."

Lilly turns as Jacqueline springs up. "I'm going to kill you, you little sneak!"

As Jacqueline races up the garden, Lilly's radio is playing "Devil Woman".

Chapter 10

Afterwards

The days after the funeral took on a pattern. In the evenings, Jacqueline got drunk on red wine and fell asleep on the sofa. It was just too short for her body – her legs jutted out over the armrest and she woke stiff-necked in the small hours and stumbled to her bedroom. Most days she slept until mid-afternoon; her dreams were flamboyant, so that she woke feeling both exhilarated and exhausted as though some other, more exciting version of herself lived by night. Sometimes, in sleep, she forgot he was dead, and so he died all over again as she lay on her back staring at the square of green velveteen that held back the awful day. She tried not to think about what was happening to him, right now, this very second. When she failed, she comforted herself with the thought that it was not him in the coffin under the earth, only his "mortal remains", that he was beyond all horrors of the flesh. It was a half comfort at most but it was all she had. Sometimes she stayed like that, lying on her back in the green room for so long she would drift back into sleep and wake to find another chunk of the afternoon painlessly disposed of. Most days she neither washed nor dressed, just stayed in the T-shirt and shorts in which she had slept, his raggedy old cardigan pulled on over them. Each time she put it on she felt herself enveloped in a sense of him that was physically calming. She went downstairs and made tea in the old pot, covered it with the singed cosy and took it to the sitting room. She switched on the TV and muted the sound, programme following programme in a shifting procession of meaninglessness. People's mouths opened and closed, they talked, quarrelled, kissed, yawned, ate, laughed, cried. Their faces expressed love, disgust, hate, fear, surprise, anger, grief. Outside the birds sang and in the room the three clocks ticked away the seconds. *"There are too many clocks in this room."*

At some point, she would fall asleep and wake to find that evening had fallen on the garden beyond the windows. The clocks still ticked and the silent screen flickered and blinked. When hunger got the better of her, she went to the kitchen where the fridge and cupboards were stuffed full of the food he would never enjoy. She had no appetite for anything but toasted cheese sandwiches and digestive biscuits. After she had eaten, she left the dishes in the sink, adding to the pile day by day, then she opened a bottle of red wine and took it to the sitting room and began the cycle all over again.

On the day she found the envelope, she had woken later than usual. She'd had one of the Lilly dreams again. In it Lilly, barefoot and wearing her blue dress, was moving through a landscape that might have been drawn by a small child. The trees were black and ill-formed and shook themselves with a sound like rustling paper. Great black, ragged birds flew screeching into the air and disappeared behind a range of dark and higgledy-piggledy hills. The sound, which in the dream had startled Lilly and made her scream, always woke Jacqueline. She got out of bed and threw on his cardigan, then went downstairs. She made tea and took it into the living room and sat on the sofa thinking about the dream. Like all the other Lilly dreams, this one had changed somewhat over the years, so that now Lilly always had her back turned to Jacqueline, which meant that she could not see her sister's face. It's because I don't remember what she looks like, thought Jacqueline. She glanced round at the framed photographs on the wall – her parents on their wedding day, Gayle and herself taken years apart but dressed in almost identical white Communion dresses, two Confirmation photographs, Gayle in her Deb's dress, Jacqueline on her graduation day, Gayle with Roy in her arms ... her father on his 70th birthday.

Jacqueline put her cup down and got to her feet.

Jacqueline remembered seeing some old photographs in his drawer, the one where they had found his will, his birth certificate and life-insurance papers sealed in a brown envelope with the words "IMPORTANT DOCUMENTS" printed in biro, provoking a further torrent of tears from Gayle. "You see," she said. "He was thinking about us."

The photographs were jumbled up with old diaries, a long-expired passport, a broken comb, a ball of twine and old currency coins. None of them were of Lilly. All the same, he had kept one near him, she was sure he had. Her eyes turned to the bookshelves. One by one, she lifted up the books and shook them gently before replacing them on the shelf. Things drifted to the floor and piled there, old bus tickets and receipts, torn envelopes and betting slips, scraps torn from newspapers, a Mass card memorial to his sister – Lillian the First, the long-dead beauty whom Lilly was reputed to have favoured. From *The Complete Works of William Shakespeare* a brown envelope floated and Jacqueline bent and picked it up. It had an English stamp and had been addressed in large block capitals to Frank Brennan. She slid her finger under the flap and tipped the contents into her hand: a book of matches and a picture postcard. The matchbook cover had a black-and-white sketch of a sprawling house – Victorian, by the look of it. There was a phone number underneath and a name, *Sea Holly Villa*. Jacqueline flipped the cover – the matches were still there, pink-tipped and intact. The postcard was a scene from an English seaside town, the name scrawled in glossy red lettering across an unfeasibly blue sky. Jacqueline turned it over – it was unused. She returned the matchbook and the postcard to the envelope and replaced it inside the book.

The photograph fell from the pages of *Tess of the D'Urbervilles*. She might have known. It had always been his favourite. The photograph had been taken in the back garden. She examined it for a moment then turned it over. Someone had pencilled a date on the back: *June 1976*. She had not realised it had been taken that year. She turned it over again and looked at the three of them, longhaired and long-limbed, squinting into the sun. That summer everyone had squinted, hiding secrets behind their eyes. She moved her thumb softly across the images, Lilly outstandingly the beauty of the three, Gayle's soft-featured prettiness, even her own querulous little face stamped with the cellular beauty of the young. Her eyes went back to Lilly's eyes and she stared at them as though they might contain a clue.

She looked at the heap on the floor of the things that had fallen from the books. Her eyes strayed to *The Complete Works of Shakespeare* again and she went to the bookshelf and picked up the book. Her fingers moved over the cloth cover. The dark-blue fabric was unravelling at the spine – the thread barely held front and back together any longer. Jacqueline opened it to the flyleaf.

August 1974
This book belongs to:
Lilly Brennan
Blackberry Lane
Ballinreel
Co Dublin
Ireland
Europe
Earth
The World
The Universe
Age 14 – Happy Birthday to Me!

Jacqueline's fingers moved slowly over the loping blue-ink scrawl. She became suddenly aware of the too-loud ticking of her father's alarm clock and then, for no reason she could clearly identify she had a memory of him saying, *"There are only two unforgivable sins in this world; sleeping late in the mornings, and putting any winged creature in a cage."*

She closed her eyes for a moment and then opened them again and carried the book to the stripped bed. As she sat down, a picture came to her, of her parents rolled together in sleep, perhaps long after they would have wished it that way. She looked around her at the room where they had shared their nights for so long. There was nothing left here of her mother except the black-and-white wedding-day photograph on the wall. She imagined him lying here alone, after her mother had gone, rolling into that furrow that they had made together. She thought of Gayle saying, "They're together again after all this time," but Gayle was a comfortable person who believed comfortable things. Jacqueline wished she could believe comfortable things, but she could not. And besides, their mother had removed herself body and mind from this house and all it had come to stand for, by her own free will – why would her spirit, if spirit there was, wish to do otherwise?

Jacqueline bent over the book in her lap, opened it and let the pages fall as they would. She looked at the passage marked by a pencilled asterisk:

"The crow may bathe his coal-black wings in mire,
And unperceiv'd fly with the filth away;
But if the like the snow-white swan desire,
The stain upon his silver down will stay."

When she closed her eyes, she saw them at the kitchen table, her father with the book in his hand, Lilly frowning deeply.

"Now what do you think he was getting at there, Lilly?"

"How would I know? Maybe if he wrote in proper English, I might know what he means."

Jacqueline flipped the pages and found the envelope. She inspected it more closely. The ink of the date stamp was faded but she could make out the month and year. July 1983. She turned to the flyleaf of the book again and placed the envelope on the opposite page. She stared from the scrawling inscription to the carefully written address on the envelope; she couldn't be sure.

She dragged herself backwards on her hands until she was sitting upright against the wall to the side of the bed; it felt cool against her back and solid. She reached out and picked up the envelope. Her thumb moved in a slow circle over the faded postmark.

She stayed there until the room darkened around her and when she got up she felt stiff and chilled. She walked to the window and looked down on the moon-silvered orchard. She shivered and turned away.

"Do you remember that boy?"

"Yes, I remember him."

Jacqueline sighed into the phone. "I haven't even told you which one I mean yet, Gayle." Gayle, understanding the loneliness of unshared memories, always insisted on keeping her company – even in the past.

But Gayle surprised her. "I think I know the one you mean. Is it the boy from the carnival, the one who was in charge of the swing boats?"

Words are wizards, reassembling the past like some magic unshattering of glass, all the jagged shards rising up into the air, dancing together, reknitting the pattern of the lost thing. Jacqueline heard it, the whoosh of flying boats in the darkness. She saw a flash of Lilly's eyes, darkly glittering in the lights from the carnival as she looked down on the figure of the boy moving about below them. Saw the faded blue of his denim shirt open at the neck, showing his dark skin, saw his black hair glistening and his white teeth gleaming when he smiled. And he smiled and smiled, and the thin gold ring in his left ear shimmered and everybody was dazzled.

"Do you like him, Lilly?"

"Who?"

"Luke."

"Not Luke – Luca. He's alright."

"Because I think he likes you."

"Yeah? Big thrill!"

"Yes, he's the one," said Jacqueline. "Luca."

"Was that his name?" said Gayle. "I couldn't quite remember. Why do you ask?"

"No particular reason. Where was it he came from – can you remember?"

"God, I don't know, Jacqueline, what does –"

"It was somewhere in England," said Jacqueline, "and it was somewhere beside the sea. I remember because once, when Daddy was having a go at her, Lilly said she was going to go and live there with him and open a chip shop on the beach."

"I remember," said Gayle. "Daddy nearly went mad."

"Can you remember the name of the town?"

"Not off-hand."

"Did he go back there afterwards?"

"I don't know – I don't know what happened to him," said Gayle.

"Do you think you could find out? Maybe Goretti Quinn would know."

"She's probably forgotten, like the rest of us," said Gayle. "Why do you want to know?"

"I just do. Where is she these days, Goretti Quinn, do you know?"

"Not really – I haven't seen her in years. She moved when she got married, to Wexford or Waterford, I can't remember which. Ask Regina if you really want to know."

"I never see Regina," said Jacqueline.

"You saw her at the funeral, Jacqueline – I saw her hugging you."

"Did I? Oh right, of course." Jacqueline remembered her surprise when a middle-aged woman with hair the colour of mouse, having muttered the requisite "Sorry for your loss", had thrown her arms around her and pulled her close. Regina Quinn; she had hardly recognised her. "I don't suppose you have Regina's number, do you, Gayle?"

"No, I don't, I'm sorry."

"Let me know if you remember where it was. That town where Luca came from."

"Okay. I will. But, Jacqueline, why do you want to know? What's going on?"

"Nothing's going on." She paused. "Gayle, did Daddy ever … do you think he could have found something out and not said?"

"You mean about Lilly? Found out what?"

"I don't know. Anything."

"Why, do you?"

"No. I don't think so."

"Then why did you ask? Did he say something?"

"No, nothing."

"Then why would you think he was keeping something back?" said Gayle.

Jacqueline stared down at the postcard in her hand. "I don't. I was just thinking aloud. How's the baby getting on?"

"She's doing really well, thanks. Getting stronger all the time. Alison thinks they'll be able to bring her home in a week or so."

"That's great news."

"Yes, it is. Jacqueline, are you alright there on your own?"

"Yes, I'm fine."

"You don't sound fine. All that stuff about that boy, about Luca ..."

"I told you, Gayle, that was nothing – I was just thinking out loud."

"All the same, it didn't feel right leaving you there all on your own."

"I live on my own, Gayle" – in a cave apparently – "and you have your family to see to."

"You're my family too. I wish you'd come over here ..."

"I don't know ..."

"Will you think about it?"

"Of course."

"No, really think about it this time, because you know we'd love to have you stay with us."

There it was: the *us* that brought them again to a full stop.

Chapter 11

1976

It is Ireland's hottest day in the whole of the 20th century and Lilly Brennan is a streetwalker.

Jacqueline's mother says, "That's no way to talk about your own daughter, Frank."

"It's easy to tell you didn't see what I saw," says Daddy. "Leaning up against the church wall they were, her and that Quinn girl with a shower of rock apes swarming round them, like bluebottles round shit."

"Don't be so vulgar, Frank."

"Mam, I swear," says Lilly, "we were just talking to a few fellas. He's making it sound like a crime or something."

"I know a streetwalker when I see one," says Daddy.

"That's enough, Frank. And your daddy has every right to be annoyed with you, Lilly – you were supposed to be at Mass, not hanging around with boys."

"I was at Mass," says Lilly, "but it was scorching and I felt like I was going to faint with the heat and –"

"Don't give me any of your excuses," says Daddy.

"It's not an excuse, it's a reason," says Lilly.

"And don't give me any of your lip, either."

Lilly runs out of the kitchen and bangs the door behind her.

"You don't have to take the door off the hinges!" Jacqueline's mother yells after her. "Is it any wonder I'm always getting headaches?"

Lilly does not come down for her dinner and Jacqueline has to do the dishes.

"But it's Lilly's turn – it's not fair!"

"Lilly is upset," says Jacqueline's mother.

"Then why can't Gayle do them?"

"Gayle has to go running."

"Gayle always has to go running."

"Yes, she does, so just do the dishes and stop giving out. In the time it takes you to complain about it, you could have them done."

"No, I couldn't," says Jacqueline. "It takes ages to do the dishes and it only takes a minute to complain about it."

"Well, your minute is up. Now do the dishes and be quiet, Jacqueline."

All the time she is washing the dishes, Jacqueline is thinking about how much she hates her mother and her sisters.

She has just finished when her mother comes back. "Here's Regina come to play with you, Jacqueline."

Jacqueline and Regina Quinn stand and stare at one another.

"Are you not going out to play with Regina, Jacqueline?"

"I don't want to play," says Jacqueline. "I was going outside to read."

"Well, you can go outside and play instead," says Jacqueline's mother. "You spend your life reading. And you have a guest now."

"She's not my guest," says Jacqueline. "A guest is someone you ask to come. I didn't ask her to come. I never ask her to come."

"Jacqueline Brennan, don't you be so rude! And with poor Regina standing right in front of you. I wouldn't blame her if she decided she didn't want to play with you after all."

Jacqueline looks at Regina again. For a wonderful moment, she thinks that maybe Regina will decide she doesn't want to play, but Regina just giggles and covers her buck teeth with her hand.

"Oh, alright then, come on if you're coming," says Jacqueline.

The door opens and Lilly comes in. Her eyes are all puffed up and red.

"I did your turn at the dishes, Lilly," says Jacqueline. "So you better do mine."

"Oh shut up!" says Lilly, and flings herself into a chair.

"Why was Lilly crying?" asks Regina, as soon as they are outside.

"Because she's a streetwalker," says Jacqueline.

"Jacqueline Brennan, imagine calling your own sister a hoor!"

"I didn't call her a hoor, I called her a streetwalker. At least, Daddy did."

"Same thing," says Regina. "Why did he call her a streetwalker then?"

Jacqueline tells Regina about Lilly, Goretti, and the boys.

"Were they kissin' and stuff?" asks Regina.

"Don't be stupid, of course they weren't kissin' – they were outside the church and Lilly said they were only talking."

"But your da called her a hoor, and in the Bible hoors do sex and stuff."

"Are there hoors in the Bible?" asks Jacqueline.

"Loads of them, only they don't call them hoors – they call them Jezebel and harlots. Have you got a Bible? I'll show you."

"Somewhere," says Jacqueline. "I'll go and get it and meet you in the orchard."

In the kitchen, Lilly and her mother are sitting close together at the table. They stop talking when Jacqueline comes in.

"What do you want?" says Jacqueline's mother. "You only just went out."

"Where's the Bible?" asks Jacqueline.

"What do you want a Bible for?"

"We want to read about something, that's all."

"Books, always books," says Jacqueline's mother. "I don't know where it is – somewhere on the shelf in the sitting room, I suppose. Just make sure you put it back where you find it."

"Mrs Quinn says the Bible is sacred and should have pride of place in the house," says Jacqueline.

As the door is closing behind her, she hears Lilly saying, "Little freak."

She finds the Bible under a stack of Daddy's National Geographic – Jacqueline thinks that Mrs Quinn would not approve. She picks it up and carries it very quietly into the hall. She stands and listens but all she can hear is a man on the radio saying, "What's the recipe today, Jim?"

Her mother smiles when she comes back into the kitchen. "You found it – good girl. Now off you go and play, or whatever it is you're doing."

"Weirdo," says Lilly. "Who plays with a bible?"

"Now, Lilly," says Jacqueline's mother, and she smiles at Jacqueline again.

Jacqueline knows they are just waiting for her to go outside so they can start talking again.

In the orchard, Regina Quinn is lying on her belly under the oldest apple tree. Jacqueline lies down next to her and, while Regina looks for hoors, Jacqueline wonders what Lilly and her mother were talking about.

"Here's a bit about Jezebel," says Regina. She reads aloud slowly, her finger moving along the page from word to word. "'She painted her eyes and adorned her head.'"

"Lilly paints her eyes," says Jacqueline. "I don't think she adorns her head but she's always washing her hair. What else?"

Regina flicks through the pages but she can only find something about an adulteress. "An adulteress is the same thing as a harlot," she tells Jacqueline.

"Here, let me see," says Jacqueline. She reads aloud. "'As bitter as wormwood and sharp as a double-edged sword.' What's wormwood?"

"I don't know," says Regina. "Will I find the abominations for you?"

"What are the abominations?"

"Things you're not allowed to do, or God will smite you. Give it back and I'll find them."

Regina finds the abominations and hands the Bible back to Jacqueline. Jacqueline reads for a moment then looks up. Regina is watching her with a delighted smile on her face.

"Are there any that aren't about periods or lepers?" asks Jacqueline.

"There are lots about the things you can and can't eat," says Regina. "Keep going."

Jacqueline keeps on reading. "I've found it – there are an awful lot of things you're not allowed to eat. Listen to this – 'camels, bats, badgers, eagles, mice, hares, vultures, buzzards ...'"

Regina rolls over onto her back and closes her eyes, while Jacqueline goes on with the list.

"'Seagulls, owls, lizards, crocodiles ... something called geckos and anything that goes on its belly and most insects, unless they have 'legs above their feet'. But you can eat grasshoppers and locusts if you want to, and 'wild goats and antelopes and frogs and all clean winged things'. I like that bit – 'all clean winged things.'" But Jacqueline has had enough. "Regina, I think the Bible is a bit silly really."

"My ma would go mad if she heard you calling the Bible silly."

"Well, it is," says Jacqueline.

"And my ma is gonna kill Goretti when she hears about her missing Mass," says Regina, "and about the fellas."

"Are you going to tell on her?"

"I will unless she gives me stuff," says Regina.

Jacqueline opens her eyes and stares at Regina. Sometimes, she thinks, the most stupid people can have the best ideas.

Regina rolls onto her back too and begins to sing softly. The song is one she has made up about a nettle and a nun in a strawberry dress. It is a very silly song and it doesn't make any sense but it always makes Jacqueline smile. She listens with her eyes closed while Regina sings it over and over again in her funny high little voice. She thinks what fun Regina can be sometimes. She is glad Regina called

*today after all, but if only she wouldn't come again
tomorrow and the next day and the day after that,
expecting to do it all again. As though one day was the
same as the next and people did not wake up feeling
differently to the way they went to sleep. Because the truth
is, Jacqueline thinks, that some days she is almost happy to
see Regina standing in the porch saying "Are you comin'
out to play?" and some days she just wants to slam the
door so hard in Regina's face that it knocks out her two
buck teeth.*

*Long after Regina has to go home to mind her little
brothers, Jacqueline stays in the orchard dreaming, with
the Bible under her head as a pillow. She hears her mother
calling her name four times before she gets up. She picks up
the Bible and walks slowly up the garden to the house.*

She sees her mother standing at the kitchen door.

*"You'd better get a move on!" she calls, "if you want to
go to the carnival."*

Suddenly it is not too hot to run.

"Who's taking me to the carnival?" Jacqueline pants.

*"Lilly and Goretti, but you'd better get ready in a hurry
or they'll go without you."*

"Is Gayle coming too?"

*"No, she's just back from her running competition and
she's worn out from the heat. Now hurry up and put that
Bible back where you got it."*

*A voice is singing in Jacqueline's head: Lilly is taking me
to the carnival – not Gayle, just me. Me and Lilly. And
Goretti Quinn – but that doesn't matter because Lilly is
taking me to the carnival.*

Gayle is eating her dinner at the kitchen table.

"Lilly is taking me to the carnival," says Jacqueline.

"Rather you than me," says Gayle. "You're only going because Daddy said Lilly couldn't go without you. And she has to be home by half ten. She's absolutely RAGING."

The Bible feels suddenly heavier and, as she carries it back to the sitting room, Jacqueline mutters under her breath: "Bitter as wormwood."

Chapter 12

Afterwards

Jacqueline told herself that if she waited long enough, whoever it was would go away – they always had before. Since Gayle and Roy's departure, she had not opened the door to a single caller. She had no wish for sympathy and no intention of making tea for people she had not invited and did not welcome. Most people did not persist beyond a second push of the bell and, more often than not, she would hear the rattle of the letterbox and something dropping onto the hall floor. There was a fat clutch of them now – sympathy cards and Mass bouquets bound together with elastic bands.

But this time it seemed that whoever it was had no intention of going away.

Jacqueline, who had been standing stiffly to one side of the kitchen door, peered around the doorway and saw a face pressing itself against the coloured glass of the front door.

"*Jacklean!*" a voice called. "*It's me – Regina!*"

Jacqueline opened the door. A car was parked in the driveway and a stout little woman with large breasts, dressed in black leggings and a speckled brown blouse, was standing in the porch. "*Oh God, Jacklean, imagine if your diddies didn't grow! Some girls' don't. I'd just die if my diddies didn't grow."*

"Hi, Jacklean." Regina Quinn smiled the same old smile and began jogging on the spot, her arms folded under heavy breasts.

"Hi, Regina," said Jacqueline. How remarkable, she thought, never to have felt the need to have anything done about those teeth.

"I thought you were in alright," said Regina, "and Gayle said I was just to keep on knocking until you heard me."

Thanks a million, Gayle, thought Jacqueline. "Sorry, I was in the garden. When were you talking to Gayle?"

"She rang me yesterday – she got my number from Ann-Marie Nugent. God, it's got very blowy, hasn't it?" Regina peered over Jacqueline's shoulder into the hall behind her. "And it was lovely earlier."

Jacqueline ignored the hint. "Ann-Marie Nugent?"

"Yeah, you remember Ann-Marie Nugent – Gayle's best friend?"

"Oh, that Ann-Marie – are they still in touch?" Jacqueline wondered why it always surprised her that friendships should endure over the course of a lifetime – other people's friendships at least.

"Don't ask me where Ann-Marie got it though," said Regina. "I hardly ever see her. From Margaret O'Sullivan probably, or it might have been Pauline Fitzsimons. No, come to think of it, it was probably Eileen Delaney. Then again it could have been Irene Casey."

Jacqueline frowned at the tangle of names. "You said Gayle rang you?"

Regina nodded. "I think she's a bit worried about you, here on your own and all."

"There's nothing for her to worry about," said Jacqueline. "So were you able to get in touch with Goretti?"

"Goretti?" Regina frowned and stopped jigging for a moment.

Jacqueline sighed. "Gayle was supposed to see if you could find something out for me, from Goretti. She didn't say anything to you?"

"No, just that she was worried about you ..."

"On my own and all, I know," said Jacqueline. "Well, like I said, I'm fine."

"I could ring her for you, if you like," said Regina.

"Ring who?"

"Goretti – if you want to ask her something?"

"What, now?"

"Sure." Regina reached into her back pocket and pulled out her phone. "Give us a second."

Jacqueline watched while she dialled.

"Here, it's ringing," said Regina. "Do you want to talk to her yourself?"

She held out the phone but Jacqueline shook her head. "Just ask her if she remembers the name of the town that boy Luca came from – Luca, the boy from the carnival."

Regina's eyes widened. "You mean the one that Lilly ...?"

"Yes, that one."

"Hi, Goretti," Regina said into the phone. "Hold on a second, will you?" She put her hand over the phone and hissed at Jacqueline, "Okay, I'll ask her. I'll just ..." She began to edge away from the porch.

Jacqueline stepped back a few steps into the hall until she was out of earshot of Regina's conversation with her sister and waited.

"Jacqueline!"

"Yes, I'm here." Jacqueline hurried to the door.

"Goretti says hi."

"Hi to her too. Was she able to remember?"

"Yeah, but it's not an address – it's just the name of the town – that's all she has."

"That's all I want – what is it?"

"Coldhope-on-Sea. She has no idea whereabouts in England it is."

Jacqueline nodded – well, there it was. She scribbled it quickly on the pad beside the phone, tore off the sheet and stuffed it into the pocket of the grey cardigan.

"Thanks, Regina, I appreciate it."

"No problem. I hope it helps." Regina folded her arms under her breasts and began to jog on the spot again.

"Thanks again, and for taking the trouble to come over and check on me," said Jacqueline.

"Right." Regina looked into the hall again, then down at her shoes, the way Jacqueline remembered her doing as a child. "Well, I suppose I'd better be off."

"Okay. Well, bye, Regina." Jacqueline made to close the door.

"Is everything alright, Jacklean?"

"Everything is fine, Regina."

"It's just with you asking about that boy from the carnival ..."

"It's nothing important, Regina," Jacqueline patted the pocket that held the piece of paper, "but thanks for this. Like I said, I appreciate it."

"Okay. Bye then, Jacklean. Mind yourself."

"You too." Then, watching Regina walking away, an impulse took hold of her and she called after her, "Regina, hang on a second!"

Regina turned quickly and Jacqueline stepped out into the porch.

"Can I ask you something?" she said.

"Sure."

"All those years ago, when we were kids, why did you want to be my friend?"

Regina smiled broadly. "Because I liked you, Jacklean."

"But why did you like me?"

"Oh God, I don't know." Regina rolled her eyes. "Because you were nice to me, I suppose."

Jacqueline frowned. "Was I? Are you sure about that? I seem to remember ..."

Regina shook her head. "No, you were, really. All those times I used to come around here, annoying you, when all you really wanted to do was to read your books. I kept waiting for you to tell me to go away, but you never did."

Jacqueline nodded. "Okay. Thanks, Regina. Sorry, it was a stupid thing to ask. I just wanted to know."

"Jacklean – about Lilly – when I asked about her just there, I wasn't being nosy. It's just that I always wonder – everyone does."

Jacqueline folded her own arms across her heart. "I know they do, Regina, but there's nothing, nothing at all."

Regina looked down at her feet again. "It's just, with Lilly, well, no-one ever thought she'd have an ordinary life, not like the rest of us. But that, nobody expected that."

"No, nobody expected that," said Jacqueline.

"Right," said Regina. "Well, I suppose I'd really better be ..."

"What about you, Regina?" said Jacqueline. "Are you happy?" She had a sudden uncomfortable memory of a wedding invitation she had declined. "You got married, didn't you?"

102

Regina smiled so widely that Jacqueline could see the dark amalgam in her lower molars. "A farmer," she said. "Can you believe it, Jacklean? Me, a farmer's wife?"

Jacqueline found herself smiling too. "And ...?" She thought she remembered Gayle gabbing about children.

"Five boys." Regina's impossible smile widened.

Jacqueline shook her head in wonderment. "And you're happy, I can see you are. I'm glad." She realised that she meant it. "You deserve to be happy, Regina."

"So do you, Jacklean."

Jacqueline had no answer to that.

"Right, well, I'll see you so," said Regina. "You take care of yourself, Jacklean."

Jacqueline said she would take care of herself. She stayed watching while Regina climbed into a dark-blue, mud-spattered Toyota Verso. You should have been kinder to that little girl, she told herself. Not for the first time she had the conviction that if, after all, there turned out to be a heaven, it would not be the big sins that kept the likes of her out, but the little failures in charity and kindness: the small daily sins of omission.

Regina waved as she drove away and Jacqueline waved back.

She walked slowly back to the house and closed the door behind her. She stood in the hall, pulled the piece of paper from her pocket and read what she had written. Coldhope-on-Sea. As she walked to the kitchen to make herself a pot of tea, she was humming a song under her breath:

"The nettle and nun in a strawberry dress
Ran down the hill and started to mess.
The sun went in and the rain came down,

103

'Mercy me,' said the nun with a frown.
'We will certainly drown.'"

On the silent television screen, a spectacularly ugly man dressed in army surplus was catching fish with a spear he had fashioned from a tree branch. Jacqueline watched him gut the fish on a stone, cook it on a makeshift spit over an open fire, then eat it with his fingers. He was succeeded on the screen by a group of women in a marquee. They were erecting conical structures made out of hundreds of little choux pastries all held together by caramelised sugar. It seemed to Jacqueline a treacherous process in which fingers got burned and tears were shed. What fascinated her were the expressions of all these people, the naked bliss on the man's craggy face as he devoured the fish, the look of total absorption in the eyes of the women as they sweated and agonised over their towers of cakes. It was almost, she thought, as if it all mattered.

How, Jacqueline wondered, do I become one of them? How do I stop being the person lying on the sofa watching? How do I get one of those lives?

She pulled the envelope from the pocket of his cardigan and examined the contents again, letting her thumb move over the smooth surface of the postcard, the little raised sketch of the house. Then she took out the matchbook, put it on her knee, picked up her phone and dialled the number printed under the sketch. She listened to the recorded message: *invalid number*. That was that then.

She went into the kitchen and began making tea. In the act of pouring water into the teapot she put the kettle down, picked up her phone again and googled Sea Holly Villa. There were a few results but none of them in the right area. She made the tea and took it into the sitting room but, before she drank it, she googled the number for UK directory enquiries, then dialled it. As she had guessed, the area code on the matchbook had long since changed, but the operator confirmed that the local number was a working one. Jacqueline thanked her and hung up and drank her tea.

The first time she tried the new number it rang out. She tried it again half an hour later and, just as she was about to hang up, a cool unhurried voice answered. "Yes?"

Jacqueline jumped to her feet. "Hello, is that Sea Holly Villa?"

"Yes."

Jacqueline realised she did not know what she wanted to say. "Are you – is this a guesthouse?"

There was a long silence, then a sound that might have been a sigh. "Yes."

There was another long silence which the woman on the other end made no attempt to end.

"Okay then," said Jacqueline. "Thank you. Goodbye."

She hung up and looked at her reflection in the door of the china cabinet. "You're a fool," she told herself. Her eyes stared back at her. People always said she had his eyes. An image came to her of him laid out in his coffin, dressed in his new suit, his shorn head slick with Brylcreme. Grief tore at her heart like a claw.

She drank less than usual that evening and went to bed properly, undressing and brushing her teeth. She fell asleep easily but woke in the night, startled and sure that some particular sound had disturbed her. She sat up and listened, but the house had done its talking and was quiet; if there had been a sound, it had come from outside. She got out of bed and crossed to the window, pulled the heavy green curtain aside and looked out on a clear starry night. There was no wind and the garden was dark and still. All that was left of her father's moon was a thin, translucent fingernail clipping. She dropped the curtain and went back to her bed.

She thought about Regina Quinn. She hoped there was an orchard on that farm of hers. How easily the names of those girls had rolled off Regina's tongue and, after all, Jacqueline found that she had not quite forgotten them: Ann-Marie Nugent, Margaret O'Sullivan, Pauline Fitzsimons, Eileen Delaney, Irene Casey. She didn't remember the individual faces but she could see them, like bit players in a film, brightly coloured tops and wide-legged trousers, giggling and leaning on one another's arms as they picked their way carefully in their high sandals across the grass toward the big white marquee tent.

She reached out to turn on the bedside lamp. The brown envelope was on the bedside locker where she had left it, having examined its contents once more before settling down to sleep. She shook it so that the matchbook and the postcard fell onto the duvet. She picked up first the postcard, then the matchbook and tried to picture the owner of the imperturbable voice on the phone. She imagined her moving about in the rooms of the big house in the little sketch. She imagined herself standing before the house, staring up at its windows. Before she fell asleep she had made up her mind what she would do.

Chapter 13

1976

Jacqueline is dressed and ready when the doorbell rings. She peers over the banister and watches them in the hall below.

"I can't believe you're allowed to go and I'm not," says Lilly. "It's just not fair."

"I know it's not," says Goretti Quinn. "Do I look okay, Lilly?"

"You look alright. You look fine."

Jacqueline doesn't think that Goretti Quinn looks fine. She is wearing the wide navy trousers that Daddy calls road-sweepers and purple platform shoes. Her top is bright orange. It is too tight and there are words written across it in big black letters, LIPS THAT TOUCH LIQUOR WILL NEVER TOUCH MINE. But it is her hair that Jacqueline cannot stop staring at.

Jacqueline's mother comes into the hall.

"Oh, you've done something to your hair, Goretti," she says.

"I had a perm, Mrs Brennan." Goretti turns and looks at herself in the hall mirror. "It was supposed to look like Farah Fawcett Majors ..."

"More like Leo Sayer," says Lilly.

"Well, I think it looks very nice, Goretti," says Jacqueline's mother. "You both look very nice."

"What's the use in looking nice when I'm not allowed go to the marquee?" says Lilly. "And when no-one can see me and I have to be home by half ten."

"People will see you at the carnival, Lilly," says Jacqueline's mother.

"Oh please, Mrs Brennan!" says Goretti Quinn. "Please, can Lilly come to the marquee?"

"Not this time, Goretti. Her daddy says no."

"But you said you'd talk him into letting me go! You said you would, but you didn't!" Lilly is almost crying.

"I tried, love."

"Well, you didn't try hard enough!"

"At least you're allowed to go to the carnival.'

"Only if I take that little sneak with me!" Lilly points up the stairs to where Jacqueline is standing on the landing, looking down. "Look at her up there, earwigging as usual. How am I supposed to enjoy myself with her spying on me and listening to every word I say?"

"Now, Lilly, I know you're upset but I won't have you talking about your little sister like that. Come down here, Jacqueline – the girls are waiting for you. And don't you be any trouble to Lilly now, do you hear me?"

By the time Jacqueline reaches the hall, Lilly and Goretti are already at the gate. She has to run to catch up with them halfway down Blackberry Lane. The whole way to the carnival Lilly sulks and doesn't speak to Jacqueline or Goretti, and Jacqueline wonders why she ever thought going to the carnival would be fun.

But it is fun, even though she has to walk behind Lilly and

Goretti so she won't make a show of them and even though Lilly calls her "creep" and "little freak" and "spoilsport" so often Jacqueline loses count. The evening air is cool and there are crowds of people at the carnival, queuing for the rides or standing around at the stalls where there are fluffy toys, dolls and goldfish to be won. There are other stalls too, selling candyfloss and sticks of rock and toffee apples.

Lilly and Goretti run straight to the bumpers and leave Jacqueline to stand and watch. When the ride is finished, they stay in the car and pay the man collecting the money for another turn. By the time they come back, Lilly is laughing and in good humour again.

"Can we go on the swing boats now, Lilly?" asks Jacqueline.

"You can go on your own – I'm not getting in with you," says Lilly.

"You can't go in the swing boats on your own," says Jacqueline. The swing boats are like a seesaw – you need two people for them to work.

"Then go on the roundabout or something, can't you?"

"I'll tell Daddy on you, Lilly. I know he gave you money for me too."

Lilly calls her a sneak again, but she takes her on the swing boats and then on the bumper cars. The man who takes the money on the bumpers says, "Here comes Miss Ireland again!" and Lilly laughs and looks happy. Jacqueline does not like the bumpers very much – they swing first one way and then another and boys keep crashing their cars into Lilly's car. Jacqueline bangs her elbow against the side of the car and it hurts but, when she asks Lilly to make the boys stop, Lilly only laughs and shouts back that she can't make them stop. By the time the ride is over, Jacqueline feels sick.

Lilly gives her money to go and buy herself sweets and Jacqueline buys a packet of Spangles and a toffee apple. She looks around for Lilly and Goretti and sees them standing at the shooting range. A boy has his arm around Lilly's waist. He is showing her how to shoot. Nobody, Jacqueline thinks, is showing Goretti Quinn how to shoot. Jacqueline sucks her Spangles and watches Lilly and Goretti for a while, then she gets tired of waiting and queues up by herself to go for a ride on the roundabout. Her horse has big black staring painted eyes and a blue mane. While it goes round and round, Jacqueline watches Lilly and Goretti. She sees them climbing into the swing boats. The man in charge of the boats has screwed-up eyes and a hump on his back. The boys in the next boat keep reaching out and trying to grab Lilly and Goretti Quinn's boat and the man with the hump shouts at them to stop.

When the roundabout stops, Jacqueline gets off and wanders around. The crowd has got bigger and, even though it is getting late, the sky is still bright. People keep bumping into Jacqueline and her elbow hurts.

From the marquee tent, she can hear the sound of music. A loud voice says over and over again: "Testing, testing, one two, three."

Jacqueline is very thirsty but all her money has gone. All of a sudden, she feels tired and dizzy and a little bit sick. She finds a place to sit and she tears the plastic wrapper from her toffee apple. It looks very nice on the outside, shiny and sticky brown, but when she bites into it, the apple tastes soft and spongy.

Jacqueline wants to go home.

She goes and stands beside the swing boats until the old

man with the hump brings Lilly's boat to a stop with his big wooden stick.

"Lilly, can we go home now?"

"Not yet. I'm not going home yet."

Goretti Quinn squeals. "Oh look, there's Pauline Fitzsimons and the others!" Then she stops and looks at Lilly. "I said I might go in with them, only because ..."

"Yeah, right, you'd better go, Goretti." Lilly bends down and fiddles with the strap of her sandal.

Jacqueline watches Goretti Quinn walking away. A crowd of girls surrounds her: Pauline Fitzsimons, Margaret O'Sullivan, Ann-Marie Nugent, Eileen Delaney and Irene Casey. They are wearing bright tops and wide trousers and their frizzy perms look huge under the carnival lights. Jacqueline watches them picking their way carefully across the field in their platform sandals, then they disappear through the flap in the big white dance marquee. When she looks down at Lilly, she is watching them too, the strap of her shoe forgotten.

Before they leave the carnival grounds, the band in the marquee begins to play, and as they start up the road they can still hear the words of the song they are singing: "Oh, What a Night."

All the way home, Lilly does not speak, but Jacqueline is too tired to care. People are coming towards them, passing them by, on their way to the marquee. There are gangs of boys and gangs of girls and couples – boys and girls holding hands or with their arms linked about each other's waists. The girls mostly have permed hair and some of the boys do too, fluffy and huge in the evening light, like giant dandelions. The boys smell of aftershave, some of it sharp and some of it sweet. It seems to Jacqueline that she

111

and Lilly are the only people going in the other direction.

Lilly whispers something under her breath, and Jacqueline can just about make it out: "It's not fair, it's just not fair."

Chapter 14

Afterwards

The streets were slick from a recent summer downpour as Jacqueline came out of the small station. A flower bed laid out to spell the name of the town in damp and ragged red and yellow blossoms welcomed her to Coldhope-On-Sea. A signpost led her through the heart of the town, along narrow streets of candy-coloured shopfronts with a gull on every chimney and bunting strung from roof to roof like someone's faded washing strung out to dry. On the wide and pretty promenade, Jacqueline would have liked to sit down, but the benches were wet from the rain. Another downpour sent her running for cover to the nearest café, and she waited out the shower with a leaky stainless-steel pot of tea. Before leaving, she asked directions to Shore Road and the way led her on a winding ascent above the town, with a clear view of the sea and the long pale stretch of sandy beach below. The sun had come out again. Jacqueline stopped to catch her breath and watched a group of boys who were crossing the sand carrying something between them: it looked like an armchair.

Even without the sign on the gates, Jacqueline would

have recognised Sea Holly Villa from the sketch on the matchbook. In reality, the house was cream-coloured with pale-blue shutters. A narrow veranda ran the length of its front and, to Jacqueline, everything looked a little shabby and in need of painting. A short drive gave way to a flagstone path that zig-zagged between flower beds smelling of lavender. Jacqueline walked up three steps to the veranda. The door was wide open and she considered the large black lion's-head knocker and the brass bell. She decided on the bell and, while she waited, a gust of wind sent petals from potted geraniums swirling like red confetti about her feet. When nobody came, she put down her holdall, grabbed the knocker with both hands and rapped smartly twice. After a second attempt at the bell, she picked up her holdall again and stepped through the open doorway.

"Hello?" Her voice echoed round the high-ceilinged hall but nobody came.

The fan-shaped stained-glass window above the open door threw a jewelled pattern on the dark tiles of the floor. Jacqueline called out again then crossed to an open doorway on her right. She took a step inside the doorway and peered about her. The room was long, dim, narrow and overcrowded with dark and cumbersome furniture. Most of it, Jacqueline noticed, had claws. The walls were papered in an ugly pattern of ruby and yellow flowers interspersed with exotically coloured butterflies and birds. Almost every surface held a clutter of ornaments and knick-knacks. From under a glass dome, the eye of some long-dead and stuffed creature glittered. The only redeeming feature in the room was the bookshelf that lined the length and width of one entire wall.

114

Catching the sound of a low humming above her head, Jacqueline went back into the hall and started slowly up the stairs, her footsteps soundless on the thick, faded carpet. The darkly gleaming handrail slid beneath her palm as she went and she caught the scent of old-fashioned lavender furniture polish. The humming led her to the second landing where a tall, thin woman was hoovering frenetically.

"Excuse me?" said Jacqueline.

The woman turned and looked at Jacqueline from blurry blue eyes set in a latticework of wrinkles. She was dressed in figure-sculpting moss-green leggings and a matching zipped-up top. Her hair, unnaturally red, was so sparse that patches of pink scalp gleamed through. After looking Jacqueline up and down for a moment, she stuck out a sinewy foot in a ballerina pump to switch the machine off.

"Hi," said Jacqueline. "I'm sorry for just walking in and I did try knocking. And ringing actually. I was hoping you had a room?"

"A room?" The woman looked from Jacqueline to her bag and back again.

"A room," said Jacqueline, "for tonight. For a couple of nights maybe – if you have any vacancies, I mean?"

The woman bent down and pulled the plug from the socket.

Watching her, a sudden fear seized Jacqueline. "I haven't come to the wrong place, have I? This is Sea Holly Villa? You take guests, don't you?"

"Did I say I didn't? People stay here, if they want to, if I like the look of them." The woman picked up the hoover and came down the stairs toward Jacqueline. "After you," she said and Jacqueline hurried ahead of her down the stairs. She waited in the hall while the woman stowed the hoover in a cupboard, then picked up a crumpled paper bag from a small table. "Liquorice Whip?"

"No, thank you," said Jacqueline.

The woman snapped off a piece of liquorice with her teeth and chewed, her eyes on Jacqueline. "So you want a room?"

Jacqueline wasn't sure if she did or not now. The sunshine through the open doorway looked inviting and she had to fight an urge to bolt, to run all the way back down the hill and catch the next train back to the airport.

"Tell you what," said the woman. "Why don't you think about it over a drink? I know I need one." Without waiting for an answer, she pattered away and disappeared round a corner of the hall.

Jacqueline looked at the open door again, then she followed slowly in the woman's wake.

The hall ended in a short flight of stone steps leading down to an enormous kitchen. Jacqueline looked about her at the blend of old and new, the flagstone floor, the ancient range side by side with modern fitted units and a hob.

The woman, her head in an ancient-looking fridge, called out, "Grab two of those long glasses from the dresser, would you?"

Jacqueline dropped her bag on the floor, crossed to the enormous dresser and surveyed the rows of exquisitely gleaming crystal. Carefully, she took down two glasses and carried them to the long table. She set them gently down on the aged wood which had been scrubbed to the whiteness of bone.

"I'll give those a rinse." The woman came up behind her

116

and set a frosted glass bottle, which contained some pale pinkish liquid, on the table.

Was it rosé or something else, Jacqueline wondered. She didn't want wine, she wanted tea.

"Why don't you sit down?" said the woman. "And by the way, I'm Dot Candy."

She held out a hand and Jacqueline took it; it was long and bony and chilled from the bottle.

"Jacqueline Brennan."

"Pleased to meet you, Jacqueline Brennan!" Dot Candy carelessly whipped up the glasses and carried them to the sink. "So what brings you to this part of England? Let me guess – you came here on holiday as a child. More than half the people who've stayed here have come looking to recapture some childhood summer idyll."

"Do they succeed?" asked Jacqueline.

"I shouldn't think so," said Dot Candy.

"Well, in any case, I've never been here before." Jacqueline pulled out a chair and sat down. "It's an interesting house," she said.

"I know," said Dot Candy. She picked up a cloth and began drying the glasses. "It dates from the 1850s. Martin inherited it from his uncle."

She came back to the table, glasses in one hand and a tray of ice cubes in the other. Jacqueline watched as her long skinny fingers pushed the ice cubes from the soft rubber tray. Dot dropped three cubes into each glass, opened the bottle and poured the pale pink liquid.

She handed a glass to Jacqueline, picked up her own, threw back her head and drained it in one go. While she refilled it, Jacqueline sipped at her own drink: it was cool and tart with an agreeable but unfamiliar flavour.

"Of course, Martin always knew it was coming to him – Peter made no bones about that. He had no other family except Martin, so there was nobody else to leave it to. Still, nobody expected him to go so soon, so all of this came to us a whole lot sooner than we expected."

Has she forgotten that I don't know who these people are, Jacqueline wondered.

"Only, as it turned out," said Dot, "there wasn't so much time to enjoy it as we thought – not for Martin at any rate."

In the silence that followed, Jacqueline could hear the sound of Dot Candy swallowing. She wondered if she should ask about Martin. But I don't know Martin, she thought, and I don't care about Martin. She looked up to find Dot Candy watching her over the rim of her glass.

"Like it, do you, the drink?"

"Yes, thank you, it's very nice, very unusual. What is it exactly?"

"It's sumac lemonade."

"Come again?"

Dot Candy smiled. "Bring your drink and I'll show you." She got up and walked through the open doorway.

Jacqueline picked up her glass and followed her outside onto a wide terrace.

Dot walked down a short flight of steps to a wide lawn. "Behold the staghorn sumac tree!" she called. She was standing before what looked to Jacqueline like a large shrub with hairy branches.

Jacqueline walked down steps which were worn dark and smooth by time, and crossed the grass to stand next to Dot.

"It doesn't look like much now," said Dot, "but you

should see it in the autumn. The leaves turn a fiery red and it's just beautiful."

"And that's what you use to make the lemonade?"

"Yes, the very same way the native American Indians used to do it. The tricky bit is making sure the berries are ready. Then all you have to do is boil them, strain them, add the sugar and Bob's your uncle."

"Isn't it a lot of trouble?" said Jacqueline.

"You could say the same thing about roasting a chicken," said Dot Candy.

Jacqueline felt unable to argue the point.

"Of course, there's a poison sumac too," said Dot Candy, "but there's no way you could mix them up – the berries are quite different – hairless, waxy, just like white grapes really. You wouldn't want to make lemonade from those babies."

"No, I suppose not," said Jacqueline faintly. "Well, I suppose I'd better be ..."

But Dot had moved away. "This one here is what the house gets its name from," she said over her shoulder.

Jacqueline looked where she was pointing, at a shrub with brilliant silver-green foliage and bluish-purple flowers.

"It's a sea holly tree," said Dot.

It reminded Jacqueline of thistles.

Her hand brushed against something soft and furry to the touch. "What's this one?" she said.

"That's lamb's ear – you can feel why."

"It's pretty," said Jacqueline.

"It's practical," said Dot Candy. "The salt sticks to the fuzz so the plant can survive." She waved an all-enveloping hand. "A seaside garden is a challenge: you have to choose plants with sea legs, plants that can cope with wind and drought and salt. That cosmos over there – looks like a puff of wind would knock it over, doesn't it? But it's tough: the poorer the soil, the more it likes it. And that lavender and the Artemisia, they reflect light away from themselves, protect themselves naturally from sizzling up in the sunshine."

Jacqueline surveyed the beauties of the garden with a vague depression. "Wasn't anything chosen just for its aesthetic qualities?" she asked.

"If I'd had my way it would have been." Dot Candy came to stand beside her. "I had big plans for this garden once. If I'd had my way this would have been the most beautiful wildflower garden you've ever seen. I wanted clover and campion, and hemlock to attract butterflies and insects and bees and – oh well, never mind." With a sudden deft movement, she whipped the glass from Jacqueline's hand. "I'll take that if you're finished."

Startled, Jacqueline watched her walk away.

"You know," Dot Candy called over her shoulder, "you'd probably be a whole lot more comfortable somewhere else. I can give you the name of some good guesthouses in the town if that's what you're looking for."

She's turning me away, thought Jacqueline, she's decided she doesn't like the look of me. Perversely, it had the effect of making her want to stay. She stood for a moment looking at the lamb's ear, which felt so fragile, but could withstand gales and storms, then she turned and walked back to the house.

Dot Candy was rinsing the glasses at the sink.

"I'd like a room, if that's alright with you," said Jacqueline.

Dot Candy turned and looked at her, then picked up a

tea towel and wiped her hands on it. "Bring your bag," she said, and walked away.

Jacqueline picked up her holdall and followed her back through the long cool hall to where a low counter cordoned off an area beneath the stairs.

Dot Candy raised the hinged counter-flap and slipped in behind. With her back to Jacqueline, she surveyed a row of hooks on the wall, from which keys were hanging. "Now where will I put you?"

While she waited, Jacqueline's eyes fell on a faded leather-covered book with one single word picked out in gilt: GUESTS.

"This one, I think." Dot Candy reached up and unhooked a key, then let herself out and lowered the counter-flap once more. "If you'll come with me," she said, her tone suddenly and disconcertingly that of the professional host.

Jacqueline followed her again through the hall.

Dot pointed to a doorway. "This is the dining room. Breakfast is served here between eight and ten. If you'd rather not stand on ceremony, you'll find me in the kitchen."

She led the way upstairs. On the second landing, she unlocked a door and stood aside so Jacqueline could pass.

The room was spacious and bright with sunshine. It was also exquisitely clean and smelled of fresh polish. A faded rug almost entirely covered the gleaming dark-wood floor. The fireplace had a mahogany mantelpiece and an old-fashioned steel fender, its twin knobs polished until they shone. A big cracked blue jug filled with dried flowers replaced the grate. There was a king-size bed and a gargantuan mahogany wardrobe, a chest of drawers and a washstand with an old-fashioned jug and basin. On a small three-legged table by the window, a silver tray was set with a silver teapot, jug and bowl; the bowl was stuffed with sachets of sugar and pods of UHT milk. There were also two glass bottles of mineral water, one still, one sparkling, and a single blue-and-gold fine-china cup and saucer – almost, thought Jacqueline, as though she had been expecting me.

"No bath," said Dot Candy, as she opened a door on a small en-suite with shower. "There's another room I could give you – it has a bath, but the views are not so good – your choice."

Jacqueline had crossed to the big bay window and was staring down at the distant sea. "No, thank you," she said, "I'll have this one, please. This is my room."

Chapter 15

1976

The old man with the screwed-up face and the hump on his back has gone. A new boy is in charge of the swing boats and the bumpers are no longer Lilly's favourites. The boy wears a black leather bag across his chest for the money he collects. He has long curly black hair and dark eyes that gleam in the lights from the carnival. The six red-and-white boats are full of girls and Jacqueline watches them showing off. They stand up while the boats are still moving, they laugh loudly and pull hard on the thick blue ropes, sending the boats flying high in one direction and higher still in the other. Back and forth, back and forth they fly so that their hair flies out behind them, red and gold and brown, and Lilly's is the darkest of them all. Their eyes are on the boy as he moves about below them. His name is Luca. He is the boy from the garden, the one who came to play his guitar and sing to Lilly in the middle of the night. Jacqueline thinks he looks a little bit wicked.

Lilly is wearing a white halter-neck top, her brown back is bare, and when she climbs into the boat for the third time, she stumbles on the shaky little wooden ladder.

Goretti Quinn laughs so much that the boat begins to rock, but Luca smiles and holds it steady for Lilly.

When the ride is over, Jacqueline hears Lilly and Goretti Quinn talking about him.

"Do you like him, Lilly?"

"Who?"

"Luke."

"Not Luke – Luca," says Lilly. "He's alright."

"Because I think he likes you, Lilly."

"Yeah? Big thrill!" says Lilly, laughing.

There are red X's on the kitchen calendar. Lilly is marking off the days until the Festival Queen Dance in the marquee.

"Why is she doing that, when she's not allowed go to the dance?" asks Jacqueline.

"Don't ask me," says Gayle.

Jacqueline goes into the sitting room. The television is on but Daddy is not watching the racing. He is combing his hair and looking at himself in the door of the china cabinet. On the top of the china cabinet there is a photograph in a brown wooden frame. Jacqueline, her mother, Daddy, Lilly and Gayle are sitting together on a blanket with the sea behind them. No matter how hard she tries, Jacqueline can never quite remember that particular day. When she tries, all the trips to the estuary and all the picnics mix themselves up in her head in a jumble of sunshine and buckets and spades, red lemonade, tea in the blue flask and sandwiches packed in bread-wrappers, so that she cannot tell one day from the other. Was the photograph taken on the day Gayle fell off the jetty into the sea and had to walk home in Lilly's petticoat, or was it another day altogether?

Jacqueline picks up the frame and peers at herself

closely. In the photograph, she is much younger than she is now. There is an apple in her hand and her face is screwed up as though she has just tasted something nasty.

"Daddy," she says, "why am I pulling a face?"

Daddy puts his comb back into his pocket. "I've told you a million times, Jacqueline."

"Tell me again."

Daddy takes the frame from Jacqueline's hand and looks at the photograph. "You were eating your apple and talking at the same time when the photo was taken and this is you with a mouthful of pips ..."

"So I spat them out ..."

"All over the blanket ..."

"And I knocked over the flask ..."

"And the tea spilled ..."

"And Mam gave out to me ..."

"And Mam gave out to you ..."

"And you gave me a piggy-back ..."

"To the end of the jetty."

There is the sound of a car outside and Daddy puts the photograph back on top of the china cabinet.

"I'm getting out of here," he says. "The flower women are coming."

Jacqueline follows Daddy into the hall.

He calls up the stairs. "Stella, your flower women are here!" and he pulls a face at Jacqueline.

Jacqueline laughs. Daddy doesn't like the flower women. They hold their meetings in each other's houses and, when it's her mother's turn, they take over the whole sitting room and do things to flowers with bits of wire and little green sponges. Sometimes Jacqueline listens but they talk about stupid things like form and texture and "repeating your lines" and say things that don't make sense, like "never cut on a nodule".

Daddy says her mother is wasting her time with all this flower-arranging nonsense. He told her she should give it up like she gave up everything else she started: the crochet and the smocking and the basket-weaving and the bloody lampshade-making. He said: why can't she try her hand at cookery lessons instead?

But Jacqueline's mother told him not to be so smart. "And if you must know, I've discovered I have a flair for flowers so you'd better get used to it, because I'm keeping it up."

Now, Jacqueline's mother comes down the stairs.

"Frank," she says, "please don't make a show of me. It's only once every two months that they come here, so please make an effort to be civil."

Daddy pulls a face behind her back and Jacqueline laughs. She doesn't like them either, the flower women: Kay and Olive and Heather and Mona and, last but not least, Florence McNally. Florence is rich and posh and, according to Lilly, thinks she is the Queen of England. She lives in a big house all by herself. Daddy says it's because no-one would have her, but Jacqueline's mother says that's all he knows. Florence had a husband once but he died tragically when Florence was just a bride. Jacqueline cannot imagine Florence McNally as a bride – Florence has short grey hair and wears tight checked skirts even though she has the biggest bum Jacqueline has ever seen. Daddy says she's nothing but an oul' snob, but Jacqueline's mother says Florence is a real lady who knows more about flower-arranging than anyone else in the flower club.

"Right, I'll be off down the town so," says Daddy,

"because God forbid I'd make a show of anyone."

"Don't try to make out that it's because of my friends you're going out," says Jacqueline's mother. "You were going out whether they came or not."

"What if I was?" says Daddy. "Since when was it a sin for a man to go out for a pint?"

"If it was only one pint," says Jacqueline's mother.

Jacqueline thinks they're going to have another row. But, instead, they go together to open the door and Daddy shakes hands with the flower women and says something that makes everyone laugh – even Florence McNally.

Jacqueline walks with Daddy to the gate. "Can I have some money for the carnival, Daddy?"

"What, are you off to the carnival again?"

"Lilly said she'd take me this evening if I want to go."

"Did she now? I hope she looks after you when you're there."

"Yes, Daddy," Jacqueline lies, because it is better to go to the carnival with Lilly and be ignored by her, than not to go at all.

As she walks back to the house, Jacqueline can hear the murmur of the flower women's voices coming through the open sitting-room window. She imagines how warm the sitting room must be, and how full of the smell of women's perfumes and the fat sweet smell of the flowers. She wonders how they can bear to be inside when the sun is shining and the sky is blue, listening to one another saying the same things over and over again. But she is bored and there is nothing to do, so she crosses the grass and stands at the window and peers in. Florence McNally has her back to the window and is bent over the table. Her skirt is stretched tight across her big huge bum and Jacqueline has to put her hands over her mouth to stop herself laughing out loud. At times like this, she almost wishes Regina Quinn was here to share the joke.

"Now remember, ladies," Florence says in her loud deep voice, "leaves should be a healthy green with no loose pollen on the petals, because that means the flowers are nearing the end of their lifespan."

Compared to Florence, Jacqueline's mother's voice is soft and high. "What do you think, Florence, should I use the pedestal or the vase?"

And Florence says, "Oh, the vase, Stella, without doubt, the vase – exquisite, absolutely exquisite. Isn't it exquisite, ladies?"

Then everyone says something about the vase.

"Stunning," says Kay, and "Lead crystal, of course," says Olive, and "It must be sixteen inches high at the very least," says Mona, and "An heirloom, I think you said?" says Heather.

And Jacqueline's mother, sounding pleased and happy, says, "Fifteen inches actually and it is lead crystal. My mother got it as a wedding gift and passed it on to me before she died."

And Jacqueline wonders again how they can bear it. She turns away from the window and that is when she notices the evergreen bush. For a moment she thinks it has blossomed overnight but, going closer, she can see that what look like red-and-black flowers are really hundreds of ladybirds. When she is tired of looking at them, she wanders down to the orchard.

There is someone in the field behind the hedge – Jacqueline can hear talking and laughing.

Lilly comes through the gap in the hedge.

She is smiling but when she sees Jacqueline she stops. "How long have you been standing there?"

"Not long."

Lilly looks over her shoulder then back at Jacqueline. "Is Daddy here?"

"No, he's gone down the town – the flower women are here."

"Oh God, not the flower women!" says Lilly and Jacqueline smiles because Lilly sounds just like Daddy.

When Lilly has gone, Jacqueline walks to the gap in the hedge. In the distance she can see a boy walking through the meadow, but he is too far away for her to be sure who he is and she stands and watches the dark head bob up and down as he moves away fast, towards the river.

Chapter 16

Afterwards

Jacqueline took off her shoes and unzipped her bag. She rummaged through her clothes until she found his cardigan. She sniffed it. She wondered if it was her imagination or if it smelled just slightly less of him. Someday she would have to wash it. She pulled it on quickly, then lay down on top of the bed. When she closed her eyes, she could hear the distant hum of the hoover. Somehow it soothed her and she fell into a doze. She was startled awake by the phone – Gayle again. She put it on silent and checked the time and found to her surprise that she had been asleep for more than two hours. Her mouth felt dry as an overbaked meringue and she drank the bottle of still water. In the bathroom, she looked at her face in the mirror. She was pale and heavy-eyed and her skin looked like the cheese on which she had primarily been existing. A staggering amount of grey was coming through at her roots and temples now and her hair needed a cut. The thought triggered a memory of her father, draped in the fluorescent pink gown and eyeing her reproachfully in the salon mirror, and she turned away from her own reflection quickly.

When she flushed the toilet, the pipes made a sound like a violently gargling giant. A second giant joined in when she turned on the taps to wash her hands.

In the bedroom, she stood at the window and looked at the cloudless sky and the distant jittery silver sea. Closer at hand, something else caught her eye. In the garden below her, a blue-and-silver bicycle was leaning against a wall, glittering and winking in the sun.

She pulled on her shoes, then picked up her shoulder bag and went downstairs. The front door was still wide open and she walked to the gate and made her way down the hill, enjoying the warmth of the sun. Halfway down, at a turn in the road, she stopped and looked at a signpost saying "Cliff Walk". Before leaving her to settle in, Dot Candy had given Jacqueline a potted guide to the town. "There are two beaches, north and south. The North Beach has the promenade and the fair – all that jazz. The South Beach is smaller and more private. There's a path leading from the beach that goes all the way to the clifftop. There's a signpost for the cliffs off Shore Road – you'll have passed it on your way up here today."

Jacqueline kept on walking; exploring would keep. Right now, she was thirsty and hungry in a way she could not remember feeling for some time.

On the promenade she bought fish and chips and two bottles of water, then walked down the slipway to the North Beach. She found a spot where she could rest her back against a rock, sat down, took off her shoes and ate her food. The tide was in and there were still a lot of people about. She watched a man go by in long shorts, sandals and socks; his shins were bright pink from the sun. A woman was trying to lay a towel flat but the wind kept snatching

131

it from her grasp. Jacqueline finished her food and poured the remains of a bottle of water over her greasy fingers and dried them with a paper tissue. She checked her phone. She had six texts and two missed calls from Gayle now. She typed a reply: **Sorry. Battery died. All OK. Will call tomorrow.**

She checked the time – if she were in Blackberry Lane she would be opening her first bottle of wine right about now. She picked up her shoes and carried her rubbish to a bin, then walked to the edge of the sea. She let the water swirl around her toes. It was very cold but it felt good and so bracing that she rolled up her linen trousers and waded out until the water was over her knees.

Her phone beeped again as she was crossing the beach toward the promenade. Walking with her head down, reading Gayle's texts, she glanced up and stopped abruptly. An armchair had been abandoned in the middle of the slipway. Jacqueline put her phone in her pocket and surveyed the chair. It was tub-shaped and very faded. Horsehair gaped through a rent in the green velvet and the headrest was festooned with seaweed. It was not his chair, it did not even resemble his chair, but nonetheless an image rose up in Jacqueline's mind, of her father as she had found him, with his dinner on his lap. A wave of grief and fatigue washed over her and she made her way slowly up the slipway and started the long walk back to the house.

The door to Sea Holly Villa was still wide open. Jacqueline wondered if it was ever shut – perhaps it stood open all night long.

Her eyes went to the counter that cordoned off Dot Candy's small triangle of office. She stood for a moment and listened, then made up her mind. She moved quietly and quickly to the counter. When Dot Candy arrived, barefoot and silent from the direction of the kitchen, Jacqueline had the guestbook open in her hands.

Dot Candy stopped and looked at her, her face devoid of any expression.

"I was just thinking that I should have signed in," said Jacqueline.

"Please yourself," said Dot Candy.

"Right, I'm not sure if I have a ..." Jacqueline rustled about in her bag and pulled out a pen. "Here it is."

When she looked up, Dot Candy was still watching her. I'm fooling no one here, she thought. But she owed it to the lie now to make it a good one, so she made a performance of signing the book. She noticed that only a handful of pages had been used and the last time a guest had signed in was three years ago.

"Don't you keep a record of all your guests?" she asked.

"Not anymore," said Dot Candy. She held out a hand and Jacqueline handed over the book. "In the early years we were sticklers for it – it was one of the first things I bought when we went into business – a guestbook and lemon soap."

"Lemon soap?"

"Shaped like shells," said Dot Candy. "I bought them as a job lot at the market and put them in all the rooms. The man who sold them to me told me they were handmade with real lemon juice. I think he told the truth because the place stank of lemons for about eighteen months."

"I suppose you haven't kept the old guestbooks?" said Jacqueline.

"They're in there somewhere," said Dot Candy. She indicated the counter with a tilt of her head. "If there's something in particular you're looking for then just say so."

"No – there's nothing," said Jacqueline. "Thank you. I'll just be off to bed now."

"I hope you're comfortable in your room? I left you a jug of fresh water. Let me know if you need anything else."

"Thank you, Dot. Goodnight."

"Goodnight," said Dot Candy.

Jacqueline was sure she was watching her walk away.

She couldn't sleep; her body felt exhausted but her mind wouldn't rest. She wondered if it was because she hadn't had a drink all day. At two-thirty she got out of bed, put his cardigan on over her T-shirt and shorts and went downstairs in her bare feet. The countertop creaked when she lifted the flap and she froze. She stood without moving for a few minutes and listened, but nothing stirred in the house. She slipped in behind the counter and switched on an old-fashioned table lamp on its top. Dot had said the old guest books were somewhere here. She dropped down on her hunkers and began rummaging through stacks of files and papers on some shelving under the counter.

"Which year are you looking for?"

Jacqueline shot to her feet.

Dot Candy was leaning against the staircase. The light was too dim to read the expression in her eyes.

"1983," said Jacqueline. Then a thought struck her. Why not start at the beginning, just in case? "Actually, no – if you don't mind I'll take a look at 1976 first."

"That would be one of the first ones. We only opened the house to guests in 1974. Come out and let me in – I'll find it quicker than you will."

Jacqueline slipped out and Dot took her place and disappeared under the counter. Jacqueline waited; she felt like a creeping thief. Dot reappeared with a wine-coloured leather-bound book in her hand.

"There you are – that covers the year you want and the next three or four as well. If you don't find what you need in there, feel free to look through the rest of them tomorrow. Only, I'd take that to bed with me if I was you – your feet will get cold."

Jacqueline reached out and took the book. "I'm sorry," she said. "I had no right. It's just that I have reason to believe someone I knew once stayed here. Only I'm not sure when exactly, so I didn't know which one I needed."

"You only had to ask," said Dot Candy. Again there was no evidence of judgement or chagrin in her face or voice. She came out from under the stairs and closed down the flap. "Fancy a nightcap?"

"No, thank you," said Jacqueline. "I won't. It's a bit late and I'd really like to get a start on this ..."

"Okay, night then."

"Goodnight, Dot, and thank you."

Jacqueline crept back up the stairs. Why hadn't she just asked earlier when she'd had the opportunity, when Dot had caught her with the book in her hand? Why did she have to go creeping around in the night? She felt like a weasel, she felt like a worm, she felt like a "little sneak". And why hadn't she accepted the offer of the nightcap?

She had reached the second landing when she thought she heard the front door opening. She peered over the rail into the hall below and saw the top of a woman's head. Another smaller head was resting on the woman's shoulder. Dot Candy came toward them and reached out and stroked the child's hair. Jacqueline carried on toward her room.

Chapter 17

1976

Something is wrong but Gayle won't tell. Jacqueline can hear them whispering in the kitchen. "Don't mind him, Gayle, he's nothing but an old creep," says Lilly. "Everyone knows that. He's always saying stuff like that to girls – just don't let it upset you."

"Who said what? Why is Gayle upset?" Jacqueline wants to know.

"Get lost!" Lilly says. "Mind your own business, Little Big Ears!"

Later, Goretti Quinn calls and Jacqueline hears them arguing in Lilly's room. She goes to the bathroom, flushes the toilet and turns on the tap, then leaves the water running and sneaks back to Lilly's door.

Goretti Quinn is shouting. "My da never said that! She's making it up!"

"Are you calling my sister a liar, Goretti Quinn?"

"Well, why is she saying those things about my da? She's making out that he's some kind of weirdo!" Goretti Quinn sounds like she's nearly crying.

"So you are calling my sister a liar," says Lilly. "Then

you can get out of my room and don't come back!"

Jacqueline makes a run for the bathroom. She is just in time. Lilly's door bangs shut and Jacqueline listens to the sound of footsteps thumping down the stairs. The front door bangs and Jacqueline smiles. Maybe Goretti Quinn will never come back.

Jacqueline wakes to the sound of shouting from downstairs. Gayle groans and her bed creaks as she turns over.

On the landing, Jacqueline leans over the banister. Lilly, Daddy and her mother are in the hall. Daddy is wearing his pyjamas and her mother is in her blue nightdress. Lilly is all dressed up in her tight purple-velvet bellbottoms and a lilac tank top. In her platform sandals, she seems to Jacqueline to tower over her parents.

"It's twenty to one in the morning," says Daddy, "and I'll ask you again, where have you been?"

"There's no need to raise your voice, Frank," says Jacqueline's mother. "Lilly, your daddy's been sitting up for hours worrying about you."

"Well, I didn't ask him to sit up and I didn't ask him to worry either."

"Now, Lilly, don't give back cheek," says her mother.

"You were with some young fella, weren't you?" says Daddy.

"I was with Goretti."

"Don't lie to me, Lilly! I saw you."

"Ha!" yells Lilly. "Did you hear that? He WAS spying on me – I knew it!"

"Frank," says Jacqueline's mother.

"What?" says Daddy. "I waited up for her, I saw her

out of the window and she was with some rock ape."

"He's not a rock ape," says Lilly. "He's my boyfriend."

Jacqueline decides to make herself comfortable. She creeps down three steps and sits on the step above the little landing. It's the perfect place to peep around the corner and see without being seen.

"I'll decide if he's your boyfriend or not," says Daddy. "Who is this Romeo anyway?"

"For God's sake, can we leave Shakespeare out of it?" says Lilly. "You don't know him so what does it matter?"

"So how old is this joker then?" says Daddy.

"Seventeen."

"Has he got his Leaving Cert?"

Jacqueline can't help smiling. Daddy always wants to know if people have their Leaving Cert.

"He's left school," says Lilly.

"So he hasn't got his Leaving Certificate?"

"Alright, he hasn't got his Leaving Certificate. Are you happy now? No Leaving Cert – quelle horreur!"

Jacqueline smiles again. Daddy hates it when Lilly talks French at him.

"Don't get smart with me, I'm warning you, Lilly."

"I'm not being smart," says Lilly. "You're always telling me to learn another language, so now I'm speaking French."

"Never mind what language it is," says Daddy. "Cheek is cheek. So if he doesn't go to school, what does he do?"

"He has a job, if you must know."

"What sort of job?"

"What does it matter what sort of job?"

"That good, is it? Well, you can stay away from him from now on."

"Frank, can you not just –"

"Don't side with her against me, Stella," Daddy says, his voice risen even further.

"I'm not siding with anyone – and don't start shouting at me, Frank. I just think you're being a bit too hard on her."

"And you're too soft on her! She has you wrapped around her finger. If it was up to you she'd be out walking the streets every night of the week!"

"What am I supposed to do?" says Lilly. "You don't like it when I hang around in a crowd, but you won't let me go out with anyone either. You just don't want me to have any friends, do you?"

"You have your sisters, don't you?" says Daddy. "And the Quinn girl –"

"Yeah, and you don't like her either," says Lilly.

"And you have your school friends, or are they not the kind of friends you had in mind?"

"So you're saying I'm not allowed to go near a boy, is that it?"

"What about that nice chap who called here around St. Patrick's Day?" says Daddy. "I gave you permission to go to a dance with him, didn't I?"

"Who? You don't mean Sexy Sexton?"

Jacqueline puts her hand to her mouth to stop herself from laughing out loud.

"Don't be vulgar now, Lilly," says her mother.

"Edmund Sexton is a lovely young fella," says Daddy.

Jacqueline thinks of Lilly calling Sexy Sexton a long streak of paralysed piss. She wishes she could see the look on Lilly's face.

"He's a drip," says Lilly. "He wanted me to go to some stupid céilí with him!"

"*What's wrong with a céilí?*" *says Daddy.* "*At least he had the manners to come to the front door and ask me to my face if he could take my daughter out.*"

"*Yeah, like it was the 18th century!*" *says Lilly.* "*My God, I'm like a prisoner in this house. You won't even let me go to the marquee and everyone else I know is allowed to go.*"

"*There'll be plenty of time for marquees when you finish your schooling,*" *says Daddy.* "*Or maybe you'd prefer to throw the towel in and just get a job in a factory?*"

"*Don't be silly, Frank,*" *says Jacqueline's mother.* "*Of course she wouldn't.*"

"*What's silly about it?*" *says Daddy.* "*If she wants to street-walk, then what's the point of sending her to school? What's the point of that pile of new schoolbooks you spent all that money on?*"

Jacqueline thinks about the stack of brand-new, sweet-smelling books piled high on the sideboard in the sitting room, just waiting to be covered. Lilly is the only one in the family who does not have to have second-hand books. Gayle has to use Lilly's books and, by the time Jacqueline gets them, they have both Lilly and Gayle's names written on the front page, and marks and scribbles all over them.

"*Of course there's a point in sending her to school,*" *says Jacqueline's mother.* "*Lilly has a good mind.*"

"*Then she'd better use it,*" *says Daddy,* "*and forget about boys and dances until she gets her exams.*"

"*Mam, did you hear him?*" *says Lilly.* "*He's saying I'm not allowed to go out with anyone now. Until I'm seventeen! It's not fair – he's mean and he's a big spy and I hate him! I hate him!*"

Before Jacqueline has time to move, Lilly is thundering

up the stairs. She almost falls over Jacqueline and stares down at her.

"Oh my God," she says, "this house is full of spies. Get out of my way!" The toe of her shoe nudges Jacqueline hard in the side and Jacqueline crouches against the wall.

Lilly pushes past her and Jacqueline hears her bedroom door slam shut.

"What's going on?" says Gayle, when Jacqueline goes back into her own room. Gayle's voice is full of sleep.

"Nothing," says Jacqueline. "Gayle, what did Slinky Quinn do to upset you?"

"How do you know about that?" says Gayle, and her voice does not sound sleepy anymore.

"I just do. What did he do?"

"He didn't do anything," says Gayle. "Just go to sleep, Jacqueline."

Jacqueline pulls the sheet over her head. She has no idea why she is crying. The kick hardly hurt at all.

Chapter 18

Afterwards

It was too early to be awake but Jacqueline knew she would never get back to sleep. The yellow room cupped the sunshine and dazzled the eyes. She got out of bed, opened the window and surveyed the day. The sun was shining, the sky was blue and the sea was bluer – she had come to the seaside, so what did she expect? She turned and glanced at the guestbook in the chair where she had left it last night – she should have just started with the book from 1983. The chance of finding Lilly's name in the 1976 book had been almost non-existent and she had known it was. But while it lasted, it had been a hope, however slender, and now it was gone.

She picked up the small kettle and went to fill it from the bathroom sink. When it had boiled, she fiddled with the miniscule UHT milk pods, the teabags and paper sachets of sugar and made her tea in the exquisite china cup. She drank it sitting in the window seat with the sun-warmed glass at her back.

After she had showered and dressed it was still only seven-thirty – she had asked for her breakfast at nine. She read for another half an hour then picked up the guestbook and carried it downstairs. The hall door was open again and she left the guestbook on the countertop and went outside into the bright sunshine.

A movement caught her eye and she turned in time to catch a puffed-up marmalade cat sloping round a corner of the house. Moving slowly, so as not to spook it, Jacqueline followed. But the cat slunk with ease through the narrow bars of a gate and threw a look over its shoulder at her.

"Okay, Skinny Malink," said Jacqueline. "No need to be so smug about it."

She unlatched the gate and let herself into a small walled garden, sketchily planted with herbs. There seemed nowhere to hide, but the cat had disappeared. In the far wall there was a second gate. Jacqueline walked toward it, opened it and went through onto the terrace at the back of the house. The cat was nowhere to be seen here either and she stood for a moment, taking in the beauty of the garden. Something winked in the sunlight and she crossed the terrace, walked down the flight of steps and crossed the lawn to a side wall.

The bicycle looked like it had seen better days. Jacqueline touched the handlebars and made to ring the bell, but drew her hand back at the last minute and walked away, following a zig-zag path through a belt of shrubs. It led her under an archway, skirted a scummy-looking ornamental pond and ended at a small stone enclosure. Two of the lichen-freckled walls had collapsed and the interior was choked with weeds and nettles. On the ground, seven aluminium bowls were laid out close together. An eighth bowl was set apart. The air smelled of cat. From here, the garden narrowed and sloped to a high boundary wall.

Jacqueline turned back. Under the archway, another cat sat watching her approach. It was entirely white but for one peculiar small black marking on its chin.

"Pretty puss," said Jacqueline.

The cat laid back its ears then hissed and bolted.

"Unfriendly lot of felines," said Jacqueline.

She retraced her steps to the house and went back to her room where she killed more time by washing her hands and checking her emails on her phone. At five to nine she went downstairs again.

She stood in the doorway to the dining room. It was not a particularly attractive room. The walls were covered in a reproduction Victorian paper the colour of overripe plums; the furniture was mahogany and ugly. On the plus side, it was a quiet and peaceful room. A single table had been set in readiness in the window, presumably for her. A band of sunshine lay across the pristine white cloth and made the silver appear to quiver. Jacqueline thought about the leather-bound book she had scanned from cover to cover before falling asleep last night. She needed to talk to Dot Candy. She sighed then turned her back on the peaceful room and followed the twin smells of frying fish and bacon to the kitchen.

"Good morning," said Jacqueline.

Dot, who was at the stove, spun round, a spatula in her hand. "Has anyone ever told you that you move like a cat?" she said.

"I'm sorry," said Jacqueline. *Little Sneak.*

"Well, never mind," said Dot. "You decided to keep me company then?"

"If it's alright with you?" said Jacqueline. She thought, I should have gone to the dining room – she didn't mean it when she said I could eat here – she doesn't want –

144

"Wouldn't have said it if it wasn't," said Dot. She waved the spatula in the direction of the table. "Sit down. I'll just open the doors and let some sunshine in, then I'll bring you your food. Have you changed your mind about a cooked breakfast?"

"No, just tea and toast will be fine, thanks," said Jacqueline.

She went to the table and pulled out a chair, hung her bag over the back of it and sat down.

Dot crossed to the door and flung it wide. Sunshine falling in a wide band across the flagged floor made a flame of her thin red hair. Today she was dressed in tight black leggings and a black, bat-winged T-shirt whose scooped neckline showed the sun-weathered skin of her neck and chest. Jacqueline wondered how old she was – early sixties perhaps.

"That's a good-looking day," said Dot.

She brought a pot of tea to the table and toast in a silver rack.

"I know," said Jacqueline. "I've been up a while. I had a walk around the garden. How many do you have for breakfast this morning?"

"Just yourself."

"Really?" Jacqueline's eyes strayed to the cooking food.

"That's for the cats," said Dot.

"Oh – actually I met them earlier. They don't appear to like me very much."

"How many did you meet?"

"Two. Why, how many are there?"

"More than two," said Dot. She placed a butter dish on the table, then a dish of marmalade, one of jam and one of honey.

Jacqueline took a slice of toast and spread it with butter.

145

"I thought I saw a child last night."

"That would be Jimmy," said Dot. She pulled out a chair and sat down at the far end of the table. "So, did you find what you were looking for last night?"

Caught by surprise, Jacqueline paused mid-bite. "No, no, I didn't. But thanks again. I left the book back on top of the counter first thing this morning."

"I saw that. Well, I'm sorry it was of no help."

"No, I'm sorry," said Jacqueline, "for snooping around like that. I don't know what you must have thought."

"No, you don't know, so why worry about it?" said Dot.

There was, thought Jacqueline, no answer to that, so she carried on eating in silence. She wondered if it was the sea air of this north-eastern town that made people so bracing, or maybe it was just Dot.

She wondered if she should remind Dot of her offer to let her look at the other guestbooks or wait to be invited.

"So, you'll be wanting to look at the rest of them, I suppose?" said Dot.

It was so exactly what she had been thinking that Jacqueline just nodded.

"What year are you after this time?" said Dot.

"1983," said Jacqueline without hesitation.

"The year Martin died," said Dot.

There was, it appeared, no getting away from Martin, so Jacqueline put her toast down on her plate. "Martin," she said, "was he ...?"

"My husband," said Dot. She leaned in over the table, stuck a thumbnail in a groove of the bleached wood and made a little sawing motion with her thumbnail. "He was killed in a hit and run."

Jacqueline shook her head. "I'm sorry," she said.

"I was in bed with flu at the time," said Dot, "and I was furious because the weather was glorious and I wanted to be outside in the garden. Martin decided to make me chicken soup. I said I didn't want any soup, it was much too hot for soup, but Martin insisted. Only we'd run out of pearl barley so he said he'd spin down to the town on his bike and get some." Dot took her thumb out of the groove and examined the nail. "Before he left he tried to kiss me goodbye, but I was so cross I turned my face away. I told him I'd give him my germs and I wouldn't let him kiss me goodbye."

Jacqueline had taken another bite of toast. In the silence, she could hear herself masticating and stopped eating.

"I fell asleep," said Dot, "and when I woke up the police were knocking at the door. But by then Martin had been dead for two hours. Of everything, that seemed to me the most awful part, that I could sleep while he was dying. I must have been quite ill because when they told me what had happened I remember thinking it was okay, because it was only a dream and I'd wake up soon. But it wasn't a dream and I never woke up."

No, thought Jacqueline, you never wake up.

Dot got up. "I'd better get these cats fed. Want to come with me to the pigsty and make friends?"

Confused by the mention of cats and pigs in the one sentence, Jacqueline hesitated. By the time she'd got to her feet, Dot had disappeared outside. Taking a quick mouthful of tea – the toast had stuck to the roof of her mouth – she grabbed her bag and hurried after her.

The pigsty turned out to be the nettle-choked ruin near

147

the end of the garden. Inside, four cats waited while Dot hunkered down and shared the contents of the pan between four of the aluminium dishes.

"Be careful," she said to Jacqueline, over her shoulder. "This place is about to tumble down. I keep meaning to knock it down, no point in it anymore – there hasn't been a pig here since Martin's uncle's day. Now come and meet Duchess, Trotsky, Sniff and Oscar."

"Which is which?" said Jacqueline.

"The stately white one is Duchess, for obvious reasons. The little white one is Trotsky, because of that little smudge of a beard. Sniff is the stuck-up marmalade piece, and the little striped tabby is Oscar. Oscar is always hungry and will come begging, so be warned. There's another three of them around somewhere."

"I've met Sniff and Trotsky already. Are they all yours?"

Dot picked up the pan and got to her feet. "None of them are mine. Who ever really owns a cat? Some of them are strays, or they just don't get enough food at home, or they just feel like coming here. They're cats." She turned to Jacqueline. "I must get on. Would you like more tea or anything else?"

"No, thank you," said Jacqueline, "but there is one thing." She opened her bag, drew out the envelope and shook out the contents into her hand. "You asked me last night if I had a reason for coming here, to this house? Well, I have these."

Dot put the pan down on a pile of rubble, reached out and picked up the matchbook. "Oh, my days!" she said. "I haven't seen one of these in years. We had them done up as souvenirs for the guests. Martin did that sketch of the house himself. Where did you get it?"

"It was among my father's things," said Jacqueline, "along with these." She handed over the envelope and the postcard, watched as Dot examined the address, then the postcard, which she turned over before looking up.

"These were among your father's things, you say?"

Jacqueline nodded. "Yes. He – he died ten days ago."

Dot looked up abruptly. "Oh, so recently," she said. "I'm very sorry to hear that."

Something in her face and voice made Jacqueline certain of her sincerity. "I think he stayed here once," she said, "in this house."

"Is that so?" Dot returned the postcard and the matchbook to the envelope and handed it back to Jacqueline. "Well, in any event, you'll want to keep these safe." She turned and picked up the pan again. "Like I say, I must get on."

She moved away quickly and Jacqueline stood and watched her go.

Chapter 19

1976

Lilly is screaming again. "I'll never, ever forgive you, never as long as I live! You made a holy show of me in front of everyone!"

Footsteps thump, coming up the stairs, and Gayle's bed creaks as she turns over.

"Not again," she mutters.

Before Jacqueline is even out of bed, a door slams shut. She is standing on the landing when her mother comes out of her room.

"Get back to bed this minute, Jacqueline."

"But what happened and why is Lilly shouting? Who made a show of her?"

"Do what your mother says," says Daddy, coming up the stairs. He goes into his room, his head down and his shoulders hunched, and Jacqueline's mother goes after him and closes the door.

Jacqueline is alone on the landing again, staring at the sign on Lilly's door and listening to her sister crying.

"So what did Lilly do this time?" says Gayle, when Jacqueline goes back to her own room.

"Oh shut up, Gayle," says Jacqueline.

Regina Quinn knocks on the front door before Jacqueline has even had her breakfast. She doesn't even bother to say hello, just "Well, did your da kill Lilly?"

"What are you talking about?" says Jacqueline. "Why would my da kill Lilly?"

Regina's little eyes open as wide as they go. "Did you not hear what happened last night?"

Jacqueline would like to pretend she heard but she wants to know so badly it is almost a pain. So she says, "Just tell me what happened, Regina."

"Don't you know? Your da only walked into the marquee and caught Lilly wearing the face off a fella!"

"Who said so?" says Jacqueline.

"Goretti said so."

"What fella?"

"The one from the swing boats and Goretti said your da dragged Lilly out in front of everyone. He made a show of her and he tore her sash."

"What sash?" Jacqueline feels lost and stupid now, and angry with herself for knowing nothing.

"Oh my God!" says Regina. "The sash that Lilly got for being chosen as a finalist in the Festival Queen competition! Did you not even know THAT? Lilly is in the final. Oh, Jacklean, imagine if she wins! Goretti said the prize is a diamond crown and a silver cup and a hundred pounds in cash."

"Then Goretti is stupid," says Jacqueline. She feels more sure of herself now. "They wouldn't give Lilly a diamond crown, not a real one. And anyway, how come Goretti knows all this? Lilly isn't even speaking to her."

"Yes, she is, they made up. They went to the dance together last night. Jacklean, do you think Lilly will win? Because I do – she's gorgeous. Even though my ma says all the Brennans think too much about their looks."

Regina is right – Lilly and Goretti Quinn are best friends again. Goretti comes knocking at the door and Jacqueline's mother sends her around to the back garden where Lilly is sunning herself on the brown blanket.

Jacqueline settles down behind the gooseberry bushes to watch them.

"What did he say?" says Goretti. "Did he kill you?"

"Do I look dead?" says Lilly. "He just said he's throwing in the towel."

"Is that all?" Goretti sounds disappointed. "Your da is always throwing in the towel."

"I know. And he said what he always says about me getting a job in a factory. Because what's the point in me getting an education if all I want to do is street-walk?"

"There's nothing wrong with working in a factory," says Goretti Quinn.

Jacqueline is sure she is thinking about her sisters – Saints Dympna, Veronica and Catherine all work in a biscuit factory.

"I know there isn't," says Lilly. "Did I say there was? But I'd rather be a hairdresser and that's what I told my dad. That shut him up. There's no way he'd ever let me leave school without doing my Leaving Cert. It's like he thinks I'll die or something if I don't get it. Just because he had to leave school when he was fourteen, he thinks everyone should be happy to shut themselves up with their stupid books and be a swot and have no fun."

"He's so mean," says Goretti Quinn.

"Tell me about it!" says Lilly. "And now he's not going to let me out of the house. How am I supposed to meet Luca?"

"Are you really going with him, Lilly?"

"Maybe ..."

"But, Lilly, everyone is saying he's a gypsy."

"He is not a gypsy, Goretti Quinn!" Lilly sits up suddenly and Jacqueline has to duck down quickly behind the gooseberry bushes.

"I'm only telling you what everyone is saying," says Goretti, "and he does live in a caravan."

"Well, everyone is wrong," says Lilly, "and just because someone lives in a caravan doesn't make him a gypsy. And, for your information, Luca only lives in a caravan when he's with the carnival. I happen to know that his family in England have a house the same as you and me. And his grandfather runs a big fair, so there!"

"Okay," says Goretti Quinn. "Don't blame me for what people are saying."

"And I'll tell you something else," says Lilly. "Luca said everyone thinks working in a fair is romantic, but it's not, it's a hard slog. He has to look after the rides, dismantle them every time they move on and then set them up again in the next place. And he does all the repairs, all the painting and cleaning and stuff and he handles the money. He works really hard and he's really, really good with people."

"And he's gorgeous," says Goretti Quinn. She giggles. "Don't forget that bit, Lilly."

Lilly laughs. "And he's gorgeous."

"Would you live in a caravan with him, Lilly?"

"If he asked me to," says Lilly. "Luca told me he has the wanderlust and he thinks he probably always will."

Jacqueline wonders what the wanderlust is – she thinks it is probably a disease.

Goretti Quinn begins to sing. "Lilly and Luca sitting in a tree, K-I-S-S-I-N-G!"

Lilly laughs and lies down again. Jacqueline waits a while but they are so quiet that she thinks they must have fallen asleep and she sneaks quietly away.

Chapter 20

Afterwards

After breakfast, Jacqueline followed the path to the cliffs. As the track curved away from the road, she followed it, and rounding a sharp bend almost fell upon the chair. This time it held a sleeping man. His legs were planted wide apart and his head had fallen slightly forward. His hair was black and lightly flecked with grey, shocked on one side by a narrow band of white: a "Mallen streak", thought Jacqueline, thinking of a Catherine Cookson novel she had read as a teenager. The chair was positioned right in the middle of the track and to get around it she would have to climb up onto a rocky bank. While she was wondering whether to bother or not, the man's head jerked upward, his eyes opened and for a moment he looked straight into Jacqueline's eyes.

"You have to give way to a duck," he said, then his head fell forward and he began to snore.

Jacqueline turned on her heel and retreated.

A small boy was watching Jacqueline solemnly from behind a pair of very ugly and very thick glasses.

"My daddy has no head," he said.

Jacqueline studied him with no real alarm; she was in no doubt but that she was dreaming. But the boy did not disappear. Instead he spoke again.

"I'm a lonely child," he said, and he pushed his glasses up his nose.

"Is that right?" said Jacqueline.

She reluctantly decided that he was real and in truth he did not in any way resemble a dream-child. His body was too chunky and he had tufty, copper-coloured hair, and brows that tilted slightly at the inner corners, giving him a perpetually perplexed expression. She thought he looked about four or five.

She looked about her. She was sitting in a red-and-white striped deckchair and her book lay at her feet. She remembered now that she had come out onto the terrace of Sea Holly Villa to read. She picked up her book, opened it and ostentatiously began to read, using it to screen the child from her vision. She had always made a point of ignoring children she did not know, and most of the few she did, and still remembered the last time she had broken her rule.

A little girl had been sitting opposite her on a train and her expression as she stared fixedly at Jacqueline was so intent and serious that Jacqueline had smiled at her.

The child hadn't returned the smile. Instead she said loudly, "She's pretty, isn't she, Mummy, even though she isn't young?"

The woman next to her leaned in and hissed something inaudible in the child's ear.

Jacqueline stared out of the window and simulated being a deaf mute.

"But she isn't, Mummy." The little girl's tone was one of patient reason. "Look, she has lines around her eyes."

It was more than five years since the incident but Jacqueline had never forgotten it. She remembered, too, going home that evening and examining and re-examining her face in a mirror.

When she glanced up, the little boy was still watching her.

Jacqueline gave a little ground. "Why are you lonely?" she asked. "Haven't you anyone to play with?"

The boy shook his head so fiercely the heavy glasses juddered. "No," he said, and he stamped his foot in frustration. "I'm a lonely child."

"He means that he's an *only* child," said Dot Candy, coming out on the terrace and ruffling the child's hair. "Jacqueline, this is Jimmy Small. Say hello."

"Hello," said Jacqueline and realised too late that Dot had been addressing the child. The error made her feel foolish. She made a show of digging her phone out of her pocket and checking the time and was genuinely astonished to find it was gone two-thirty. She got up. "I'd better get a move on and go get something to eat."

"You know you're welcome to make yourself something here," said Dot.

"Thanks, but I think I'll go into the town," said Jacqueline.

"Suit yourself." Dot smiled down at the boy. "Shall we go walk the course, Jimmy?"

The child squinted and nodded vigorously and Jacqueline watched them moving hand and hand down the steps and across the garden.

She had her lunch in a small seafood restaurant on the

promenade. She put away a plate of pasta with prawns, and on a whim ordered the 'Tart of the Day'. It turned out to be treacle tart and, as she chased the last crumbs round the plate with her fork, Jacqueline was assailed by a memory of her father, eating apple pie and custard on the day of his haircut. And on the back of that came a wave of other memories. She saw him, grinning puckishly over the rim of his whisky glass, thought of how he always refused to be hurried but would suddenly break into the funny little shuffly run he had. She remembered how he would never wear a hat, however cold the weather got, but hunched down instead, inside the upturned collar of his overcoat. Like every memory of him, these hurt her like a physical attack, but this time the pain was alloyed with the sudden conviction that one day all these would be happy memories. All she had to do was wait.

She left the restaurant and strolled down the slipway to the beach. The afternoon was warm and she sat on the sand and took off her shoes, wrapped her jacket around her bag and made a pillow of it, then stretched out and closed her eyes.

When she awoke and checked her phone, she realised she had been dozing for more than two hours; she wondered if she had some kind of sleeping sickness. It was still pleasant but not as warm as it had been. She unwound her jacket from her bag and put it on, then sat looking about her.

The tide had come in and she got up and walked to the shore. She waded into the sea. The water foamed about her calves in lace-like patterns that stretched and tore and then reformed.

The light on the water was dazzling and she closed her

eyes. Keeping them shut, she took a couple of steps. The sand heaved softly under her feet and she swayed a little, then she took another step and another. She thought: I could just keep on going …

"Some people leave their clothes in a neat little pile beside the water."

Jacqueline opened her eyes and spun round. A man was standing at the water's edge. The sun caught the streak of white in his hair and made it gleam and Jacqueline recognised the man from the chair.

"Why do they do that, do you think?"

Jacqueline was not even sure that he was addressing her; his eyes were fixed on the sea. He was dressed in a dark-blue greatcoat, and trousers that looked too big for him, the ends of which flapped and billowed in the wind. Jacqueline decided he had been talking to himself. She turned her back on him and decided to ignore him. She put some distance between them, moving slowly sideways in the water. The afternoon was still as beautiful but somehow, now that she knew he was there, she could no longer enjoy it.

"People don't thrash around gasping like you might imagine. Sometimes they float for a while. Sometimes they just go under quietly."

Giving him a wide berth, Jacqueline began to wade toward the shore.

"When water is inhaled there is associated coughing and vomiting, followed by loss of consciousness."

"I'm not interested!" Jacqueline called over her shoulder. "Go away and annoy someone else."

"You're Irish," he said. "Dublin."

Jacqueline kept on walking. She picked up her shoes and

hurried toward the slipway. When she looked back, the man was still standing where she had left him, facing out to sea. Just a madman, she thought, but she felt shaken and angry. Why pick on her when the beach was dotted with other solitary walkers? As she made her way up Shore Road, a flock of birds flew above her; she stood and gazed up at them. They formed a perfect V as though one spirit moved them. Watching them, an appalling sense of loneliness washed over her and she moved on again quickly.

The door to Sea Holly Villa was open and the house was very quiet. As she went upstairs, Jacqueline remembered that she only had a couple of pages left to read in her book. Dot would hardly mind if she borrowed a book. She doubled back and wandered into the lounge with the awful wallpaper and the claw-legged furniture and the dead things under glass. She crossed to the bookcase. Moving slowly, she read the titles of the books, running her fingers over the spines, and finally pulled out a collection of Somerset Maugham's short stories. As she opened it, a gentle creak made her turn sharply and she realised with a small shock that she was not alone.

In a corner of the room, a girl was reclining in a rocking chair. The child Jimmy was in her lap, his upturned face pale and moony in the dim light, his eyes fixed on Jacqueline.

"I'm sorry," said Jacqueline. "I didn't mean to disturb you."

The girl looked up and met Jacqueline's gaze but did not acknowledge her presence by so much as a flicker of her eye.

"Well, I'll leave you to it so," said Jacqueline and hurried from the room, the book in her hand. Cool little madam, she thought, as she went back upstairs.

As soon as she opened the door to her room she saw it on the chair by the window. Somerset Maugham was forgotten as she picked up the guestbook and carried it to the bed.

It took her less than five minutes to find his name.

Chapter 21

1976

Daddy comes into the sitting room. "This fine young man wants a word with you, Lilly."

The fine young man is Sexy Sexton.

Jacqueline looks at Lilly. She is lying on the floor with her elbows on a cushion, watching Opportunity Knocks, *and barely glances over her shoulder at Sexy Sexton.*

"Hiya, Eddie," she says, then she goes back to looking at the television.

Sexy Sexton is standing in the doorway, his shoulders stooped as he tries not to bang his head.

Jacqueline decides to ignore him too and stares at the screen. The advertisements have come on and a man is pouring a pint of Guinness. A voice says, "This summer sit back, relax and enjoy the long cold spell ..."

Jacqueline thinks that it is just one more thing that does not make sense.

"Lilly, where are your manners?" says Jacqueline's mother. "Eddie, come on in and sit down. Gayle, move up on the sofa and make some room for Eddie."

Gayle's face goes bright red but she moves up and Sexy

Sexton sits down beside her. While Daddy is talking to Sexy about the weather and the match on Sunday, Jacqueline inspects him. He is very tall and skinny and his hair is greasy. Jacqueline tries to find the puss-ball that Lilly says is like a third eye, but there are so many spots and pimples on Sexy Sexton's face it is hard to tell one from the other.

Daddy says, "You know I was at school with your father, Edmund?"

"Were you really, sir?" says Sexy Sexton.

Jacqueline makes a loud snorting sound – nobody has ever called Daddy "sir" before – but Daddy gives her a look and she stops.

"In the primary school this was," says Daddy. "Of course your father went on to the Christian Brothers and the University after that. Most of the rest of us had to leave and go out and get work and –"

"Oh Daddy, please tell me you're not going to bore poor Eddie with how you had to go out and sweep chimneys when you were ten," says Lilly. "Because, if you are, I'll just go and get my violin."

Daddy smiles. "Do you hear the way she cheeks me, Edmund?" he says. "If you must know I didn't sweep chimneys. My first job was as a nipper on a building site and I wasn't ten, I was thirteen. Different times, Edmund, different times, but at least your father did a bit better for himself. But what made him want to go and be a solicitor?"

"Frank!" says Jacqueline's mother.

"Well, I only mean that I always had the idea he wanted to be a doctor."

"Actually, sir, I think it was my grandfather who wanted him to be a doctor," says Sexy. "Dad always had an interest in the law."

163

"Ah, well sure, you'll be the doctor now," says Daddy, "so everyone wins. And I suppose your dad will end up a judge before much longer, with all your grandfather's connections in Leinster House. Has he still got that fine boat of his?"

Sexy Sexton smiles and looks at his feet. "It's not a very big boat," he said, "but, yes, sir, Grandad loves his sailing."

"Never mind," says Daddy, "he'll get a bigger one soon, I'm sure. And please, Edmund, call me Frank. Now, Lilly, are you going to make this young man a cup of tea or something?"

Lilly, without turning round, says, "Eddie, do you want a cup of tea or something?"

"I wouldn't mind a glass of water," says Sexy Sexton. "It's awful warm."

"Okay, come on into the kitchen and I'll get you one then."

Everyone watches them go.

"What did you go and do that for, Frank?" says Jacqueline's mother.

"Do what?"

"Embarrass Lilly like that, bringing that young fella in without a word of warning."

"Who needs warning?" says Daddy. "Edmund had the manners to knock on the door and ask me if he could take Lilly to the pictures. What's the harm? And he said Lilly knew he was coming."

"That's not the point."

"If you ask me," says Daddy, "it's nice to see a bit of manners for a change. And, anyway, Lilly didn't seem to mind, did she?"

And that is the question Jacqueline keeps asking herself – why didn't Lilly mind?

Nothing makes sense. Lilly is going with Sexy Sexton. Sexy Sexton the Crater Face, Sexy Sexton the Creep, Sexy Sexton the Long Streak of Paralysed Piss. He has called to the house three times now in his car, and Lilly has gone with him to the pictures, to bowling and once, on Sunday, just for a drive.

Jacqueline is not absolutely sure what people do when they go with other people – "sex and kissing" Regina Quinn says, but no matter how she tries Jacqueline cannot imagine Lilly kissing Sexy Sexton.

"Why did Daddy let her?" Jacqueline asks Gayle. "He said he didn't want Lilly going out with boys. Sexy Sexton is a boy."

"Don't call him that," says Gayle. "Yes, he's a boy, but he's different."

They are lying in the garden on the brown blanket. Gayle is wearing her blue swimsuit. She says she is tired of running. She wants to get a proper suntan for once – just like Lilly's.

"How is he different?" asks Jacqueline. "Is it because his father is loaded?"

"I don't know if he's loaded," says Gayle.

"Well, his grandad has a boat and they have a fountain in their garden."

"I don't know about a fountain …"

"You don't know much," says Jacqueline. "Regina Quinn says Sexy has a fountain in his garden."

"Maybe he has, but anyway that's not why Daddy doesn't mind Lilly going out with Eddie. I think Daddy

165

likes Eddie because he's going to university to study medicine when he leaves school and because he has nice manners and, well, because he's nice."

"He's not nice," says Jacqueline. "He smells funny and he has spots and his hair always looks wet."

"He doesn't smell funny," says Gayle. "Don't be silly, Jacqueline – that's just aftershave and I think it smells nice."

"Well, I think he stinks," says Jacqueline, "and I think he's a long streak of paralysed piss. Lilly said so and she's right, so why is she going with him? I don't understand."

Gayle sits up quickly. "Is that a car in the lane?"

"I think so. It's probably him again."

"Who?"

"Sexy Sexton, who do you think?"

Gayle jumps to her feet. "Go and see, will you, Jacqueline?"

"Why do I have to go and see? I don't care if it's him or not – you go and see if you're that bothered."

"I can't go, I'm in my swimsuit," says Gayle. "Please, Jacqueline, I'm begging you. And if it's Eddie bring him into the house, okay?"

"Okay, okay," says Jacqueline.

"And don't call him Sexy."

Jacqueline watches Gayle running all the way to the house. She gets up slowly and walks up the garden and round to the front of the house. Sexy Sexton's car is in the drive and Sexy Sexton is standing in the porch. His back is to Jacqueline and both of his hands are on top of his head, smoothing down his hair.

"Lilly's not here!" shouts Jacqueline and Sexy Sexton jumps and turns round.

"You frightened the life out of me," he says, then he smiles at Jacqueline. "I didn't hear you coming."

Jacqueline does not smile. She looks Sexy Sexton up and down. He is wearing white shorts, a white T-shirt and white runners and he has a white band around his forehead. Who does he think he is, Jacqueline wonders, Bjorn Borg? She tries to imagine Lilly kissing him.

"Have you any idea when she'll be back?" says Sexy Sexton.

"No."

"Right, well, maybe you could give her –"

"Have you really got a fountain in your garden?" asks Jacqueline.

"We do," Sexy Sexton says with a smile. "Would you like to see it?"

"No," Jacqueline lies.

The front door opens.

"Hiya, Eddie."

Jacqueline stares at Gayle. She is wearing a cream dress and white sandals. Her hair is loose around her shoulders and her plait has left it in long wide ripples. She looks, Jacqueline thinks, like somebody else.

Jacqueline says, "Is that Lilly's dress you're wearing?"

Gayle's face goes red and Sexy Sexton says, "Hi, Gaye, I was just asking your little sister to give Lilly a message for me."

"It's Gayle," says Jacqueline, "her name is Gayle not Gaye. And that IS Lilly's dress. She's going to kill you, Gayle."

Gayle ignores her. "Do you want to come in and wait, Eddie?" she says. "Lilly will probably be back soon."

"Sure," says Sexy Sexton.

Jacqueline tries to follow them into the house but Gayle shuts the door in her face. Jacqueline marches round the back of the house and in through the back door.

They are in the kitchen. Sexy Sexton is sitting at the table and Gayle is pouring red lemonade into two glasses. She hands a glass to Sexy Sexton.

"I want some too," says Jacqueline.

"Then get it yourself," says Gayle.

Jacqueline watches Sexy Sexton drinking his lemonade. She stares at the funny little ball under the skin of his neck that bobs up and down.

"Thanks, Gaye," says Sexy Sexton. "I was parched. Playing tennis in this weather – I must be mad."

The front door bangs and Jacqueline hears Lilly calling, "Eddie? Are you here, Eddie?"

Sexy Sexton jumps up and Gayle stares down at Lilly's dress. Jacqueline smiles.

Lilly comes into the kitchen. "There you are, Eddie, I saw your car. That's a very nice dress, Gayle. Do you want to come into the sitting room, Eddie – at least we'll have a bit of privacy there?"

Jacqueline and Gayle watch them go.

"Do you think she noticed?" asks Gayle.

Jacqueline is too busy wondering why Lilly and Sexy Sexton want privacy.

The door opens again and Lilly sticks her head around it. "You're dead, Gayle Brennan!" she hisses. "Now get my good dress off this minute!" For once, she does not bang the kitchen door.

"I think she noticed," says Jacqueline.

Chapter 22

Afterwards

Dot Candy was on the terrace, reclining in one of the striped deck chairs. The terrace was still lit with sunshine although much of the garden was in shadow. She had a glass of wine in her hand and she turned her head when Jacqueline appeared in the kitchen doorway.

"Hello – join me in a drink?" she said.

Jacqueline noticed that there was a second glass on the table before her. She's been expecting me, she thought. "Sure." She came out onto the terrace, pulled out a chair, and sat down. "But just the one, I'm heading into town to get something to eat."

Dot poured her some wine and topped up her own drink. "Cheers!"

"Cheers." Jacqueline took a sip of the wine. It was good, in fact it was wonderful and she took a second, decent draught. "Thank you for finding that guestbook for me. I hope you didn't go to too much trouble."

"Did you find what you were looking for?"

"Some of it," said Jacqueline.

"Yes and no then," said Dot. She leaned her head

against the back of her chair and for a while there was no sound but the song of the invisible birds.

Perverse woman, thought Jacqueline, full of questions when they're not welcome, but now when I'm willing to offer information she doesn't want to know. She leaned back too and closed her eyes. When she opened them again Dot was watching her.

"You have good hair," said Dot, "nice and thick. I envy people with good hair."

"Thanks." Jacqueline's hand went involuntarily to her head. "I think I get it from my father – he had good hair too. Actually, it was his name I found in the guestbook. He did stay here after all."

"Is that so?" said Dot. She leaned in and replenished both glasses.

"In 1983," said Jacqueline.

Dot took a sip of her drink and settled back in her chair once more.

"His name was Frank," said Jacqueline. "Frank Brennan."

Dot's head nodded on her stalky neck. "You look a bit like him. It's the eyes, I think."

Jacqueline put her glass down on the table. "You remember him. But why didn't you say so before?"

"I wasn't certain at first – it was a very long time ago."

"And yet you remember him," said Jacqueline.

"Some people you just remember," said Dot.

"Tell me," said Jacqueline.

"Nothing much to tell. He came, he stayed a while and then he went away again."

"But why did he come?" said Jacqueline.

"He never really told me in so many words," said Dot

Candy, "but from what I gathered, there was a child ... or a young girl ..."

"My sister. My sister Lilly. She disappeared in 1976 and was never found. And he was looking for her here?"

"Like I said, he never actually told me the details, but I believe that's why he came. The poor man ... oh, hello, Marilyn."

Jacqueline turned. A girl was standing on the terrace behind her. She had very dark, very long, straight black hair and was wearing a short navy-blue dress and very high, black, strappy shoes. She looked very different with her face heavily made-up, her lips dark red and glossy as cherries, but Jacqueline recognised the girl from the rocking chair. Right this minute, Jacqueline wished her back there.

"I don't think you two have met officially," said Dot. "Jacqueline, meet Marilyn. Marilyn, this is Jacqueline Brennan."

"Hi, Marilyn," said Jacqueline.

The girl barely acknowledged her greeting. "He's asleep," she said, looking at Dot.

"Fine, you get off then," said Dot.

"Thanks, I won't be late." Marilyn walked away, her body canted unnaturally in the ludicrous heels.

"She *will* be late," said Dot, "but who can blame her?"

"You watch the child for her?" said Jacqueline.

Dot nodded. "She needs to get out sometimes and have a bit of fun."

"She seems very young to have a child," said Jacqueline.

"She looks about fifteen, doesn't she? But she's just gone twenty-two."

"The little boy," said Jacqueline. "He told me his daddy has no head."

Dot winced. "Did he say that? I'd hoped he was starting to forget. You see, Marilyn's boyfriend, Jimmy's father, was decapitated."

"Jesus!" Jacqueline put her hands to her own neck.

"Poor little Jimmy overheard Marilyn one evening, when she was drunk and hysterical and not exactly watching her words. Unfortunately, the salient facts seem to have lodged in his brain. It's a pity, because Jimmy doesn't have any actual memory of his father."

"How did it happen?" asked Jacqueline.

"An accident on a building site," said Dot, "and to make matters worse he was working here illegally – he was Bulgarian – no insurance, nothing. Marilyn lost the run of herself for a while and they got evicted from their flat. She was in danger of losing Jimmy – she came very close to having him taken away by social services."

"Has she no family of her own?"

"None that want to know – but they're okay now, they're here. Oh hello!" Dot sprang to her feet. "What's up, Jimmy? Couldn't you sleep?"

Jacqueline twisted in her chair again. This time it was the child who was standing behind her. He was dressed in purple pyjamas decorated with green dinosaurs, his feet were bare and he was holding some kind of cuddly toy animal, so ratty it was hard to tell what exactly – a squirrel perhaps from the look of its tail. He gazed fixedly at Jacqueline, then without warning he broke into a run, his arms spread wide, swooping past the two women, the squirrel flying wildly above his head. Careering down the steps he ran about the lawn, making loud aeroplane noises. Then, as suddenly, he was back again, circling Jacqueline's chair. She drew in her feet, tightened her hold on her glass to avoid the flying squirrel and waited for him to stop.

Her sigh of relief when he finally swooped down to the garden again was audible and, meeting Dot's eye, she could see the woman's amusement.

"He likes you," said Dot.

"I don't think so," said Jacqueline.

"He does. Children are like that – they take best to people who don't fawn over them."

"Perhaps," said Jacqueline. She buried her nose in her glass.

Dot picked up her glass from the table and drained it. "I'd better go put that child to bed," she said, "but you stay and have some more wine. I shouldn't be more than ten minutes – he's tired out."

"I should go," said Jacqueline, but she stayed where she was. Watching Dot running across the lawn after the boy, she didn't think he looked tired out. He squealed and yelped and evaded Dot's grasp several times before she finally caught him, swept him up in her arms and carried him into the house.

Jacqueline thought about her dinner but after the heavy lunch she could wait, and she needed to talk to Dot Candy. And it was very peaceful now the boy had gone. So she refilled her glass and tried to relax and enjoy the pleasant evening. Two butterflies danced by in a jazzy synchronicity and she watched them for a while, mesmerised.

She had refilled her glass a second time before Dot returned, another bottle of wine in her hand.

"Sorry," she said. "That took longer than I thought – three stories in fact. And when he finally got to sleep, it was all I could do to stop myself cleaning that room."

"Jimmy's room?"

173

"Well, Marilyn's room – it's a bombsite up there."

"You don't clean it?"

"No, I don't. Marilyn is not a guest, she lives here. She's supposed to look after herself, keep her room clean and all that. I keep promising myself I'll ignore it, but it's not easy. Oh well, never mind, not your business, forget I said anything." She filled her own glass and offered Jacqueline a top-up.

"No, thanks. I helped myself while you were gone."

"So what? Have some more," said Dot.

"I'd best not – not on an empty stomach."

"Look, why don't I get you something to eat?" said Dot. "Unless you really want to go into town."

"No, it's too much trouble," said Jacqueline, "and your work is done for the day, you're relaxing."

"Would you eat an omelette?" said Dot, already on her feet. "I would. I haven't eaten yet myself. You stay here and I'll be back before you know it."

Resistance, Jacqueline felt, was futile and the truth was she had no real desire to walk all the way back down the hill again. She could get a taxi, she supposed, there or back or both but it was so much more pleasant to sit here and sip her wine and she really did want to talk to Dot.

When Dot had hurried off, Jacqueline, her glass full once more, succumbed to her own languor and settled back in her chair. And it did seem like no time before Dot was back with the omelette and with it a basket of French bread and a tossed salad.

As they settled down and began to eat, Dot picked up the threads of their conversation almost as though there had been no break. "I shouldn't talk about Marilyn like that – it's not easy for her. You know, she says he comes to her at night sometimes."

"Who does?" said Jacqueline. "By the way, this omelette is heaven."

"Thanks. Calvin, Jimmy's father – his name was Calvin Schmalz."

Biting into the still-warm bread Jacqueline realised she had misheard. It was Schmalz, not Small.

"Though the state that room is in, it's a miracle he can find her," said Dot musingly.

Jacqueline couldn't help smiling. "What does she say he does?"

"I don't think he does anything much by the sounds of it," said Dot. "Just stands there and smiles at her. And once, she said, he kissed the top of Jimmy's head and told her he was happy."

"I suppose it's good she can believe that," said Jacqueline.

Dot's eyebrows rose. "A twenty-eight-year-old man who's had his head sliced off his body, and he comes to her smiling?" Her tone was bitter. "What's he got to be happy about?"

"Does he carry it under his arm?" said Jacqueline.

"Does he carry what under his arm?"

"His head," said Jacqueline, and then at the expression on Dot's face added, "I'm sorry, it isn't funny, I shouldn't have said that."

"No," said Dot, "it's not funny."

Then her face contorted and suddenly they were both laughing uncontrollably.

When they stopped, Dot said, "The truth is, I envy Marilyn. After Martin died, I looked for signs everywhere, any sort of sign that he was still here. You know, all that rubbish that people talk about – white feathers and the spirit of the dead returning in the form of a bird or a cat." She shook her head.

"But the dead don't come back," said Jacqueline. "No matter how much you want them to." She pushed her plate away.

"No, I don't believe they do." Dot's voice was gentler than Jacqueline had heard it yet.

"About my father …" said Jacqueline.

"Shoot," said Dot.

"You said you believed he came here looking for my sister. Did he find her?"

Dot took a sip of her wine. "No, I don't believe he did. No, I'm certain he didn't although I always had the feeling that he found out something …"

"Found out what?" said Jacqueline.

"I have no idea," said Dot, "I honestly haven't. It was just a feeling I had …"

"Based on what? People don't just have feelings for no reason – it's always based on something, some fact, something they've seen or heard …"

"Alright then," said Dot. "Based on the way he was when he left here to return home."

"What do you mean? How was he?"

"Different. Just different to the way he was when he first arrived here. If I had to put a word on it, I'd say he seemed hopeful – as though something had happened to make him more hopeful." She shrugged her shoulders. "That's the only way I can explain it and I was probably wrong."

"No, I don't think you were wrong," said Jacqueline. "I think something did happen while he was here. Because that's how I remember it too. He went away and when he came back he was different. For a while he was different, better, like the spark was back for a while. And then it went out again and it never returned."

Dot stirred in her chair. "I'm very sorry," she said. She leaned forward. "You know we were speaking about grief just now?"

Jacqueline nodded.

"Well, you probably know this already, but the Victorians set out the periods of mourning considered appropriate – two to three years for a husband, one for a parent."

"Yes, I've heard that," said Jacqueline.

"I've often wondered about that," said Dot, and she settled back in her chair again. "I know I mourned Martin for a lot longer than three years. But I imagine after the time allotted was up and they'd packed away all that paraphernalia they went in for, the jet beads and what-have-you, those Victorians still went on grieving inside, the same as us."

"I imagine so too," said Jacqueline.

"But the time comes," said Dot, "when you stop willing them to come back. At first you think that could never happen and when it does it feels like a sort of betrayal. It isn't, of course, it's natural. Otherwise we, the people left behind, would never get on with our own lives. We'd just stay forever crippled by grief."

Dot's eyes were fixed on Jacqueline's face. She's not talking about herself, thought Jacqueline, she means me. Is that what I am, forever crippled by grief? She looked up at the sky. While they had been talking, the bright sharp stars had cut their way through. She got to her feet.

"Okay, well, it's late, and I'm tired. Let me take those dishes."

"No, please leave them," said Dot.

"But you cooked it," said Jacqueline. "The least I can do is wash up."

"I like to keep busy," said Dot and the brittle nature of her smile stopped Jacqueline's protest in its tracks.

"Okay, if you insist," she said. "Thank you, Dot, for the wine and the food and for ... for everything. Goodnight."

As she walked away, Dot called after her. "Jacqueline! You should speak to Magpie."

Jacqueline turned. "Who's Magpie?"

"You'll see him around the town," said Dot. "Your father and he used to go about together a bit. He's Irish, used to be a fisherman at one time – the best place to find him is at the harbour. Ask anyone there and they'll point him out to you. He might remember something or he might not." She shrugged her shoulders. "No guarantees with Magpie, but speak to him."

Chapter 23

1976

There is room for only two more X's on the calendar and then it will be the day of the Festival Queen Dance.

Daddy comes in with the newspaper in his hand. "Would you believe it, there's a horse called Golden Gayle running in the 2.15 at Newmarket!"

"Where?" Gayle jumps up, nearly spilling the milk.

Daddy spreads the paper on the table and the two of them lean in over it. "There!" Daddy stabs the paper with his pencil. "Eight to one."

"It's even spelled the same way as my name," says Gayle. "Are you going to back it, Daddy?"

Daddy winks at Jacqueline. "I suppose I'll have to."

"Like you need a reason to back a horse," says Jacqueline's mother.

"Ah but I have a good feeling about this one," says Daddy. "I think I'm in for a lucky spell."

Jacqueline's mother rolls her eyes. They are going to start arguing again, Jacqueline thinks, about Daddy wasting money on backing horses and going to the pub. She picks up Billy Bunter Butts In *and goes outside and*

179

down to the orchard.

She has only just settled herself with her book when Regina Quinn comes rustling across the grass. She has a towel rolled up under her arm.

"Are you comin' down the river, Jacklean?" she says.

Jacqueline is about to say no, but even under the trees it is too hot to read today. She thinks about how cool the water will feel running over her hot skin. "Alright, but I'm bringing my book."

In her bedroom, Jacqueline takes off her clothes, puts her swimsuit on and gets dressed once more. On the landing, she gets a towel from the hot press and goes downstairs.

Regina is waiting for her in the orchard. They cut through the gap in the hedge and walk through the meadow to where the river is waiting for them, cold and silver.

It is even better than Jacqueline has imagined. The stones are mossy and smooth and they feel cold under her feet. She closes her eyes with happiness, lies back and lets herself float so that the sound of the flowing water blocks out Regina's chattering. They stay in the water for a long time and afterwards they spread their towels on the grass and lie down. The sun dries their swimsuits in next to no time so that they are able to put their clothes on over them for going home.

On the way back they meet Slinky Quinn. He has his gun in one hand and a bag across his shoulder.

"Howya, Da," says Regina.

Jacqueline looks at the bag and knows there are dead things in there. She imagines them curled up together with blood on their fur, and the day sours like milk in the sun.

When she looks up, Slinky Quinn is watching her and smiling. Jacqueline feels the label of her T-shirt rubbing against her sunburnt neck. She looks down quickly and stares at the rows and rows of blue elephants dancing rings around her shorts, at the hairs above her knee-bone, pale and shimmery in the sunlight.

"How's young Brennan today then?" says Slinky Quinn. "You're growing into a little topper, you are, a right little topper."

Jacqueline thinks that she is glad Slinky Quinn is not her daddy.

"I wish I didn't have to go home," says Regina, when Slinky Quinn has gone.

"Why?" Jacqueline asks, wondering if Regina can read her mind.

"I was supposed to mind Popeye but I snuck out, and now my da will tell my ma he saw me down the river."

"Will she slap you with the wooden spoon?"

Regina nods her head.

"How many times is that this week?" asks Jacqueline.

Regina counts silently on her fingertips. "Four," she says, "so far."

Poor Regina, Jacqueline thinks, going home to Slinky and Mrs Quinn and the wooden spoon, but at least she gets gravy.

When she is back in her own bedroom, Jacqueline stares at herself in the mirror and thinks about what Slinky Quinn said. Is she growing into a little topper? Does she even want to be a little topper? She has never thought about the way she looks before, not really. She knows she is not like Gayle, who is very tall, with fair hair and blue eyes and broad shoulders. She supposes that she herself is more like Lilly, except that her own hair is light brown and her nose is a different shape, and she has too many freckles. Lilly never gets freckles. Jacqueline sighs and takes off her clothes and lies down on her bed in her swimsuit and tries to pretend she is still floating in the cool shining water of the river.

Daddy is cooking a heart for his dinner. He takes the tray out of the oven and the fat spits and hops. Jacqueline watches him stab the heart with the long fork then lift it onto the big blue-and-white plate which has a picture of a river with a little humpback bridge and there is a man under the bridge, fishing from a boat. The heart rolls across the little humpback bridge and into the river.

"That's disgusting," says Lilly.

Daddy cuts into the heart and the blood flows, making the blue water red.

"Oh look, Daddy!" says Jacqueline. "Your heart is broken."

"Lilly must have broken it so." Daddy smiles at Lilly, then his head goes to one side. "Is that a flaw on your face, Lilly?"

"It's not a flaw, Frank," says Jacqueline's mother. "It's a spot and you'd hardly notice it, Lilly."

Lilly says, "Tell that to the Bionic Man," but she smiles at Daddy. "I forgot to tell you, Daddy. Eddie wants to take me to the marquee dance on Saturday night. I told him you didn't want me to go but he says he's going to ask you anyway."

Jacqueline's mother says, "You're seeing an awful lot of that fella all of a sudden. I hope he's careful in that car of his."

"Of course he's careful," says Daddy. "Edmund is a sensible young fella. As long as he's taking you and seeing you home, I don't see why not. Tell him to come and talk to me."

"Okay, Daddy, I'll tell him." Lilly sounds as if she doesn't care but Jacqueline sees the little smile on her face when Daddy isn't looking.

Gayle says, "But it's not fair – I want to watch Eamonn Coughlan in the Olympics."

"He's not even running tonight," says Jacqueline's mother. "It's only the opening ceremony. You can switch over after New Faces."

"But the Olympics are more important than stupid old New Faces," says Gayle.

"In your opinion," says Jacqueline's mother.

Jacqueline gets up and goes over to the window. If she ruled the world, everyone would have their own television, then there wouldn't be so many arguments. Daddy could watch Match of the Day and The Sky at Night, Lilly could watch Charlie's Angels, her mother could watch Crossroads and …

A blue car comes through the gateway and up the drive.

"Here comes Sexy Sexton again," says Jacqueline. "Why is he always here?"

"Jacqueline Brennan!" says her mother. "Come away from the window this minute, and go and let Edmund in. And stop calling him Sexy Sexton – how many times do you have to be told?"

Gayle jumps up from the sofa. "I'll go."

Jacqueline watches her hurrying out of the room, her fingers touching her plait. When she comes back, her face *is very red and Sexy Sexton is behind her.*

He shakes hands with Daddy and Jacqueline's mother, and Daddy says, "Sit yourself down, Eddie."

Sexy sits down on the sofa and Gayle sits down next to him.

"Eddie," she says, "what do you think is more important, Eamonn Coughlan in the Olympics or New Faces?*"*

Sexy Sexton looks at Gayle as though she is talking double Dutch and Jacqueline's mother says, "Never mind about that now, Gayle. Jacqueline, love, will you go and tell Lilly that Edmund is here, please."

Jacqueline gets up and goes into the hall. She stands at the bottom of the stairs and shouts as loudly as she can. "Lilly, Mam says you're to come down now! Sexy Sexton is waiting for you!"

In the living room, everyone starts to talk at once.

Jacqueline's mother says, "Isn't it very hot for the time of night, Eddie?"

Gayle says, "Are you still playing tennis, Eddie?"

Daddy says, "So, Edmund, what do you give for Eamonn Coughlan's chances of a medal?"

Jacqueline smiles and goes upstairs.

Lilly comes out of her room. She is wearing her navy bell-bottoms and a white crinkly top with little bits of what looks like glass all over it. The pieces of glass have been sewn on with red threads and they glitter like mirrors in the sunlight that is streaming through the landing window.

"Sexy Sexton is waiting for you, Lilly," says Jacqueline.

Lilly smiles. "You know you're not supposed to call him Sexy, don't you?"

"I know," says Jacqueline.

"Well, anyway, stop staring at me," says Lilly.

184

"The cat has leave to look at the queen," says Jacqueline. "Why is it called cheese cloth, Lilly?"

Lilly looks down at her top. "I don't know. Why do you always ask such weird questions?" She pushes past Jacqueline and Jacqueline leans over the banister and watches her going slowly down the stairs in her platform shoes.

"You look lovely, Lilly!" she calls.

Lilly bends her head backwards and smiles up at her. "Thanks, Jacks."

Jacqueline feels her heart flip in her chest. "Lilly," she says, "why are you going with Sexy Sexton?"

Lilly stops and looks up again. "Why shouldn't I go with him?"

"Because you're so … and he's … he's Sexy Sexton."

"Mind your own business, Miss Nosey Parker," says Lilly, but she is still smiling.

Jacqueline follows her down the stairs.

Chapter 24

Afterwards

Jacqueline woke at half-nine with half a hangover and a headache. She had lain awake late into the night wondering about a man called Magpie, about her father coming to this place all those years ago, in the summer of 1983. 1983, when Dot was mourning her dead husband and Jacqueline had finished her first year of university and taken her first summer job. She remembered how she had spent her days in a pokey newsagent's, selling cigarettes and newspapers, scooping ice cream into cones or weighing out boiled sweets. On Saturday mornings, trying and often failing to keep her patience with the hordes of children as they deliberated endlessly between Black Jacks or Fruit Salads, Jelly Snakes or Chocolate Mice. She had disliked it all but gritted her teeth and got on with it, pretending not to notice how the men who came in for their ten Rothmans or twenty Carrolls eyed her up as she turned to reach down the packets of cigarettes. What she struggled with most were the times when the shop wasn't busy and she had to come out from behind the counter to sweep the floor or clean the fridges or, worst of all, wash the window inside and out. She felt exposed then – anyone, people she knew, girls she had gone to school with, the flower women even, could come along and catch her working like a skivvy.

She had been washing windows on the day he left. She remembered walking home, dusty and hot and mortified, and the front door opening before she reached the porch.

Her mother had said, her tone flat but her eyes a little wild, "Your father's gone."

For a moment Jacqueline had thought that her father too had disappeared. But this time at least there had been a note, which if it did not explain anything much, promised he would return. Jacqueline had read it so many times she had memorised it.

Stella,

I will be gone for a few days. Please don't worry. I will explain when I come back.

Love,

Frank

P S I will come back

And he had phoned. Jacqueline had been at work but Gayle, who had caught a flight home from London, took the call and Jacqueline had had to rely on Gayle's version of events.

"Word for word, Gayle," she demanded.

"I can't remember word for word." Gayle was huffy. "I'm not like you."

"Try."

"Okay. Well, the phone rang and I answered it and it was Daddy and I said, 'Daddy, where are you?' and Daddy said, 'I'll be home soon, love, don't worry. Now put your mother on.' So I got Mam and she said, 'Frank, where the hell are you?' and … well, I don't know what Daddy said because I couldn't hear him, but Mam said, 'What do you mean "it doesn't matter"?' and then she just said 'yes' and 'no' a few times and then she said, 'Goodbye, Frank' and she hung up. I asked her where Daddy was, but she didn't answer me and now she's in her room lying down again. Jacqueline, do you think he's going to come back?"

"I don't know," said Jacqueline. "He said he will, so I suppose he will."

"But where did he go, and why did he go?" Gayle had wanted to know but Jacqueline had no answer to that either.

Thirteen days later, he returned. When they asked where he had gone and why, he said it didn't matter where he had gone, but he had needed a bit of a break. And that, thought Jacqueline, was how he had seemed, like someone who had badly needed a break and felt a little better for it. More hopeful, Dot Candy had said. Had he been hopeful, Jacqueline tried to remember. Certainly he had seemed less hopeless and it had lasted at least until after Christmas and then he had changed again. So what had happened while he was here? What had he found out or thought he had found out? She needed to speak to Magpie.

The hall had the now familiar morning smell, an intermingling of fish and bacon. Jacqueline took a quick look into the dining room but no table had been set for her in the window this morning. In the kitchen, a corner of the big table had been laid for one and, as Jacqueline was about to sit down, Dot Candy came in through the open door, a frying pan in one hand and a spatula in the other. She was dressed in a long orange garment that covered her body from neck to toe; it reminded Jacqueline of a wigwam

Gayle had once got for Christmas.

"There you are," she said.

"Sorry I'm late," said Jacqueline.

"No worries. Sit down. There's tea in the pot on the table, it's not long made. Have some while you wait and I'll make you some fresh with your breakfast. Is it tea and toast again, or can you manage the full works?"

"Maybe some fried eggs with the toast this morning," said Jacqueline – her new wolfish appetite kept taking her by surprise. "If it's not too much trouble."

"No trouble at all." Dot crossed to the sink and dumped the pan and spatula there. "I've just been feeding the cats – we have the full complement of eight this morning. "I'd take you down to meet them only I've rooms to do, once I've fed you."

She makes me sound like one of the cats, thought Jacqueline. She poured herself some tea. "Are you expecting guests?"

"Not particularly," said Dot, cracking eggs into a pan. "If they come they come."

"I don't understand," said Jacqueline. "You do this every morning – cook a breakfast for all these cats as well as cleaning all those rooms. But you don't advertise and you turn people away if, as you say, you don't like the look of them. Why?"

Over her shoulder, Dot shot her a look and Jacqueline thought, I've overstepped the mark. She waited for a put-down but Dot was concentrating on the eggs.

"You don't understand because you don't know how it was," Dot said at last. "You see, long before Martin knew this place would be his, he came here on holiday as a little boy. He never forgot those weeks he spent here, with just

189

him and his mother and his Uncle Peter."

The toaster popped and Dot put the bread on a plate and carried it across to Jacqueline. "Would you like some fresh tea?"

"No, no, this is fine, thanks," said Jacqueline.

Dot went back to the eggs. Jacqueline buttered her toast and waited for Dot to elaborate but Dot said nothing further until she had served up the eggs. Then she pulled out a chair and sat down, again at the far end of the table.

"You see, Peter lived here alone all his life and, even as a child, Martin said he knew that wasn't right, that this house was too big for just one person. So as soon as Peter died and the house came to Martin, the first thing he did was tell me he wanted to open the house to guests. He wanted to fill all those empty rooms with people because, he said, this was a house that was meant to be lived in and enjoyed by as many people as possible."

"How did you feel about that?" said Jacqueline. "By the way these eggs are glorious."

"Thank you," said Dot. "Frankly, I was not delighted. The idea of filling my home with strangers, paying or otherwise, filled me with no joy. But even I could see the sense of using all that extra space to bring in an income. And," she turned and gazed out through the wide-open doorway, "I loved the garden. And so we moved here and people came and Martin was happy."

"And you?" said Jacqueline.

"I did the practical things – the cooking and cleaning. I made the beds and I cooked eggs and bacon and kippers and beans. And what was left over I gave to the cat." She looked at Jacqueline. "I haven't always been a batty cat lady. In the beginning there was only one cat, the others came with the years. Besides," she smiled, "someone hands you a house with six bedrooms, one of them an actual night nursery – who could blame a person for believing she might one day fill some of those rooms with actual children as well as paying guests?"

Jacqueline looked up enquiringly.

Dot shook her head. "What a stupid word – *miscarry* – like holding a bag upside down."

"I'm sorry," said Jacqueline.

Dot got up and wandered to the doorway. "But with Martin gone and the guests growing thin on the ground, greatly encouraged by me it has to be said, I just kept on doing the rooms. It gives me something to do, and the cats get the breakfasts instead of the leftovers." She turned back to Jacqueline. "I believe that's what they call a win-win situation? But enough of my story. What about you, Jacqueline Brennan? What do you do for a living? Something fancy I'll warrant, in a fancy office."

"I work as a freelance editor," said Jacqueline. "A fancy office?"

She smiled, thinking of the small room with the pale grey walls and the ceiling-to-floor bookcase, the shelf that held the tools of her trade: thesaurus, reference works and manuals, her decades of dictionaries. Was it sad that she could list them, trail her fingers mentally along their spines in the order they stood on the undusted shelf? Left to right with regard for neither chronology nor aesthetics, the much-mauled three-volume 70s Webster's nudging a 1940s Concise Oxford with a sniff of mould about the browning pages, a tatty 80s Collins side by side with the cool slippery sheen of the New Oxford Dictionary of English.

"Believe me," said Jacqueline, "there is no fancy office."

191

"Right," said Dot. "Well, I'll leave you to enjoy the rest of your breakfast in peace."

"Actually," said Jacqueline, "before you go, I was hoping you could tell me more about this Magpie you said used to hang around with my father, the Irish fisherman guy?"

"Ex-fisherman – he doesn't go out on the boats anymore. Do you like seafood chowder?"

Jacqueline shook her head at the random change of subject. "Seafood chowder, yes, I suppose so – why?"

"Good, then I'll meet you in the hall at a quarter to one for lunch in Toby's."

"But, what about this Magpie?"

"Chances are he'll be in Toby's too," said Dot, "though I can't vouch for the condition he'll be in. And for all I know he can't tell you what you want to know."

"I understand," said Jacqueline, "but he's all I've got, so it's worth a try surely?"

Dot nodded. "Fair enough. And now I must dash."

Shortly afterward, Jacqueline heard the hum of the vacuum cleaner somewhere above her head.

Chapter 25

1976

"Jacqueline, go and get your bike, will you? I need some ham from Sweeney's."

"Why do I have to go?" says Jacqueline. "I'm reading. Why can't Gayle go?"

"You're always reading," says her mother, "and Gayle's gone running, that's why."

"Then why can't Daddy drive you down?"

"He's still in bed – he's on nights this week, remember? Now stop arguing and go and get your bike. Florence is coming for lunch and I've nothing to give her."

"But it's too hot to cycle…"

"You can get yourself an ice lolly with the change."

"Alright, then."

"Just don't dawdle, and be careful on that bike."

It really is too hot to cycle. Jacqueline goes as slowly as she can without falling off her bike. It is cool under the trees in Blackberry Lane but, as soon as she comes out onto the main road, the sun is hot on her head and arms and she starts to sweat. She freewheels all the way from the top of the hill to the bottom. The rush of air is so cool and *wonderful it makes her feel as light as a puff pastry. Jacqueline laughs aloud at the idea. She thinks about cycling back to the top of the hill just so she can do it all again, but tells herself she'd better not: God forbid she might keep snooty Florence waiting for her lunch. The airy feeling does not last long and, by the time she reaches the village, Jacqueline is dripping with sweat.*

She parks her bike against the wall of the sweet shop and goes inside. The girl behind the counter is reading a magazine. She looks a bit like Lilly, with long dark-brown hair, which she is curling around one finger.

"An ice lolly, please," says Jacqueline.

"Which one?" The girl is turning the pages of her magazine and does not look up.

"I don't know," says Jacqueline.

The girl looks up and rolls her eyes then she puts her magazine down, gets up and lifts the lid of the fridge. "Take your pick."

Jacqueline leans over the fridge. The cold feels like a burn against her skin – below her, the frost curls like white sparkly fog. Jacqueline lets her head hang down and the fog moves around her like a smooth, soft, icy tongue that licks her face.

"Make up your mind, will you?"

The girl sounds a bit like Lilly too, cross and impatient.

Jacqueline cannot make up her mind. Does she want a Super Split or a Little Devil? Although she does really like the jelly bit in a Tip Top ... in the end she chooses a Dracula.

She eats it sitting outside on the bench at the bus stop, under the shade of a tree. She licks but does not bite so that it will last longer, but it is gone too soon and all she is left with is the wooden stick, sticky fingers stained dark red and lips that taste of blackcurrant.

"How are you enjoying this weather, young Brennan?"

Jacqueline says she is enjoying it fine. She does not like the smell in the butcher's shop, and it is worse today in the heat. Mr Sweeney looks sad, but he always looks sad. Jacqueline wonders if it is because he spends all day looking at dead things. When she pays him for the ham, she is careful not to touch his fingers because of the blood under his nails.

The cycle home seems even longer and hotter. Jacqueline thinks she might even melt and turn into a puddle. At the bottom of the hill, she gets down from her bicycle and walks it all the way to the top. Then she gets up on it again and cycles the rest of the way to Blackberry Lane. Just before she turns the corner, she hears someone shouting.

"Get out of my way, Lilly, I mean it!"

"Will you just listen to me, Eddie, please?"

"I don't want to listen to you anymore – just get out of the way!"

Jacqueline gets down off her bike. She pushes it up against the hedge then tiptoes to the corner and peeps around. Lilly is standing in the middle of the lane in front of Sexy Sexton's car and Sexy Sexton's head is sticking out of the window.

"But I told you it was nothing, I swear it was nothing," says Lilly.

"It wasn't nothing, Lilly! I saw you with him. I saw you with my own two eyes."

"And I told you we were only messing. I swear it, Eddie. Can you not just forget about it, please?"

"No, I can't forget about it. I'll never forget about it. Now, will you please get out of my way, Lilly?"

Lilly does not move. "But what about tomorrow night?" she says. "Will you at least call for me, Eddie? You know my dad won't let me go if you don't call for me."

"Are you serious?" says Sexy Sexton. "You actually want me to call for you so you can go meet your gypo? You must take me for a right fool, Lilly! Now, I won't ask you again – get out of my way!"

He blows the horn so loudly that Jacqueline jumps in fright.

When Lilly still does not move, he sticks his head out of the window again and shouts, "I said MOVE!"

The car shoots forward and Lilly gives a little scream and jumps aside. Jacqueline presses herself against the hedge just in time, as Sexy Sexton's car speeds past. Her heart is beating so fast that it is a minute before she can move again. Then she runs to her bike, pulls it out of the hedge and cycles as fast as she can around the corner.

Lilly is walking ahead of her and Jacqueline calls out, "Lilly, Lilly, are you alright?"

Lilly turns and stares at Jacqueline and her face is wet from crying. "Why are you here?" she screams. "Why are you always here? Just go away, will you! Go away and leave me alone!"

Jacqueline drops her feet to the ground and leans on the handlebars of her bike. She stays that way, watching as Lilly runs up the lane and in through the gate. She tries to push off on her bike again but her legs feel like jelly and she has to get off and walk the rest of the way home.

"Take this up to Lilly, will you?" says Jacqueline's mother.

"And tell her to take these tablets, and don't dawdle on the stairs – and make sure you knock first."

"I'm not her servant, you know," says Jacqueline, taking the tray. There is a glass of hot milk and a saucer with two aspirin on it.

Lilly's door is closed. Jacqueline hasn't seen her since what happened in the lane. She stands for a minute looking at the sign on the door: STOP THE WORLD, I WANNA GET OFF!

She knocks but there is no answer, so she pushes the door open and waits for Lilly to shout at her. Lilly does not shout. The curtains are drawn and the room is dim and Lilly is lying on top of her bed. Jacqueline goes closer and stands over her sister with the tray in her hands. Lilly is lying on her back. Her eyes are closed and her arms are wrapped around her radio. There are sounds coming from it – music but mostly hissing and spitting.

"Mam says you're to take this," says Jacqueline.

Lilly opens her eyes and looks at the tray. She pulls herself up against her pillow, reaches out, and takes the glass of milk.

"And these." Jacqueline picks up the saucer with the aspirin.

Lilly looks at them, then looks at Jacqueline, her lips open, and Jacqueline can see the white wet gleam of her sister's teeth. Lilly's tongue comes out, her eyes still fixed on Jacqueline's. She's waiting for me to serve her, Jacqueline thinks, and slowly she picks up one of the tablets, and places it in Lilly's mouth. Her fingers brush against Lilly's tongue: it is soft and warm, a damp cushion. Lilly brings the glass to her lips and swallows, then her mouth opens again and Jacqueline places the other tablet on her sister's tongue.

197

After a second sip of milk, Lilly says, "Take it away."

She slips down in the bed again and her eyes close. Jacqueline puts the glass on the tray and looks around her at Lilly's room. From the walls the many eyes of David Cassidy stare back. After a while, Lilly's breathing grows louder, her arms on the radio loosen and Jacqueline can see the gleam of a silver dial.

"Lilly," she says, very quietly.

Lilly does not answer and Jacqueline bends down and touches one finger to the silver dial. Lilly's eyelids roll upward.

"Mmm?"

"Do you want me to turn the radio off so you can go to sleep?" asks Jacqueline.

"No. It's OK." Lilly's voice is gentle and sleepy.

"But it isn't even proper music, Lilly. Do you want me to change the station for you?"

"No, I want this one," says Lilly.

"But you can't even hear it, Lilly."

"It doesn't matter. I like it."

"Why do you like it, Lilly?"

"Because it's Radio Caroline," says Lilly, "and because of where it comes from ..."

"Where does it come from, Lilly?"

"From the sea ..." Lilly's voice is a murmur now.

"How can it come from the sea, Lilly?"

"From a ship on the North Sea, imagine that." Lilly's eyes open and Jacqueline follows her gaze to the window. "Imagine that somewhere out there on the sea, in the wind and rain and the dark, someone is playing records just for me."

"But, Lilly," Jacqueline is looking at the light round the

edges of the curtain, "it isn't dark and there isn't any wind and rain ..."

Lilly's eyes open wide. "Take the milk away now, Jacqueline," she says. "The smell of it is making me sick."

"Okay, but Lilly?"

"What?" Lilly's voice is impatient now.

"I wish I could have a loan of your radio sometime."

"Well, you can't!" Lilly snaps. "Now go away, Jacqueline, and leave me alone. I'm tired and I want to sleep."

"Okay, Lilly." Jacqueline picks up the tray. "But I bet I know what you wish for."

"What are you on about now, Jacqueline? I said I want to go to sleep."

"I bet you wish you could go to the dance in the marquee tomorrow night," says Jacqueline.

Lilly pulls herself up against the pillows again. "Who says I'm not going?" she says.

"But if Sexy Sexton won't take you," says Jacqueline, "then Daddy won't let you go."

Afterwards, when Jacqueline closes the door behind her, Lilly's radio is playing "Don't Go Breaking My Heart".

Chapter 26

AFTERWARDS

She spent the morning on the terrace reading, until the child came out once more to disturb her. For a long time he just stood in the doorway watching her and she eyed him surreptitiously over the top of her book, all the time pretending not to notice he was there. Eventually he came outside to the terrace, sat down cross-legged much too close to her chair and set out a cluster of toys. In among the rubber dinosaurs and the helicopter was the ragged squirrel. Every now and then he looked up as though to check whether Jacqueline was watching. She observed the decencies by admiring his collection then went back to her book. Immediately, he began a new game which involved him tearing about the garden making *vroom-vroom* noises with the helicopter held aloft. Jacqueline promptly got up and carried her book upstairs. As she did she noticed that the *vroom-vroom* had come to a sudden end. But it started again as soon as she was in her room, so she shut the window and lay down on the bed. She intended only to rest her eyes but the room was stuffy and she dozed off.

She woke just before one and had to hurry to get ready.

As she came downstairs she could see Dot through the open doorway. She was kneeling on the flagstone path, her poppy-red head bent over a flower bed. She had changed into a white strapless sundress with a ruched bodice embroidered with bright red cherries and her legs jutted out beneath the skirt like long brown twigs ending in purple flip-flops. She leapt to her feet, agile as a teenager, when Jacqueline came out.

"I was just doing a bit of weeding while I waited," she said. "I'll go wash my hands and be with you in a tic. Oh, and we're walking by the way – I don't drive."

"Is that your bicycle I saw in the garden?" said Jacqueline.

Dot nodded. "Feel free to use it any time the fancy takes you."

"Thanks," said Jacqueline, "but I haven't cycled in years." More like decades, she thought.

She waited by the gate and was joined by Dot, a wicker basket over her arm, and they walked downhill side by side. It was a day of wind and sparkle, the sea below wrinkled and silvered in the sun. In the town, the awnings flapped and the bunting billowed.

Toby's was a greasy-spoon café at the heart of the harbour. Inside it was dim and crowded with weather-beaten men. The floor was stone-flagged and the low beamed ceiling was hung with dusty-looking fishing nets strewn with life-sized plastic crabs and lobsters. The only free table was a rickety affair next to a smeary window. Jacqueline picked up the laminated menu and studied the fare which was limited to seafood chowder, Fish of the Day, double egg with sausage and chips, or scrambled eggs on toast. Dessert was a choice of spotted dick and custard or treacle sponge and custard.

"You're not impressed," said Dot. "But you wanted to talk to Magpie and this is where he eats – when he eats."

"No, no, it's fine," said Jacqueline and she looked about her with more enthusiasm.

"He's not here right now," said Dot, "so relax and enjoy your lunch. This place might not look like much, but the seafood chowder is the best in town – all the fishermen eat here."

A waitress came over and Dot ordered for both of them: two seafood chowders and two Black Sheep.

"That okay with you?" she said, as the waitress walked away. "Beer goes well with the chowder here."

Jacqueline nodded and Dot leaned back in her chair.

"I love it here," Dot said, gesturing at the window. "That's a real working harbour, that is, not just some picture-postcard version of one."

Jacqueline looked through the dirty window. It looked real alright, with the pallets and crab pots stacked high and the trawlers and pleasure craft coming and going on the water – but it was charming too, with the sun on the sea and the row of brightly coloured huts that lined the harbour wall.

"This Magpie," she said, "he sounds very elusive, but you said that he and my father struck up a friendship?"

"I'm not sure I'd call it a friendship," said Dot. "But I saw them together a few times and I know they had a drink together a couple of nights. And once I saw them out there, sitting on that very wall, deep in conversation. Don't ask me what about."

The beer came at the same time as the food. The chowder was steaming hot and served in big mismatched bowls with ragged hunks of bread on the side. Jacqueline had to admit that all of it was good.

Once again, she found she was ravenous as a gull and had almost finished her food when Dot said, "There's your man."

Jacqueline looked up, peering through the window. "Which one?"

"He's leaning against the pink hut."

"That's Magpie? Are you sure?"

"Of course I'm sure!"

Jacqueline looked again at the man. She had recognised him at once as the man from the beach, the drunk from the chair; and now he was not so much leaning against the hut as slumped there.

"What's up?" said Dot.

"Nothing," said Jacqueline. "It's just I've seen him around. Was he, was he always this way?" She was trying to imagine her father and this man together.

Dot put her spoon down. "If you mean, did he look like that in 1983, the answer is no – none of us look the way we did back then. Magpie must be hitting sixty now and he'd only have been in his late twenties then."

"I didn't mean looks – so much as, is he – is he homeless?" She had just stopped herself from asking if he was some sort of tramp. "He looks like he might be homeless."

"Let's just say he has his demons." Dot picked up her spoon and went back to her chowder. "He goes a bit crazy on the booze sometimes, so he can't hold down a job or pay his rent. But at the moment he has one of those fishermen's cottages we passed on the way down here."

"You said he used to be a fisherman himself?"

203

"Yes, but there was some kind of accident. It was back in Ireland. I don't know the details but people were drowned. It messed Magpie up and he's never gone back to the sea. Instead he gets a bit of work here and there, doing maintenance on the boats – other men's boats." Dot put her spoon down and sighed.

Jacqueline wondered if the sigh was for the empty bowl or Magpie. "So what happens when he goes crazy and can't work and doesn't pay his rent?" she said.

"He relies on the kindness of strangers," said Dot.

"Strangers like you? You let him stay at Sea Holly Villa, don't you?"

"Why not? Hadn't you noticed? I take in all kinds of waifs and strays."

Jacqueline looked up quickly, but Dot seemed absorbed in rubbing a piece of bread round her empty bowl.

Jacqueline's eyes went back to the slumped figure. "I should go and talk to him," she said.

"I wouldn't," said Dot. "Believe me, despite present appearances, on a good day that man is as sharp as a tack. Today, however, is not a good day, not for Magpie. Best leave it for now."

Jacqueline said nothing and for a while both women sat and stared through the window at the pink hut and the man it supported.

Dot finished her drink. "Would you like something else?"

Jacqueline shook her head and they got up and walked to the bar and asked for the bill then tussled mildly over who should pay.

"I invited you," Dot insisted and Jacqueline conceded defeat.

After the dimness of Toby's, the sunshine seemed more

brilliant than ever. The harbour smelled of fish and tar and the tang of the sea.

"I have some shopping to do," said Dot, "if you want to come along?"

"No, you go on," said Jacqueline. "I'm going to hang around for a bit. You're right, this is an interesting place."

"Suit yourself, but you won't get any sense out of him today."

Before Jacqueline could reply, Dot was gone, her basket swinging on her arm. Jacqueline crossed to the harbour wall and sat and watched Magpie for a while from the corner of her eye. His head had fallen to one side and she thought he was probably asleep. She got up and began strolling in his direction. At each of the coloured huts, she stopped and made a pretence of examining the posters advertising fishing and pleasure trips from the harbour, while all the time surreptitiously studying Magpie. His body was enveloped in the same dark greatcoat and he was wearing trainers with the laces missing and no socks. Up closer, it was clear that he was indeed asleep – asleep and snoring in broad daylight.

Jacqueline turned her back on him and walked away.

Back in the yellow room, she drew the curtains on the glitter of the day then lay on the bed and thought about her father and that man. She tried to imagine them sitting on the harbour wall with their heads bent together. What had brought them together and what had they talked about? She closed her eyes on the puzzle and woke two hours later. Definitely sleeping sickness, she thought. She got up and reached for a bottle of water, then remembered she had drunk it earlier. She had a raging thirst. She picked up the empty bottle and carried it downstairs.

They were in the kitchen; she could hear them talking as she walked down the hallway. Nobody looked up as she came down the steps to the kitchen and Jacqueline stood and watched them grouped around the table. They looked, she thought, like a family. Dot Candy was pouring orange squash into a tall blue plastic beaker, Jimmy was playing with paint and pieces of dry pasta and Marilyn, her chin in her hands, was calmly watching the mess he was making.

"Now don't forget, Marilyn," said Dot, "my train leaves at seven fifteen on Monday morning, so mind you come home on Sunday night."

"I won't forget," said Marilyn. Looking up, she caught sight of Jacqueline standing in the doorway.

"I was wondering if I could get some more water," said Jacqueline.

Dot turned and smiled. "That'll be the chowder – there's a price to pay for everything in this world." She got up and went to the fridge.

"It was worth it," said Jacqueline.

"You're welcome to sit down and join us," said Dot, handing over two icy-cold bottles of water.

"Thanks," said Jacqueline, "but I think I need to go out and get some air."

As she walked away, she could hear Dot saying, "Now mind, Marilyn: seven fifteen. Don't go letting me down."

Chapter 27

1976

"Is it alright if I go up the river for a swim, Mam?"

"Is Regina going with you?"

"No, she had to go home. Mrs Quinn says she has to mind the brats this afternoon."

"Don't call them brats," says Gayle. "I'm sure Mrs Quinn didn't call them that, and the baby is a little dote."

"Regina calls them brats," says Jacqueline, "and they're her brothers. So why shouldn't I?"

"It seems a shame Regina had to go home on such a lovely day. Couldn't she have brought the children here to play in the garden instead?"

"I don't want them with me," says Jacqueline. "The baby never stops crying and Leo Quinn keeps sticking his tongue out at me. And, anyway, I want to go for a swim."

"Alright – well, you can go, but don't swim for at least half an hour – you ate half a sliced pan with your lunch."

The banks are crowded. It seems to Jacqueline that everyone has come to the river today. There is hardly room to move in the water: girls are shouting and splashing and boys are diving and ducking one another. She keeps on walking and does not stop until she has rounded the bend in the river and found a quieter place to swim, where there are just a couple of small boys catching minnows with jam-jars on strings. She stays in the river for a long time then climbs out and stands on the bank, shaking the water from her hair. When she bends down to spread out her towel, she sees a movement in the bushes. A man is watching her. He moves away quickly, but she recognises Slinky Quinn. The little boys have gone and suddenly the idea of stretching out on her towel does not seem such a good one to Jacqueline. She pulls her shorts and T-shirt on over her still damp swimsuit and hurries home. It is the first time she has ever felt nervous to be alone in the fields.

Gayle and her mother are in the kitchen when Jacqueline gets home.

"You didn't stay long up the river," says Gayle.

"I didn't feel like it," says Jacqueline. She gets herself a glass of milk and sits down at the table.

The door opens and Lilly comes in. "Is Daddy up yet?" she says.

"Not yet," says Jacqueline's mother, "but I think I heard him moving about."

"Did Eddie ring?"

"No – are you expecting him to?"

"I thought he might." Lilly walks to the window and back again to the table.

"What's wrong with you?" says Jacqueline's mother. "Sit down and stop prowling around, will you?"

Lilly sits down at the table.

"There you are, Frank," says Jacqueline's mother as

Daddy comes in. "I just put a chicken in the fridge for our dinner tonight."

"Grand," says Daddy. "What are you all doing inside on a beautiful day like this?"

"I was up the river," says Jacqueline. She thinks about telling Daddy about Slinky Quinn hiding in the bushes watching her, but she stays quiet.

"We can have it with a bit of salad," says Jacqueline's mother.

"Salad again," says Jacqueline. "Why can't we have stew or something?"

"Who wants stew in this weather?" says Lilly.

"I do," says Jacqueline. "The Quinns had stew the other day."

"Good for them," says Jacqueline's mother, rinsing her hands under the tap. "Maybe you'd like to go and live with the Quinns then? Because we're having chicken salad and we're having it early, so don't go wandering off."

"Why are we having it early?" says Jacqueline.

"Because I have my flower club at Florence's tonight and Gayle is off to her training. And that way your daddy can have his dinner with us before he goes to work. Oh, and Jacqueline, you'll be on your own for an hour or so when Lilly goes to her Festival Queen Dance."

Jacqueline looks at Lilly and Lilly looks at Jacqueline.

"But I'll be back by half eight. Oh, look, Lilly," Jacqueline's mother is pointing at the calendar on the wall, "you didn't mark off the last X on the calendar."

"I forgot," says Lilly.

"Now how could you forget that?" says Jacqueline's mother. "It's all you've talked about for the past two weeks."

Lilly catches Jacqueline's eye again and then quickly looks away.

In the orchard Jacqueline is pretending to read, but all the time she is watching Lilly. Closer and closer she comes, until Jacqueline can see her toenails: they are painted and glitter in the sunlight like little bright-pink helmets. Lilly is wearing her new platform sandals – espadrilles, she calls them, not sandals. They have laces that criss-cross Lilly's brown legs, and the heels are chunky and high as two half-pounds of butter. Her dress is light blue and crinkly and it sways above Jacqueline's head and, when Lilly stoops, there is the scent of newly washed hair – lemons among the apple trees.

Chapter 28

AFTERWARDS

Cliff Walk ended in a large park that extended all the way to the cliff's edge. At its centre was an elaborately turreted bandstand and it was toward this that Jacqueline slowly made her way. As she came closer, she saw that there was a man sitting at the top of a flight of steps running up to the bandstand. His head was hanging forward and Jacqueline, staring at the tell-tale Mallen streak, quickened her pace.

She stopped at the base of the steps, shaded her eyes with her hand and squinted up at him through the glare of the sunshine. "Hi there."

Magpie showed no sign of having heard. Jacqueline wondered if he was asleep again.

She tried once more. "I believe you're Magpie. My name is Jacqueline Brennan. You don't know me but I was hoping I could talk to you about something. It's about my father."

Magpie's head lifted almost imperceptibly. The fall of hair hid his eyes but Jacqueline had the sense that he was watching.

"His name was Francis Brennan and I think you met him when he came here to this town. It was a long time ago, but I think you knew him, spent some time with him. And I've been hoping I could talk to you about him."

Magpie said nothing, but reached a hand into a pocket of his greatcoat and brought out a packet of cigarettes. Jacqueline watched as he flipped the lid of the packet one-handed, extracted a cigarette and put it between his lips then slowly returned the pack to his pocket. She wondered if he was being deliberately slow in his movements. She waited while he brought out a box of matches, lit up, stowed the matchbox back in his pocket and took a long pull on his cigarette. He leaned forward and rested his elbows on his thighs. He let his head hang down so that his hair touched his thighs.

"Like I say," said Jacqueline, "it was a long time ago and I'm not sure if you'd remember him. 1983 to be exact."

"Are you taking the piss?" said Magpie.

"Excuse me?" said Jacqueline.

Magpie's head came up with a jerk and Jacqueline saw his eyes for the first time: they were very dark grey under hooded lids. "I said, are you taking the piss?"

Now, for the first time, she caught his Irish accent.

"No, I'm not taking the piss," she said. "I'm deadly serious. Somebody told me you spent time with my dad when he was here. And, yes, I know it was a long time ago, but I was just hoping you might remember something."

"Somebody told you." Magpie pulled savagely on his cigarette and exhaled, eyeing Jacqueline through the stream of smoke. "Who? Who told you?"

"Dot Candy. She runs a – she lives at Sea Holly Villa –

it's –" She stopped, remembering that Dot had said he stayed there sometimes.

"I know who she is," said Magpie, shaking back his hair. He had riotous eyebrows, with more grey in them than black. There was grey in the bristles on his chin too and red veins on his cheeks. Dot had said he was about sixty; Jacqueline would have put him at a weathered mid-fifties.

"So you're up there with Dot Candy, are you?" he said. He ran his eyes over her and nodded his head. "Yeah, I can see how you'd fit her bill alright."

Jacqueline wanted very much to ask what he meant by that but she resisted the urge. She had an uncomfortable feeling it had something to do with waifs and strays.

"Dot said you talked to him," she said, "to my father – that you spent some time with him. Do you remember him at all? I think he came here looking for someone – his daughter, my sister."

"I don't know anything about anyone's daughter or sister," said Magpie, and he pushed himself to his feet.

Jacqueline took a couple of steps backward. Looming over her like that in his great flapping coat, he seemed giant-like and a little alarming.

"He was Irish," she said. "His name was Francis Brennan. It was the summer of 1983 and …"

Magpie came down the steps. "You think I can remember some bloke from 1983? Don't make me laugh. I can barely remember what happened yesterday." He moved away, loping swiftly across the grass.

Jacqueline watched him go. "*I think you could!*" she called after him. "*I think you could remember if you tried! You used to sit on the wall at the harbour talking to him. I just need –*"

"*I don't give a fish's tit what you need!*" Magpie yelled over his shoulder.

Jacqueline followed the path that led down to the South Beach. It was a lot smaller than the North Beach and the shingle was strewn with shattered shells and other things that had been smashed and discarded by the sea: odd shoes, a woman's handbag, a rubber glove, the claws and torsos of crabs. Jacqueline kicked at it all as she walked. She felt low and angry – angry with Magpie and with herself and, yes, she was angry with her father. Why had she been surprised to think of them together, her father and that man? They were both drunks after all – admittedly, when it came to her father, not of the falling-down-in-the-street variety. Even that was not true – she could remember a time when he had lain down on a wall over a fast-flowing river and gone to sleep in the middle of the afternoon. They had been at a wedding – he, Jacqueline and Gayle. Her mother had refused to go, even though it was Aunty Carol's oldest daughter who was getting married. Jacqueline tried to recall when that had been – the summer of 1985, she thought. For some reason her mother had been getting worse and worse that past year, as bad as when it had all begun really, but in a different way this time – quieter, not lashing out, not accusing anyone, but unhappy, desperately unhappy. In the middle of the meal, her father had disappeared and when she and Gayle had gone to look for him, they found him asleep on the wall of the bridge, flat on his back, quite still, his hands on his thighs like an effigy on a tombstone. The wall was very narrow, just about wide enough to accommodate his prone body. The bridge was in the middle of the little country town and a small crowd had gathered round him. A man was trying to wake him by prodding his stomach.

"*Don't do that!*" Gayle had screeched. "You'll startle him and he'll fall in and be drowned!"

The man stepped back and Jacqueline and Gayle approached their father very quietly. Jacqueline sat down on the wall next to his head and looked down at his sleeping upside-down face; he was smiling and he looked, Jacqueline remembered, very comfortable.

"Try to wake him now, Gayle," she said. "But we have to be ready to grab him if needs be, alright?"

"Alright," said Gayle. She leaned in and whispered "Daddy" so gently that Jacqueline rolled her eyes, but he opened his eyes immediately and looked up at her, his gaze wondering and childlike.

"What's going on, pet?" he said.

Gayle flung herself bodily across him, shouting hysterically, "*Don't move, Daddy, you're on a wall! Don't move or you'll fall into the river and be drowned!*"

To this day Jacqueline did not understand how all three of them had not ended up in the water.

But, right this minute she understood how he had drunk himself into that position on the wall. Right this minute she knew she too could be a drunk like him and Magpie, if she could only summon enough energy to fulfil her potential. As she crunched angrily across the shingle, she told herself she would go into the town now and buy a couple of bottles of whiskey, then come back here and find a nice cave, one where the sea was sure to come in. Then make herself comfortable and just sit down and wait. Why not? She could not think of a single good reason why not. So she would do it, she would just go and do it.

The intention stayed with her all the way to the town, but once there her anger cooled and she knew that she did not want whiskey, nor to drink it in a cave on the beach. The moment had passed but she would have a glass of wine in a pub, somewhere quiet and comfortable – that would do.

Only it was half past seven and there were people everywhere in the town. She put her head inside the door of a couple of bars, but everywhere was crowded. In the end she settled for a small Italian restaurant for the simple reason that it was only half-full. The tables were covered in red, white and green oilcloths and every table had its own stump of candle in a waxy wine bottle. The portly and diminutive lone waiter reminded Jacqueline of Danny DeVito. She ordered a bottle of wine and drank two glasses before her food came. When the bottle was empty, she ordered another half bottle. Along with the bill, Danny De Vito brought her a liqueur on the house.

As she left the restaurant, she stumbled a little and he caught her elbow to steady her. He stood in the doorway and bowed her out. When Jacqueline looked back, he was still there and he blew her a kiss. It made her giggle and she swung her bag as she walked along the seafront.

The wind had dropped and the air felt balmy. People were walking about in twos and fours. Jacqueline felt a sudden surge of love for the world and all the people in it. She sat on a bench and looked at the moon-slicked sea. The narrow band of light ran from shore to horizon like an enchanted pathway in a fairy tale. It should, thought Jacqueline, be possible to step onto that path, glide skater-like toward the horizon and just keep on going. Then it occurred to her that this was the third time in as many days that she had thought about walking into the sea, one way or another, and not coming back. Was that why that Magpie person had said those things to her about drowning – not because he was crazy, but because of something he had sensed in her? In an instant, she felt sober and she thought about how stupid she had been about Danny DeVito; he must have had a good laugh about her, staggering out into the night like that. What did she think she was doing anyway, taking herself to this place on a whim? And now that she was here, she had no idea what she was doing, except making a laughing stock of herself. Depression and self-hatred slipped over her like a dark veil.

She was too weary for the uphill walk and took a taxi back to the house. For the first time since her arrival, the door was locked. Somehow it seemed fitting. Jacqueline let herself in with the key Dot had given her and went straight upstairs. The last thing she wanted was to encounter her host looking for a repeat of last night. Momentarily she was reminded of Regina Quinn calling for her to come out and play, expecting to take up where they had left off the previous day. The yellow room was dim and pleasantly cool and Jacqueline sat on the bed and eased off one of her shoes. When she rubbed her foot, the skin felt like yeasty dough, warm and swollen.

There was a knock on the door and she dropped her foot to the floor. "Come in."

The door inched open and Dot head appeared. "Sorry to disturb you, I heard you come in. About Magpie ..."

"Forget it," said Jacqueline. "Thanks for trying to help but it doesn't matter."

Dot pushed the door wide and stepped inside the room. "I wouldn't be put off by today if I were you."

217

Why did people say that, Jacqueline wondered – *if I were you*? If you were me you'd do exactly what I do.

"Magpie goes in cycles," said Dot. "Tomorrow he could be a whole different man. You can talk to him then."

"The thing is, Dot, I've already spoken to him."

"Really, at the harbour, in the state he was in?"

"No. Later on in the park at the top of the cliff." She pushed off her second shoe and it dropped to the floor.

"Sleeping it off in the bandstand, was he? And how did that go? Not so well, I'd guess."

"It doesn't matter," said Jacqueline. "I very much doubt that anything that man has to say would be of interest to me."

Dot's hand went to her throat. "I can see you're disappointed but if –"

"Dot, I appreciate you trying to help," said Jacqueline, "but it doesn't matter. Really it doesn't." As Dot made no move to go, she said, "I was just about to go to bed."

"Sure," said Dot. "But there's just something I wanted to run by you. Day after tomorrow, I won't be here – an old friend is coming out of hospital after a hip-replacement operation. She needs me to pick her up in a taxi and get her home safely. She hasn't got anyone else."

Jacqueline waited. What did any of this have to do with her? All the walking had given her a pain in her lower back. The only thing she wanted was to lie flat, turn out the lights and go to sleep. She didn't give … what was that awful phrase – she didn't give a fish's tit about Dot Candy's friend.

"It means catching the early train and staying over," said Dot, "which means you'll be on your own for breakfast."

"Oh, is that all? It's fine, don't worry."

"It's two mornings – there'll be no charge of course."

Jacqueline waved away talk of money and Dot closed the door.

Jacqueline had just closed her eyes when her phone rang: Gayle. Jacqueline's finger hovered between 'answer' and 'reject'.

"Hi, Gayle, how are you doing?"

"I tried the house twice." It sounded like an accusation.

"I was out," said Jacqueline. "How are you doing anyway?"

"Not great. I just can't believe he's gone. And I hate the idea of you there all alone in that house, Jacqueline. If only we were nearer to one another."

Now is the time, Jacqueline thought, to say, "Actually I'm nearer than you think." Instead, she said, "I wish we were too, Gayle."

Chapter 29

1976

Daddy comes home from work while Jacqueline is having her breakfast. He ruffles Jacqueline's mother's hair and she wriggles away from him.

"That's a great morning out there," he says.

"Easily known you've finished your nights for another month," says Jacqueline's mother.

Daddy smiles. "I sure have and all's well with the world and it'll be even better when you get me a cup of tea, Stella love."

Gayle comes into the kitchen, yawning.

"Good morning, sleepyhead," says Daddy.

"It's not my fault I'm sleepy. Lilly woke me up in the middle of the night, playing her radio."

"She must have been playing it very loud," says Daddy, "if you could hear it in your room."

"She wasn't playing it at all," says Jacqueline's mother. "You must have been dreaming, Gayle. Lilly wasn't even here last night – she was baby-sitting for the Kellys."

Daddy looks up from his tea. "What do you mean she was baby-sitting? What happened to this Festival Queen

Dance she had our hearts broken about? I thought Edmund was taking her to it? I hope she hasn't gone and had a falling-out with that nice lad."

"Don't ask me," says Jacqueline's mother. "I was at Florence's house for the flower demonstration. All I know is she went baby-sitting for the Kellys – isn't that right, Jacqueline?"

Jacqueline has her mouth full of Rice Krispies and nods her head but keeps her eyes on the tablecloth.

"And Joe Kelly said they'd probably be late and they must have been because I looked in on her earlier and her bed hadn't been slept in. I don't know why they have to stay out so late but at least they let her sleep over when they do."

Jacqueline looks up in surprise. She catches her mother's eyes and looks down again quickly.

"But I was sure I heard Lilly's radio," says Gayle. "It was so loud I thought it was in my room."

"Well, you were definitely dreaming," says Jacqueline's mother, "because Lilly never goes to the Kellys' without taking her radio along – imagine, they still have no television! Oh well, I just hope they pay her properly."

"And good luck to them trying to get her out of the bed," says Daddy.

Jacqueline pushes her chair back and gets up carefully, keeping her hand pressed against her stomach. She is at the back door when Daddy calls her.

"Yes, Daddy?" Jacqueline turns slowly.

"You'll be needing this."

"Oh!" Jacqueline comes back and takes the book he is holding out to her. "Thanks, Daddy."

"Now is there any chance a man could get a bit of

breakfast so he can go and get some shut-eye?"

Jacqueline stands for a moment under the oldest apple tree in the orchard. She would like to lie down here but someone might hear. She keeps on walking, out through the gap in the hedge and far enough into the field until she feels safe. Then she sits down and pulls Lilly's radio out from under the waistband of her shorts. She fiddles with the silver dials until the sound is just right, puts it down on the grass next to her, stretches out and closes her eyes. She wonders where Lilly is and why she has not come home yet, then remembers that as soon as Lilly does come she will want her radio back. A song comes on and Jacqueline leans over and turns the sound up just a little higher, then settles herself on the grass again. She likes this one, she really does. She hopes that Lilly won't come home too soon, and she hums along to "Heaven Must Be Missing an Angel".

"Is Lilly back yet?"

"Not yet," says Jacqueline's mother. She is standing at the sink washing lettuce. "Now go and wash your hands before you sit down."

"Not salad again," says Jacqueline.

She goes upstairs and reads the sign on Lilly's door: STOP THE WORLD, I WANNA GET OFF! She knows it isn't locked, she knows that Lilly isn't there, but she knocks gently before she opens the door to Lilly's room. After the heat of the garden, the room feels lovely and cool. Her silky eiderdown looks cool too, all white and smooth because there was no Lilly to disturb it last night. Where did she sleep, Jacqueline wonders, where is she now? When she pulls the radio out from under her blouse, all of David Cassidy's eyes are watching her.

"*What are you up to, Jacqueline?*"

Jacqueline spins round.

Her mother is standing in the doorway. "You know you're not allowed in here. Is that Lilly's radio you have there?"

"*I was just looking at it," says Jacqueline.*

Her mother comes closer and holds out her hand. "It's still warm," she says and she looks at Jacqueline. "Gayle said she heard this last night – have you had it all the time?"

Jacqueline shakes her head, then she nods it. "Lilly said I could have it."

"*Then why didn't you say so this morning?" says her mother. "And why were you so surprised when I said that Lilly had stayed over? Is there something you're not telling me, Jacqueline?"*

Her mother sits down on the edge of Lilly's bed and puts the radio in her lap.

Jacqueline shakes her head again.

"*So you're telling me that Lilly went off baby-sitting for the Kellys," says her mother, "and she left her radio with you? Well, now I know for sure that you're lying. When has she ever gone to the Kellys' without taking her radio with her? Now tell me what's going on, Jacqueline."*

"*Nothing," says Jacqueline. "Lilly gave me her radio for a loan, she did – she gave it to me before she went to ... before she went baby-sitting."*

Jacqueline's mother picks up the radio and turns it over in her hands, then she looks at Jacqueline again. "I'm going to give you one more chance," she says. "Now you told me last night that Martin Kelly came over in the car and asked Lilly to baby-sit. Was that or was that not true, Jacqueline?"

"*Lilly said so," says Jacqueline, and that, she thinks, is true.*

"*That's not what I asked you, Jacqueline. Did Martin Kelly come over and did you see Lilly go with him in his car?"*

Jacqueline looks down at her feet. "I don't know."

Jacqueline's mother gets up quickly. There are wrinkles on Lilly's eiderdown in the place where she sat. She comes closer to Jacqueline, and there is a look in her eyes that Jacqueline has never seen before.

"*What do you mean you don't know?" she says. "Either you saw them or you didn't. Did Martin Kelly call over for Lilly or didn't he?"*

"*I don't know," says Jacqueline again.*

Her mother comes even closer. "You're not making sense, Jacqueline. Did you see Martin or not? I won't ask you again. Don't make me lose my temper."

Jacqueline shakes her head.

"*You didn't see Martin? But you said that Lilly gave you her radio before she went out?"*

"*She did."*

"*But she wasn't going baby-sitting, was she?"*

"*I don't know," says Jacqueline.*

"*I think you do know," says her mother. "Alright then, what was she wearing when she gave you the radio?"*

"*I can't remember," says Jacqueline.*

She was wearing her blue dress, she thinks, and in her head she can see Lilly moving toward her under the apple trees. Closer and closer she comes until Jacqueline can see

Lilly's toenails: they are painted and they glitter in the sunlight like little bright-pink helmets. Lilly is wearing her new cream platform sandals, except Lilly calls them espadrilles, not sandals. They have laces that criss-cross her brown legs, and the heels are chunky and high as two half-pounds of butter. The material of her dress is crinkly. It sways above Jacqueline's head and, when Lilly bends down, there is the scent of newly washed hair – lemons among the apple trees.

"Well, try to remember!" *Her mother is too close now and her eyes are angry.*

"I can't remember!" *Jacqueline shouts.* "I didn't see! I was reading, the sun was in my eyes. Leave me alone, it's not fair! I didn't do anything, I didn't do anything!"

Jacqueline's mother turns and rushes from the room.

"Frank!" *she calls.* "Wake up, Frank, I need you!"

Jacqueline is so surprised that for a while she does not move. Nobody ever wakes Daddy after he's been on nights. She goes and stands on the landing, listening to the sound of voices from her parents' room.

"I know that, Frank," *her mother is saying,* "but something is wrong, I know it is. I need you to get up and go and find Lilly and bring her home."

Daddy will be so angry, Jacqueline thinks, but when he comes out of his room he does not look angry, just sleepy. He passes Jacqueline on the landing without saying anything and she watches him hurrying down the stairs. Her mother goes after him, still holding Lilly's radio. The front door bangs shut and there is silence in the house.

Jacqueline goes back into Lilly's room. She stands at the window and watches the car until it passes through the gateway and she cannot see it any longer. When she goes downstairs, the lunch is laid out ready on the kitchen table. There is salad, but there are corned-beef sandwiches too. Jacqueline does not feel like eating now. She picks up her book from the table where she left it and takes it down to the orchard. She sits under the oldest apple tree and thinks about how much trouble Lilly is in this time. After a while, she opens her book and tries to read. The people in the story are having a picnic and, as she reads the words, Jacqueline can imagine them moving through the fields under the trees. The women are wearing white dresses and carry parasols and all the men have tall hats. Jacqueline thinks that if she really tried, she could hear their voices as they talk among themselves, could almost taste the food they eat – game pies and chicken and fruit – how lovely it all sounds. Jacqueline looks up from the page and stares around her at the trees in the orchard and the scorched grass. But it would not, she thinks, be that way in real life. In real life, someone would be in a bad humour or someone would be complaining about the weather. Someone would be stung by a nettle, or step in cow dung, or there would be too many midges or flies in the jam. That was the trouble with books – things got left out. Things like banging your elbow or your socks falling down because the elastic has gone, or the label in your jumper scratching your neck or something getting in your eye. Things like bits of burnt toast getting into the butter or the expression on someone's face changing the way you feel about absolutely everything. What it all comes down to, Jacqueline thinks, is that there isn't any point in trying to be like the people in books – it just doesn't work. Not only are they not real but the world they live in is not real either. She puts her book down and thinks how thirsty she is, and how hot and

226

uncomfortable. She thinks how nice it would be to go inside and lie down on Lilly's white bed in Lilly's cool room. But she stays where she is and she tells herself that everything will be fine when Lilly comes home.

Chapter 30

AFTERWARDS

Considering, Jacqueline thought, the amount she had drunk, she felt surprisingly rested and clear-headed. She got out of bed, stood at the window and looked at the sky: it was an unbroken blue. Beneath it everything glittered in the sunlight: the sea, the nap of dew on the grass. Downstairs, she was surprised to find the door actually locked and she drew back the bolt and went outside. She went around to the back of the house and stood on the terrace. The garden had the almost spellbound quality that early morning sometimes lends. Remnants of mist lingered in the grass and shimmered in the sunlight. *"Mist in the hollow, fine weather to follow."* Once again, she heard his voice as clearly as if he had been standing beside her. Then the thought that he would never see another morning like this one made grief lurch at her insides. She walked down the steps and across the grass and stood in front of the sea holly tree. Why did you come here, Dad, and what the hell am I doing here now?

A sound startled her and she spun round.

Magpie was standing on the terrace watching her.

"Jesus, you nearly frightened the life out of me!" said Jacqueline.

"Sorry." He swiped at his hair, rummaged in the pocket of his greatcoat. "Smoke?"

"No. No, thank you." Jacqueline walked back slowly toward him as he lit up.

He took a long slow drag on his cigarette then leaned against the wall of the house, showing no sign of speaking.

"Did you want something?" said Jacqueline.

Magpie took another drag, watching her slit-eyed through the smoke. "As I recall, it's you that's looking for something."

"You've remembered something?" Jacqueline came up the steps to the terrace.

Magpie shrugged, straightened up and looked down at the cigarette in his hand. "Bits and pieces – if you want details you have no chance."

"I'm grateful for anything you can give me," said Jacqueline. She indicated the deck chairs. "Do you want to sit down or …?"

"Mind if we walk as we talk?" Magpie turned away without waiting for her reply.

"Not at all." Jacqueline followed him. "In fact, I was thinking of walking into town and getting some breakfast – will you join me?" She knew she sounded too eager, too grateful, but that was exactly how she felt.

"What's wrong – Dot not looking after you?" He flung the question over his shoulder.

"No, of course not, I just –"

"Like your own company? Me too, and I've eaten, thanks." Going down the hill his coat, which was much too big for him, flapped wide in the wind.

His long legs ate up the road and Jacqueline had almost to break into a trot to keep up with him. "So what can you tell me?" she panted.

"About your dad? He was looking for some kid when I came across him."

"What kid? My sister?"

"No – one of the Earlys from the fair."

"Luca," said Jacqueline.

"The very one," said Magpie.

"Did he find him?"

"No, he was long gone. But your dad went sniffing around the show at the North Beach."

"What show?"

"The funfair – the kid's uncle was Ned Early – he ran that show back then."

"And?" said Jacqueline.

"And Ned Early wouldn't entertain him, basically told him to sling his hook. But your dad wouldn't take no for an answer." Magpie glanced back at Jacqueline. "I suspect you take after him. Anyway, the result was he got himself knocked about a bit."

Jacqueline came to a standstill. "Are you saying this Early guy beat him up?"

"Not Ned himself. A couple of his sidekicks did it." Magpie looked back again, saw Jacqueline's face and stopped walking. "It wasn't as bad as all that – they just roughed him up a bit and turfed him out the fair gates onto the seafront." He grinned unexpectedly. "Luckily your dad had a fair few drinks on him at the time so he didn't really feel it – not until the next day, anyway."

Jacqueline did not even pretend to see the funny side of it. "How do you know all this?" she asked.

Magpie began walking again but he slowed his pace so that Jacqueline drew level with him. "Because I happened to be on the promenade at the crucial moment," he said. "You know, promenading myself? So I picked him up and dissuaded him from going back for a second round."

"You helped him." She turned and looked him in the eye. "Thank you for that."

"Don't mention it," said Magpie. "I'm heading up this way."

They had reached the turn for Cliff Walk.

"Me too," said Jacqueline. "So then what happened?"

"I took him for a pint." Magpie smiled at her sideways. "That is to say, he joined me on a bender."

"Sounds about right," said Jacqueline. "Did he talk to you about my sister, about Lilly?"

Magpie looked at her. "He said his kid had gone missing, and one of the last people to see her was this lad from the carnival."

"One of the last, yes," said Jacqueline. "So Dad came over here to see Luca? But why then? That was 1983, seven whole years later. Did he know something – had he found out something?"

"I don't know for sure," said Magpie. "He had some notion ..."

"About Lilly?"

"Yeah, nothing definite, mind, just something someone had heard from someone else, that kind of thing."

"What had they heard?" said Jacqueline.

"That this kid Luca had been seen recently," said Magpie. "Someone on holiday had spotted him – in France, I think it was."

"And?" said Jacqueline.

"He was with a girl – and this person, whoever it was who saw them, said the girl looked just like your sister."

"They saw Lilly?" Jacqueline felt something loosen in the pit of her stomach.

"They said they saw a girl who *looked* like your sister," said Magpie. "Calm down, don't jump the gun – like I said, it was just hearsay. Your dad wasn't certain – even the person who'd told the story to begin with couldn't be sure. Apparently, Luca and the girl disappeared into the crowd and they only saw her for a split second."

"But they thought they saw Lilly with Luca. In France. I can't believe this."

In her head, she was thinking: I'm hearing this and I'm carrying on walking and the sun is still shining and nothing has changed. It was just like all the enormous things in life – when they happened, they never felt the way you thought they would.

"So did Dad ever talk to Ned Early?"

"Not that night, he didn't – I talked him out of it. But he came looking for me the next day, your dad did. Apparently, I'd told him I knew Ned Early, which I did – I used to do a bit of work around the fairground from time to time. Anyway, apparently I'd made your dad a promise that if he slept on it and let things cool down, I'd have a word with Ned for him."

"Apparently?" said Jacqueline.

"So your old man told me. He asked around the town, found out where I lived and came round hammering on my door. Talk about total recall."

Jacqueline smiled. "That was him alright."

Magpie turned and looked at her quickly. "I could be wrong, but I have a feeling he's not around anymore?"

"He died," said Jacqueline, "not so very long ago."

"I'm sorry," said Magpie. "And do you mind me asking – this conversation we're having –?"

"Why didn't I have it with him?"

"Something like that," said Magpie.

"I didn't know this place existed until a few days ago. I found something in his things. It seemed likely my dad was here once, and as it turns out I was right. So I came here. I thought I might be able to find out whatever it was that he found out, or even," she spread her hands, "I don't know, something he missed. He never told anyone about this France thing. I don't believe he ever told my mother about it."

"Strange."

"Yes. So did you talk to Ned Early for him?"

"I did in the end, to get him off my back."

"Did you ask him about Luca and Lilly in France? What did he say?"

"He knew nothing about that, said it was a load of old rubbish." Magpie glanced at Jacqueline. "You have to understand that he was very bitter about it all. About what had happened to Luca in Ireland, the cops and all that. They gave the kid a right old hiding. You could hardly blame the old man for feeling the way he did."

Jacqueline stopped walking. "No, that didn't happen," she said. "The police didn't beat Luca – his uncle must have got the wrong end of the stick. They wouldn't have done that to Luca."

Magpie stopped too and turned and looked at her. "I think you'll find that it was Luca who got the wrong end of the stick." He flicked his cigarette-butt away.

"You're saying they beat Luca up? I don't believe it – why would they?"

Magpie lit up another cigarette, shielding the flame from the wind with his hand. He took a long pull and said, "Well, according to Early they did. His story is that they tried to get Luca to make a confession and, when he wouldn't, they locked him in a cell for two days. Frightened the shit out of him and gave him a right old hiding while they were at it. And that's what Early told your old man too."

"You got him to agree to talk to Dad?"

Magpie grinned. "Who could resist this face?" A girl bounced past them on the cliff path, a high ponytail swinging behind her. Magpie turned his head and watched her. "How do they make them do that?"

"Do what?" Jacqueline was thinking about the big detective with the red-gold hair and the smiling blue eyes.

"Girls and ponytails – how do they make them swing that way? Is it accident or design?"

"I have no idea," said Jacqueline.

Magpie was on the move again and she hurried to catch up with him.

"But why would they do that to Luca? Why would they even try to force him to confess? There was never really any question about Luca being to blame – too many people saw him that night, long after Lilly left the carnival. And she was seen later on, when Luca had an alibi, more than one alibi."

"Maybe they were the wrong kinds of alibis," said Magpie. "Anyway, in the end, Early told your old man that Luca had gone, left the country. According to him, he wasn't sure where the lad had gone exactly – France, as far as he knew."

"France," said Jacqueline.

234

Magpie nodded. "But the kid hadn't kept in touch. Early seemed very put out about it – it's not the way they do things. That fairground shower are clannish as a rule – they stick together – but this lad had gone his own way, and Early blamed what had happened to him in Ireland for that. He said it changed his outlook on life."

"How did my dad seem to you after he'd talked to Ned Early?" said Jacqueline. "I mean, do you think he still believed that Lilly was out there somewhere, in France maybe?"

"Hard to say," said Magpie, "but he definitely believed Ned Early was keeping something back."

"He told you that?"

"Yes, he did."

"But he never found out what that was?" said Jacqueline.

"Not as far as I'm aware," said Magpie. "But I know he left his Irish address with Ned and asked him to keep it and contact him if he found out where Luca was. And he gave Ned an address for your sister too, the one who lived in England …"

"Gayle?" said Jacqueline. "He gave Ned Early Gayle's address? Why?"

"He said that if Ned knew where Lilly was, and if she didn't want to get in touch with him, maybe Ned would ask her to let your sister know she was alright, alive. Then your dad wouldn't worry about her and promised he would leave her alone from then on – if that was what she wanted."

And somehow that pathetic request seemed to Jacqueline like the saddest thing she had heard so far. Perhaps the pain showed in her eyes because Magpie, glancing toward her, suddenly stopped walking.

"This is hard on you," he said. "Has to be."

"I wanted to hear the truth," said Jacqueline, "and you're telling me the truth. So this Ned Early …?"

"Long dead – and, before you ask, as long as I've been in this town I've never set eyes on this Luca character."

"But there must be someone I could ask about all this," said Jacqueline. "Someone who knew them?"

Magpie appeared to hesitate, then he said, "Well, there was a sister – her name was Dawn. She was a fair bit younger than Luca. Ned was raising the two of them – I think the parents were dead."

"Did my dad know about her – did he speak to her?" said Jacqueline.

"I don't think so," said Magpie. "He never mentioned her to me. As far as I can remember, she wasn't around here that summer … but, you know, this was all a very long time ago."

"I realise that, and I appreciate the efforts you've gone to. It's just that one little thing you remember might make all the difference."

Magpie did not reply.

They were in the park now. Magpie kept on going until there was nowhere else to go. It was too close to the edge for Jacqueline's comfort and she stood at a safe distance and watched as the wind lifted his coat. He'll take off in a minute, she thought.

"*And there's definitely nothing else you can remember?*" she called to him.

"*Afraid not!*" Magpie called back over his shoulder. Then he walked away from her, stalking along the cliff-edge, his coat-ends flying behind him like wings.

Jacqueline walked slowly back along Cliff Walk and on down to the town. She wanted to eat her breakfast alone this morning, with no smell of frying fish and no Dot Candy chattering, so that she could think about what she had just heard. On a whim, she decided on Toby's and ate scrambled eggs on toast while watching the comings and goings in the harbour through the smeary window. Afterwards she walked to the seafront and strolled along the promenade, stopping at the entrance to the fairground. The big wheel was still at this hour of the morning. Walking back, she looked at the sea and thought how nice it would be to swim, to move her muscles and clear her brain. Not now, and not here where the beach was already crowded, but later perhaps, and off the South Beach where it would be quieter. But she hadn't brought a swimsuit. Still, she could always buy one – the seafront was lined with shops selling every form of seaside tat, from buckets and spades to giant inflatable dolphins.

She found a shop that specialised in surfboards, wet suits, psychedelic shorts, very brief bikinis – and swimsuits. There were only two suits in her size and she dithered between a choice of blue with yellow flowers or purple with green stripes.

"You like to try?" The sales assistant gestured to a corner of the shop where there was an alcove with a mirror on the wall and a drooping curtain hanging from a length of string. He was very young, with mahogany-coloured skin and dreadlocked hair, and he was watching Jacqueline with an unreadable smile on his beautiful face.

She shook her head. "I'll take this one," she said. She handed over the blue-and-yellow suit. "And I'll take that blue-and-white beach towel too."

Walking up the hill, with the bag in her hand, she second-guessed her decision – would the suit fit, would it look too young and make her look ridiculous? And in any case the weather would probably turn and she would never even get to wear it. What did it matter, what did any of it matter? Someone believed they had seen Lilly with Luca in France.

At Sea Holly Villa, Dot was in the hall polishing the mirror. "Did Magpie catch you?"

"Yes, he caught me. Thanks for that, Dot, and you were right. He did spend some time with my father, drinking mostly, by the sound of it."

"Well, I didn't like to say, but Magpie was good to him, brought him home here a couple of nights a bit the worse for wear ..."

"Legless, you mean," said Jacqueline.

Dot smiled. "With one leg between them, let's say. Was he able to help you at all?"

"Yes, some – at least he tried. He's a funny fish, Magpie."

"But not a bad one," said Dot. "I can tell you more about him if you come to dinner tonight."

Jacqueline hesitated. Come to dinner sounded a lot more formal than the impromptu sharing of an omelette. She opened her mouth to decline but Dot was too quick for her.

"I'd enjoy the company," she said. "And you know you'd like to find out more about Magpie." She gave Jacqueline a spiky grin. "Come on, you have a curious nature, why deny it? And besides, it can be my way of making up for abandoning you the next couple of mornings."

"Oh, but I don't mind that," said Jacqueline.

"But I do," said Dot, "and I'd really like you to have dinner with me."

It seemed to Jacqueline that the only way out was downright rudeness, so she said, "Well, yes, then, thank you. If you're sure it won't be a lot of hassle."

"Great. We'll say seven o'clock, if that suits you."

Jacqueline, who was thinking that none of it really suited her, said that seven o'clock would be lovely.

Chapter 31

1976

"Now, Goretti, I'm going to ask you to go over it again for me one more time."

"But I already told you, Mr Brennan!" Goretti's eyes are red from crying.

"I know you did," says Daddy, "but I need to be sure I have all the facts straight. So if you don't mind, Goretti."

Jacqueline thinks that Goretti Quinn looks like she does mind but Mrs Quinn says, "Of course she doesn't mind, Mr Brennan. That's what we've come here for."

Mrs Quinn is sitting on the sofa next to Goretti. On the table in front of them there is a little golden woman standing on top of a red-and-gold pillar.

"Is it Lilly's?" Jacqueline wanted to know when Goretti had brought it into the sitting room. "Is she the Festival Queen?"

Daddy told her to shut up, and Jacqueline was so surprised she has not spoken since.

"If you could start from when they called out Lilly's name please, Goretti."

"Alright. Well, they called out Lilly's name and a man

240

put a sash on her that said, 'Festival Queen 1976'. Then the man gave Lilly the trophy and an envelope with a hundred pounds in it and someone took Lilly's photograph. Then she came down from the stage and everyone crowded around her. All the girls wanted to hold the trophy and some of them wanted to see the hundred pounds too."

"And then?"

"And then Lilly said she wanted to show Luca what she'd won so we went outside –"

"Hang on a minute, Goretti," says Daddy. "You're forgetting something. Didn't you say that Lilly made a comment about how she didn't think this Luca character would be too impressed that she'd won a beauty competition?"

"Oh right," Goretti nods her head, "I forgot about that. Yeah, Lilly said, 'He'll probably turn his nose up because he didn't want me to enter the competition in the first place.' She said she'd told him anyone else would be proud of their girlfriend, but that he thinks beauty competitions are just an excuse to have good-looking women parading around like cows. And then she said, 'But wait until he sees my big hundred pounds!' I can't remember exactly, Mr Brennan, but it was something like that."

"Good girl," says Daddy. "So you went outside and what happened then?"

"We went outside and we saw Luca over at the swing boats. I don't think he saw Lilly because he just kept on working. Lilly thought he was ignoring her on purpose so she called him and after a while he came over to her. Lilly took the money from the envelope and held it up and said, 'What do you think of that?' Then Luca took her to one side ..."

"Took her to one side or pulled her to one side? Can we be clear?" says Daddy. "Last time you said that Luca pulled Lilly to one side. Which was it, Goretti?"

"I'm not sure. He put his hand on her arm. I think he didn't want to argue in front of me."

"But he definitely put his hand on Lilly?"

"Yes, he did, he definitely did."

"And then what happened?"

"Well, like I said, I heard them arguing but they had moved away so I couldn't really hear much, except when they started shouting and I already told you about that."

"Tell me again, please, Goretti."

"Tell Mr Brennan again, Goretti," says Mrs Quinn.

"Alright, alright, I'm telling him, aren't I? I couldn't hear what they were arguing about but I presumed it was about Lilly parading around like a cow, because Luca seemed very annoyed. Then Lilly walked off in a huff and I went after her – and Luca went back to the swing boats. We hung around for a while. Lilly kept looking over at Luca – I think she was waiting for him to come over to her, but he didn't – he just stayed at the swing boats. Some girls came out of the marquee and they were all over him …" Goretti looks at Mrs Quinn then back at Daddy. "I mean like, flirting and stuff, you know, and Luca was laughing and joking with them. That was when Lilly shoved the trophy at me and told me I might as well have it. And then she ran off. I started to go after her, but she shouted at me to leave her alone – she was in a temper. I wish I had gone after her, Mr Brennan, I really do …" Goretti starts to cry again.

Daddy waits until she has stopped and blown her nose. "Are you sure this Luca didn't follow Lilly?"

Goretti looks up from her hanky. "He didn't – he was collecting money and talking to the girls – I don't think he even looked round. And anyway, after Lilly left me there on my own, I went over to some of the girls on the swing boats and Luca was there – I saw him."

"You're sure about that, Goretti?"

"Yes, I'm sure."

"And you say that Lilly was wearing her blue dress and her new cream sandals," says Jacqueline's mother.

"Yes, Mrs Brennan – she looked lovely, she really did." Goretti begins to cry again.

Jacqueline's mother does not seem to notice. She nods her head. "Yes, those are the only things missing from her wardrobe, as far as I can see."

"Just a few more questions, Goretti," says Daddy. "We know now that Lilly did not go baby-sitting for the Kellys as she said she was doing. She lied about that."

Goretti Quinn nods her head and looks down at her feet.

"But you say she didn't go to the dance with Edmund Sexton either, that she met you at the entrance to Beechlawns and you walked down together. Is that right?"

"Yes, we walked down together."

"And she didn't meet Edmund at the dance later on?"

"No, I don't think he even went to the dance. I didn't see him there at all."

"That's what he told me too," says Daddy. "That he had no plans to take Lilly to the dance. So she never meant to go to the dance with Edmund and she never meant to go baby-sitting. What the hell was she playing at?"

"I don't know, Mr Brennan," says Goretti Quinn. "Can I go home now, please? I don't want to answer any more questions."

"Now, Goretti," says Mrs Quinn, "don't take that tone with Mr Brennan."

"That's alright, Agnes," says Jacqueline's mother. "We're all just worried and upset but I'm sure Goretti has told us all she knows."

It is the first time Jacqueline has ever heard her mother calling Mrs Quinn "Agnes" and, when she gets up to go, Mrs Quinn takes Jacqueline's mother's hand in her own.

"If there's anything I can do to help, Stella, anything at all …"

Perhaps, Jacqueline thinks, she could try turning around three times saying, "Please, Saint Anthony, look around. Something's lost that can't be found" and see if Lilly will walk in the door.

Daddy and Jacqueline's mother are talking about Lilly.

"They filled out a form, that's what they did," says Daddy. "They asked me a lot of questions and filled out a flippin' form. What was Lilly wearing when she left home, the colour of her hair, her eyes, her height, her weight? I don't know what she weighs – I told them she was a skinny little thing. They think she's most likely gone to stay with a friend and that she'll come back of her own accord."

"But then they're not even looking for her," says Jacqueline's mother. "They're not taking it seriously enough. Did you tell them we've already checked with all her friends? Did you tell them that, Frank?"

"Of course I told them that – they said she's probably with someone we don't know about. They seem to think there are lots of places a fifteen-year-old girl might go that her parents wouldn't think of. They wanted to know if she had a boyfriend."

"What did you tell them?"

"I told them she saw a bit of young Edmund Sexton but that I'd already been around to Edmund's house and he didn't see Lilly last night, that he told me he had no plans to see her. What the hell was she up to, Stella? Oh, and I told them about that – that gypsy from the carnival too. They're going to send over a couple of detectives to talk to us here in the house later on."

There are two detectives. One is Gerry O'Sullivan and the other is Donal Devine. Donal Devine is small and thin and quiet – Jacqueline thinks of him as the Other One. Gerry O'Sullivan is the one who asks all the questions. He has red hair and blue eyes and he is the closest thing to a giant that Jacqueline has ever seen and he smiles at her and tells her she can call him Detective Gerry. He wants to know everything about Lilly. He has a little notebook with a black cover, and when he asks a question he writes the answers down. Jacqueline likes to think about her name being in Detective Gerry's little black book.

"Does Lilly have a bank account?" he asks.

Jacqueline's mother says no, only a Post Office savings book. Detective Gerry asks if he can see it and Jacqueline's mother goes upstairs and comes back with the book in her hand.

"The money is all still there," she says, as she hands the book to Detective Gerry. "Lilly isn't much of a saver." She sits back down next to Daddy on the sofa and starts to cry. "Look, I want to know what you're doing to try to find her!"

Detective Gerry says, "Mrs Brennan, I want you to believe that no stone will be left unturned. Lilly is under sixteen and we're putting out a full alert."

"But what do you think has happened to her?"

"The simplest and most likely answer is that she's with a friend, someone you haven't thought of yet, or someone you don't even know about. There is another possibility – Lilly may be injured …"

Jacqueline's mother opens her mouth to say something but Daddy is too quick for her. "Now, Stella, the man is only saying it's a possibility."

Detective Gerry nods his head. "And, believe me, Mrs Brennan, we'll do everything we can to find your daughter and bring her home. Now, I've just a few more questions I need to ask you."

"Alright." Jacqueline's mother sits back down on the sofa next to Daddy.

"Would Lilly be in the habit of walking home on her own?"

"Well, not at night," says Jacqueline's mother, "not on her own. During the day, she would, they all do. They're up and down to Beechlawns all the time. Isn't that right, Frank?"

"That's right. Lilly and Jacqueline are friends with the Quinn girls. Goretti and Regina are always up here."

Jacqueline watches Detective Gerry writing. The hairs on the back of his hands are a shade lighter than the hair on his head. Jacqueline really hopes that he won't put Goretti Quinn in his black notebook.

"And if they're going into the town, they take their bikes," says Jacqueline's mother. "Well, Gayle and Jacqueline do. Lilly used to cycle a lot but not so much anymore …"

Because, Jacqueline thinks, you can't cycle properly in platform shoes.

"*And they walk down to the town to get the bus to school. Lilly and Gayle go to St. Teresa's Convent School.*"

"*I'll need a list of all her school friends,*" says Detective Gerry.

"*And in the winter Frank drops them down in the car, if he's not working, don't you, Frank?*"

"*Would Lilly ever take a shortcut home?*" says Detective Gerry. "*Say through the fields and across the river?*"

"*Not at night, she wouldn't – she has too much sense.*" *Daddy looks at Jacqueline's mother. "She wouldn't, would she, Stella?*"

"*I don't think so,*" says Jacqueline's mother. "*At least not on her own, she wouldn't.*"

"*I'll see you out,*" says Daddy when the two detectives get up to go.

Jacqueline follows them out into the hall.

She hears Detective Gerry saying, "We do have to face the possibility that Lilly may have been taken against her will, Mr Brennan."

Chapter 32

AFTERWARDS

In the afternoon, Jacqueline returned to the South Beach. She brought the blue-and-yellow swimsuit rolled up in the new towel under her arm. She had not made up her mind to swim but it was easily the hottest day of the summer so far and there was no excuse. She just wished she had put the suit on under her clothes. She had not yet tried it on, and in the sunlight it looked yellower than she remembered. She struggled into it under cover of the new beach towel, conscious that, to anyone looking, she must look like a ridiculous prude. Except that nobody was looking, and if nobody was looking why was she bothering to cover up? The suit seemed to fit her well enough and once she was in the water she forgot about how she looked and enjoyed herself immensely. Afterwards she lay on the towel and let the sun dry her skin but when she tried to doze she remembered what Magpie had told her and the questions started all over again. To stop the loop, she forced herself to read and when her thoughts began to stray she went back into the sea again and swam as hard and fast as she physically could.

She stayed on the beach longer than she had intended and arrived back at the house with just enough time to shower and change in time for dinner with Dot Candy. She caught sight of herself in the bathroom mirror and was startled. Her face and shoulders had taken the sun and her nose was peppered with freckles – it made her look healthy and vital and almost young. She put on a lot of moisturiser, did her make-up quickly, dried her hair roughly and put it up. She hesitated over what to wear. Would Dot dress up? It made no difference anyway – the closest to dressy she had brought with her was a black skirt and a white T-shirt. She put them on, decided she looked like a waitress with her hair up and let it down again.

Downstairs, she followed the scent of cooking to the kitchen. The door to the terrace was wide open and Dot was there, wineglass in hand, surveying a round table laid with a white cloth and dressed with yellow flowers and tea lights.

"You look nice," Dot said. "It's such a lovely evening, I thought we'd eat outside again. What do you think?"

Jacqueline noticed that the table had been set for three. "Good idea. The table is lovely. Is Marilyn joining us?"

"I think I heard the door." Dot dashed away, calling over her shoulder, "Sit down and help yourself to a drink!"

Jacqueline had just sat down when Dot returned with Magpie. She introduced them like two people who had never met and Magpie met Jacqueline's eye and shook her hand firmly, saying nothing. He was dressed in a suit of very creased, but perfectly clean-looking grey linen with an open-necked suit shirt, so white it had to be new. It was the first time Jacqueline had seen him without the greatcoat and somehow without it he seemed taller and, but for the drinkers' paunch, quite lean.

"I'll go get the starters," Dot said. "Help yourselves to the wine."

The sound of her flip-flops slapping across the terrace seemed to reverberate loudly.

Magpie sat, then leaned across and picked up a bottle of wine. "Drink?"

"Please."

"Say when."

Jacqueline watched the dark-red wine rising in her glass. "When. Thank you."

Magpie filled his own glass. "Cheers!"

"Cheers!"

They drank and were silent again. Jacqueline picked up the paper napkin next to her plate and inspected it. It was bright yellow and depicted a scene from the Mad Hatter's Tea Party. It seemed to her perfectly fitting.

"From the look on your face when I walked in," said Magpie, "I take it she didn't mention I was coming."

Jacqueline looked up. "No, it wasn't that, I just wasn't expecting …"

Magpie grinned at her over his glass. "'Nobody expects the Spanish Inquisition.'"

Jacqueline smiled. "Why is that funny?" she asked. "I've never really understood."

"Me neither," said Magpie. "It just is."

He swiped at a fall of hair and Jacqueline thought, I am just like Dot Candy, I like good hair too.

Dot returned as though on cue, bearing aloft a spectacularly dressed salmon mousse on a silver tray. She took over the business of talking and while they ate segued breezily from subject to subject. From time to time, Magpie contributed a wry comment but mostly he just ate, consuming everything put before him with obvious relish.

When eventually she brought in the dessert, Dot said, "If you don't mind, I'm going to go and get the coffee and then I'll leave you two to it. I have a very early train to catch in the morning."

Jacqueline looked at Magpie quickly and wondered if he was dismayed at the idea of being left alone with her, but his eyes were on the cheesecake.

Dot returned with a pot of coffee. "Don't worry," she said, "I've already loaded the dishwasher and put it on. Just leave what's left in the sink and I'll take care of it in the morning. And there's plenty more wine, so help yourselves. Goodnight."

Magpie got to his feet.

He's leaving, Jacqueline thought. She felt relieved and piqued all at the same time. Then he opened his arms and Dot went to him, tangling her arms about his neck. When they broke apart, Dot kissed him on his face – close to his mouth, Jacqueline noticed, and she looked away. She reminded herself that he had been a guest in this house, God knew how many times, and of the non-paying variety too – but what of it anyway?

Then Dot came at Jacqueline, arms outstretched. "Goodnight, Jacqueline."

Jacqueline got to her feet, surprised and confused, and felt herself enfolded in Dot's arms. "*Talk to him!*" Dot hissed in her ear, then released her and was gone.

They sat down and Magpie picked up his spoon and began on his cheesecake. Jacqueline pecked at hers and sipped her wine and floundered inside her head for something to say. Should she try to explain to him that this had not been a set-up, or if it had, not of her planning? Or should she just try to act naturally? While she hesitated, the silence lengthened and she felt so awkward that she grabbed at a floating thought in desperation.

"So how long were you a fisherman?"

As soon as the words were out, she remembered there had been some kind of accident. She grabbed her glass and took a nervous gulp, eyeing Magpie anxiously.

"Since I was fifteen."

He showed no sign of unease and Jacqueline relaxed a little.

"Fifteen? Isn't that very young?" she said. "Did you run away to sea or something?"

Magpie made a sound in his nose. "You like your romance, don't you? I didn't have to run away – I had an uncle who skippered a trawler, he took me willingly."

"You weren't much more than a child all the same."

Magpie did not appear to hear her. "My God, that thing was some rolly bitch. Roll the milk outta' your tea, she would." He pronounced it 'tay'. "I spent the first three days in my bunk. The first time I threw up, I tried to hide it in my boot – I soon ran out of boots though. After that I just did it anywhere." He gave a sudden shout of laughter. "When we docked after five days at sea, I scuttled up that ladder so fast I was off her before she was made fast."

"But you went back," said Jacqueline. "I suppose it was in your blood, with your uncle being a fisherman?"

"Maybe. Anyway, I went back, first as galley boy, then as a deck hand."

"So what's it like?" said Jacqueline.

"Nothing like you imagine, that's for sure."

"No?"

"It's much better and much worse."

"Tell me," said Jacqueline. She liked the way he spoke without looking at her. She was no longer tense and realised that she was interested in hearing what he had to say.

"Well, for starters, it's much louder," said Magpie. "There's always the sound of the engine so everyone is always shouting to be heard above those noises. And then there are the smells: the seawater itself and the diesel and iodine and fish heads in the bait buckets ..."

"Charming," said Jacqueline.

"But there was the best of food – roast beef, legs of lamb, the best of steak and tons of milk and loads of apples and vegetables. On the downside, the bunks are often damp and you have to use damp cloths under the dishes to try to hold them down on the tables. You spend a lot of time looking at the sky – you see shooting stars and satellites, but always with one eye on the boat. And there's too much time to think, especially on winter nights."

"What do you think about?"

"UFOs and mermaids," said Magpie.

"Did you ever see one?"

"Which, a UFO or a mermaid?"

"A mermaid," said Jacqueline. "Everyone knows there are no such things as UFOs."

Magpie laughed aloud and Jacqueline smiled, pleased that she had amused him.

"I never saw one," he said, "but I knew a man that did. He said she was beautiful and friendly. Some nights you'd dream of gold – those Armada wrecks in the Irish Sea now, they'd be full of gold. And the things we pulled out from the seabed – a plane controls once, and a World War I

253

pilot's mask – all dried out and rotten, but still recognisable. And the gulls and gannets would land alongside the boat and when it rolled they'd fight over a loose fish. Gannets have the most remarkable eyes, light blue they are. And I once saw a cod that was about forty years old, so it was around longer than I was at the time. You feel a sort of respect for that."

His eyes had a glazed faraway look so that when he abruptly changed the subject, Jacqueline was taken by surprise.

"So what about you – where's home for you?"

"Donegal," said Jacqueline, "near Gweebarra Bay."

"I know it," said Magpie. "Lots of birds and bats and flowers and butterflies. Hard landscape, hard weather and remote too – sound people but not too many of them."

Jacqueline bowed her head – there was that.

"How did a Dub end up way up there?" said Magpie.

"I went on holiday one summer. I rented a house for a couple of weeks, found I liked it and decided to stay."

They sat in silence for a while, then Magpie said, "There was a place he used to talk about, something to do with fruit. I remember thinking it sounded green and leafy."

Jacqueline put her glass down. "Blackberry Lane," she said. "You remember that?" An image of her father came to her, bent and thin, leaning on the gate, his eyes on the fields, lean and griefy.

"Blackberry Lane, that was it. He made it sound like Walton's Mountain without the mountain."

"It was hardly that," said Jacqueline. "Actually, my mother couldn't stand *The Waltons*."

"He used to talk about her," said Magpie, "your mother. What a great woman she was."

"What else did he say about her?"

"That he was afraid she was going to leave him. Did she leave him?"

Jacqueline ran her finger around the rim of her glass. "She died, nine years ago, of pancreatic cancer. But yes, she left him long before that. She stayed for a long time, but in the end she did leave him."

She remembered her father's voice on the phone, bewildered, incredulous: "She's gone, she's left me."

"Who's gone, Dad?"

"Your mother, she's gone."

"Gone where?"

"She's moving in with one of those flower women."

"Did you have a row, Dad?"

"No row. She just opened the birthday card I'd left on the table for her, read it and said, 'Frank, I'm leaving you.'"

"What did you put in the card, Dad?"

"I put fifty quid in it," he had sounded outraged, "so she could get herself something. You know I never know what to buy her."

Jacqueline said patiently, "I meant, what did you write in the card, Dad?"

"I don't know what I wrote – I wrote what I always write, I suppose – 'To Stella, Happy Birthday, Frank' – what's that got to do with anything? I'm telling you, she's gone to live with Florence McNally and she says she's not coming back, ever. She said she's made up her mind and she doesn't want to discuss it. She said she doesn't want to live this way anymore. I don't understand it, Jacqueline, I just don't understand it. Who does something like that on the spur of the moment?"

Jacqueline got up and walked across the terrace, aware

of Magpie's eyes on her. The light was failing but there was a streak of amber between the earth and the darkening sky. She could remember almost exactly the moment when she too had made up her mind to desert him. It was a Sunday, a filthy day in February. She had roasted a chicken for their dinner, but long after the meal was ready he had still not come back from a walk. She knew exactly where to look; it was the place he went back to time and again. On this occasion he was standing in the rain, leaning on the gate, his chin resting on his folded arms. Next to him was a grey woollen glove that someone had shoved on the gatepost; it had furred in the rain and resembled a small rabbit, perched and ready to spring. He was soaked through, his hair flattened by the rain, and did not answer when she called him, but stood gazing out across the land as though there was something to see other than the crows picking over the newly turned field. As she watched him, she had been reminded of the first time she had come upon him in that exact place, the time he had said that thing about poppies and disturbed soil. Remembering, she had shivered – not from the cold and rain but from the realisation that she could not live her life this way, in this place. It was not as though she had not thought about her sister's body – how it would have passed through the stages of decomposition into something else entirely, becoming part of the soil and the stones that surrounded her. The parts of her that would remain: her strong white teeth, her bones and the way that death would have disassembled them – how someone turning over a field might come upon a femur or a tibia, pieces of her sister disjointed.

He was unresisting when she put her hand on his arm and she led him wordlessly back to the house. The wool of his jumper felt wet and fuzzy and swollen under her fingers, the way she imagined sheep to be after heavy rain. Two months later she signed the lease on the house in Donegal.

When Jacqueline turned around, Magpie's eyes were on her.

"In the end we all left him," she said. She came back and sat down. "Tell me what else he told you."

Magpie sighed. "It was a very long time ago. He was drunk or I was drunk, mostly the two of us were drunk together – either ways it didn't make a lot of sense to me."

"It doesn't need to make sense to you," said Jacqueline. "Tell me anyway. Please."

"Fair enough." Magpie hunted in the pocket of his jacket and took out his cigarettes. "He talked about his girls – I was never sure how many of you there were exactly."

"There were three of us: Lilly was the oldest, then Gayle, then me."

"Right, well, he talked a lot about Lilly – he told me that thing about France. He never actually told me in so many words what had happened to her. I just put it together from what Ned Early said."

"She went to a dance one night and she never came home," said Jacqueline.

"Jesus!" Magpie pulled on his cigarette. "He was worried about one of you – the little one, he called her. He said she was sharp as a tack but the spark had gone out of her. That she blamed herself and he didn't know why."

Jacqueline looked down at her glass. "He couldn't have known that," she said.

Magpie looked at her through the smoke of his cigarette. "I hated my younger brother, you know. I used to plan how I was going to kill him. I had it all worked out. I was going to lure him into the freezer in a game of hide and seek. We had one of those old-fashioned chest-type ones, I used to imagine him in there, frozen up and stiff like a leg of lamb."

"I didn't hate my sister," said Jacqueline.

"There's nothing unnatural about it if you did. In nature, when resources are limited, competition is fierce. Sharks kill in the womb – did you know that?"

"Now you're starting to sound just like you did the first day I saw you," said Jacqueline. "When you were drunk and accosted me on the beach."

"Accosted you on the beach, did I?" Magpie shrugged his shoulders. "What can you do? Drinkers drink."

"I suppose they do," she said. She put her glass down on the table. "About my father – you have no idea how much it means to me, hearing all these things – what he did, what he said about me and my sisters. Was there anything else, anything at all?"

"Just what I told you – his girls, how great you all were. The lane and, yeah, I think he mentioned an orchard once, nothing more specific. I'm sorry there isn't more."

"There's nothing to be sorry about," said Jacqueline. "It was a great deal for a man who claimed to remember nothing."

Magpie looked at her full-on for a second. "Some days I remember everything," he said.

The look in his eyes made Jacqueline avert her gaze. He's thinking about the accident now, she thought, and it's my fault.

"I'm sorry," she said, "I shouldn't have said that. And I really do appreciate all you've told me."

258

Magpie shrugged. "You're welcome. If I think of anything else I'll let you know."

"Thank you." Suddenly she felt very tired. She got to her feet. "You know, if you don't mind, I think I'll just tidy up here and get to bed."

Magpie looked at her for a minute, then he drained his glass, picked up his cigarettes and matches and restored them to his pockets.

He got to his feet. "You're an attractive woman, Jacqueline," he said, "so it's a shame."

I am not going to ask him, thought Jacqueline, I'm not going to ask.

"What's a shame?" she said.

"That look in your eye, like something's gnawing at your ankle. The past has its teeth in you and that's a shame."

"Doesn't it in all of us? Doesn't it in you?"

"I don't count," said Magpie. "Goodnight, Jacqueline."

Chapter 33

1976

Daddy has an alibi. Jacqueline knows what that means. In Agatha Christie books, people need an alibi when someone has been murdered so they can prove they were somewhere else and couldn't have done it. But often, Jacqueline thinks, it is the person with the best alibi who turns out to be the murderer in the end.

"Are they mad?" says Jacqueline's mother. "Why are they wasting precious time questioning you, when Lilly is out there somewhere?"

"They have statements," says Daddy. "People who say I dragged Lilly kicking and screaming from the marquee tent. Apparently, I ripped that sash from her back."

Jacqueline's mother puts her hand to her mouth. "Who said that?"

"They wouldn't tell me who said it, but it's all written down in black and white and signed and sealed like it was the absolute truth. I swear to God, Stella, it wasn't like that. That sash got snagged on something in the doorway of the tent, when Lilly went running off ahead of me."

"Sweet Jesus – but that was a week ago. Why are people

bringing that up, what are they thinking?"

"You know right well what they're thinking," says Daddy, "and they're not the only ones thinking it. Sexton crossed the road to avoid me today."

"Edmund's father? Why would he? You're imagining things, Frank."

"I'm imagining nothing," says Daddy.

They are talking about Lilly on the evening news.

"Gardaí are appealing for the public's assistance to help trace the whereabouts of 15-year-old Lilly Brennan who has not been seen since she left her home on Friday 23 July this year. Lilly is 5'7" and weighs 8 stone 10 pounds. She has dark-brown eyes and long, very dark-brown hair. When last seen, Lilly was wearing a blue cheesecloth dress and cream-coloured canvas platform shoes."

Jacqueline thinks how happy Lilly would be if she were here now to see all the fuss being made over her. People come to the house: Auntie Carol, Mrs Quinn, Sexy Sexton's mother, all the flower women, people Jacqueline does not even know. They bring sandwiches, cakes, even whole dinners. Jacqueline's mother looks at the plates and casseroles as though she does not understand what she is supposed to do with them. Gayle takes them. She smiles and says, "Thank you, that's very kind of you" and she writes down the cooking instructions for the stews and casseroles: "Warm at 450°c for 20 minutes." – "Moderate oven for about half an hour."

There are so many women and so many casseroles, Gayle worries about whether or not they will manage to give the right dish back to the right woman. Jacqueline thinks that there has never been so much food in the house, but nobody feels like eating it. She wanders around the kitchen, lifting the lids and frowning at soups and stews.

The flower women lower their voices when she comes near, but she hears them talking. "I believe they're asking anyone who was on the road on Saturday night to come forward. And they're questioning that boy from the carnival. I hear that he and she were …"

"So I believe – he's a gypsy, isn't he?"

Not everyone is thinking about Lilly. Olive O'Rourke is talking about her daughter's wedding. "It's the 4th of October – we're praying for good weather."

Jacqueline goes into the sitting room. Her mother is sitting on the sofa between Florence McNally and Mrs Sexton.

Mrs Quinn is sitting in Daddy's chair, drinking tea. "Don't worry, Mrs Brennan," she says. "God knows exactly where Lilly is and, wherever that is, He's there with her."

Jacqueline's mother puts her cup down on the coffee table and stands up. She is not wearing any lipstick and the skin under her eyes is almost navy blue. "I'm sorry, Mrs. Quinn," she says, "but I just don't believe that." She walks out of the room.

Mrs Quinn shakes her head. She stares at Sexy Sexton's mother. "That's a very nice costume you're wearing, Mrs Sexton. Did you buy that in Switzers now?"

"Actually, no," Mrs Sexton keeps her voice low, "I picked it up in Rome." She looks at the sitting-room door. "Perhaps someone should go after her …"

"I'll go," says Florence Mc Nally, and she gets up and hurries from the room.

Jacqueline follows her and stands in the hall watching

Florence's bum wriggling in her tight skirt as she hurries up the stairs.

Olive O'Rourke comes out of the kitchen and smiles at Jacqueline. "I'm praying for your sister to come home safely," she says.

Perhaps, Jacqueline thinks, that is the problem: there are too many prayers, and sometimes the really important ones get lost among the silly ones, the ones for sunshine or dresses or Dublin to win the All Ireland.

Upstairs, she can hear them talking in her mother's bedroom. "People are saying that Frank …"

"No-one believes a word of it," says Florence McNally.

"But they do, I know they do. The police went to Frank's work. They asked his boss and the men he works with a load of questions – what time Frank got into work that night, when he left, that sort of thing, and now people are talking."

Florence McNally says, "They're asking the same questions of a lot of people – they have to. It's their job, Stella. But only very stupid people or very narrow-minded people believe that Frank could …"

"That's nearly everyone then, isn't it?" says Jacqueline's mother.

Jacqueline goes back downstairs.

Detective Gerry wants to talk to Jacqueline. He tells her that she is not in trouble and all she has to do is tell the truth. "Do you understand, Jacqueline?"

Detective Gerry smiles and Jacqueline says she understands.

"Good," says Detective Gerry. "Now tell me about the last time you saw Lilly."

263

"I was in the orchard, reading my book," says Jacqueline, "and Lilly came. She said I was to tell Mam that she was going baby-sitting."

"What was Lilly wearing, Jacqueline?"

"Her new shoes and her blue dress," says Jacqueline.

"Did Lilly usually get dressed up to go baby-sitting?"

"I don't know – I don't think so."

"Did you see or hear anyone come to the house to collect Lilly?"

"No, I didn't see anyone. I was in the orchard reading."

"And you didn't hear a car?"

Jacqueline shakes her head.

"And did Lilly mention that she was meeting anybody, or that she was planning on going to the dance in the marquee?"

"No."

"How did Lilly seem to you, Jacqueline? Was she happy or sad or worried?"

Jacqueline thinks, I wasn't looking at her face. She says, "I don't know, I was reading."

"Alright, just one or two more questions now, Jacqueline. Have you ever noticed anyone hanging around the house – a boy or a man perhaps?"

"Only the boy in the garden with the guitar," says Jacqueline, "but that was Luca."

Detective Gerry looks up from his notebook. "Luca was in the garden here, with a guitar? When was this?"

"I don't know," says Jacqueline. "Before the festival started. He was singing to Lilly in the middle of the night. Daddy chased him away."

Detective Gerry says he will ask Daddy about that. "Was there anyone else?"

"The boy in the field," says Jacqueline.

"Who was the boy in the field?"

"I'm not sure. I only saw his hair – it was black. I think that was Luca too. Lilly came through the gap in the hedge out there and afterwards I went to the gap and looked and I saw him running away towards the river."

"Is there anything else, Jacqueline, anything at all?"

"No."

"You understand how important it is to tell us everything, no matter how small it might seem?"

"I understand," says Jacqueline.

The man on the television is talking about Lilly again. "Today Gardaí combed the countryside and woodland near the home of missing teenager, Lilly Brennan."

Jacqueline imagines men in uniforms and hats moving through the fields, pulling behind them a giant comb attached to a rope – the big wide teeth rake through the grass and the ditches.

"Local people turned out today to assist in the search. Garda divers also searched the river near the missing girl's home. Meanwhile questionnaires have been issued to establish what cars have been seen in the area where Lilly Brennan was last seen, as police fear she may have been abducted – plucked from the side of the road as she walked home alone."

Jacqueline thinks it makes Lilly sound just like a flower.

Chapter 34

AFTERWARDS

There was a soft but persistent knocking. Jacqueline knew it was her mother come to say she was sorry about the corned-beef sandwiches but when she opened her eyes Dot Candy was standing in the doorway of her room.

"Sorry to wake you so early, but I'm in a fix."

Jacqueline sat up in bed, mentally adjusting herself to the trauma of being not eleven and gratified but forty-eight and bemused. "Is something wrong? What time is it?"

"It's nearly six-thirty and I have to catch a train in fifteen minutes. Marilyn hasn't come home."

Jacqueline shook her head. "Are you worried about her? Can't you ring her?"

"I tried that – her phone's off. It would only be for an hour or two."

"What would?"

"The boy, Jimmy, I can't take him with me to the hospital. I need someone to look after him."

"You mean me?" It was too early and Jacqueline was too surprised to pretend. "Oh, I don't think so."

"I know it's an imposition," said Dot, "and I wouldn't

266

dream of asking if I wasn't completely stuck. But it wouldn't be for long – Marilyn is probably on her way back right now."

"If she was on her way back, wouldn't she have answered her phone?" said Jacqueline.

Dot shrugged her shoulders in a gesture of helplessness. "I don't know what else to do. Jean is depending on me and I can't let her down. She doesn't –"

"Fine. I'd better get up then, hadn't I?" Jacqueline didn't want to hear any more about Jean. She flung the duvet off and swung her legs to the floor.

"Thank you," said Dot, "you've saved my life. I'll let you get dressed." She shut the door, then opened it again immediately. "Oh, and I know it's an infernal cheek, but is there any way you would feed the cats?"

As she came down the stairs, Dot was in the hall pacing. Behind her the door stood open.

"Jimmy is still asleep," she said. "With any luck he'll stay that way for a while."

"You'd better go," said Jacqueline curtly. "You'll miss your train."

"Yes, I'd better hurry. So I'll see you tomorrow then." Dot gazed at Jacqueline, a rueful expression on her face. "You have no idea how grateful I am."

"Don't mention it," said Jacqueline.

Dot turned away and left, leaving the door wide open behind her. Jacqueline went to the kitchen and switched on the radio, just in time to catch the end of the weather forecast: "*Fog patches will clear early, giving way to widespread haze, so look forward to long sunny spells ...*"

She opened the door to the terrace. It did look fair.

Perhaps it wouldn't be so bad, perhaps he wouldn't wake up, perhaps Marilyn really would come home very soon.

She filled the kettle and was just sitting down with a mug of tea when the boy marched into the kitchen. He was wearing his purple dinosaur pyjamas and his glasses, and his squirrel was dangling from one hand. He looked, Jacqueline thought, a bit too perky for so early in the morning.

"Where's Dotty?" he said.

"Dotty had to go out." Jacqueline gave him a smile so unnaturally big it almost made her jaw ache.

"Where's Marilyn?"

"Marilyn isn't ... Marilyn is still out, but she won't be long. Would you like me to make you some breakfast?"

Jimmy turned and ran.

Jacqueline put her cup down and got up slowly.

"Damn you, Marilyn, and damn you, Dot Candy," she said.

She went after the child and found him in the lounge, kneeling up on the sill of the big bay window.

"Come on, Jimmy," she said, "come and have some breakfast and before you know it, Marilyn will –"

"*I want Marilyn!*" he cried and began thumping the glass with the flat of both hands.

"Don't do that, Jimmy," said Jacqueline. "You could hurt yourself."

She crossed the room and reached out to touch him but he pulled away from her and bounded from the sill to the floor. Then he ran across the room and flung himself into the rocking chair where he curled himself up like a little purple peanut and began to howl.

"Oh, give me strength!" said Jacqueline.

For ten minutes she stayed with him. Crouched over him and finally kneeling next to him, she tried every tactic she could think of, but Jimmy would not be comforted, coaxed nor cajoled from the chair. In the end, she left him there, still howling. She told herself that the best thing she could do was to make him some breakfast. Eventually hunger would get the better of him and he would have to stop crying in order to eat. Better yet, Marilyn would come home and solve the problem.

The howling stopped abruptly as she reached the kitchen. She went and stood in the open doorway and breathed in the quiet of the morning. Then she turned back into the kitchen and wondered about what to make for him. There was a bowl of fruit on the kitchen table with a couple of bananas – she had a notion that children ate a lot of bananas. But maybe eggs would be better, eggs in a cup with toast soldiers, and if he didn't eat it she would – she was hungry now.

Something brushed against her leg and she almost leapt out of her skin. "*Oh, for God's sake!*" she yelled and Oscar hissed then shot across the room and out through the open doorway where he sat eyeing her from a safe distance and lashing his tail. "Yeah, I know, you want feeding too – well, join the queue."

She found a tray and carried Jimmy's meal to him in the lounge. The rocking chair was empty. She set the tray down on the sideboard and went into the hall, calling his name. A frightening thought struck her: what if he'd run off to try to find his mother? She hurried out the front door, down to the end of the drive and peered down the hill. If he's run off, she thought, if he's knocked down and killed they'll blame me. The unfairness of it all made her want to weep.

Back inside the house she searched the entire ground floor then she went upstairs. Marilyn's room, she knew, was on the first floor but she had no idea which it was. The first door she tried turned out to be some sort of linen cupboard, the perfect hiding place, she would have thought, but it did not contain a crying child. Two further doors opened on bedrooms, obviously unoccupied but pristine and spotlessly clean as though in readiness for expected guests. How many rooms were there in this house anyway?

"Bingo!" she said finally as a door opened on a room with a just-burgled look – she had no doubt that this one was Marilyn's. But no child was visible.

The huge room opened on an ancient-looking bathroom, complete with an enormous and ancient-looking bath which stood side by side with a modern shower unit. She went inside and had a quick look around. No Jimmy.

She emerged and stood, surveying the bedroom. Everywhere was chaos. The large double bed was unmade and strewn with clothing – at its centre sat an upended handbag, the contents tumbled in a heap with a single high-heeled sandal sitting on top. Jacqueline got down on her knees to look underneath the bed. The match of the shoe was there, along with a hairbrush and some scrunched-up paper tissues, but Jimmy was not. Getting to her feet, she gazed about her. Everywhere she looked, there were items of clothing – tops and jeans, skirts and dresses and bras and knickers. They hung from the open drawers of a tallboy, they drooped from chairbacks and littered the floor. In the enormous mahogany wardrobe, its doors flung open, the hangers hung empty, while beneath them on the floor of the wardrobe lay another tangle of clothes and belts and fallen scarves, jumbled together with bags and shoes and boots.

One thing was certain: there was no child hiding in there. Then Jacqueline noticed the bed under the window. It was a child's wooden bed and it had been painted fire-engine red. Its bedclothes were rumpled. Jacqueline stepped gingerly, avoiding shoes and discarded towels, and crossed the Rubicon into Jimmy's bedroom. That was how it felt – these were two separate living spaces – Marilyn's and the child's. His was a room within a room. The wardrobe had been painted red to match the bed and to one side a row of red shelves held Jimmy's clothes: carefully folded T-shirts, shorts and jumpers as pristine as if they were on display for sale in a clothes shop. On the far side of the wardrobe another row of shelves held a selection of toys, all neatly displayed according to type: cars, stuffed animals, plastic models. Everything neat and orderly. Jacqueline shook her head at the conundrum that was Marilyn, then she pulled open the doors of the small wardrobe. His clothes had been divided into sections: shirts, trousers, jackets, winter coats, everything neatly hung.

Beneath it all was Jimmy himself, hunched down, his face buried in his knees.

Thank God for that, thought Jacqueline.

"I made egg and toast soldiers for you," she said.

"*I want Mummy!*" the child wailed and he sprang up and darted past her.

"Stop the world, I wanna get off," said Jacqueline.

She hurried out onto the landing, hearing him already scampering across the hall below. She raced down the stairs and stood in the hall, looking frantically around her. Had he gone outside?

Perhaps he'd gone back to the rocking chair?

She plunged into the lounge. No Jimmy.

Then a sound from behind her sent her haring back into the hall. "*Please be Marilyn, please be Marilyn!*" she chanted under her breath like a mantra.

Magpie was leaning against the porch wall, head on his chest, his arms folded.

"You!" she said, too disappointed to hide her feelings. "Dot's not here and it's a bad time."

Magpie raised his head lazily. "Good morning to you too. And it was you I was looking for … but I won't keep you so." He straightened up and turned away.

"I'm sorry – I thought you were Marilyn – she didn't come home last night and I'm supposed to be looking after her son. He ran off and I only just found him – but now I seem to have lost him again. I don't suppose you saw him outside?"

"Yeah, he was on his way into town for a pint," said Magpie.

"It's not funny," said Jacqueline. "Something could happen to him."

"Look behind you," said Magpie.

Jacqueline spun round.

Jimmy was standing in the hall, his eyes puffed and pink under the thick glasses.

Magpie moved forward and past Jacqueline into the hallway. He knelt down before the child, "Having a bad day, little chap?"

Jimmy nodded solemnly.

"He hasn't stopped crying since he got up," said Jacqueline.

"I haven't had my breakfast," said Jimmy. "I'm hungry and I want toast."

Magpie got to his feet and turned back to Jacqueline.

"He wants toast," he said.

Jacqueline opened her mouth to defend herself but closed it again – what was the point? "Do you want to have something too?" she said to Magpie instead.

Magpie shook his head. "I only came to tell you I've tracked down Luca's kid sister, or at least I think I have."

"How, when? You said nothing last night."

"I didn't know anything last night," said Magpie, "but after I left here I met a bloke in the pub who knows where she's living now."

He put a hand in his pocket and rummaged about, then pulled out a packet of cigarettes.

"Well, where is she?" said Jacqueline impatiently.

"She's living in a town about fifty miles up the coast. I don't have her address though."

"How big a town – what's it called?"

"Northby. Not a very big place – a seaside town a lot like this one."

"Then I'll find her. Is her name still Early?"

Magpie shook his head. "The bloke I talked to said she was married but he didn't know who to. Has an idea where she's working though."

"Then I'll find her," said Jacqueline. "Just tell me what you know."

"I'm hungry," said Jimmy. "I want my toast."

Jacqueline ignored him. "This is great news," she said to Magpie. "Maybe she'll know something."

Magpie lit up and took a long slow pull on his cigarette before he answered. "She might. I think she and her brother were very close. And I could be wrong, but once I got the impression that Early suspected she might have kept in touch with Luca. But, if she did, she kept it to herself.

273

The thing is, I wouldn't be at all surprised if she goes on keeping it to herself."

"Why do you think that? Did you know this girl well or something?"

"Not very well – I just saw her about a bit years ago, but I know how the Earlys operate. Think about it – you're a stranger and into the bargain you are who you are. I'm just saying, that's all."

"And what if you were with me? Would that make a difference?"

"Might, might not."

"Then would you come with me? Please?"

Magpie looked at her before raising his face to the sky and staying like that for a few moments. Then he flung the cigarette-butt down, grinding it underfoot.

"Come on then," he said.

"What, now? I can't go now. You know I can't – I have Jimmy. Can we not go later on today?"

"Like the man said," said Magpie, "it's now or never – so make up your mind. Take the kid with you, why don't you?" He turned to Jimmy. "You like the train, don't you, Jimmy?"

Jimmy nodded frantically.

"I can't take him with me."

"Why not?"

"You can't just go off with someone else's child. What if Marilyn comes back?"

"Do you really think that little jade cares where he is?"

A sudden image came to Jacqueline – mother and child curled in the rocking chair, the girl's lips on the child's forehead – then the split-personality bedroom upstairs.

"Actually, I think she does really – she just wants her

own life too."

"Is that what it is? Right, well, it's up to you. There's a train in forty minutes – are you coming or not?"

Chapter 35

1976

Detective Gerry says, "There's been a possible sighting. A couple were travelling home from a wedding in the early hours of the night Lilly disappeared. They've come into the station now to report seeing a young girl fitting her description."

Jacqueline's mother puts her hand to her chest.

"Where?" says Daddy.

"The girl was walking along the side of the road, just past the turn-off for Beechlawns. The woman heard a description of Lilly on Garda Patrol *and it jogged her memory."*

"But that's only a mile down the road," says Daddy.

"Why didn't they stop?" says Jacqueline's mother. "How could they just drive off and leave a young girl walking alone in the middle of the night?"

"Was she alone?" asks Daddy.

"She was alone," says Detective Gerry, "and, as I say, they cannot be certain it was your daughter. They are an elderly couple. The gentleman in particular is uncertain."

"Did they describe her?" says Jacqueline's mother.

"The description is of a tall, dark-haired young woman in a white dress –"

"But Lilly's dress was blue," says Jacqueline's mother.

"I appreciate that fact, Mrs Brennan," says Detective Gerry, "but in a certain light, a pale-blue dress might possibly look white."

"Why didn't they stop?" says Jacqueline's mother again, but nobody answers her.

"The couple made a further statement," says Detective Gerry. "They report having seen a man on the same stretch of road. He was coming through a gap in the hedge at the crest of the hill."

Jacqueline knows the gap – people use it as a shortcut to the fields and the river. Nobody is talking now and she can hear the three clocks ticking.

"A man or a boy?" says Daddy.

"The woman says definitely a man, a not very tall man. Unfortunately the description is poor – she only caught a glimpse of him as the car went past."

"Did the man do something to Lilly?" says Jacqueline.

Her mother starts to cry.

"Shut up, Jacqueline," says Gayle.

"She was so close to home," says Daddy. "Just down the road."

It is Lilly's birthday. She is sixteen and there should be presents and a birthday tea.

"A birthday tea, not a party, mind," Jacqueline's mother always says. "Just a cake and a few candles."

But it always feels like a party when after the dinner she says, "Everyone stay where you are!" and begins clearing the plates and putting out the biscuits and buns. Then "No looking now!" she says, and everyone has to close their eyes while she takes the cake out from wherever she has hidden it. Then there is the sound of the match striking and in a little while she begins to sing "Happy Birthday to You" and everyone opens their eyes and joins in while Jacqueline's mother puts the cake down in front of the birthday person so they can make a wish and blow out the candles.

But it is not like that now and when Jacqueline's mother starts putting out the plates of biscuits and buns, it does not feel like a party at all. Nobody closes their eyes and when the cake comes out of the press, Daddy says, "Jesus Christ!" under his breath. There are sixteen candles on the cake but Jacqueline's mother does not light them. She just sits down at the table again. Everybody waits and nobody speaks.

Jacqueline stares at the back door, and for a minute she thinks that maybe, just maybe, Lilly will walk in. But Lilly does not come.

After a while Daddy gets up and says, "Gayle, will you help your mammy clear the table, love?"

That is when Jacqueline's mother gets up, picks up the birthday cake and drops it into the bin.

That is when Gayle starts to cry.

"Don't upset yourself, Stella," says Daddy. "It doesn't mean anything – it's just one more day."

Jacqueline's mother spins round. "It means everything, everything! Nobody in this world wanted to be sixteen as badly as Lilly did. If she could come home, this is when she would have come. Now, today, right now."

Daddy gets up and puts his arms around her but Jacqueline's mother pushes him away. "Jesus Christ,

Francis, what if they never find her? We won't ever have a place to put her, not a grave, not a stone – where will she be, where will she be?"

"We will find her, love," says Daddy. "Of course we will."

"No, I can't stand it, Frank!"

Jacqueline's mother runs out of the room and Daddy goes after her.

Jacqueline and Gayle follow them into the sitting room. Jacqueline's mother is pulling down the photos from the wall, photos of Lilly on her Communion and Confirmation days, a photo of them all taken at Christmas with Lilly wearing a red dress and a green paper hat.

"Now don't do that, Stella," says Daddy.

"Why not?" *Jacqueline's mother is shouting,* "I want them gone, do you hear me? I want them gone! I can't bear to look at her beautiful face day after day and know I'll never see her again!"

Gayle is sobbing. "Stop it, Mam, stop it!"

"Stop it, Stella – you're upsetting the girls now," says Daddy. "Give the photos to me, Stella – I'll put them away, for now."

Jacqueline's mother holds out her hands and Daddy takes the photographs from her.

When everyone has gone, Jacqueline stays behind and looks around her. There is only one photograph of Lilly left – it is the one on the top of the china cabinet, the one with Jacqueline holding the apple.

Later on, when her mother has taken two Beecham Powders, and is asleep on the sofa, and Gayle is crying in their bedroom, Jacqueline hears Daddy moving around in the attic.

279

After she says her prayers that night and just before she falls asleep, Jacqueline whispers, "Happy birthday, Lilly."

Jacqueline wakes to the sound of screaming and for a minute she forgets and thinks: Lilly is in trouble again. Then she remembers and sits up.

Gayle's bed is empty and the bedroom door is open. Jacqueline gets up and goes out onto the landing. Lilly's door is wide open and it takes a little while for Jacqueline to understand what she is looking at. Gayle is lying on Lilly's bed and their mother is lying on top of her. Gayle's face is turned toward the door and Jacqueline can see her wide-open mouth and her staring eyes. Her face is bright red and her legs and arms are thrashing about as she struggles to be free.

Daddy is shouting, "Let go of her, Stella! Let go of her this minute, I said! Jacqueline, help me get her off."

The skin of her mother's back is warm under her nightdress as Jacqueline helps Daddy pull her, wriggling and kicking, off Gayle.

Jacqueline says, "Mam, you're hurting Gayle."

"I found her in Lilly's bed!" her mother screams. "What was she doing in Lilly's bed? I thought it was Lilly, I thought it was Lilly!"

"Come on, love," Daddy says. "Gayle didn't mean any harm."

Afterwards, when they are back in bed, Gayle says the same thing over and over again. "She pulled my hair out – Mam pulled my hair out!"

Jacqueline says, "Why did you go in Lilly's bed?"

"I don't remember," Gayle is crying, "I don't remember. I must have walked in my sleep."

It is the last time that Gayle walks in her sleep. Jacqueline thinks that maybe it is because, even in her sleep, Gayle knows now that it is not safe to get out of bed.

Three nuns call to the house from St Teresa's Convent of Mercy: there is a small fat one, a small thin one and a tall thin one. The small fat one is Sister Agatha. Jacqueline does not like her. She has a mean face, a baggy chin and a mole with a hair growing out of it next to her nose. Jacqueline hears her mother telling Daddy to be civil to them.

Sister Agatha says the sisters are having Masses offered for Lilly's safe return. "Such a beautiful girl, such potential."

Daddy says he is going out to get some fresh air.

When they are leaving, Jacqueline hears Sister Agatha telling her mother that the Lord is mighty and not to fall prey to the sin of despair. It is almost, Jacqueline thinks, exactly what Mrs Quinn had said – only this time her mother does not tell Sister Agatha that she does not believe.

"Stupid old mickey-dodgers," says Jacqueline as the door closes behind them.

"Don't be mean," says Gayle, coming down the stairs. "They're kind and they care. Everyone cares. Everyone just wants Lilly to come home."

Jacqueline wonders if the church is the only cold place in the world this summer. She puts her pennies in the slot and lights a candle. There are six other candles already lit, but she is the only one here. She wonders what the other people prayed for, or if one person prayed for six things or ... she gets up and walks up the aisle to the front pew, every sound she makes echoing in the silent church. She kneels down and stares very hard at the tabernacle, the place where everyone says God is. Jacqueline wonders why God needs a tabernacle when He is already everywhere, and also in heaven. She wonders if God has a comfortable seat in heaven, she wonders why the seats in the church have to be so hard ...

Jacqueline gives her a head a shake and tries to stop her mind wandering – it is always the same, even at Mass. Jacqueline does not really like Mass – it is very boring. She wonders if God gets bored with it, she wonders if God gets fed up listening to the same things over and over again, the same way she does. She realises that she is doing it again and she wishes she was holy. Once, she thought she wanted to be a nun. It was after she saw The Sound of Music for the first time. It lasted for a whole week and every day she put a white sheet around her head and a black towel on top of that and she sang "Climb Every Mountain" to herself in the mirror. But when she really thought about it, she realised that she didn't want to be a nun, she wanted to be Maria Von Trapp and have adventures and trick the Nazis, only she didn't think she would like being a governess to seven children and she didn't want to get married, even to the Captain. Really, she just wanted to be like Julie Andrews, and run singing up the highest mountains ...

Jacqueline shakes her head again and brings her mind back to the reason she has come. She puts her palms together and says her short prayer, "Please, God, make Lilly come home."

Chapter 36

AFTERWARDS

"I'm coming," said Jacqueline.

Magpie stuck out his hand to Jimmy. "Come on then and we'll get you some toast. We'll have to be quick though if you don't want to miss the train. Jacqueline can go and get your clothes."

Jacqueline watched as Jimmy took Magpie's hand. As they walked away down the passageway to the kitchen, Magpie looked over his shoulder and winked at her, and she heard Jimmy saying, "Marmalade, I want marmalade on my toast."

Jacqueline fumed as she hurried up the stairs – the trouble she had taken with that child – all her efforts at comforting and reassuring him, but that man had only to smile and stick out his hand and the wretched child trotted off with him like a trusting pup.

In Marilyn's room, she grabbed a blue-and-white striped T-shirt from the top of one pile and pair of long green combat shorts from another. She pulled a dark-blue sweatshirt from a hanger. Shoes, he would need shoes – she picked up a pair of brown sandals and hurried from the room. In her own room, she changed her top and put on some blusher, lipstick and mascara, then grabbed her bag and hurried downstairs. Halfway down the stairs, she remembered underwear for Jimmy and ran back up again. They were waiting for her on the terrace.

Jimmy was eating toast and marmalade and chatting away to Magpie as though he had never known sorrow in his short life.

He pointed at the clothes in Jacqueline's arms. "They don't go together."

"You're probably right," said Jacqueline, "but this is as good as it gets. And if you want to come with us, you'll put them on. Or we can go without you?"

Quick as a flash, Jimmy put his toast down and came to her. He pulled down his pyjama bottoms and his underpants came with them. In another split second he had wriggled his pyjama top over his head and stood before her naked. Jacqueline blinked: she had never seen such skin and bone, such pallor in a living child. But when, she asked herself, had she last seen a naked child at such close quarters?

"Get on with it," said Magpie. "Don't just stare at the child. We're going to miss that train." And he began to walk away.

Panicked, Jimmy with one leg in his underpants and one leg out, flapped his hands and hopped frantically. "Don't go without us!" The tears were back in his voice.

"He won't," said Jacqueline. "Will you, Magpie?"

Magpie shook his head. "No," he said, unsmiling, "but get a move on." He strode across the terrace and disappeared around the side of the house.

Jacqueline grabbed Jimmy's T-shirt. "Put your arms up."

Jimmy's arms shot into the air and Jacqueline slipped the top over his head. His head poked through the neckhole and his flattened hair sprang up again as though it were made of elastic.

By the time she got to the footwear Jacqueline was in a lather of sweat. Who knew there was so much fuss and fiddling to dressing one small child?

"Those are my inside sandals," said Jimmy

"Well, today they can be your outside sandals," said Jacqueline.

She helped him on with a sandal and, as Jimmy lifted one scrawny foot, he suddenly put his two hands on the back of her head and leaned on her. And now there'll be marmalade in my hair, she thought, but the touch of him, like a light warm cushion resting on her head, somehow had the effect of gentling her mood.

"Good boy," she said, and she smiled up at him.

"You don't smile properly," said Jimmy, his voice loud and accusatory.

And you, thought Jacqueline, are an odd-looking little ogre. This was why she avoided children: their lies were transparent, their truths devastating. "I'll just have to work on that then, won't I?" she said. "Now let's go in so I can lock up."

She found a pen and some paper in a kitchen drawer. She scribbled a note for Marilyn, keeping it deliberately brief and she hoped, suitably accusatory:

Marilyn, as you did not return and I needed to go out, I have taken Jimmy with me. Jacqueline Brennan

She left it on the kitchen table, weighted down by Jimmy's blue beaker. Then followed by Jimmy, she locked up the house.

He found a book which he insisted on taking with him. "It's my dinosaur book," he said.

"Oh alright then," said Jacqueline, "but hurry up."

Magpie was waiting for them at the end of the drive, leaning against one of the gateposts, face upturned to the sky, eyes closed.

"Sorry," she said. "It took longer than I thought."

"Jesus wept," said Magpie. He hunkered down. "Up you get."

Jimmy skipped forward and clambered up onto his shoulders.

"Hold on tight now," Magpie instructed the boy. "I'm just the horse, you're the jockey."

And that was how they hurried down the hill to the town, Jimmy riding high on Magpie's shoulders, arms looping his neck like pale ribbons.

At the station Magpie stabbed at his pockets but Jacqueline said firmly, "You're doing me a favour, this is on me" and he didn't argue. She wondered how little money he had at his disposal and then she wondered what they were doing together, she and this man she did not know and this odd little child, setting off together on a journey.

On the train, Jimmy sat next to Magpie and demanded of Jacqueline, "Where are my snacks?"

"There aren't any snacks," said Jacqueline.

"Marilyn brings snacks on the train."

"Does she? Well, I'm afraid I didn't. If there's a trolley, I could get you something … some biscuits or crisps?"

"Sugar rots my teeth," said Jimmy, "and crisps could make me choke. Marilyn brings rice cakes and grapes."

"Does she really?" Jacqueline was genuinely amazed.

When the service trolley came around, she bought him

an apple. Jimmy wanted it cut into pieces and Magpie took a Swiss Army knife from his pocket and did the honours, carefully and with great good humour.

Half an hour into the journey, Jimmy suddenly slid down from his seat and came and stood beside her, his book in his outstretched hand.

"Read it, please, Jacky Lean."

That's a new one, thought Jacqueline, but it made her smile. Taken by surprise, she took the book from Jimmy and opened it to the first page. It was mostly pictures with very few words. She began: "'*A long, long, time ago a very lazy little dinosaur wished he did not have to –*'"

"Speak up!" said Jimmy. "I can't hear you."

Jacqueline glanced up, conscious of listening strangers all around her. She met Magpie's amused eyes, cleared her throat and started over again.

"Again," said Jimmy, as soon as she had finished.

"You can't want the same story twice in a row," said Jacqueline.

"Oh, I don't know," said Magpie. "I used to read the same story over and over again too. It was one about a mermaid."

Jimmy went back and climbed up next to Magpie again and said, "Tell me the story about the mermaid."

Jacqueline closed the book on her lap and grinned at Magpie. "You're on."

Chapter 37

1976

In September, the weather is like a seesaw: first cool then warm, then cool then warm again. Up and down, up and down, as though summer cannot make up its mind whether to stay or go. Dublin beats Kerry in the All Ireland: Jacqueline thinks that at least someone's prayer has been answered.

In school, the classroom window shakes in the wind and when she moves her feet under her desk, Jacqueline's new black patent shoes creak like a branch in a breeze. She's in sixth class now and Miss Moore says they must work hard because secondary school is just around the corner.

Regina Quinn's desk is empty because she has been kept back a year.

"It's because she's thick," says Maria O'Brien, and the other girls snigger.

"She's not thick," says Jacqueline. "She's just taking her time." It is not what she meant to say, but she feels the need to defend Regina and it shuts people up.

Miss Moore has long straight shiny black hair and eyes the colour of chocolate buttons and Jacqueline would like to please her. But sometimes in the middle of a lesson, when Miss Moore is talking about Cúchulainn or the rivers of Ireland or long division, Jacqueline suddenly thinks about Lilly. Then she can see her sister moving toward her under the apple trees, her pink toenails coming closer and closer and suddenly it is as though a jar of humming and buzzing flying things has spilled open inside her head.

Miss Moore asks Jacqueline to stay behind at lunch one day. She asks Jacqueline how she is feeling and Jacqueline says she is feeling fine. She gives Jacqueline a copybook with a hardback silver cover: it looks like Christmas tinsel and it is the nicest copybook Jacqueline has ever owned. Miss Moore tells Jacqueline she has a gift with words and that maybe she would like to write down the things she is feeling in the silver copybook. Writing about how you are feeling, Miss Moore says, can sometimes make you feel better and nobody, she tells Jacqueline, need ever see what is in the copybook but Jacqueline herself. She does not say anything about Lilly, but Jacqueline knows she is thinking about her. Everyone is always thinking about Lilly.

The first thing Jacqueline writes about in the silver copybook is the dream she keeps having about Lilly. She is washing Lilly's hair. Lilly is leaning over the bath and Jacqueline is rubbing in the shampoo – it smells of lemons and makes a lot of suds. Suddenly Jacqueline pushes Lilly's head under the water and holds her there. Lilly struggles and struggles but she cannot get away from Jacqueline's hands. The water runs black, Lilly's head shrinks to the size of Jacqueline's fist, then it snaps like a piece of thin soap and dissolves like a bath cube. Jacqueline watches it gurgling down the plughole.

Writing the dream down does not make Jacqueline feel better at all.

In the playground, girls whisper and stop when Jacqueline comes near.

She hears a girl saying, "That's her – it was her sister that disappeared."

At the turn-off for Beechlawns, Jacqueline says goodbye to Regina Quinn and looks for Daddy. She cannot see him yet, but she knows he will be waiting for her at the top of the hill. He never says it, but Jacqueline knows he does not like her or Gayle to walk anywhere on their own anymore. He would, she knows, like to pick her up at the school gate if she let him, but Jacqueline remembers what Lilly used to say, "Only posh girls and babies get collected from school instead of walking home with their friends."

Halfway up the hill, she sees Daddy waving to her and she waves back.

A car goes by with the windows wide open and the radio blaring "Dancing Queen". Jacqueline is reminded of Lilly's radio. When she comes to stand beside him, Daddy does not turn around. He is leaning on a gate staring at something in the cornfield even though there is nothing to see – no golden corn waving in the wind, only stubble and some crows picking over the ground. Jacqueline thinks he must be looking at the poppies.

"I like them too, Daddy," she says. "They're my favourite flowers."

Daddy turns. "What's that, love?"

"I was just saying that I like poppies too."

Daddy turns away again and looks at the field. "They

290

say poppies thrive in disturbed soil."

Jacqueline does not really know what he means, but a cold feeling comes over her and suddenly more than anything in the world she wants Daddy to look at her and not at the flowers in the cornfield.

"Are you coming home, Daddy?" she says, but he just stands looking at the field as though he has forgotten she is even there. "Daddy," she says again, but he pays no attention.

She tries to think of something to do or say to make him notice her. She looks around her – there is nothing. She bends down and picks up a stone. She sniffs it and holds it out.

"Smell that, Daddy," she says. "I bet you didn't know that a stone has a smell?"

Daddy looks around and down at the stone in Jacqueline's hand. "Go on ahead, pet," he says. "I'll be right behind you."

Jacqueline lets the stone fall to the ground. She walks away, turning every few minutes to see if he is following her, but Daddy is still standing where she left him.

In Blackberry Lane, her feet kick up a dust cloud that takes the shine off her new patent-leather shoes. She notices things, things she has seen many, many times but has not stopped to think about before. Like the dark corners where the sun does not reach, the way the ditches are choked with nettles and how the trees meet and block out the light. She stops at the gap in the hedge for the buttercup field and waits in the band of sunlight for Daddy to catch her up. He does not come and Jacqueline walks home alone.

She lets herself in at the back door. Her mother is sitting at the kitchen table stirring tea in a blue mug. When

Jacqueline comes in, her mother stops stirring and looks up quickly.

"Oh, is it that time?" she says.

What it sounds like to Jacqueline is "Oh, it's only you."

Her mother begins stirring again. She has dressed herself today, but her hair looks like it has not been brushed. A thought comes into Jacqueline's head: she could brush her mother's hair for her. She imagines herself going upstairs to her parents' room. She sees herself walking to the cream wood dressing table, she can even see her own reflection in the hanging mirror that tilts forward or backward until it is just the way you want it. She reaches out and picks up her mother's hairbrush – it has a white handle and a big flat back with a painted-on bunch of pink and yellow roses. When she turns it over, Jacqueline can see a little fuzzy tangle of her mother's dark hair caught in the black plastic teeth of the brush. She sees herself coming down the stairs with the brush in her hand, sees herself coming up behind her mother very quietly and, without saying anything, beginning to brush her mother's hair. Long, slow, strokes. She is very gentle so as not to snag the brush on any knots, so as not to hurt her mother.

"What's for the dinner?" asks Jacqueline.

Her mother looks up again. "Are you hungry?" she asks. She sounds surprised. "I could make you something …" She looks at the press as though she is trying to think of the names of things that people like to eat – she hardly ever eats anymore – she mostly just drinks tea.

"It doesn't matter," says Jacqueline. "I'll wait until Daddy comes in."

"Good girl." Her mother begins stirring again.

Jacqueline goes into the sitting room and switches on

the television. She sits on the sofa and stares at the screen. The Smash advertisement comes on – the one that always makes Jacqueline laugh. The aliens look like they have been made out of tin cans and they make fun of humans: "They are clearly a most primitive people."

Jacqueline does not even smile.

Near the end of September, the weather changes again. The days are hot and sunny as though summer has come once more. Jacqueline wakes one night, sure that something in particular has disturbed her. She kneels up in bed, pulls back the curtain, and presses her face to the cool window glass. She picks out the shape of the magnolia flowers, but there is nothing else to see. She sits back down in bed and listens to Gayle making funny little noises in her sleep. Jacqueline is thirsty so she gets out of bed quietly and goes downstairs to the kitchen. She takes a glass from the press and turns on the tap. When she looks up she sees something through the window – a flash of blue and something moving among the trees in the orchard. She puts the glass down in the sink and turns off the water.

She runs into the hall, calling, "Daddy, Daddy, there's somebody in the orchard! I think it might be Lilly!"

She waits until she hears footsteps overhead before running back to the kitchen. Before she has the back door unbolted, they are all behind her and then they are in the garden, the four of them, running across the damp grass.

Jacqueline's mother is shouting, "Lilly, Lilly! Where are you, Lilly?"

It is not Lilly, just some boys stealing apples. One of them is slower than the others, who by the time Jacqueline reaches the orchard have all disappeared through the gap in the hedge. The boy who is left behind turns and Jacqueline sees his terrified eyes caught in the light from Daddy's torch. Apples tumble as he runs and there is a last flash of his blue T-shirt before he too disappears.

Afterwards, Jacqueline's mother will not come inside. She moves around under the apple trees in her white nightdress, calling Lilly's name. She is still calling it when, between the three of them, they drag her inside the house. When she gets away from them, she runs upstairs to Lilly's room and curls up on the bed. They try to coax her back to her own room, as if she were a little girl, but she claws at the blankets on Lilly's bed and makes a noise in her throat that starts out quiet but ends up as a scream.

Daddy has to call the doctor and Dr May comes and gives Jacqueline's mother something to make her sleep. She sleeps in Lilly's bed all night and most of the following day. Before she wakes up, Daddy has already taken an axe and hacked the branches from every single apple tree.

Chapter 38

AFTERWARDS

As soon as they stepped from the train, Jimmy said he needed the toilet.

Magpie looked at Jacqueline, "Right, I'll leave you to it and go see if I can find Dawn."

"Can't you wait for us?" said Jacqueline. "We'll only be a few minutes?"

But Magpie is already moving away. "Best if I see her on her own first. I'll meet you on the pier in half an hour."

Jacqueline watched him go and Jimmy tugged at her hand.

"I need to go to the bathroom NOW."

She took him to Burger King. In the women's toilet a small queue of people were waiting but when Jimmy began jigging on the spot the woman ahead of her insisted they take her place in the queue. When their turn came, she hesitated again. Did she go with the child into the cubicle and how much could he do for himself and how much was she expected to do for him? While she was deciding, Jimmy pushed in ahead of her and slammed the cubicle door in her face.

"Let me know if you need any help," Jacqueline told the door.

"*I'm able to do it myself!*" roared Jimmy.

"Glad to hear it," said Jacqueline, and when she turned every woman in the queue was smiling at her. They think I'm his doting mother, thought Jacqueline.

Jimmy reappeared with his clothes awry and his glasses in his hands. Without them, his face looked unguarded and somehow vulnerable. No longer magnified by the thick lenses, his eyes seemed softer too.

"They fell off," he said, handing them to Jacqueline, "and I stood on them."

"Are they broken?" Jacqueline inspected them. "Ah feck it, yes, they are. Can you see without them?"

Jimmy nodded.

"Good lad, now you wash your hands and I'll wrap these in some tissue and put them in my bag until we get back."

The hand-washing ritual seemed to take forever.

Magpie kept them waiting. Jacqueline sat on a bench on the pier while Jimmy raced backwards and forwards making some sort of flying noises. It was he who spotted Magpie at last and he ran to him, yelling in delight. Jacqueline watched as the man swooped the boy up in his arms and swung him overhead.

"Well?" she said, as Magpie approached. She thought she could smell alcohol on his breath.

"She's not happy about it, but she's agreed to meet you."

"That's great. When are we meeting?"

"Not now, she's working. She'll meet us when her shift is over."

"When is that?"

"Six o'clock."

"Six o'clock! But that's hours away! Does she not have a lunch break or something sooner than that?"

"Beggars can't be choosers – it's six o'clock or nothing."

"Fine, but what are we going to do for the next six hours?"

"*Dinosaurs!*" yelled Jimmy. "Can I have one, please?"

Jacqueline looked where he was pointing at a girl selling foil helium balloons on the pier.

"I suppose so."

She reached for her bag, but Magpie was already rummaging in his jacket pocket.

"I'll get this one."

They walked over to the girl and Magpie handed over the money. "I'll take that nice pretty pink one – Snow White, is it?"

Jacqueline watched Jimmy's face fall.

"What's up? You don't like Snow White?" Magpie asked.

Jimmy shook her head.

"How about Cinderella then? No?" Magpie winked at the girl. "Give him the dinosaur there, will you?"

Jimmy watched, avid-eyed, as the girl freed a garish balloon emblazoned with an unlikely orange dinosaur against a backdrop of an erupting volcano. He took the string in both hands and stared up beatifically at the balloon sailing above his head.

They walked the length of the pier, the boy with the balloon between them. We must look like a family, Jacqueline thought. A crowd of young girls came toward them, dressed in short shorts and skimpy floral skirts. They passed, trailing a scent of floral perfumes and she saw Magpie give them the once-over.

He caught her watching and grinned. "A rage of maidens," he said.

Later, on the beach, he bent down and wrestled the shoes from his feet. He was sockless and his feet were pink and clean-looking, the way Jacqueline remembered them when he had first spoken to her on the beach.

"Can I take my sandals off, Jacky Lean?" said Jimmy.

Jacqueline nodded and he sat down on the sand and let her unbuckle his sandals, then he leapt up and raced away across the beach, roaring ferociously, the balloon in his wake.

Watching him, Magpie said, "I don't get this fascination with dinosaurs. Dinosaurs and vampires – that's all the young care about nowadays." He dropped down and stretched himself out on the sand.

Jacqueline looked down at him. His eyes were closed and the wind whipped his remarkable magpie hair clear of his brow. She said, "Weren't you fascinated by anything when you were little?"

"Gods," said Magpie.

"Gods?"

"I used to recite the names of gods before I went to sleep. I had them off by heart – first the Gods of War, they were my favourites, Ares, Enyo, Pallas Athena – then Hephaestus, God of the Forge and Fire, Workman to the Immortals – Aeolus, King of Winds, I liked him a lot. Then the goddesses – Ate, Goddess of Mischief – Eris, Goddess of Discord – I can't remember the rest."

Jacqueline raised her eyebrows. "What sort of little boy chants the names of gods?"

He shrugged.

Jimmy came back and Magpie raised himself on one elbow and watched him roar away again. "He's an odd-looking little chap, isn't he?"

"Don't say that!" Jacqueline snapped.

"Why? Because he's a child and all children are beautiful?"

"No, of course not," said Jacqueline. She knew she was being unaccountably defensive, particularly considering that she had only recently been entertaining identical thoughts about Jimmy. "He is a little odd-looking but he doesn't know that yet."

"*Ha!*" Magpie gave a shout of laughter. "No, I don't suppose he does, but he'll find out soon enough."

"Yes, I imagine he will," said Jacqueline.

They watched the boy in silence.

Jacqueline thought about that short span in a person's life before they saw themselves as the world saw them, when they were both beautiful and not beautiful and before they knew that it mattered.

"Poor Jimmy," she said.

Jimmy came running past them once more. "*I'm a cloud!*" he sang. "*I'm a cloud!*"

Magpie met Jacqueline's eye. "He's a cloud, Jacky Lean," he said.

They smiled.

Jimmy badgered them to take him paddling in the sea and Magpie took off his coat and rolled up his trousers, exposing long and hairy calves.

Afterwards they took him to the big amusement park and let him ride on the merry-go-round, then they walked among the stalls three-abreast. At the Hoopla stall, Magpie won Jimmy a dinosaur beanie and a cheap-looking water pistol.

Jacqueline bought them fish and chips and Magpie suggested they have them in the bandstand out of the wind.

While they were eating, Jacqueline remembered something. "Oh my God," she said, "I forgot to feed the cats."

"They won't starve for one day," said Magpie.

Afterwards, Jimmy wanted ice cream and Jacqueline bought three 99s and a yellow bucket and spade for Jimmy. She sat with Magpie on a bench on the seafront while Jimmy ate his on the steps leading down to the beach, the bucket and spade next to him.

"Does he look a bit pink to you?" said Magpie

"Now that you mention it," said Jacqueline. "That's my fault, I suppose. I should have got some sunscreen for him. Hold this, would you?"

She handed Magpie her cone, pulled Jimmy's sweatshirt from her bag and took it to him. Up close, his arms did look alarmingly pink. She came back and took her ice cream.

"He'll probably be whinging all night now," she said, "but at least it won't get any worse. Thanks to you."

Magpie made a sound like a grunt. Jacqueline glanced at him. His tongue was busy lapping and his eyes held the intense, almost spellbound expression peculiar to humans who, regardless of their age, are intent on the business of consuming an ice-cream cone out of doors on a summer's day.

"You do know," she said, "that the first time I set eyes on you, you were fast asleep in an armchair, in the middle of the path to the cliffs?"

"Jaysus!" said Magpie. "I must have been pissed. When I'm pissed I do a lot of things I don't remember. What was an armchair doing on the cliff path anyway?"

"I don't know actually." For a second Jacqueline wondered if the chair was real at all – perhaps it was a figment of her imagination. "I think some kids left it there." She looked at Magpie again. "What I don't get is how you reconcile *this* you with the drunken you who falls asleep in a chair on a public pathway and doesn't even remember it? Doesn't it bother you?"

Magpie finished the last of his cornet, licked his lips and rubbed his hands on his trousers. It was so long before he spoke that Jacqueline wondered if she had offended him.

"I took him out with me," he said, "my nephew Joe. He was fifteen years old and he wanted to be a fisherman. His mother, my sister Deborah, was dead set against it but I thought I knew better. I'd got my own boat at the ripe old age of twenty-eight and I was the king of the world. So I took him out with me. I decided that if he was going to have a love affair with the sea, he should at least take the time to find out what it was he'd be loving." He took out his cigarettes and lit up in his usual leisurely fashion, took his first pull and gazed at the sea. "I was asleep when it happened. The boy was in the wheelhouse with another one of the crew. I'd told them to keep her going, to follow the line and not to alter for anyone. They were to call me when we reached a certain point, but she got caught in a northerly gale, a sudden big swell. There mustn't have been time for anyone to even come and wake me. All I know is I woke to a crash and a wallop. I heard the sound of someone roaring. I can't be certain but to this day I'm certain it was Joe. I ran up and made for the wheelhouse, but there was no time – she just heeled right over. I was thrown clear. And after that I don't remember anything at all. I have no memory of being in the sea."

"But you were saved," said Jacqueline.

Magpie pulled viciously on his cigarette. "I was picked up," he said. "There was another boat in the area dodging the weather."

"And Joe?"

"He was lost along with the rest of the crew. Five in all."

"My God."

"My sister couldn't look at me. She wouldn't even have me at the funeral. Her husband, Tom, the mildest fairest-minded man I have ever met, said the best thing I could do was stay out of sight for a while."

"That must have hurt you," said Jacqueline. "But it was an accident, not your fault. And you were only young yourself. How long ago did this happen?"

"1982. Ah well, luckily there's not much ails a body that can't be fixed by the judicious application of caffeine, water, aspirin and alcohol."

Jacqueline did the maths. If he was twenty-eight in 1982 that made him fifty-nine now. Not so old really; not that it mattered.

"So what did you do?" she said.

"I cleared out."

"Where did you go?"

"I went someplace," said Magpie, "and after that I went someplace else, until I washed up here. I don't remember it all and, even if I did, it wouldn't interest you."

"Sorry," said Jacqueline.

"Don't be sorry," said Magpie, "but now I've told you mine, you can tell me yours."

Taken by surprise, Jacqueline looked away. "Who says I've got one?"

"You've got one," said Magpie.

Jimmy was running along the edge of the water, his arms spread wide on either side, his balloon bobbing above him like a second sun.

Jacqueline got to her feet. "I'd better go and get him," she said. "It's almost time to go and meet Dawn."

Chapter 39

1976

It is October and the weather is cool. Early in the morning, while the whole house is still asleep, Jacqueline takes her bike and cycles all the way to the estuary. She likes this time of the day: everything has a crisp, clean feel to it, as though it has nothing at all to do with yesterday or any of the days that came before that. Like everything really could start over again and be different. Someone has cut the grass along the banks at the side of the road. Cut grass smells differently in October than it does in July – Jacqueline had never noticed that before. The wooden jetty is still there, but some of the slats are missing. The little stony beach looks the same. Jacqueline thinks that if she tries hard enough she will find it, the exact place where they sat when the photograph was taken. She thinks she can remember it now, her mother and Daddy, Lilly and Gayle and herself sitting on the brown blanket that always smelled of last summer's salt and grass. Her mother pouring dark tea from the fat blue flask and spooning sugar from a twist of paper. And herself, not paying attention to what she is doing, biting down on her apple. She can almost taste the bitter pips in her mouth. Her thick wet plait is heavy and is making a damp patch on the back of her dress – she has been swimming, Jacqueline thinks she can remember that too. How it felt beneath the waves, away from the dazzle of the sun, cool and quiet, the world above her like tiny pins of light and then coming up with water diamonds on her lashes. But there is nothing to show where they sat, where the blanket flattened the grass, where the spat-out apple-pips fell, nothing at all. And there is nothing to show that Lilly was here the night she disappeared.

But that is what Sexy Sexton told the police, and what he started to tell Daddy when he called to the house.

"You're not welcome here," Daddy told him.

Sexy Sexton asked Daddy to hear him out. He said that he had just come from the police station where he had given his statement.

Daddy said, "Like I said, you're not welcome here."

Sexy Sexton said, "I can understand that you're angry, sir. I wasn't one hundred per cent honest with you and then – well, then it seemed too late. I should never have left her alone like that, I know that ..."

"How many other lies did you tell?" said Daddy.

"Mr Brennan, sir," said Sexy Sexton, "I swear on my mother's life I told the honest to God truth to the police, and I'm here to tell it to you now ..."

Daddy shut the door in Sexy Sexton's face.

As soon as Jacqueline gets home, she goes into the sitting room and picks up the photograph. She has it in her hand when Daddy comes in.

"Daddy ..."

"Not now, Jacqueline."

305

MARIA HOEY

"But I just want to know who took the photograph."

She cannot believe that she has never thought about it before, all those times she has looked at it, examined it, her face, the apple in her hand. If everyone is there, sitting on the blanket, then who was behind the camera?

"Just some man, a birdwatcher," says Daddy. "Your mother wanted a photo with everyone in it for once, so she asked the first person she saw to take the picture."

Jacqueline tries to imagine the man, the stranger, his face half hidden behind the camera, his eyes upon them, capturing them forever with one press of the button. "Daddy, tell me again –"

"That's enough now, Jacqueline – the time for stories is over. I have things to do."

In the evening, Jacqueline sees a great, inky cloud behaving as no cloud she has ever seen before. As she watches, the cloud changes shape. It grows longer and longer, staining the pale sky as though someone has spilled oil on it. Jacqueline knows what it is. Daddy has told her about murmurations of starlings, but she has never seen one before with her own eyes. She wants to tell Daddy about it, but keeps thinking about what he said: "The time for stories is over."

When she goes into the sitting room, the photo on top of the china cabinet has gone.

Jacqueline lies in bed remembering the stories Daddy used to tell them when they were small, so scary sometimes that afterwards, when they could not get to sleep, Jacqueline's mother would tell Daddy off. "For the love of God, Frank, can you not just tell them a bedtime story fit for little girls?"

306

Almost all Daddy's stories were about little children who got lost in a forest full of dark trees and frightful swollen toadstools. Gayle always wanted to know if the children found their way home in the end and Jacqueline could never understand why she could not just wait for the story to unfold – she herself never had any wish to hurry the lost children out of the forest. "Make the wind howl, Daddy," she would demand and Daddy would round his lips and make a long thin whistling sound that rose and fell and rose and fell and Jacqueline would shiver and imagine she saw, in the shadows of the room, the figures of the poor lost children moving slowly beneath the dark trees.

Then Gayle would interrupt and spoil it all, "Did they live happily ever after in the end, Daddy?"

Once, Jacqueline remembers she lost patience with her sister and said, "Why does every story have to end with happy ever after? It's so boring!"

And Daddy laughed and said, "Ah but the story never really ends at the happy-ever-after bit."

Jacqueline was not sure what he meant by that.

Once she asked him if there really were monsters under her bed, like Lilly said.

"Well, do you think there are?" asked Daddy. While Jacqueline was still thinking about what the right answer might be, Daddy said, "Because if you believe there are monsters under the bed, then there are monsters under the bed."

"I don't believe it," Jacqueline told him.

Daddy smiled. "Then you have nothing to worry about."

Chapter 40

AFTERWARDS

Luca's sister was over half an hour late. They waited for her in the café on the pier. Jimmy grew restless and kicked Jacqueline repeatedly on the shins. She lost her patience and snapped at him and he stopped kicking but began tearing open the small paper sachets of sugar and salt and spilling them into hills.

"Stop it," said Jacqueline, "you're making a mess!"

He sulked for a while, then began sucking violently on the straw in his empty can of orange. He would not stop until Jacqueline ordered him another drink. His face, she noticed, looked pinker than ever.

In the end, Dawn came in unnoticed. She slipped quietly into the seat next to Magpie, an unremarkable-looking woman in her mid-forties, neither plain nor pretty, and dressed for a working day in black jacket, black skirt and white T-shirt. Her hair was cut short, mid-brown showing some grey at the temples, and her eyes were brown, but smaller and lighter than her brother's. Jacqueline realised that she had been expecting a young woman – more than that, she had been picturing a girl – a beautiful female version of Luca. Dawn barely acknowledged Magpie's introductions and refused the offer of tea or coffee and then they all just sat, nobody saying anything.

Jimmy made a particularly loud slurping noise. Dawn glanced at him and smiled as though he had done something funny or endearing – they left that bit out when they made me, thought Jacqueline. She glanced at Magpie. He inclined his head almost imperceptibly in the direction of the woman next to him and Jacqueline realised that everyone was waiting for her to begin. She put her mug down too hastily on the table and tea splashed.

"*Stop that!*" Jimmy shrilled. "*You're making a mess!*"

Dawn smiled at him again.

Jacqueline said. "Thank you for agreeing to see me, Dawn. I don't know how much Magpie told you –"

Dawn cut across her. "He told me who you are, and I told him I wanted nothing to do with you."

Discommoded by the hostility in her voice, Jacqueline looked at Magpie again, but he was stirring a spoon round and round in his coffee cup and did not meet her eyes. She looked at Dawn.

"But you still came."

"I came because Magpie asked me to," said Dawn. "So what do you want to know?"

"Well, I suppose I just ..." What do I want to know, she wondered. "I suppose I want to know anything you can tell me. You see, my father came here – I don't mean here – I mean to the fair your grandfather owned in –"

"He didn't own it," Dawn cut across her again. "He had the lease on it. He owned the bigger rides and let pitches to other showmen. My family, what's left of it, still have standing rights. Look, I don't have a lot of time for this.

What is it that you want to know?" Her eyes were hostile and fazed.

Jacqueline turned to Magpie again. This time he met her gaze, sighed and settled his spoon next to his mug.

"Dawn, Jacqueline here is trying to fit the pieces together so she can maybe make some sense of what happened to her sister. Isn't that right, Jacqueline?"

"That's right," said Jacqueline. She smiled gratefully at Magpie then turned back to Dawn. "Anything at all you can tell me – about where Luca is now – or even anything he might have told you about what happened in Ireland, what happened to my sister."

Dawn rested her arms on the table and leaned in. "None of that had anything to do with Luca. None of it." She had thin lips and tiny teeth and anger made brown diamonds of her eyes. "They just made a scapegoat of him, that's what they did. None of it was true."

Jacqueline kept her voice deliberately measured and low. "But Luca was seeing my sister, that part was true. And, from what I could tell, Lilly was in love with him."

"For all the good it did him!" Dawn made a bitter disparaging sound.

"Or her," said Jacqueline.

"Are you saying that what happened to your sister was Luca's fault?" Dawn's chin jutted forward aggressively.

"Of course not, I never thought that. As far as I'm concerned there was never any question of that."

"Well, it's a shame you couldn't have told that to the Irish police then."

"Dawn," this time it was Jacqueline who leaned in, "I was eleven years old when it happened, a child."

"And Luca was seventeen," said Dawn, "not much

more than a child either. But that didn't stop them taking him in – for questioning, they called it. They kept him for two days and two nights and they tried to make him say he had killed that girl ..."

Jacqueline drew back involuntarily.

Magpie said reproachfully, "Dawn ..."

"It's true," said Dawn. "They only let him go because they had to, because they couldn't keep him any longer without charging him. And they couldn't charge him because they knew he was innocent. He had witnesses – independent witnesses who could say they saw him nowhere near where the girl disappeared." She glanced at Jacqueline. "Your sister, I'm sorry, I know she was your sister."

"It's okay," said Jacqueline. "Luca must have been very frightened."

"Yes, he was frightened – he was terrified. They kicked him and knocked him about. But you know what frightened him most? That place they kept him in. Luca told me it had no windows, no natural light and he thought they were never going to let him out. When he told me that, he cried like a girl. And those men, those Irish police, they thought he was crying because of what they had done to him, because of how they'd hurt his body. But it wasn't that at all. Luca was crying because he was thinking that was how prison would be, no window, no sky, no trees."

Listening to Dawn, Jacqueline had a sudden clear memory from that summer – Lilly telling Goretti Quinn about Luca's wanderlust. She looked at his sister now and said, "I don't know what to say to you. That was so wrong, what they did to Luca, so very wrong."

"But that other boy," Dawn's eyes grew fierce with

anger, "the one whose father was a policeman?"

"A solicitor," said Jacqueline automatically. "Edmund Sexton."

"Did they kick and beat him? I think not."

"No, I don't imagine they did," said Jacqueline and imagined the anger was quelled a little in the other woman's eyes.

"Luca told the truth about what happened the night your sister went missing," said Dawn. "To the police, to your father, to anyone who asked. He saw her, they quarrelled, she ran off and he didn't see her again after that. And he never left the fairground that night. People saw him there, a lot of people. Only they were the wrong people, carnival people, and because of that the police chose not to believe it. But still they couldn't prove a thing against Luca, because there was nothing to prove."

"Where is he?" said Jacqueline. "Where is Luca now?"

"I don't know. Far away from here."

The two women looked at one another.

"You're asking me to believe," said Jacqueline, "that you don't know where your brother is?"

"You don't know where your sister is," said Dawn and Jacqueline recoiled physically.

"Ah Jaysus, Dawn," said Magpie, "give her a break!"

Dawn turned on him. "You don't know what it did to him. He came back from Ireland and he wasn't the same Luca. He was at war with the world and then he fell out with Ned and went away again. And he was never the same. Never."

"And you blame what happened to him in Ireland," said Jacqueline. "I understand that. But I have a very good reason for asking about him. Somebody told my father

312

they'd seen Luca in France and they said there was a girl with him who looked like my sister, who looked like Lilly."

"I know all that," said Dawn. "I was there when he came."

"When my father went to see your grandfather? I didn't realise you'd been there."

"Well, I was," said Dawn. "Grandfather didn't know I was there but I was and I listened. My brother, the person I loved most in the world, just slipped out of my life and no-one ever explained why. I knew something had happened to him, that he'd been in danger, might still be for all I knew. But nobody would tell me anything, so when your father came shouting the odds at my grandfather, I listened."

Jacqueline couldn't keep from smiling, "That, I understand," she said.

"Your father told Grandfather all about this sighting in France. He seemed to think that your sister was with Luca, that maybe Luca had helped her get out of Ireland in the first place. But how could he, when the police were watching him the whole time until he left Ireland to go home again? And Grandfather told him that Luca had no idea where Lilly was."

"He also told him he didn't know where Luca was," said Jacqueline, "but my father didn't believe him, did he? So much so that he left an address, in the hope that Luca or even Lilly might get in touch."

Dawn's eyes were expressionless. "I know nothing about that," she said, "but I know that you're calling my grandfather a liar. Have you ever thought that it might be your sister who was the liar, just like my grandfather said she was? He had the measure of her alright – a liar and a

313

troublemaker he called her – but she didn't fool him and she didn't fool me. Luca was better off without her."

Dawn leaned back in her chair and Magpie stirred his cup with unnecessary vigour.

Jacqueline made a conscious effort not to lose her temper. When she spoke again, her tone was even, "How could your grandfather make those judgments on someone he didn't even know?"

Dawn looked down at her nails. "Luca told him all he needed to know," she said, her voice sullen.

"Luca was in love with Lilly," said Jacqueline, "so why would he badmouth her like that? And how was she a liar?"

"I have nothing else to say to you," Dawn pushed her chair back and got to her feet, "and anyway I need to go now."

Jacqueline got to her feet too. "Dawn, you must know where Luca is – at least tell me that."

"I don't know," said Dawn. "I can't help you. I'm sorry."

As she rushed out, Magpie said, "Leave it for now, Jacqueline. I'll go after her and I'll see you outside in five minutes."

Jacqueline watched him go, then she turned to Jimmy.

"Come on," she said, "the party's over."

"It isn't a party if there isn't a cake," said Jimmy.

"And sometimes there's cake and no party," said Jacqueline. "That's life for you. Now hurry up."

When she had paid and taken Jimmy to the bathroom again, they went outside.

Magpie was standing by the sea wall staring at the water. He turned when she came up behind him and looked at her ruefully.

"Well, you gave it your best shot," he said.

"She wouldn't tell you where he was either? I'm not surprised – she obviously hates my guts. But I just don't believe she doesn't know where he is."

"Let it simmer," said Magpie, "just let it simmer."

"How long am I supposed to let it simmer? She knows something, I feel it in my gut."

Magpie shook his head. "Like I say, give her time." He turned back to the sea. "Rain's on the way."

"Where?" Impatiently, Jacqueline gazed with disbelief from the glassy water to the blue sky.

"That bank of fog on the horizon," said Magpie. "Weather's coming in from the sea."

"I suppose you'd know," said Jacqueline doubtfully.

Magpie turned to her. "You mean that I'd always see a storm coming? Not always."

Oh, you cretinous idiot, Jacqueline berated herself and tried to think of what to say next.

Magpie grinned unexpectedly. "But it's fine weather today and I don't know about you but I could murder some pints. Coming?"

Jacqueline looked down at Jimmy. "I should really get him home ..."

"Fair enough." Magpie bent down and patted Jimmy's head. "See you around, young man." Then he was gone, moving swiftly along the seawall and Jacqueline, taken by surprise, could only stand and watch him go.

The air was still warm as they walked to the station. Jimmy dawdled, dragging his spade noisily along the ground behind him.

When, for the third time, he asked why Magpie was not coming with them, Jacqueline lost her patience. "He isn't

315

coming because he doesn't want to come," she said bluntly but Jimmy looked so crestfallen it made her feel ashamed.

She held out her hand. The boy looked at it for a moment then he put his hand in hers and they walked the rest of the way to the station hand in hand.

Just before the train pulled out, a man hurriedly approached, his head down. For a moment Jacqueline thought it was Magpie and she raised her hand to wave him over. The man looked up. Jacqueline saw the face of a stranger and dropped her hand quickly. She sat back, feeling curiously flat and disappointed.

Jimmy fell asleep almost as soon as the train began to move, his body pushed up against Jacqueline's. As he slept the fingers that held the string loosened and the dinosaur balloon floated into the air. She made a grab for it and caught it, but as she did the bucket and spade fell from Jimmy's lap. She tried to retrieve them but the child's head lolled and fell forward into her lap, and lay there like a dead weight. Looking down at him she sighed. How did people do it, not just for one day but every day? How did they endure the endless I-wants and the countless look-at-me's? She reached down and pushed a wayward strand of Jimmy's coarse hair from his eyes. His face was roaring red now and she was filled with compunction. Resting her head against the window glass, she closed her eyes and immediately images of the day paraded through her mind. Jimmy screeching, "*I'm a cloud!*" – Luca's sister, small brown eyes so bright and hostile and full of resentment – Magpie's eyes on her as he said, "She's trying to fit the pieces together ..."

How could he know, she wondered, that that was how I felt, how I have always felt? Like a figure in a jigsaw puzzle with bits of me missing, the clues to who and what I am meant to be lost, wedged beneath a sofa cushion or fallen down behind a sideboard. And what were the names of those gods again, the Gods of War – Ares, Enyo, Pallas Athena ... she started awake. The balloon had escaped her fingers too and she made a grab for it, pulling it down and tying it to her wrist.

When the train pulled into their station, Jimmy was still sleeping soundly. She tried to wake him, tapping him on the cheeks and finally gently pinching his nose, but he went on sleeping. In the end she had to carry him from the train along with his bucket and spade. Outside the station, she hung about looking out for a taxi, hoping vaguely that the fresh air would revive Jimmy. But with no taxi in sight and the child still sleeping soundly, she set off on foot. He was not so very heavy, but when the yellow spade slipped from her grasp she almost dropped him in the effort to recover it. In the heart of the town people were milling about and it did not take her long to pick up a taxi. She bundled Jimmy into the back seat and as she climbed in beside him she felt a gentle tugging at her wrist. She leaned back out and glanced up: the balloon was bobbing furiously. She thought, it wants to go free. With a quick tug she pulled it down and into the car and closed the door so that it could not escape.

As she fumbled for the key in her bag, the door sprang open. Marilyn fell on her and almost clawed the sleeping child from her arms.

"Where have you been?" she said. "How dare you take him and not tell me?"

"I left you a note – did you not get it?" said Jacqueline.

"A note, what good is a note? I've been waiting for more than six hours for you to come back. Who does that, takes someone else's kid and just goes off? What are you, some kind of menopausal freak?"

In some objective chamber of her mind, Jacqueline argued the insult – she was not actually menopausal. She did the maths: it was just gone seven-thirty now which meant that Marilyn had not returned until after one o'clock.

She said calmly, "I'm sorry you were worried, Marilyn, but you weren't here and I needed to go out. If you had come back when you said you would, I wouldn't have had to take Jimmy with me."

"Look at him!" Marilyn drew her fingers gently over Jimmy's hair, bringing it back from his face to reveal the extent of his war-wounds. "His poor little face is burned and look at his legs and arms. I never let him burn in the sun – couldn't you see his skin is too fair? And where are his glasses?"

"I'm sorry about the sunburn. I didn't think and by the time I realised it was too late." She rummaged in her bag. "I'm sorry about his glasses too – he stood on them and they got broken."

Marilyn snatched the toilet-tissue-wrapped glasses from Jacqueline's hand, "I don't believe this! What were you even doing with him? I left him with Dot."

"Dot had an early train to catch. Don't you remember, Marilyn? She asked me to look after Jimmy until you got back but you didn't come back in time and I needed to go. I had no choice but to take him along with us."

"Us?" Marilyn's small glittering teeth nipped at the pronoun. "Who's us? You're saying you took my kid off with some stranger?"

Jacqueline opened her mouth and closed it again. She had been about to say that no, it had not been a stranger, but thought better of it. Magpie knew Marilyn, so doubtless Marilyn knew him also and Jacqueline was not at all sure that the introduction of his name would help matters.

"Unbelievable!" Marilyn turned back into the house in disgust.

Jacqueline followed her slowly into the hall and watched her moving swiftly up the stairs. Jimmy's head hung over her shoulder, his upended hair swinging like a dirty yellow mop-head. When they had gone, she dropped his bucket and spade onto the hall table, opened her bag and added his water pistol, his book and the dinosaur beanie. She untied the string from her wrist and watched as the balloon floated upward toward the high ceiling. Marilyn would have to get a stepladder to try to retrieve it tomorrow. Serve her right, she thought.

In her room, she undressed and pulled on her T-shirt. It was beginning to smell and she told herself that she needed to either do some washing or buy new stuff.

As soon as she climbed into bed, her phone beeped. She reached out and picked it up: four missed calls and a host of texts, all of them from Gayle. She tapped out, **All fine. Talk tomorrow** – then put it on silent.

She closed her eyes and immediately the reel in her head began replaying the day. She tried to turn off her thoughts but without success. If only, she thought, she could be like Jimmy, and she remembered enviously how easily sleep had come to him. She imagined him tucked up now in his little red bed, or perhaps Marilyn had taken him into her bed tonight. That little jade, Magpie had called her – an old-fashioned phrase but he was full of old-fashioned phrases – a rage of maidens, indeed. In fairness, Marilyn was right to be furious at her for allowing the child to get burnt like that. She remembered the soft, light weight of him as she had carried him as he slept. People, a lot of people, said children made sense of things. For a moment, lying there in the darkness, Jacqueline let herself wonder if it could have been that simple. But in her heart she knew that had never been for her. She would not have wanted it, she had never wanted it, and even if it had not been too late, she did not want it now. That man on the train, she had been almost certain it was Magpie, that he had changed his mind and come after them. How ridiculously pleased she had been, her heart lifting like a teenager's and all because some old drunk ... Poor Jimmy, his arms and legs must hurt like hell. A waste of space, she told herself, that's what we are, me and Magpie, like those awful people in *Trainspotting*, the ones who had let the baby die from sheer neglect. What was it Dawn had said about her grandfather? That he had the measure of Lilly, that she was a liar and a troublemaker. *"But she didn't fool him and she didn't fool me. Luca was better off without her."* What exactly had Dawn meant by that? That Lilly had not fooled her? Just how exactly did anyone get the measure of someone they had never even met?

Chapter 41

1976

It is Halloween. Jacqueline's mother forgets to buy her a Halloween mask. She is always forgetting things now. Last year Lilly went trick or treating in Beechlawns with Goretti Quinn. Daddy went to collect Lilly at nine o'clock to bring her home in time for apple-bobbing before Jacqueline had to go to bed.

"But I don't want to bob for stupid apples!" said Lilly. "The bonfire wasn't even over and it was brilliant. I wish I lived in Beechlawns."

"So you're always saying," says Daddy. "What's so brilliant about burning tyres and bangers? It's like bloody Beirut up there tonight."

"At least it isn't miles from everywhere like this stupid house!" says Lilly.

"What are you on about? It's less than a mile from here to Beechlawns."

"And another mile to the village," says Lilly.

"What's in the village that's so attractive?" says Daddy.

"Life," says Lilly.

Jacqueline and Gayle are playing Snakes and Ladders on

the sitting-room floor. Daddy said to turn the television off so as not to disturb their mother, who has fallen asleep in the armchair. Jacqueline can hear all the sounds in the room: the ticking of the three clocks, the sappy logs sizzling in the flames, the rustling of Daddy's paper as he turns the pages. If someone were to peep in through the window, they would never know, she thinks. They would think that nothing had happened and we were just a normal family.

"Why didn't you let her go to France?"

Daddy looks up from his paper and Gayle, her hand in the air, stops shaking the cup of dice.

Jacqueline looks at her mother. She is not looking at Daddy, but at the fire.

"What are you talking about, Stella?" asks Daddy.

"The one thing she wanted most in the world," says Jacqueline's mother, "and you said no."

Daddy drops his paper on his lap. "But that was more than a year ago, Stella. And you know why we said no – Lilly was sick, she –"

"You said no, not we!" says Jacqueline's mother. "You said it!" Her voice is rising. "Every girl in her class was going. She begged and she pleaded and she cried, but you said no."

"But, love," Daddy's voice is low and gentle, "she'd been in bed for nearly two weeks. We had Dr May in, remember? And he said Lilly had a touch of pleurisy. We were all very worried. Why are you bringing this up now, Stella? It was a long time ago …"

"The one thing she wanted more than anything else and you couldn't let her have it!" Jacqueline's mother gets up and walks out of the room.

Gayle says, "Are you alright, Daddy?"

Daddy does not answer – he drops his face into his hands. In the fireplace, the coals crumble and fall soundlessly.

Chapter 42

AFTERWARDS

While she was dressing, a series of shrill cries drew Jacqueline to the window. In the garden below, Jimmy was running in circles, the dinosaur balloon following where he led. At least, thought Jacqueline, the sunburn had not affected his voice. And Magpie had been wrong about the weather: the sky was clear and blue and the sun was shining. She finished dressing and went downstairs to the kitchen, the cats on her mind.

The door was open to the sunshine and made a bright frame for Marilyn who was on the terrace, stretched out on one of the sun loungers. She was lying on her back, wearing just the bottom half of a skimpy and brilliant yellow bikini. Jacqueline, thinking wryly of her own modest swimsuit, turned away and went to the fridge. The egg tray was full and the shelves were stuffed with vacuum-packed kippers.

"Unbelievable, isn't it? A whole fridge-load of food just for a pack of cats."

Jacqueline spun around. Marilyn was leaning against the doorjamb, one hand on her hip. Jacqueline averted her gaze from the small, pert breasts and bubblegum-pink nipples.

"Oh, I don't know," she said. "The cats come so she feeds them."

Marilyn rolled her eyes and Jacqueline thought: I'm defending the batty cat lady now. "How is Jimmy by the way? I hope his sunburn isn't too bad. And I'm sorry about the glasses …" There were so many things to be sorry about that she left it at that.

"Don't worry about it." Marilyn pattered across the kitchen floor barefoot. "I'm off for a shower."

"I'll watch Jimmy then, will I?" Jacqueline called after her. No answer.

Muttering under her breath, she grabbed two packets of kippers and got to work. It wasn't until she was scrambling the eggs that the ridiculousness of the situation struck her – here she was making breakfast for a stranger's cats. She thought about the decision she had made on waking this morning: she would stick to her guns and get out of this madhouse for today at least.

As soon as she stepped out onto the terrace, Jimmy came careering up the steps toward her.

She tightened her two-handed grip on the pan. "Don't come too close, Jimmy, this is very hot."

He was wearing a new pair of glasses today and they were even more hideous than the usual ones, their bright red rims clashing with the deep pink of his nose. His arms had been coated in something white and chalky – calamine lotion, thought Jacqueline. The air felt muggy and close as she made her way to the pigsty and she was surprised to see a massing of purple-black cloud in the distance. There were no cats in sight and, as she knelt to divide the food, she had a mental image of them arriving yesterday to find the dishes empty; perhaps they would never come again.

She got to her feet and turned to find Jimmy standing watching her.

"Can we go again?" he said.

"Go where?"

"On the train to the place with the dinosaur balloons and ice cream and a picnic with chips?"

"You enjoyed yourself then?" said Jacqueline.

Jimmy nodded. "It was quite good fun."

Quite good fun – who could have known?

"But you live right next to the beach – surely your mother takes you all the time, doesn't she?"

"But I want to go on the train with Magpie," said Jimmy. "Why is he called Magpie? A magpie is the name of a bird not a person."

"So it is, but Magpie is probably just a nickname, on account of his hair because it's black and white, sort of like a magpie's wing. I'm sure he has another name, a Christian name." Jacqueline wondered what it was – something prosaic like John or Michael most likely.

"So can we go?"

"I don't think so," said Jacqueline.

As she walked away, Jimmy came hurrying alongside her. "Why not?"

"Well, I don't think that Magpie could. I mean he's probably busy and can't just go off anytime he likes." Busy drinking, thought Jacqueline, or busy sleeping it off. She wondered where he had spent the night.

"But we could still go," said Jimmy.

It took Jacqueline a moment to understand his meaning. "You mean me and you, without Magpie? Well, I don't know." The idea that the child would want to spend time in her company startled her but, that aside, would she ever want to spend another sticky-fingered day like yesterday?

She climbed the steps to the terrace and Jimmy stayed on the grass staring up at her. The sun glinted off the glass of his even-more-terrible spectacles.

"So can we go and can we have a picnic?"

Jacqueline opened her mouth and closed it again. She had been about to say "We'll see," but even she knew that children hated we'll-see's. "I don't know, your mum might not like it and anyway, I might not be here for much longer."

"Why not?"

"Because I might be going away."

"Going away where?"

"Just somewhere."

"But when you come back?"

"Oh alright," said Jacqueline. "If I come back and if your mum says it's okay and if I can ..." Surely that many ifs would put him off?

"Then do you promise?" said Jimmy.

Jacqueline bowed her head. "If all of those things happen, then I promise."

Jimmy gave a loud whoop and galloped away across the grass with the balloon still bobbing above him.

In the kitchen Dot was making coffee.

"You're back," said Jacqueline.

"Yes, I just got in. All went according to plan." She held out her hand and took the pan from Jacqueline. "I'll take that – thanks for looking after them for me."

"I'd hold off on the thanks if I were you," said Jacqueline. "I forgot to feed them yesterday and I made a mortal enemy of Marilyn and almost let Jimmy get burnt to a crisp by the sun."

"You've been busy," said Dot. "Tell me all about it."

They sat at the table and Jacqueline gave her a potted version of the previous day's events.

"So you and Magpie – sounds like you got along like a house on fire," said Dot.

Jacqueline looked down at her cup. "I wouldn't go that far. But he told me about his accident with the boat and all that. It explains a lot."

"In my experience, knowing the full story tends to do that," said Dot. "So what now?"

"Well, for a start I won't need breakfast tomorrow morning," said Jacqueline.

"You've decided to go home?"

"Not home," said Jacqueline, "not just yet." She put her cup down. "I'm not even sure if I have a home." She had not meant to say it and she looked at Dot, surprised.

"Then why don't you stay? You know if it's a question of money, there's no problem."

"Oh no, it's not that," said Jacqueline and hid her face in her coffee cup.

Stay here in this house and become of one of Dot's waifs and strays for real? Stay in this seaside town – was it even a real place? She felt that it would not surprise her to learn that it evaporated at the end of every summer and did not reappear until the winter was over. She thought of the deserted beaches and arcades, the seasonal shops and kiosks with their shutters down, the striped deck chairs and awnings all packed away and the sky mirroring the winter sea.

She looked up and Dot was watching her. "Thank you, Dot," she said. "I mean it, thank you. Listen, there's somewhere I need to go, but if it's alright with you I won't give my room up just yet?"

328

"No problem."

"And there's something else, something I've been meaning to ask you. My father coming to stay here, in this house I mean, was that just pure chance?"

"Chance and the fact that every hotel and guesthouse in the town was full," said Dot. "He came at the height of the season, the town was choc-a-block with tourists. He told me I was his last chance, that someone had sent him up the hill to me. Why, what did you think?"

"I thought there might have been something behind it," said Jacqueline. "Something definite. That envelope I showed you, the one with the postcard and the matches? I thought it might have been Lilly who sent it."

Dot shook her head. "Oh, Jacqueline, I wish I'd known that, I do indeed. I'd have told you it was me who sent that envelope. After your father had gone home, I found a fountain pen in his room and I decided to send it back to him. He'd also left a postcard behind. I wasn't sure if he had intended to post it or if he just bought it as a souvenir. In any event, I stuck it in with the pen. His address was in the guestbook. The matchbook must have been one he took away from here himself." Dot eyed Jacqueline sorrowfully. "I'm sorry. I had no idea you had linked it to your sister."

"No, it's my fault for making mysteries out of nothing when in reality there's usually a simple explanation for everything. But it doesn't matter." Just another road to nowhere, she told herself. "But I have one more question – and I hope you won't be offended by my asking it, Dot. Was there, was there ever anything between you and my dad?"

"What made you think that?"

Jacqueline thought that if Dot was offended she did a good job of hiding it.

"All those people who must have stayed here," she said, "and yet you remembered him so easily. It made me wonder."

Dot folded both hands around her cup. "I'll tell you what there was between us," she said. "The afternoon your father arrived here I had a line of sleeping tablets laid out all ready to take." As Jacqueline looked up, Dot smiled weakly. "It wasn't very long after Martin had died, you see, and it still hurt to breathe. All I wanted to do was go to sleep and not wake up, and that night I'd decided to do just that."

"And then Dad came knocking?" said Jacqueline.

"And then your dad came knocking," said Dot, "and he just kept on knocking. He would not go away. Afterwards he told me it was because he knew there was nowhere else for him to go. But in any event, in the end, I opened my bedroom window and yelled at him to go away. I told him I was too sick to take in guests. He just yelled back that he wouldn't want me to do anything, not even cook breakfast – all he wanted was a place to lay his head for a day or two."

"So you let him stay," said Jacqueline.

"There was something about him," said Dot, "standing there looking up at me. He seemed so tired and sad, I hadn't the heart to turn him away. I didn't even go down to let him in. I just threw the key down and told him to let himself in and pick whatever room he wanted. Then I went back to bed. The tablets were still there, laid out on the bedside table waiting for me, but I could hear him moving about downstairs and somehow I found I couldn't take them after all. I put them back in the bottle. Later on I heard him outside again, calling up to me. 'Missus!' he called me. 'Are you there, Missus?' I got out of bed and went to the window. I asked him what he thought he was doing standing outside yelling at me. He said he didn't know which room I was in and he was just wondering if I would mind if he made himself a bit of dinner. He said he'd clear up after himself, only he couldn't bear eating in a restaurant in front of strangers."

"That sounds like my dad alright," said Jacqueline.

"What could I do? I told him to feel free and that the next time he needed me, my room was the second door on the second landing. But if it was all the same to him, would he just leave me in peace? A couple of hours later he came knocking at my door. He said he'd made a coddle but there was too much food for one person and would I have some? I told him to go away, that I wasn't hungry, but he said he'd leave it outside my door on a tray, in case I changed my mind. He said not to mind the way it looked – that it tasted great."

Jacqueline was smiling – she couldn't help herself.

"After he'd gone, I started imagining I could smell it." Dot smiled wanly. "I hadn't eaten a proper meal in so long I was probably suffering from malnutrition. Anyway, in the end I opened the door and took the tray inside and I ate it. I was surprised to find that coddle was a stew of sausages and rashers and potatoes – I'd never eaten it before and I've never eaten it since, but it was wonderful. In the morning I got up and cooked him a breakfast. He stayed almost two weeks and after he was gone I thought about the sleeping tablets and what I had planned to do, but somehow the moment had passed." Dot got up and walked to the open doorway. Over her shoulder, she said, "You asked me if there was anything between your father and me. I suppose you could say in a way that he saved my life. And that was all. Oh, once or twice we sat here at this table late at night and drank whisky or brandy and got maudlin together. And once, I admit it, I kissed him or he kissed me, I can't remember who did what to be honest, but that was all it was, a kiss. He slept in his own bed every night and I slept in mine." Dot turned back to Jacqueline. "Don't ever think otherwise, Jacqueline – he was a good man, your father."

"I know he was," said Jacqueline, "and I'm glad he came here when he did. I mean I'm glad for you, Dot." She got to her feet. "Thank you for telling me all of this, but I need to be going. Would you like me to settle my bill first?"

"No need for that – you're coming back, aren't you? Your room will be ready and waiting in any case."

"Thank you, Dot. I appreciate it."

Dot waved her thanks away. "Listen to that," she said. "Thunder, and by the look of that sky rain is on the way."

Jacqueline stared through the window at the darkening sky. Magpie saw it coming after all, she thought. He saw it coming a long way away.

Chapter 43

1976

A dog found Lilly's sandal. He picked it up in his mouth and brought it back, and laid it down at the feet of the woman who owned him. The woman's name was Nancy O'Dwyer. She picked up the sandal and took it home and then took it to the police station because, she said, she had "a feeling it might mean something".

Jacqueline knows all of this because Detective Gerry rang Daddy and told him and Daddy told Jacqueline's mother so she would know what to expect when Detective Gerry came.

Now they're all in the sitting room waiting, Gayle and Jacqueline's mother side by side on the sofa holding hands, Daddy in his chair and Jacqueline sitting next to him on the floor, her head against the armrest. Nobody says anything. They are all listening for the sound of Detective Gerry's car on the gravel outside. Jacqueline counts the row of brass elephants marching along the mantelpiece. She knows there are seven, but she counts them anyway.

The three clocks tick and it seems to Jacqueline that they have never been louder. Daddy must be thinking the same thing because all of a sudden he says, "There are too many clocks in this room." He gets up, goes and stands at the window and stays there until the car comes.

Daddy goes out and comes back in with Detective Gerry and the Other One. Detective Gerry has a clear plastic bag in his hand and he does not wink at Jacqueline.

Daddy asks if they would like to sit down but Detective Gerry says, "We're fine where we are, Mr Brennan."

He puts the bag down on the coffee table, almost exactly, Jacqueline remembers, where Lilly's golden girl had stood. The golden girl is at the back of the press under the stairs now – Jacqueline saw it when she was searching for her skates.

Detective Gerry says, "Right, now I am going to ask you all to look carefully at the item in this bag."

This time it is the Other One who puts his hand in his pocket and pulls out his notebook.

Jacqueline's mother reaches out her hand to touch the plastic bag but Detective Gerry says, "I'll have to ask you, Mrs Brennan, not to remove the article from the plastic bag. But look at it carefully if you would, and tell me if you can identify it."

Jacqueline's mother picks up the plastic bag and holds it up to the light. Jacqueline leans in closer but all she can see is a dirty, light-coloured thing and her heart gives a little jump. That's not Lilly's sandal, she thinks. Lilly's sandal was lovely and clean and new and the colour of butter.

"It's hers," says Jacqueline's mother. "It's Lilly's sandal."

Espadrille, thinks Jacqueline – it's not a sandal, it's an espadrille.

Gayle makes a funny little sound in her throat and

Daddy says, "Are you sure, Stella?"

Jacqueline waits for her mother to start shouting and screaming because Lilly's sandal is an article and it means something.

Her mother does not shout and she does not scream. She holds the bag with the sandal and looks at it and she says, "Where was it found?"

Detective Gerry tells them it was found at the bottom of the hill, half a mile from the turn into Blackberry Lane. "Which fits in with the possible sighting," he says.

"But you searched that whole road," says Daddy. "I've walked it myself again and again."

Detective Gerry bows his head. "As I said, the dog appears to have dragged it from a ditch. I can assure you, Mr Brennan, the entire area will be scoured again for clues by a team of Garda searchers."

Daddy asks the question that Jacqueline has been thinking inside her head. "But what does it mean – Lilly's sandal?"

Detective Gerry says, "There's the possibility she dropped it and didn't notice. If she was carrying it and took a lift ..."

"Or was dragged into a ditch," says Jacqueline's mother.

"Jesus Christ, Stella!" says Daddy.

"It's what you're thinking," says Jacqueline's mother. "It's what everyone is thinking but no-one will say it."

Gayle starts to cry and Detective Gerry says he will leave them in peace.

"And I'm sorry, Mrs Brennan, but I'll need to take that for now."

"I'll want it back," says Jacqueline's mother.

She hands the plastic bag with Lilly's sandal to Detective Gerry.

He bows his head and says, "I'll make sure it gets returned to you, however long it takes."

Later that week Lilly's sandal and the ditch where it was found are on Garda Patrol. *Jacqueline thinks, I wonder if Lilly knows she's on the telly again.*

Chapter 44

AFTERWARDS

The house was in a quiet suburb of York, one of twelve in a small crescent. It was semi-detached and overlooked an oval green planted with shrubs and flowerbeds. There were two cars in the driveway; everything looked well-tended, perfectly pleasant and respectable. A far cry, thought Jacqueline, from the shabby block of flats where, all those years ago, she had surprised them. She pulled her hood back and rang the bell and watched through a panel of wavy, frosted glass as the distorted image came nearer and nearer. She had no doubt it was him – *long streak of paralysed piss.*

The door opened.

"Hi, Eddie," said Jacqueline. "Long time, no see."

He was beginning to lose his hair but otherwise, it seemed to her, he had changed very little. He was still gangly and lean, with the same sloping shoulders and the prominent Adam's apple. The skin around his mouth showed the ravages of acne, as though his adult body harboured the ghost of his teenage self. He appeared neither dismayed nor surprised to find her on his doorstep.

Perhaps, thought Jacqueline, he had been expecting her for some time.

Behind him, a figure appeared and Roy's high clear voice called, "Auntie Jacqueline! Mum, Auntie Jacqueline's come!"

In the narrow hallway, Gayle hugged Jacqueline. "I can't believe you're here. But why didn't you let me know you were coming? Come in out of that rain, will you – you look like a drowned rat. Why on earth didn't you say you were coming? We'd have picked you up from the airport. I suppose you caught a train here? Give me that jacket, will you, and come into the lounge and sit down – you must be shattered. And where are your bags? You haven't any bags."

She did not wait for an answer but chattered on and, while Jacqueline unzipped her jacket, she noticed that Eddie had folded his arms and was leaning against the wall watching her. Midway up the stairs, Roy had settled himself on a step and was gazing down on her benignly. She smiled at him and followed Gayle into the lounge. It was a large room with a lived-in appearance. The brown leather suite was a little shabby but it looked comfortable. In one corner a big widescreen television flickered.

Gayle picked up the remote and the screen went blank.

"Sit down, sit down, Jacqueline."

Jacqueline sat down on the armchair Gayle indicated and Gayle sat down on the sofa opposite.

"Oh, Jacqueline, you've no idea what this means to me! And, you know, you couldn't have picked a better time to get here. I just got back from the hospital – Alison spends almost every day there. But it's Eddie's turn to go tonight and Alison will come home for a few hours' sleep – she'll be thrilled to see you, Jacqueline. But why didn't you tell me you were coming, and where are your bags?"

"They're at the guesthouse," said Jacqueline.

"What guesthouse? You're not staying at any guesthouse. You'll stay here. Eddie can go and get your bags – you'll go and get Jacqueline's bags, won't you, Eddie? You have time before you have to go the hospital?"

"Sure," said Eddie quietly, and sat down in the armchair furthest away from the two women. "I have time. If that's what Jacqueline wants – just tell me where to go."

"It's not that simple." Jacqueline ignored him and addressed herself to Gayle. "I haven't come from the airport."

"Where have you come from then?" said Gayle. "You're being very mysterious, Jacqueline."

"I don't mean to be," said Jacqueline. "I've been staying at a guesthouse, that's all, but not in York. In that place I asked you about on the phone – Coldhope-on-Sea?"

"You don't mean ... but that's where Luca ..." Gayle stopped abruptly but Jacqueline saw how her glance went to Eddie, the way her face changed, the pleasure in her eyes changing to surprise and, if she was not mistaken, dismay. "You mean you've been staying there, you've been in England? For how long?"

"Just a few days." As she said it, Jacqueline thought how much longer it seemed.

"But you never said. I've been ringing you every day, and texting you, and all the time you were over here staying in some guesthouse?"

"Sea Holly Villa," said Jacqueline, like that altered anything.

Gayle was gazing at her, her face a study in bewilderment.

"But why didn't you say anything? There I was, thinking you were at home in that house all on your own."

"I didn't see any point in worrying you, Gayle," said Jacqueline. "I only came today because I needed to talk to Eddie."

Eddie, who had appeared to be studying the pattern of the carpet, looked up abruptly and met her gaze.

"Why would you want to talk to Eddie?" said Gayle and Jacqueline noticed the change in her tone, as though a note of wariness had replaced the earlier indignation.

"Because I do," she said.

"Fine by me," said Eddie.

"But not by me," said Gayle. She leaned forward, her eyes on her husband. "Did you not hear what she just said, Eddie? She's been over here for days and she didn't even bother to let me know. And now she just turns up on our doorstep because she's taken a notion. Not to see me or Alison or the baby, oh no, but because she wants to talk to you. How long is it since Jacqueline talked to you, Eddie?"

Eddie shook his head as though the puzzle was beyond him. "I don't know, but I don't have a problem talking to Jacqueline."

But Gayle was not looking at Eddie now – her shimmering eyes were on Jacqueline. "My God, you've got some nerve, Jacqueline Brennan. As long as we've lived in this house, I've been begging and pleading with you to come and stay. You wouldn't. But now, out of the blue, here you are demanding to interrogate my husband. Well, I'm not having it."

"It's alright, Gayle," said Eddie, gently. "I want to speak to Jacqueline too."

"I said I'm not having it, Eddie! I want her to go." She

jumped to her feet.

"But Mum," said Roy, "it's Auntie Jacqueline."

Jacqueline looked at his soft stricken face and felt grieved to be the cause of it.

"Roy," said Eddie, "go get your Auntie Jacqueline a cup of tea, please."

Jacqueline got up. "I don't want any tea – and if Gayle wants me to go, I'll go."

"There's no need for that." Eddie got up and went to Gayle. He encircled her waist with both hands and, his voice soothing and conciliatory, said, "You know you don't really want Jacqueline to go, Gayle."

Jacqueline snapped. "That's for Gayle to decide, not you!"

Gayle broke away from Eddie and turned on her, "If you don't mind, Jacqueline, I'd like to talk to my husband in private." She walked out of the room followed by Eddie.

Roy fixed mournful eyes on Jacqueline and she smiled.

"It'll be okay," she said.

"I think I'll go up to my room now," said Roy and he slouched out.

As the door closed behind him, Jacqueline sank back into the armchair.

"Jesus wept!" she said.

They were gone for some time and after a while, Jacqueline got up and crossed to the sideboard. She picked up a photograph in a silver frame: Eddie and Gayle on their wedding day. Eddie was looking down his nose at his bride, Gayle's face was upturned to his, solemn and seraphic.

Jacqueline imagined them arguing about her in the kitchen. Or perhaps they didn't argue, but talked things through reasonably. Gayle and Eddie as a couple: what did she know of them at all?

Moments ago, standing outside their front door, she had been reminded of the last time she had turned up unannounced on Gayle's doorstep. Then, as now, Eddie had opened the door to her, only then they had been living in a grubby little flat, and she had not been prepared for him, nor for that matter had he for her. She could still remember how he had gasped at the sight of her, the comedic quality of his astonishment. And she had gaped right back, standing there with her little case in one hand and a great stupid bunch of daffodils in the other. She had bought the flowers on impulse at the train station because they were Gayle's favourites. Just before she ran off, she had shoved them into his arms and Eddie's mouth had opened in a silent fishlike O. At the top of the road, she had looked back just once and he was still standing there in the doorway with her flowers. They had glowed golden-yellow against the drabness of the street, the greyness of the day. Then she had seen Gayle burst out the door and come running after her.

The door to the living room opened so quietly Jacqueline was unaware of Gayle's presence until she spoke.

"It's pretty awful, isn't it?" She held out her hand and Jacqueline handed her the photograph.

"I'm lost for words," she said. She watched as Gayle replaced the photograph then went back to sit on the sofa once more.

Jacqueline hesitated a moment, then went and sat next to her.

"So did you ever make that list?" said Gayle.

"What list?" It was the last thing she had expected, and for a moment she had no idea what Gayle was talking about.

"The list for the memorial cards for Dad."

"Oh, that list – no, not yet. I didn't get round to it. I'm not a great one for making lists, as you know."

"Well, you had other things to do," said Gayle.

She did not, Jacqueline thought, even sound sarcastic.

"I suppose there were more Mass cards after I left?" Gayle asked.

"Yes, quite a few actually."

"Who from?"

"God, I can't think off-hand."

"You haven't even opened them, have you?" said Gayle.

"No. I haven't, I'm sorry."

"It doesn't matter," said Gayle.

Something in her tone made Jacqueline feel depressed. She did not think it mattered either, but it should matter to Gayle. She looked at her sister, leaning back on the sofa with her eyes closed. Her face looked thin and worn, almost haggard. Jacqueline experienced a surge of compassion.

"You look tired, Gayle."

Gayle's eyelids parted and opened slowly as though the act took a great effort of will. She looked at Jacqueline, her eyes forlorn.

"You've never forgiven me, have you?" she said.

"Forgiven you for what?"

"For Eddie, for being with him, for marrying him and having the kids with him."

Jacqueline looked down at her feet in her sandals – her toes had gone quite brown. "It's not about forgiving," she said.

"Then what is it about, Jacqueline? Tell me."

"I don't know – it's about understanding, I suppose."

343

Gayle sighed. "Pick whatever word you like, Jacqueline – you're the editor – but what it comes down to is that you've held it against me ever since."

Jacqueline frowned. "I don't think I have. I just never understood how you could marry him when," she hesitated, choosing to go gently, "when there was even a shadow of a doubt."

Gayle made a sound in her throat. It was hard to tell if it was a laugh or a groan. "For God's sake, Jacqueline, you just don't get it. For me there is no doubt, there never has been."

"What, not a shadow?"

"Not a shadow. My God, Jacqueline do you think I could have married Eddie and had a family with him, lived with him for all these years if I hadn't felt absolutely certain in my own mind?"

"Then you're very lucky, Gayle. I wish I had such certainty about anything."

"But I am certain, Jacqueline. That's what I would have told you that time you came to London to surprise me, if you'd given me a chance. Remember that, Jacqueline?"

"Of course I remember," said Jacqueline. "I was only thinking about it a minute ago. I'm hardly likely to forget it."

"Like I've never forgotten the things you said to me when I ran after you that day," said Gayle. "Cruel, hurtful things. You called me a booby prize, you said that Eddie had only ever wanted Lilly and that he had just settled for me."

"I was eighteen," said Jacqueline. "I'd come to London to visit my sister, I had no idea you were living with Eddie. I mean, I knew you were in touch with him over here, or at least I guessed, but how could I know you'd shacked up with him?"

"Eddie isn't going to be a doctor anymore, Daddy. He's moving to England to study to be a pharmacist."

"That's some comedown, isn't it? Selling face creams and aspirin. How the mighty are fallen. And how come you know so much about what Eddie Sexton is doing, Gayle?"

"I just heard, Daddy, that's all."

Gayle was looking at her. "You always knew what was going on, didn't you, Jacqueline? Nobody could ever keep a secret from you. And I understand you were shocked to find me and Eddie living together, but to say those things …"

"I was shocked," said Jacqueline, "and angry and confused and disappointed. I'd brought you flowers …" She looked down at her hands – she had no idea why she had mentioned the flowers. It was a stupid thing to say and inconsequential and she had no idea why it suddenly made her want to weep.

"It wasn't true, what you said," said Gayle. "Eddie and me, it just happened naturally. It started out as a friendship, just keeping in touch by letter and then when I came over to London too it just seemed like the most natural thing in the world to look each other up. And it grew out of there. Eddie fell in love with me, Jacqueline, he really did."

"I don't doubt that much, and I'm sorry I hurt you that time. I didn't come here to hurt you this time either. I would like to speak to Eddie but not if it's going to make you unhappy. But you said yourself that you have no doubts, so what is there to be afraid of?"

"I'm not afraid," said Gayle. "I just don't know why you want to go raking things up."

"Then don't think of it as raking – think of it as tidying. There are some loose ends that I need to tidy up, that's all, and maybe talking to Eddie will help me do that."

"But he's already told everything he knows."

"Has he? Does anyone ever tell everything? There are things I haven't told you about that summer and I'm sure there are things you haven't told me. Admit it, Gayle – everybody keeps things back."

The stricken look on Gayle's face took Jacqueline by surprise, then the door opened and Eddie put his head around it.

"If Jacqueline wants to talk to me, it had better be now because I'll need to start out for the hospital in half an hour."

Jacqueline looked at Gayle. "Are you okay with this?"

Gayle got to her feet. "If you have to talk to him, talk to him."

Eddie stepped in and as she passed him he put his hand briefly on her shoulder. Then she was gone and the door closed quietly behind her.

"You have no idea what it was like, Jacqueline." He had settled himself in the armchair and was leaning back, his eyes closed.

The impatience she had always experienced in his presence prickled Jacqueline's skin like a heat rash. "Then tell me, Eddie," she said. "What was it like?"

"Well, for starters, I didn't go after her – oh, I'm not saying I didn't try, I tried plenty of times. I even approached your father that time I asked her to go with me to the céilí – you probably know that. But it was obvious she wasn't interested. Why would she be? She was Lilly Brennan for

God's sake – she could have anyone she wanted." He opened his eyes. "So I gave up. And then one night, right out of the blue, she rang me. She was so nice and sweet to me, kept saying my name – Eddie this and Eddie that. 'Eddie, I never see you around now – I'm starting to think you don't like me anymore.'"

Consciously or unconsciously, as he spoke, something happened to Eddie's face and the tone and inflections of his voice underwent a subtle change.

He was a good mimic and Jacqueline wanted to yell at him to shut up.

"Honestly, I thought it was a joke. I kept expecting that friend of hers, what was her name?"

"Goretti Quinn."

"I kept expecting Goretti Quinn to start laughing in the background – you know how they were together. But Lilly really seemed to be on the level, so I told her that of course I still liked her and she said I should come over to the house in that case and call for her. She said your old man was old-fashioned about things like that. So I did, although I still half thought it was a trick and I kept expecting Lilly and the Quinn girl to jump out from behind a hedge and shout 'Fooled you!' – or something like that. God, I don't think I ever sweated so much in my life." He made a swipe at his receding hairline as though the ghost of his damp teenage hair was in danger of dripping onto his brow. "Your dad brought me in to the living room and you were all there, just looking at me. But your mother was lovely, everybody was lovely. And Lilly was really nice to me – that was the day she asked me if I wanted her to go with me, you know, be my girlfriend. Can you imagine how I felt? Of course I wanted it – I was never so happy in my whole life. It was

347

like a dream."

Watching him, Jacqueline had the unnerving sensation that she was looking at a middle-aged man but seeing a seventeen-year-old boy.

"But she wouldn't let me kiss her," he said.

Oh good girl, Lilly, thought Jacqueline.

"She said she didn't want that yet, and I was fine about it. I never asked for anything from her, except to be with her. And I couldn't believe that she wanted to be with me too."

"Except she didn't want to be with you, Eddie, did she?" said Jacqueline.

"No, she didn't, but I didn't know that then."

"The dogs in the street could have told you," said Jacqueline. An eleven-year-old child could have told you, she thought, and she watched Eddie's face for some reaction to her cruelty – anger, pain, something – but she found nothing.

"Maybe they could," Eddie's voice sounded almost placid, "but I didn't see it."

"You never guessed that she was using you?"

Eddie shook his head.

"But you found out," said Jacqueline.

"Someone told me they'd seen her down at the river. She was with that guy from the carnival and they were kissing. I went and saw for myself." Eddie's hand crossed his face, briefly obscuring his eyes. "So I drove over to your house to have it out with Lilly. She denied it, but I could tell she didn't really care that I'd found out. All she cared about was if I was still going to call for her so she could go to that dance. She wanted to be in that Beauty Queen Final thing, be with that guy. She said if I didn't take her, your father

348

wouldn't let her go. Needless to say, I told her that was her problem not mine. I said I wouldn't be calling for her because I wasn't going to the dance, that I wasn't going to be made a fool of any longer. I think I threatened to tell your father about the carnival guy too. And then I drove off and left her standing there."

"And almost ran me over while you were at it," she said.

"Were you there?" Eddie seemed only mildly surprised. "I don't remember that. Anyway I ended up going to the dance after all. I wasn't planning to, but I found some booze at home and the more I drank the sorrier I felt for myself. I started thinking about Lilly and that guy together and it made me feel angry. I decided to go after all, so I got in the car and drove down to the club grounds. It was pretty late at that stage though, about midnight, and things were starting to wind down. I had a look inside the marquee tent but Lilly wasn't there and I couldn't see the carnival guy either but –"

"Luca," said Jacqueline, "his name was Luca."

"Right, well, he was outside in the carnival part of the field with a gang of women hanging off his arms but none of them was Lilly. So I decided she probably hadn't been allowed to go to the dance after all and I decided to head off home again. I was pulling out into the road when I saw Mick Conroy. I stopped and asked him if he'd seen Lilly around and he told me he'd seen her about an hour before, walking toward the estuary." Eddie sat back in his chair again. "But you know all this already, Jacqueline – it was in my witness statement."

"I was eleven years old, remember? In any case, no-one saw your statement, because it never went to court."

"Because there was no charge, Jacqueline, and a lot of people gave statements. But I made no secret of what was in mine. And I'm sure the Gardaí told your father what I had said – so you would have heard him talk about it." He looked at her. "Seems to me you were pretty much always there, listening, weren't you, Jacqueline?"

Jacqueline held his gaze but did not reply.

"But I get it," said Eddie. "I get that you would want to ask me face to face, adult to adult. The only thing that surprises me is that it took you this long. I'll finish the story, will I?"

He didn't wait for a reply. "I drove down toward the estuary and I met Lilly coming toward me. She was alone. She was walking in the middle of the road but she moved over to the side as I drove up. She bent down and peered in. She said, 'Go away, Sexy Sexton, I don't want you.'" Eddie smiled wanly.

"And then what?" said Jacqueline.

"Then I asked her what she'd been doing down at the estuary – it was pretty obvious she'd been drinking and I couldn't help wondering who'd given her the drink, who she'd been with. Lilly said it was none of my business, that maybe she'd been planning to run away to sea, something silly like that, I could never remember exactly. And then she said, 'Anyway, don't speak to me like that – I'm a Beauty Queen now, you know.' She seemed to think that was very funny. She started laughing and then she began walking again. I drove a bit down the road until I found somewhere to turn the car and then I caught her up. I slowed down again and asked her if she wanted a lift home – by this time I was actually worried about her – she kept wandering into the middle of the road – she really was drunk."

"You'd been drinking yourself," said Jacqueline. "You said so."

"I know that, but I'd never seen Lilly drunk before that. I tried to tell her that she shouldn't be walking by herself in that state, that she'd get herself knocked over. And that was when she said, 'You know, you are really a very nice boy, Sexy Sexton – much too nice for me.'" Eddie was silent for a moment and sat staring at the ceiling. "So then I offered her a lift again and she said no again and that was when I drove off and left her there. I left her there and I have to live with that, because maybe if I hadn't ... I thought about stopping the car just past the entrance to the club grounds and waiting to see if she went back to the carnival. Back to," he met Jacqueline's eye, "to Luca, but then I decided I was better off not knowing. I saw Mick Conroy along the road again and I stopped and picked him up and ended up going back to his gaff and crashing there for the night."

"Why didn't you go home to your own house?" said Jacqueline.

"My folks were away. I didn't fancy the idea of being on my own in an empty house and Mick asked me, so I went."

"Eddie Sexton," said Jacqueline, "did you harm my sister Lilly?"

"Jesus Christ, no, Jacqueline!" He straightened up. "I swear to God I never laid a hand on her. Do you actually, really believe I did?"

"So why did you lie to begin with? When my dad called to your house that day?"

"You mean the day after the dance? But I didn't know anything had happened to Lilly then, did I? And when it came down to it, I didn't want to get her into trouble. And, I'll admit it, I didn't particularly want to tell your father I'd left his daughter alone on the estuary road in the middle of the night. I should have told him straight off, I knew I should, just like I should have given the police my statement right away. But, in the end, I told them everything."

"You certainly took your time about doing it," said Jacqueline.

"I know I did," said Eddie, "but you know how it is. You keep shtum about something you shouldn't have, then time passes and the longer it goes the harder it is to tell the truth." He got up suddenly and walked to the window. "I didn't have to tell anyone, you know – nobody saw me with Lilly on the estuary road. Or if they did, they never came forward."

"You couldn't be sure of that," said Jacqueline. "And what about Mick Conroy?"

Eddie turned back to her. "Mick had gone when I decided to drive down to the estuary to see if Lilly was there."

"And you never told him about it?"

"No, I didn't. We didn't talk about Lilly at all that night. We talked about football and snooker and anything at all except your sister. Mick was a pal – he could see I was upset and he asked no questions. We just got drunk together – his folks were away too – and then we crashed in the sitting room. But that wasn't the reason I gave the statement, Jacqueline. It wasn't because I was afraid that someone had seen me and would say something. I did it because it was on my mind the whole time, eating me up. And so I told my old man and –"

"And he kindly accompanied you to the Garda station," said Jacqueline. "Did they lock you up for two nights and knock you around, by any chance?"

Eddie looked at her in obvious bemusement. "No, of course they didn't. You've lost me, Jacqueline – what are you on about?"

"Nothing," said Jacqueline. "Forget it."

Eddie came back and sat down. "Jacqueline, I am guilty of leaving Lilly on that road that night and I take full responsibility for that – but that's it." He put his hands to his thinning hair. "Look, what's the point of going over all of this again anyway? I nearly drove myself into a madhouse trying to make sense of it back then."

"You went off to England pretty quickly afterwards," said Jacqueline, "and you gave up medicine – why was that?"

"I went to England to finish my studies. I'd never really wanted to be a doctor – that was my grandfather's dream not mine. He hadn't managed to force my father to be a doctor and now he was trying it with me, but I'd decided I wanted to be a pharmacist. He was putting the pressure on so I went to England to get away from that. And yes, I'll admit it, I wanted to get away from the memory of what had happened with Lilly too, but –"

There was a gentle tap on the door. "Eddie, Jacqueline," said Gayle, "I don't like to disturb you, but Eddie needs to be going if Alison is to get home at a reasonable hour tonight."

"Okay, sweetheart," said Eddie, "I'll be right out." He looked at Jacqueline. "I'm sorry but I'll have to go. And I don't know what else I can tell you anyway."

"You'd better go," said Jacqueline. "Alison will be waiting for you.

Chapter 45

1976

Detective Gerry's car is parked in front of the house when Jacqueline comes home from school. In the kitchen Detective Gerry and the Other One are sitting at the table drinking tea and eating Rich Tea biscuits.

"Detective O'Sullivan has some more questions he needs to ask you," says Jacqueline's mother. "Sit down there now like a good girl."

Jacqueline sits down.

Detective Gerry smiles at her over the top of his blue-and-white striped mug and pushes the plate of biscuits towards her. "Want one?"

Jacqueline takes one and Detective Gerry puts his mug down and opens his notebook. He takes out his pen.

"Jacqueline, did Lilly ever seem unhappy to you?"

Jacqueline nods her head – her mouth is full of biscuit.

"Don't nod, Jacqueline," says her mother.

Detective Gerry leans in a little closer. "She did seem unhappy?"

The hairs on the back of his hand are red but golden too and Jacqueline wonders whether, if he grew a beard, he would look like Henry the Eighth. She is reading Murder Most Foul *and right now she wishes she could go upstairs and bury her head in it instead of answering questions about Lilly.*

"Only about not being allowed to go to the marquee dances," she says.

"And did Lilly ever talk about running away from home or anything like that?"

Jacqueline nods her head again quickly and her mother looks up from the cup she is holding in both hands.

"When – when did she say that?" she asks.

"When Daddy wouldn't let her go to the marquee dances, Lilly said she was going to run away."

Detective Gerry nods his head now and smiles, but he does not write anything down. He's disappointed, Jacqueline thinks, and she wishes she could tell him something that would please him.

"Was Lilly frightened of anybody, Jacqueline?" asks Detective Gerry.

"I don't think so." Jacqueline looks down at her shoes. There are scuffs and scratches on them now and they don't look so new. "Only ... maybe ..."

"Maybe what, Jacqueline?" Detective Gerry is leaning in closer again.

"Speak up, Jacqueline," says her mother.

"Slinky Quinn gave her the creeps," says Jacqueline.

Detective Gerry and the Other One look at each other.

Jacqueline's mother says, "Jacqueline, do you mean Regina's daddy?"

Jacqueline nods her head.

"She's talking about Tommy Quinn." Jacqueline's mother puts her cup on the table next to the tea-caddy.

355

The tea-caddy once belonged to Jacqueline's granny: it is black and red and gold and it has a picture on it of a fat man with a ponytail. He is lying on a pile of cushions with a row of girls dressed in kimonos walking toward him. The girls are carrying trays of things for making tea and, every time Jacqueline looks at it, she thinks he will never get his tea.

Detective Gerry is writing something down in his notebook. "Good girl, Jacqueline," *he says.* "Now, do you have any idea why Slinky – why Mr Quinn gave Lilly the creeps?"

"Because of the way he looked at her."

"Is that what Lilly said? That it was because of the way he looked at her?"

Jacqueline nods her head.

"What way did he look at Lilly, Jacqueline?"

Jacqueline shrugs her shoulders, "Weird," *she says.*

"Was there any other reason?" *asks Detective Gerry.*

Jacqueline nods again.

Her mother shouts, "Jacqueline Brennan, will you answer the questions and stop nodding your head!"

Jacqueline shouts back, "I don't know! Ask Gayle, why don't you?"

"Why, Jacqueline?" *asks Detective Gerry.* "What does Gayle know?"

"I don't know, she wouldn't tell me," *says Jacqueline.* "She would only tell Lilly. All I know is that Slinky Quinn made her cry."

Jacqueline's mother gets up from her chair and goes out of the kitchen.

Jacqueline can hear her in the hall loudly calling up to Gayle.

"Gayle, come down here now, please!"

Detective O'Sullivan says, "Good girl, Jacqueline – you did the right thing in telling us about this."

Jacqueline's mother comes back with Gayle. Jacqueline sees that her arm is around Gayle's shoulders.

"Gayle, I want you to tell Detective O'Sullivan how Mr Quinn made you cry," she says.

"I don't want to tell," says Gayle, and she starts to cry.

"There's no need to get upset, Gayle," says Detective Gerry. "Just tell me in your own words."

Gayle looks down at the floor. "It's disgusting. He said, he said I was to let him know if ... if I was ever stuck for a bit of sex or anything."

Jacqueline's mother puts her hand to her mouth.

Detective Gerry says, "Who said this to you, Gayle?"

"Slinky Quinn did." There are tears running down Gayle's face.

"This is Mr Thomas Quinn of Beechlawns Estate?" Detective Gerry is writing in his notebook.

"Yes, Slinky Quinn – Tommy Quinn," says Gayle.

"Was there a witness to this incident, Gayle?"

"No, I was on my own."

"Why didn't you tell me or your daddy about this, Gayle?" says Jacqueline's mother.

"I told Lilly and she said it was nothing. She said that I wasn't to mind him, that Slinky Quinn was always saying things like that to her."

"Filthy little man," says Jacqueline's mother. "Frank was right about him."

"Right about what?" said Detective Gerry.

"Frank has always said there was something not right about Tommy Quinn."

"He says he's a weasel," says Jacqueline. "And Slinky Quinn was hiding in the bushes when I was swimming in the river – I only saw him when I came out of the water."

"When was this?" says Detective Gerry.

"The day of the Festival Queen Dance," says Jacqueline.

"Why did you never tell me that?" says her mother.

Jacqueline shakes her head. "I don't know, but I told you now."

"You should have told me when it happened," says her mother.

Jacqueline thinks that it is just one more thing she has done wrong, one more thing to make her feel sad. Sad and bad.

"What happened after you saw Tommy Quinn in the bushes, Jacqueline?" says Detective Gerry.

"Nothing happened," says Jacqueline. "He just went away and then I went home too."

"Did anything like that ever happen before or since," says Detective Gerry. "I mean did you ever notice Mr Quinn watching you? Did he ever say anything to you, anything inappropriate – that is to say, anything he should not have said to you, Jacqueline?"

"No, just that I'm getting as good-looking as my sister," says Jacqueline. She looks at Gayle. "I think he meant Lilly."

"Can I go now, please?" says Gayle.

"Just one more thing, Gayle," says Detective Gerry. "Are you aware that Tommy Quinn ever watched Lilly, followed her, accosted her, anything of that nature?"

"He said things to her," says Gayle. "She told me he did but I don't think he ever followed her or watched her. She never said so if he did. But I don't think Lilly minded

*Slinky Quinn, very much. She told me just to ignore him.
But I don't think it's that easy. Maybe it was for Lilly but
not for me."*

Detective Gerry tells Gayle she can go and Jacqueline
watches her leave the room with their mother's arm around
her shoulders.

Detective Gerry smiles at Jacqueline and tells her again
that she is a good girl. The Other One smiles at her too but
he says nothing.

*"Did you not wonder why she'd go baby-sitting in her new
shoes and her blue dress?"*

"Leave the child alone, Stella," says Daddy. *"How
many times does she have to tell you? She had her head in
a book – it's not her fault."*

"I know whose fault it is," says Jacqueline's mother.

Daddy puts the paper down. He gets up slowly and goes
out of the room. Gayle slips her hand into her mother's.
Jacqueline looks at them sitting side by side on the sofa,
then she gets up and goes into the kitchen.

Through the window, she can see Daddy walking down
the garden. She wishes she could go after him and ask him
to take her up the fields. She thinks about all those
mornings long ago when they would set out: her, Daddy,
Lilly and Gayle walking single file under the trees in the
orchard and out through the gap into the meadow.
Sometimes the mist was so thick it was easy for her to
pretend that they were walking in the clouds. By the time
they reached the wooden bridge, the mist would have lifted
and the sun come out and beaded the grass so that it
sparkled under their feet. Then they followed the river up
to Beech Row where the trees were twisted giants and the

woods smelled of wild garlic. Once, they startled a heron on the bend of the river and the great bird took to the sky, faster than seemed possible, its long neck stretched, its legs sticking out behind and its wings beating the sound of its panic. But Daddy likes to go up the fields alone now. Jacqueline keeps watch until he has disappeared among the branchless apple trees.

Chapter 46

AFTERWARDS

Shortly after Eddie left, Gayle came in with a bottle of wine and two glasses. Jacqueline noticed her face was flushed and that one glass already contained wine.

"God, it's stuffy in here," said Gayle. "I'll open a window and let some sweet air in."

Jacqueline wondered if it was a way of saying she was looking particularly sour.

"It's raining heavier than ever," Gayle came and sat next to her on the sofa, filled Jacqueline's glass and topped up her own. "Cheers! There'll be some food soon. You look well, Jacqueline – wherever you've been the air must have suited you."

She's talking too fast, thought Jacqueline, and she's too cheerful. "I got some sun, that's all," she said.

"It suits you." Gayle leaned back against the headrest. "How are you doing anyway, about Dad, I mean? I'm still struggling to come to terms with it. It just doesn't seem possible that he's gone."

"I'm struggling too."

"At least he had a good turn-out," said Gayle. "I know

361

it sounds nuts but he'd have hated to have a poor turnout. And I'd have hated it for him too."

"I suppose I would too," said Jacqueline. "Mam always said he didn't have any friends, only drinking buddies but in the –"

"Yes, well, Mam wasn't always right about everything," said Gayle.

Something in her voice made Jacqueline look up from her wine but Gayle's eyes had already softened.

"Remember the way he used to tell us we were ..." Gayle paused and shelved her hands, one above the other.

Jacqueline smiled and they finished in unison: "That little bit above" and they laughed a little at the common memory.

"He wanted us to think we were better than everyone else," said Gayle. "I wonder if that was because *he* didn't believe he was really. Remember how he hated the flower women?" She laughed. "But he lumped them all together and that wasn't fair, because some of them were very nice people."

"Probably," said Jacqueline, "though I couldn't stand Florence McNally. I thought she was such a stuck-up snob though she turned out to be a good friend to Mam. All the same, Dad was right to be suspicious of her because Mam left him and went to live with Florence in the end. Do you think she realised what people were saying, that she'd gone to live with her lesbian lover?"

"That was nonsense," said Gayle. "Florence just gave Mam somewhere to go until she found her feet."

"Only she never did find her feet," said Jacqueline. "All those years living in Florence's big house, just up the road from Dad– no wonder it sickened him."

"Yes, well, I think she was happier there, and that's what counts, isn't it?" Gayle's fingers were worrying the arm of the sofa.

"I don't think she was happy anywhere," said Jacqueline. "How could she be? Still, she liked messing around in the ridiculous big flower room Florence had."

She was thinking of one day in particular, maybe a year or so after her mother had moved in with Florence. She had stood, unobserved, in the doorway to the flower room watching her mother busy with an arrangement, her movements deft and sure. She had shrunk to birdlike proportions, so much so that it was hard now to understand how they had failed to guess what was growing inside her.

Jacqueline had asked, "What are you doing, Mam?"

Her mother had looked up sharply. "I'm wiring my Gerbers."

"Your whats?"

Her mother had smiled. "Gerber daisies." She jabbed a piece of wire though the green base at the top of the stem.

Jacqueline winced. "Ouch, I bet that hurts. Why do you have to wire them?"

"Right now I'm doing it for anchorage – it helps to support the heavier blooms and stop them drooping. Some flowers can snap off the stem too easily."

Watching her, Jacqueline had said, "You're really good at all of this."

"Oh, I'm not that great – I'll never be a patch on Florence."

"I don't just mean the flowers," Jacqueline had said. "I mean …" and spreading her hands vaguely she had looked about her. What did she think was great? That somehow, the things her father had mocked, the flowers and the stuck-up women friends, were the things that had saved her mother, kept her connected to people and allowed her to live in the world despite her loss? "I mean everything," she had said. But what she had wanted to say, was "I think you're great, Mam." But then, Florence McNally came in with a silver tray that held tea and floral china and homemade biscuits and the words went unsaid.

"Why do you think she left him on that particular day, Gayle?" said Jacqueline. "Her 52nd birthday. I mean it's an odd number, not a significant birthday or anything."

Gayle got up abruptly and walked to the window. "I don't imagine it had anything to do with it being her birthday. I imagine she'd been thinking about going for some time."

"She didn't exactly get very far," said Jacqueline. "Just up the road to Florence's house. That never really made much sense to me."

"I suppose our house just held too many memories for her," said Gayle.

"I would have thought that was a better reason to stay than to go," said Jacqueline. "Poor old Daddy, he was useless without her."

"Poor old you." Gayle came and sat down again. "That was when you had to leave your lovely little flat and come home and be with him."

"It wasn't all that lovely and I didn't have to."

"But you felt you had to," said Gayle, "and that's the same thing. And you did like it – you loved being on your own, I know you did." She picked up the wine bottle and refilled their glasses. "So, Eddie said he told you everything he remembers. Was it enough?"

"I don't know. It was a start."

Gayle frowned. "But you can't still believe that Eddie had something to do with it?"

"I don't believe anything. I'm just trying to make sense of things. But one thing I do know – Dad believed Eddie had something to do with it."

"No, he didn't," said Gayle. "I know you've always believed that, but it's just not true."

"I think it is true, and so do you, Gayle. Otherwise why were things always so weird between them? I mean, look at what happened when Alison was born."

"Alison?" Gayle's head snapped up. "What do you mean?"

"The way you kept the whole thing a secret. For God's sake, Gayle, we didn't even find out that you were pregnant until after the baby was born. Who keeps something like that from their own parents?"

"But you know why that was, Jacqueline. We explained why we –"

"I know you explained," said Jacqueline. "There were complications, you didn't know if you'd go full term, you didn't want to disappoint Mam. But none of that explains why you didn't bring Alison home until she was six months old."

"You've got it all wrong, Jacqueline, all wrong."

"Have I? Then why were Mam and Dad so weird about Alison? Sure, Mam got a bit weird about everyone and everything in the end, but why was Dad so funny about her?"

"He wasn't funny about her," said Gayle. "Dad loved Alison and you can't say he didn't. He was very fond of Roy but he adored Alison."

"Yes, he adored her, but I still say he was odd about her, he was always odd about her. His voice changed whenever her name was mentioned. Now I come to think of it, he did it just before he died. We were talking about Alison and her baby and it happened again – that funny look came over his face. And I don't know how many times I caught him looking at her, when you'd bring her home with you on holiday."

"I think you're imagining things," said Gayle, "and why wouldn't he look at her? She was his granddaughter."

"That's not what I mean. I don't care what you say, Gayle, he was never comfortable with the way things turned out. He was too fair a man to hold it against Alison or Roy, but there's no way you can convince me Dad was happy knowing Eddie Sexton was the father of his grandchildren. He could hardly bear to look Eddie in the eye, and you know that as well as I do."

Gayle was shaking her head, more in weariness than anger or denial, it seemed to Jacqueline. "You don't understand, Jacqueline." She got up and walked about the room, tidying everything in her path. "If Dad held a grudge against Eddie it was because – I don't know – maybe it was because he thought that if Eddie had taken her to the dance that night ... look, why all these questions all of a sudden anyway? Has something happened, have you found out something?"

"Stop fluffing cushions and come and sit down," said Jacqueline. "Then I'll tell you."

Gayle sat down, not next to her this time but in the armchair opposite and Jacqueline told her about the postcard and the sketch of Sea Holly Villa.

"At first I thought the house itself was significant, but I

know now that it wasn't. It was just a place where Dad stayed while he was looking for Luca, and the reason he was looking for Luca was because he believed Lilly might be with him."

She looked at her sister expectantly but Gayle was looking at her own hands, so she told her about Magpie and all she had learned from him, and about Ned Early and going to meet Dawn.

"I still think that Dawn knows something she's not telling me, and I intend to find out what that is. But before I do that I need to be sure in my own mind that Dad was right in what he believed, that Lilly was out there somewhere, that she was alive. That's why I came to talk to Eddie."

When Gayle looked up it seemed to Jacqueline that there was nothing in her eyes but dullness and weariness. "What Dad believed was based on what?" she said. "That story about France, something someone thought they might have seen?"

"Dad believed it," said Jacqueline, "and it was more than that – there was Ned Early. Dad knew in his gut that Ned wasn't being honest with him, just like I'm sure Dawn knows more than she's letting on. That's why Dad was around Sea Holly Villa trying to find out more."

"But he didn't find out more, did he?"

"No, he didn't, but maybe that's because he gave up too soon. But I don't have to."

"Oh Jacqueline, don't –"

"Don't what?"

Gayle got up and began pacing again. "I just think you should leave it alone, that's all. You're just tormenting yourself with all this ... this ..."

"All this what?" Jacqueline put her glass down. "All

367

this trying to find out if my sister is alive or dead? Is that what you mean, Gayle? Whereas you actually believe that Lilly is dead, don't you, Gayle? Why is that? Is it because of something you know that I don't?"

Gayle spun round. "If you mean because of something to do with Eddie, then no. I swear to God, no. Will you listen to me, Jacqueline, once and for all – *Eddie did not harm Lilly*."

For a while there was silence, then Gayle came and sat down in her chair again.

"You're right about one thing, Jacqueline," she said. "I do believe that Lilly is dead. I do and I'm sorry if that's hard for you to hear."

Her hand stole to her sleeve and Jacqueline watched as the inevitable hankie was produced.

"It's what I believed too," Jacqueline said, "for a long time. That last time when they reviewed her case, I asked Detective Gerry to tell me honestly if he thought we would ever find Lilly alive."

Gayle looked up quickly, her eyes brimming with tears, "What did he say?"

"That he didn't believe so, that people leave trails, credit histories, subscriptions, bills, whatever. Living people leave trails, he said, and Lilly's trail had grown cold." Gayle was openly weeping but Jacqueline paid no heed. "Actually he's Inspector O'Sullivan now but I can only ever think of him as Detective Gerry."

Gayle smiled bleakly over the top of her hankie. "You had the most almighty crush on him, I remember that."

"Did you know that?" Jacqueline was genuinely surprised.

"Of course I knew it." Gayle tucked her hankie away,

leaned in and picked up her glass. "You used to light up when he came to the house and you'd follow him out to the car when he was going and stand at the gate until he'd driven away. God, you were a gas little creature!"

"Was I?" Jacqueline frowned. "How exactly was I gas?"

"You were funny and clever and so inquisitive. Your head was always in a book and then you'd come up for air, terrified you might have missed something. That was one of the saddest things about what happened, what it did to you, the way the spark went out of you."

"That's what Dad told Magpie," said Jacqueline.

"This Magpie, is he the reason you look so well?"

Jacqueline shook her head vigorously. "Don't start, Gayle – anything less romantic than Magpie you cannot even begin to imagine."

"That's a pity," said Gayle, "because imagine if Dad had somehow led you to that place just so you could meet Magpie and –" She stopped when she saw the expression on Jacqueline's face. "What? It could happen. Life is weird like that."

"Weird is one word for it alright," said Jacqueline.

"Weird but with wonderful bits dotted through it," said Gayle.

"Brilliant passages connected by long prosaic interludes," said Jacqueline.

Gayle smiled. "Brilliant passages, I like that. That summer, 1976, that was a brilliant passage – until it happened of course." She stopped smiling and straightened up in her chair. "Jacqueline, what did you mean earlier when you said there were things about that summer you'd never told anyone?"

Taken by surprised, Jacqueline looked down at her glass.

"You don't have to tell me if you don't want to," said Gayle.

But Jacqueline found that, after all, she wanted to.

She had told it exactly as she remembered it and, as she stopped talking, Gayle got up and came to sit next to her on the sofa once more. She roped her arms about Jacqueline's neck and pulled her close.

"I had no idea you blamed yourself," she said. "Poor Jacqueline, all this time!"

Jacqueline let herself be held for a few moments, then she gently wriggled free and picked up her glass. "It's fine, Gayle."

"No, but Jacqueline," said Gayle, her voice urgent, "you have to stop blaming yourself. You have to stop beating yourself up for being human. I know it's hard, because you never had any chance to put things right, but you have to forgive yourself." She leaned forward, "I'm going to tell you something, Jacqueline. I used to wish that Lilly would die. Not because I really wanted her to die, but just so that Eddie could see me. Because with Lilly there he couldn't see me. And afterwards, when she was missing, I used to feel sick with guilt."

Without looking at her, Jacqueline reached out and touched her sister's knee. "It's alright, Gayle," she said. "All that proves is that you're human too."

For a while they sat side by side in silence.

"You know it's the anniversary tomorrow," said Jacqueline.

"I know it is." Gayle's fingers went back to worrying the armrest.

"The house will be empty," said Jacqueline. "It will be the first time. I'd thought you'd mind about that?"

"I don't think I do, not really. I think it's probably for the best. After all, there has to be a first time, doesn't there?" Gayle looked up suddenly. "You're not going to give up, are you, Jacqueline – you're going to keep on searching for her."

It was not a question and Jacqueline shook her head. "No, I'm not going to give up," she said.

"Jacqueline, there's something else ..." Gayle stopped as the door was flung open.

Roy came shambling in, his face creased with uncertainty. "Is it okay if we put on the match now?"

Gayle stared at him blankly for a moment as though she hardly knew who he was or why he had appeared in her living room, then she jerked to her feet and went to stand at the window.

Without turning round, she said, "Do what you like, Roy."

Chapter 47

1976

It is Jacqueline's birthday and she is twelve years old. She wanted a poncho and a mood ring but her mother gave her a card with money in it and Daddy said, "Here you are, pet, buy yourself something nice." Auntie Carol sent her a postal order.

Jacqueline thinks about Lilly saying, "Money is better than presents" – it sure doesn't feel that way.

Last year, Lilly gave Jacqueline a box of Weekend chocolates. When Jacqueline opened them and offered her one, Lilly said, "No, those are for you. Oh, okay, I'll just have one," but she had eight and four of them were caramels. Jacqueline didn't really mind, even though caramels were her favourite. This year, her only present is from Gayle, it is Five Go to Billycock Hill *and Jacqueline has already read it. And, anyway, she is too old for Enid Blyton now, but she smiles and says, "Thanks, Gayle."*

Jacqueline's mother is "making an effort". There is no birthday cake but there are two Swiss Rolls and Bourbon Creams. After the tea, she says she will just go upstairs for a lie-down. She does not come down again. Jacqueline watches Bonanza *with Daddy and Gayle and when it is over, Daddy says he's "just popping down the town for the one".*

Jacqueline is asleep in bed when the sound of the car horn wakes her.

Gayle is already awake. "It's cold, Jacqueline," she says. "Make sure you put your slippers on this time."

They don't even bother to look out of the window. Jacqueline cannot find her slippers so she puts on her socks. Jacqueline's mother is out on the landing before them.

"He can't keep doing this," she says, pulling her dressing gown around her, and they go down the stairs one by one.

Outside, the sky is navy blue. The stars look very sharp and the moon is shining down on the roof of Daddy's red car. The wind blows and Jacqueline hunches her shoulders against it. When she moves her socks stick to the glittery, frosty pebbles.

Through the car window, they can see Daddy's head bent forward over the steering wheel.

Jacqueline's mother tries to open the door but it's locked from inside.

"Come on, Francis!" She raps the window. "For God's sake, wake up and stop that racket and unlock the door!"

The horn just keeps on going.

Jacqueline's mother bangs on the roof of the car. "I said wake up, Francis – it's the middle of November for God's sake and the girls will catch their death of cold!"

They take turns to rap and knock and rattle, they call and shout but Daddy does not move.

Then Jacqueline leans over the bonnet of the car and taps gently on the windscreen.

373

Daddy raises his head and peers through the glass at her and smiles. "There's my little girl!"

"Come to bed, Daddy," says Jacqueline.

"I'm grand where I am, pet."

"No, Daddy, you have to come in to bed," calls Gayle. "You can't sleep in the car."

"I could sleep on a bed of nails," says Daddy.

"Francis Brennan, this is the third time in two weeks you've done this," says Jacqueline's mother, "and I for one have had enough of it. You're a drunken disgrace is what you are, and if you don't come in to bed this minute, we'll lock up the house and leave you out here all night to freeze!"

"Oh no, Mam, we can't do that!" says Gayle.

"Don't 'oh no, Mam' me," says Jacqueline's mother, but she stops when Daddy opens the car door.

Between them, they help him into the house.

"He can sleep on the sofa tonight," says Jacqueline's mother. "We nearly broke our backs trying to get him up the stairs the last time."

When Daddy is asleep on the sofa, Gayle says, "I'll go and get him some blankets."

"You do that," says Jacqueline's mother. "I'm going back to bed. And I mean it – the next time he does this he can sleep in the car."

The next time it happens, Daddy's head falls backwards instead of forwards onto the steering wheel and the horn does not go off so nobody finds him until the morning.

"Howaya, Jacklean!"

Regina Quinn is standing at the bottom of the steps, leaning on the handles of the Quinn's big blue pram. The

Quinn baby is sitting up and smiling and waving his arms at Jacqueline. He says something she does not understand. His face is red and he hasn't very much hair. Only two bottom teeth show when he smiles but Jacqueline is disappointed that he is not really pop-eyed after all. Leo Quinn is in the pram too, he is sitting sideways at the baby's feet with his legs dangling over the side, and there is something on his face, which Jacqueline thinks could be jam or might be blood. He sticks out his tongue at her.

"Why did you bring them?" asks Jacqueline.

"My ma said I wasn't allowed out unless I brought them," says Regina.

"Well, you shouldn't have bothered – my mother said you can't come into our house anymore." Jacqueline likes the way it makes her feel to say this. She thinks that she would like to close the door in Regina's face but she waits to see if maybe Regina will start to cry.

Regina looks down at her shoes. "My ma said I'm not allowed to play with you anymore either."

Jacqueline is so surprised she forgets her plan to slam the door. "Why are you not allowed to play with me?"

Regina looks up again. "My ma says your ma told lies to the guards about my da."

"No, she didn't, my mother doesn't tell lies."

"I didn't say she did," says Regina. "My ma said it."

"Your ma says a lot of stupid things," says Jacqueline.

"Yeah, but the coppers made my da come down to the station. He had to answer a load of questions about where he was the night Lilly went missing. But my ma says the coppers better not try and blame him, because she'll say my da was asleep in bed, and that's the truth."

"Well then," says Jacqueline.

"Yeah but people are talking."

"About your da?" asks Jacqueline.

"Yeah, they're saying he's a Peepin' Tom or a weirdo or something."

"Yeah, well, that's not my mother's fault," says Jacqueline.

"People are sayin' stuff about your da too, you know."

Jacqueline does not know. "What sort of stuff?" she asks.

Regina looks down at her feet again. "I don't know nuttin'."

Jacqueline tries to keep her patience. "If you don't know nothing, that means you know something. So why don't you just tell me what you know, Regina Quinn? What are people saying about Daddy?"

"That maybe Lilly ran away because your da is too ..."

"Because he's too what?"

"You know," says Regina, "the way he never let her go with anyone."

"He let her go with Eddie Sexton," says Jacqueline. This is so stupid she wishes she had not said it out loud.

Regina looks like she is thinking the same thing. "Yeah but ..."

"What else are people saying?"

"You know, that he dragged her out of the marquee and tore her sash and everything."

"What about it?" says Jacqueline. A pain has started in her stomach, the sort of pain she gets when she's eaten too many crab-apples. "That was an accident."

"Yeah, I know, but people are saying how mad your da was and how everyone thought he was going to hit Luca ... or Lilly even."

"He never hit Lilly," said Jacqueline. "Daddy never ever hit Lilly. That's a big fat lie, Regina Quinn."

"That's what I said when I heard it," said Regina. "I said I didn't believe your da ever hit Lilly."

"Well, if you hear people saying stuff like that again you better tell them ... tell them ..." But Jacqueline cannot think what Regina should tell them. *"So why are you even here if you're not allowed to play with me?"*

"Because I wanted to," says Regina.

"Skinny Malink, melodeon legs, umbrella feet!" sings Leo Quinn.

"Shut up, Leo!" says Regina.

"Went to the pictures and couldn't get a seat!"

"Shut up, Leo!" says Jacqueline.

"When the picture started, Skinny Malink farted. Skinny Malink, melodeon legs, umbrella feet!"

Jacqueline stares out over the top of Regina's head. "You'd better go before my mother sees you, Regina."

"Okay. But I'll still come if you want me to, Jacklean."

"No, don't, you'll get into trouble," says Jacqueline.

"I don't mind, I'm always getting into trouble."

"How many times did you get the wooden spoon this week?" asks Jacqueline.

"Six times, I think," says Regina. "I've sort of stopped counting."

"Goodbye, Regina," says Jacqueline.

"Bye, Jacklean."

"Bye, Skinny Malink," says Leo, as Jacqueline closes the door on Regina Quinn's glittery eyes.

Chapter 48

AFTERWARDS

"Are you staying the night, Auntie Jacqueline?" Roy, oblivious to any tension in the room, had hurled himself in an armchair and pointed a remote at the big TV. *The Simpsons* lit up the screen in bright yellow and Homer's voice boomed.

Gayle turned back quickly from the window. "Are you, Jacqueline?"

Jacqueline hesitated a fraction too long and Gayle's face seemed to light up from within. And that seemed to settle it.

"Brilliant," said Roy, "and that means you can come with us to the hospital tomorrow to see Alison and the baby."

Gayle, who was collecting up the glasses and the wine bottle, looked up and laughed. "I'm not so sure about that, Roy – your Auntie Jacqueline is not exactly a baby person."

"I'll have you know," said Jacqueline, "that I spent an entire day yesterday taking care of a four-year-old." As Gayle's eyes widened she added, "Much against my will, I have to admit."

Gayle rolled her eyes. "I'm just going to get the room ready for you." She hurried off, seemingly happy once more.

"The match doesn't start for another fifteen minutes, Auntie Jacqueline," said Roy. "Will I stick on the news for you or something?"

"No, watch what you like, Roy, don't mind me. I'll just relax here."

"I'll mute it until the match comes on." Roy pointed the remote and Homer fell silent.

As he leaned over his phone again, Jacqueline found herself smiling. After all, it was nice to discover you liked the people to whom you are deemed to belong. She leaned her head back against the headrest of her chair and closed her eyes. When she opened them again, *The Simpsons* had given way to a local news bulletin and an image on the silent screen caught her attention.

"Could you turn that up a minute please, Roy?"

Roy looked up from his phone. "Huh? Sure."

"... body is that of a white man believed to be in his late fifties or early sixties. Officers investigating the murder are appealing for witnesses or any information from the public ..."

The door opened and Gayle came in. "I'm putting you in the box room, Jacqueline – don't worry, it isn't really a box, it's quite roomy actually. I'd give you Roy's room only it smells and I can't put Alison out of her room, not when –" She broke off as Jacqueline pushed past her. "Where are you off to, Jacqueline?"

"Sorry. I need to make a phone call."

In the hallway, she dialled the stored number and paced as it rang.

379

Behind her, Gayle closed the door to the lounge and she could hear the murmur of her and Roy's voices.

"Come on, Dot, answer!" but the phone kept on ringing.

The door to the lounge opened. "Is anything wrong, Jacqueline?" Gayle asked.

"Maybe, I don't know." Jacqueline ended the call: "I'm going to have to go, Gayle."

"Go?" Gayle followed Jacqueline back into the living room and watched her picking up her bag. "But you said you were going to stay. I've made up the room for you. Is this about Eddie?"

"No, this is nothing to do with Eddie or any of that. I just need to go, Gayle." She saw the look on Gayle's face and went to her. She put her hands on her sister's shoulders. "I mean it. This is not about you or Eddie or any of that, I swear. It's just that something has happened and I really do have to go."

Gayle and Roy followed her to the front door and watched as she zipped herself into her still damp jacket and pulled up the hood.

When she opened the door and saw the rain, heavier than ever, Gayle gave a small dismayed gasp. "You can't go out in that rain, Jacqueline – would you not wait until it eases off?"

"I don't think it's planning to ease off anytime soon," said Jacqueline. "I may as well go now."

"Well, here, at least take this." Gayle came forward and pulled an umbrella from a stand next to the door.

Jacqueline took it. "Thanks," she said.

For a moment they just looked at one another and then Gayle leaned in and took Jacqueline's face between her hands.

"You know you have people, don't you, Jacqueline, even if you don't want them?"

When Jacqueline said nothing, Gayle let go and Jacqueline turned away and hurried off into the slanting rain.

At the top of the road, she turned and looked back. Gayle and Roy were still there in the doorway, their arms around one another, looking after her.

Jacqueline raised her arm and waved to them. "*I promise I'll come back!*" she yelled. She wasn't sure if they could hear her but suddenly the figures in the doorway raised an arm each in a frenzy of waving.

She waved back and then turned away into wind and rain.

She had tried the number twice from the train and once from the taxi so that when she walked into the kitchen of Sea Holly Villa she was surprised to find Dot there making tea.

"Didn't you hear the phone?" said Jacqueline. "I was ringing and ringing. Was it Magpie?"

"I was out, I've only just come in," said Dot. "I got soaked to the skin and by the look of it so did you. Was what Magpie?"

"It was on the news, a man in his late fifties was murdered. His body was found in a bandstand. I didn't hear the whole news report but it was Northby, I know it was. I recognised the beach and the bandstand – it was the same one where we had our chips yesterday, me and Magpie and Jimmy. I recognised it straightaway."

Dot's hand went to her breast. "Oh my days, surely not?"

"They haven't identified him," said Jacqueline, "but it was the same bandstand and he's always in bandstands."

"But then it could be anybody," said Dot. "Why would you think it was Magpie? My, you've given me a shock. And didn't he come back with you last night?"

"No, he stayed there," said Jacqueline. "He said he had something to do but I knew he was planning on going on a bender."

"That still doesn't mean it was him."

"I think it was," said Jacqueline. "I just know it was. And if so, it will be my fault. He wouldn't even have been there yesterday if he hadn't been trying to help me."

"You're jumping to conclusions," said Dot. "Did you get a description of this poor man?"

"Part of one – the age was right – and that bandstand ..."

"So he likes bandstands, I like bandstands, lots of people like bandstands. What about his hair? You couldn't mistake that streak in Magpie's hair?"

"I didn't see a picture – I only caught the end of the news bulletin. There was a number but I didn't take it down – I'm so stupid!"

"You've had a shock – you need to calm down. Now give me that jacket and go and change out of those wet clothes, and then come back down and I'll get you a brandy. We'll have it in my sitting room, it's comfortable there. In the meantime I'll ring 999 and see what I can find out."

"I can do that," said Jacqueline.

"No – I'll do it. You go and get out of those clothes. Let me help you with that jacket."

She thinks it was Magpie too, thought Jacqueline, and she doesn't want me overhearing. But why should it matter

382

so much? He's nothing to me, I hardly even know him.

She gave in and let herself be helped out of the dripping jacket, then she hurried upstairs to her room. The hood and umbrella had kept the worst of the rain from her hair but from the waist down her clothes were sodden. Even when she had stripped, her skin felt cold and damp. She would have welcomed a hot shower but it would have to wait. She towelled her body, pulled on clean underwear, her linen trousers and a T-shirt. She pulled on socks and dug her feet into her trainers, without unlacing them and then, because she still felt chilled, drew on his grey cardigan and hurried downstairs again.

"I'm in here," called Dot.

Jacqueline followed the sound of her voice to a room off the hall. Dot was sitting in a wingback armchair, a glass of brandy in one hand. On a table before her was her phone and a second glass of brandy.

"Well?" said Jacqeuline.

Dot leaned forward, picked up the second glass and held it out to Jacqueline. "They haven't identified him yet," she said. "They think it was someone who was sleeping rough. I had to give them my name and address, in case they want to question me further. And they took my number so they can call me, in case, well, in case it turns to be Magpie after all. Now will you sit down and drink that, please?" She took a gulp of her own drink.

Jacqueline sat down in the match of Dot's chair and took a sip of her brandy. The heat in her belly was a reminder of how chilled she still was and she took a more generous gulp.

"They wanted his real name," said Dot, "but, you know, I have no idea what it is. I told them about his hair,

383

of course, but I didn't know the colour of his eyes. Blue, I thought…"

"Grey," said Jacqueline. "Storm-cloud grey."

Dot looked at her. "I should have let you make the phone call. When we see him again, we'll ask him what his real name is."

Looking about her at the pleasant peaceful little room, Jacqueline thought that Dot was right – it was comfortable with its one long window and its walls lined with bookshelves.

"Here, have another brandy."

"I shouldn't," said Jacqueline. "The first one has gone to my head." But she held out her glass for a refill.

"You care about him, don't you?" said Dot.

"Do I care?" said Jacqueline. "I don't know. When my father died, one of the things my sister asked me to do was to let our Auntie Carol know what had happened. I didn't do it. Gayle was very angry with me – our Auntie Carol is my father's – was my father's only sibling. I said I was sorry, and I was sorry, but only because it gave Gayle a stick to beat me with."

"So you forgot," said Dot. "You had things on your mind."

"No, I didn't forget," said Jacqueline. "I just didn't think about Carol, how it would affect her – other people's lives have never seemed very real to me."

"Are you talking about a lack of empathy?" said Dot. "Because I think if that were the case, you wouldn't be here."

"You mean because I want to know what happened to my sister – to Lilly? That's true, but it's for myself I want to know. Both my parents are dead now and they died without knowing. So whatever I find out now comes too late for them, and still I want to know."

"You're too hard on yourself," said Dot.

"Am I?" Jacqueline looked up. "Tell me something, Dot – aren't you ever afraid that people, people like Marilyn and Magpie will ..." She hesitated.

"Take me for granted?" said Dot.

Make a fool of you, was what Jacqueline had been about to say, but she nodded agreement.

"I'm much more afraid of being pointless than of being made a fool of," said Dot, reading her mind.

"Why would you be pointless?"

"Rattling around in this place after Martin's death, it all felt pretty pointless. I wasn't stuck for money, Peter left Martin some money along with the house, and there was the life insurance. All I know is that the first time I took a chance on someone, and welcomed them into this house without asking if they had the money to pay for it, that was the first time my life made any sense again."

Jacqueline bowed her head. "You can't argue with that," she said. She put her glass down and got to her feet. "I think I'll go to bed, it's been a long day. If you hear anything, would you call me, please?"

"Of course, but it's not him," said Dot.

In spite of her exhaustion, it took Jacqueline a long time to get to sleep. The long day played itself out on the underside of her eyelids, and on the very verge of sleep she suddenly saw her mother's face as it had looked in the last days of her life, every peak and trough of the skull visible beneath the paper skin. She opened her eyes against the image, and lay there wide awake once more. Why, she wondered, with the loss of her father so fresh in her mind, was it to her mother's death her thoughts kept turning? Was she in some way comparing griefs? But the two had been quite different – at least with her mother there had been some warning.

"What does very little time mean?" Jacqueline had wanted to know. "How long exactly has she got – months, weeks …?"

"I'm afraid we are looking at days now."

Thirteen days; it had taken her thirteen days to die.

They comforted one another that she did not suffer, that stuffed with painkillers as she was she was more often asleep than awake. What suffering there was belonged to those who watched and waited, Gayle, her father, and sometimes Florence McNally. To Jacqueline it felt peculiarly like she was watching a stranger die. Except on the thirteenth day, between her dying and her being dead, there was a moment when her mother opened her eyes and looked directly into Jacqueline's eyes. Her expression was so compelling that the other two could not fail to see it too.

"I think she wants you, Jacqueline," said Gayle.

Her father touched her arm, urging her forward. "Go to your mammy, pet."

Jacqueline, her eyes locked into her mother's gaze, told herself that this was the moment when things long withheld might be whispered, and still she did not move. She imagined herself moving, she saw herself stepping forward until she stood by her mother's pillow. She saw herself bending low and then lower still until she was close enough that her lips almost brushed the translucent curve of her mother's earlobe. And while she was busy imagining, her mother, with one soundless outward breath, gave life and Jacqueline the slip forever.

In the yellow room, Jacqueline sighed aloud into the darkness.

Chapter 49

1976

It is a week to Christmas and the turkey is delivered to the door, still warm. Jacqueline looks away quickly, but not before she sees the dangling neck and the dead eyes.

Daddy comes up behind her. "I'll take that."

Last year Gayle helped him to pluck the turkey. Jacqueline remembers watching them spreading old newspapers over the kitchen table. And how Lilly came in while they were in the middle of plucking and held her nose and ran out of the room and they all laughed at her. And how Daddy chased Jacqueline around the house with a turkey claw. He knew how to pull on it so that the claw moved as though it were still attached to a live bird, and Jacqueline laughed and squealed all at the same time and almost made herself sick.

This year, Daddy takes the turkey from the man and hangs it from a nail high on the wall in the shed. Jacqueline sees it when she goes out to get coal for the fire. He plucks it himself without telling anyone.

Sometimes Jacqueline forgets, like on Christmas Eve when

she is watching Walt Disney's Million Dollar Duck *and it's so funny that she laughs out loud. When the film is over, she goes into the kitchen where Gayle is stirring the custard for the Christmas trifle. The sound the spoon makes when it scrapes the bottom of the saucepan makes Jacqueline's teeth hurt.*

Jacqueline's mother is sitting at the table with one hand wrapped around a cup. She is holding her other hand up close to her eyes, as if she is admiring the stones in her engagement ring, but Jacqueline does not think she is really seeing the ring at all.

The back door opens and Daddy comes in with a pile of logs stacked into a pyramid against his chest – he is holding them steady with his chin.

Jacqueline remembers something she has been meaning to tell him. "Daddy, I think I know now what the thing about the crow and the swan means."

Daddy stops and looks at her. "What are you talking about, love?"

When he speaks, the log at the top of the pyramid trembles. Daddy lowers his chin to steady it.

"You know, the crow and the swan, in Shakespeare? Do you not remember, Daddy?" *Jacqueline begins to recite:*

"The crow may bathe his cold black wings in mire
And unperceived fly with the –"

"Coal-black wings," *says Daddy,* "not cold."

Jacqueline smiles because Daddy has not forgotten Shakespeare. "I know what it means," *she says.* "It means that if someone does a lot of bad things and then they do one more bad thing, no-one notices ..."

Daddy starts walking again.

"... but if a person is good most of the time and hardly

388

ever does anything wrong, and they make just one mistake, then everyone notices, everyone sees ...”

When Daddy passes her, Jacqueline's hand brushes against his jacket and she can feel as well as smell the cold of the outdoors on him.

Jacqueline calls after him, “But that isn't really fair, Daddy, is it?”

Daddy does not answer and Gayle stops stirring and looks up from the pot. “Why are you quoting Shakespeare at him?” she says.

Jacqueline follows Daddy into the hall and watches him pushing the sitting-room door open with his foot. The door swings shut behind him. Jacqueline stays in the hall listening to the logs tumbling into the box beside the fire. When Daddy comes out, he walks past her without saying anything and goes upstairs.

When she goes back into the kitchen, Jacqueline's mother is still staring at her hand and Gayle is still stirring the custard.

It is Christmas Day, but hung upside down and gutted like the turkey.

Daddy has whiskey even before his breakfast and Jacqueline's mother will not get out of bed. She hides under the blankets with nothing showing above the bedclothes only the hair on the top of her head.

“It's not fair on the girls, Stella,” says Daddy. “We have to at least try to make an effort.”

He has another whiskey while he is watching them opening their presents and Jacqueline tries not to look at the ones still under the tree, the ones with Lilly's name on them.

Gayle makes Daddy open a present. He pulls out a soap on a rope and looks at it and says, "That's grand. I'll smell like a garden with that, love."

"We can do this, girls," says Daddy in the kitchen and they help him get the dinner ready.

Gayle makes the stuffing and Jacqueline whips the cream for the trifle.

Daddy says, "I'll go up and see if your mammy is getting dressed."

When he comes down his eyes are red.

Jacqueline looks at Gayle but Gayle just smiles and smiles.

At the dinner, Daddy says, "You did a smashing job, girls."

"Dark meat or light meat, Daddy?" says Gayle and when Daddy pokes at the food on his plate she says, "Eat your food, Daddy," and Jacqueline thinks she sounds just like their mother.

Daddy blinks at Gayle and tries to smile. He lifts his fork to his mouth and he chews and Jacqueline watches the tears streaming down his face.

In the afternoon, Daddy drinks wine, then port, then Guinness, then Jameson.

"Daddy, would you not go for a little sleep?" says Gayle.

Daddy says, "Ah, I'm sound as a trout here, pet."

Gayle puts on Top of the Pops *and she and Jacqueline watch Legs and Co doing a stupid dance and then Johnny Mathis sings "When a Child is Born".*

In the evening, Jacqueline's mother comes downstairs

wearing a blue cardigan buttoned up wrong. She says she will have a cup of tea and a piece of Christmas pudding but nothing else. They all watch The Morecambe and Wise Christmas Show *and when it is over Jacqueline's mother says she is going back to bed.*

Chapter 50

AFTERWARDS

Today is Lilly's anniversary – the thought came into Jacqueline's head before she even opened her eyes. Her second thought was: Magpie. She sat up, threw back the duvet, crossed to the window and drew the curtains. It was still raining heavily and the sea and the sky were an indistinguishable blur of grey. As she turned away from the gloom, she saw the envelope on the floor. It lay just inside the door as though it had been pushed under from the other side. Jacqueline picked it up and stared at her Christian name. It had been printed in careful capitals. Then she tore open the envelope and drew out a folded sheet of paper. Something drifted to the floor. She looked down at what appeared to be a photograph. It had fallen face down and had the curled appearance of something much fingered. When she had finished reading the brief note, she bent down and picked up the photograph and carried it across to the bed. She read what had been scrawled in pencil on the back, then she turned it over slowly.

For a long time she sat and stared at the two smiling faces. When she looked up she was aware for the first time of a chill in the yellow room. She dropped the photograph and the letter onto the bed and got to her feet again.

After she had showered and dressed and pulled on the old grey cardigan, she put on her jacket and picked up her bag. She was about to leave the room when she went back, picked up the note from the bed and stuffed it into the pocket of her jacket.

Despite the rain, the front door was open. Jacqueline stood for a moment and watched the dance of raindrops on the flagstone path. Then she went to the kitchen where Dot was cooking kippers and eggs.

Jimmy, who was sitting at the table swinging his legs and eating cereal, looked up and greeted her with, "Hello, Jacky Lean."

Dot spun round. "No news," she said, "and there's been nothing on the radio, or the internet. At least nothing more than we already know."

"Right," said Jacqueline. "Hello, Jimmy, I see you've got your glasses fixed." She pulled the note from her pocket and showed it to Dot. "I found this under my door – any idea where it came from?"

"It was on the doormat when I came down this morning," said Dot. "Is anything wrong, has something happened?"

"No, nothing's wrong, nothing's happened." Her fingers closed on the note and scrunched it into a ball which she shoved back into the cardigan pocket.

"You look a bit peaky," said Dot. "Will you have some proper breakfast?"

"No, thanks. I'm going to head down to Toby's and take a look around."

"I'd go with you," said Dot, "but someone –" she

nodded in Jimmy's direction, "forgot to come home again last night."

Jacqueline took Gayle's umbrella from the stand in the hall, but the wind almost whipped it from her hands as she hurried down the hill.

Toby's was even more jammed than usual and the smell of rain competed with the aroma of fish. The waitress who had served Jacqueline and Dot their lunch was working and when asked, said Magpie had not been in since the day before yesterday. Jacqueline left the café and headed for the promenade. She walked the length of it, putting her head in at every café and restaurant. Afterwards she carefully negotiated the slipway, and stood on the beach looking left and right. The sand felt fudgy underfoot but there was no-one on the beach except one man and his dog.

Jacqueline made her way back into the town but the bars were not yet open and there was no sign of Magpie in any of the cafés. She gave up, bought herself a bottle of water and started up the hill. The wind was in her face now and she folded away the umbrella before it took off and took her with it.

At the turn for Cliff Walk, she hesitated. She was wet through and sweating uncomfortably under the bulk of the wool cardigan and her rain jacket. Surely in this weather he wouldn't – or would he? She decided it was worth a try and set off on the steep climb, her body curved into the high wind.

Crossing the park, she spotted the huddled figure in the bandstand and knew with certainty that it was Magpie.

Climbing the steps, she stood and looked down on the blue-black hair, slick from the rain, and muttered involuntarily under her breath: "You absolute gobshite!"

"Who are you calling a gobshite?" Magpie lifted his head like a heavy thing, and his eyes opened a crack as he peered up at her.

"You're drunk," said Jacqueline.

Magpie dropped his head again. "You have marvellous powers of observation."

"Here, have some of this." Jacqueline hunkered down and held out the bottle of water.

Magpie studied it without moving then heaved himself to a sitting position and reached out to take it. His fingers brushed Jacqueline's – they felt cold and calloused.

"You're frozen," she said. "And do you know that people thought you were dead? A man's body was found in that bandstand where we ate the fish and chips yesterday."

"I have no people," said Magpie.

Jacqueline looked at him, slumped over the bottle. She opened her mouth then shut it again. He's hopeless, she thought, shipwrecked, washed up here, best leave him to it. She got to her feet and turned to go. Shoving her hands into the pocket of her jacket, her fingers touched the balled-up note. She pulled it out and turned back to Magpie.

"Did you leave this for me?"

Magpie looked up and stared at the crumpled paper blankly.

"It's a note from Dawn," said Jacqueline. "There was a photograph with it. I'm assuming you remember who Dawn is?"

Magpie gave her a look before nodding slowly. "She came back looking for you. She felt bad. I told her you'd already gone so she wrote that down and asked me to give it to you. She had a whole bunch of photos with her. She made me look at every last one of them – her brother as a kid, on his own, with her, standing on his bloody head ... and one of him the way he looks now."

"How does he look now?" asked Jacqueline.

"A lot of oily hair and a bit of a gut," said Magpie.

Jacqueline closed her eyes on an image of beautiful Luca run to fat. Opening them again she said, "Thank you for bringing the note to me – it was very good of you. I assume you know what's in it?"

Magpie nodded.

"Right," said Jacqueline. "Look, are you going to be okay?"

"Sound, not a bother on me," said Magpie.

Jacqueline sighed. "Do you want to know why I called you a gobshite just now? It was because, in spite of what you say, you actually do have people, even if you don't want them."

Magpie said nothing. He had taken the lid off the water bottle and was twiddling it between a finger and thumb.

"When was the last time you spoke to any of your family?" said Jacqueline. "Do they even know where you are, or if you're alive or dead? Your brother, you said you had a brother – don't you think he wonders where you are? And, for all you know, maybe your sister does too. What happened to you and your nephew and those men was an accident. People soften, they learn to forgive."

Magpie's head jerked up. "Is that so?"

He put the top back on the bottle and set it down on the wooden floor next to him. He patted his pockets, drew out his cigarettes and matches and lit up. "Who'd have thought it, Jacqueline? You still believe in happy endings."

Jacqueline thought about the contents of the note in her pocket. "Not for everyone," she said, "but I like to think it's possible." She looked out at the slanting rain. "Look, I know you like dossing in bandstands, but I'm wet and I'm hungry and I want to go home now. Only I can't go until you do." Home, she thought, I called it *home*. "So I'm staying here until you come with me. Now come on, Dot's there too, waiting to hear if you're alright, because like a fool she's been worrying about you too."

For a moment they held one another's gaze.

"You're a very bossy woman," said Magpie, "but anything for a quiet life. Just give me a minute till I smoke this."

Jacqueline waited.

When he had flung the butt away, he got slowly to his feet. She thought he looked supremely unstable so she gave him the umbrella to use as a walking stick and, side by side, her hands ready to steady him if he stumbled, they made their slow way back to Sea Holly Villa.

Dot Candy made much of Magpie, taking his sodden greatcoat and sending him upstairs to shower and change into dry clothes. While he was gone she started breakfast. Jacqueline hung her own jacket on a hook behind the back door, first slipping the note from the pocket into her bag. The kitchen filled with the smell of sausage and bacon. Jacqueline refused the offer of food and made herself some tea.

Magpie reappeared looking unlike himself in a too-tight check shirt and half-mast combat trousers that exposed a length of hairy calves. Jacqueline wondered if the clothes had belonged to Martin.

As Dot served him his food, she suddenly exclaimed, "Would you believe it, the rain has stopped."

She walked to the door and opened it to look out. Oscar streaked in past her, arched his back, rubbed his wet backside against Jacqueline's legs and mewed.

"Get out, Oscar!" said Dot. "You don't live here!"

"You don't really like cats, do you, Dot?" said Jacqueline.

"Not really," said Dot.

Jacqueline met Magpie's eye and he laughed out loud.

"What?" said Dot.

"Nothing," said Magpie and Jacqueline in perfect time.

Still smiling slightly, Jacqueline went to the sink and rinsed her cup. "I'm going upstairs to change out of these wet clothes," she said.

Once in her room, the first thing she did was to pull the note from her bag and read it again slowly:

I am sorry about your sister. I hope no harm came to her. But Luca does not know where she is now. He is happy and married to a girl he met in France. This is a picture of them on their wedding day.

Jacqueline picked up the photograph and read again what was written there:

Luca and Adela 16th June 1985.

She held the photograph up to the light and stared into the eyes laughing down at her. Luca looked a little older, twenty-four, twenty-five perhaps, but he was still beautiful then. The girl by his side was short enough so that she could rest her dark head on his shoulder. Her colouring was similar but nobody, thought Jacqueline, even from a distance, could mistake this girl for Lilly. She touched the stranger's face – a pretty girl, but the wrong girl. Jacqueline hoped she had been the right girl for Luca.

It was not until she was drying her hair that she thought about the wording of the note. She picked it up and sat on the bed and reread it. What had Dawn meant by Luca did not know where Lilly was *now* – why now? She tried to shake it off, told herself that she was reading something into nothing. She had come to a dead end and she simply had to accept it.

There was a knock at the door. "It's only me," said Dot.

Who else would it be, thought Jacqueline. "Come in, Dot."

Dot came in with a tray on which was a pot of tea, a plate of toast and a dish of honey. "I know you said you didn't want anything but I thought you might fancy having this in the privacy of your room." She put the tray down on the table and glanced at Jacqueline. "You look a bit down in the mouth. He's perfectly fine, you know. I sent him for a lie-down."

"Who?" said Jacqueline, her mind still on the photograph.

"Magpie." Dot sat down in the window seat and surveyed Jacqueline. "I thought you might be worrying about him, but clearly not."

"I'm sorry, I was thinking about something else. But, like you say, Magpie is fine."

"Then it was bad news after all." Dot gestured to the note in Jacqueline's lap. "Is it about your sister?"

"That's the problem. I thought it might have been, but it turns out not."

"I'm sorry, that must be disappointing," said Dot, "but I wouldn't give up. Missing people are found all the time, you know. Only the other day I saw on the news where a woman who had been missing for more than twenty years was found alive and well. She wasn't the first, and I'm sure she won't be the last."

"I don't think that's going to happen this time," said Jacqueline.

As Dot closed the door quietly behind her, Jacqueline picked up the note and read it once more. Looking up, she caught sight of herself in the mirror and thought about what Dot had just said.

"The last lost girl," she said quietly.

She wondered if it was Lilly she was thinking about or herself.

Someone was knocking at the door again. Jacqueline turned over onto her side on the bed and ignored it. The knocking sounded again, more insistently this time.

Oh, go away, Dot, thought Jacqueline, go away and leave me in peace.

"*What?*" she called out, not caring that she sounded impatient and rude.

"There's a couple of people here to see you," said Dot. "I've put them in my sitting room. Come down when you're ready."

Gayle and Eddie Sexton were sitting side by side on the small two-seater sofa. There was a tray on the table before them, a pot of tea and a plate of biscuits, but nothing looked as though it had been touched. Gayle's head was on Eddie's shoulder but she straightened up when Jacqueline came into the room. There was a paper tissue in her hand, as though she had just been crying or was just about to start.

Jacqueline looked from one to the other of them.

"It's not Alison, is it," she said, "or the baby?"

When Gayle shook her head, Jacqueline said, "Then what is this? Why are you here together?"

"We came to talk to you, Jacqueline," said Eddie.

"Really? I thought you'd told me all you had to tell,

Eddie?" Jacqueline wondered that her voice could sound so light when a cannonball seemed to have materialised in the pit of her stomach.

"He did," said Gayle. She shifted as though she were uncomfortable and moved to the edge of her seat. "I mean he told you all he could, but it's not that simple, Jacqueline."

"Why isn't it simple, Gayle?"

Gayle glanced at Eddie. "Because we haven't been honest with you, Jacqueline, none of us have." She pawed at the tissue in her hand. "But the time has come for the lies to stop. I realised that yesterday when you told me all that stuff about finding Luca's sister. It made me realise that you still thought there was some chance of finding Lilly. And that thing you told me about the radio – I had no idea you'd been blaming yourself like that all this time. I knew then that we couldn't let you go on like this, spending your life on some wild goose chase."

"Why is it a wild goose chase, Gayle?" said Jacqueline. Now her voice sounded to her as curiously toneless, as though no violent emotions were churning inside her, as though the world had not shifted on its axis.

"Because there are things you should have been told a long time ago, and I'm sorry you weren't. But it wasn't up to us then – there were other people to consider. And when I spoke to Eddie he agreed."

"Was it Eddie after all?" Jacqueline turned and looked at him. "Was it him?"

"No," said Gayle, her voice sounding weary, "it wasn't Eddie. Eddie did nothing."

"Then what? For God's sake what, Gayle? Tell me."

"That's why I've come here today," said Gayle. "To tell

401

you. And hard as this is going to be for me to tell, I know it will be even harder for you to hear. But, if you'll listen, I'm going to tell you now what happened to Lilly."

Chapter 51

1976

It is New Year's Eve. Jacqueline hates New Year's Eve, she has always hated it. "Christmas is for children," her mother used to say, "and New Year's Eve is for adults" and her and Daddy would get all dressed up and go to a dinner dance or something. Before Lilly was old enough to do it, a baby-sitter would come, Nanny before she died, Aunty Carol sometimes, or sometimes a girl from the town who always tried to give Jacqueline bull's-eyes to go to bed early, but Jacqueline did not like bull's-eyes.

This year Jacqueline doesn't think her mother even knows it is New Year's Eve, or if she does she doesn't care, because she spends the whole morning in bed. Daddy goes down the town as soon as he has his lunch and, standing at the window watching him go, Jacqueline notices something white under the evergreen bush. She thinks it might be snowdrops. She remembers reading somewhere that it is good luck to ring the bell of the first snowdrop you see in the New Year. It isn't quite the new year yet but Jacqueline thinks there is no harm in being early. She lets herself out of the house. It is a bright sunny day but very cold. She is right – there is a clump of snowdrops under the bush, as though they are sheltering from the cold wind. She gets down on her hunkers, reaches out and very gently rings the tiny white bell. She rings another one just for luck and makes a silent wish. It is the same wish she makes all the time now. "Please let Lilly come home."

In the evening, Daddy goes down the town again, Gayle watches Z-Cars *in the sitting room and their mother falls asleep on the sofa in her dressing gown. Jacqueline sneaks out of the sitting room and goes upstairs to her parents' room. It doesn't take her long to find Lilly's radio. It has been pushed into a corner at the bottom of the wardrobe, behind her mother's summer shoes and sandals. Jacqueline takes it and goes to sit on her parents' bed. She turns the radio over in her hands and wonders if anyone has switched it on since the morning she played it in the field, waiting for Lilly to come home. She pulls up the aerial as far as it will go, then turns one of the silver dials until the buzzing noises stop. A man's voice says,* "And now on this New Year's Eve we'll continue with the hits of 1976. This one is from the Electric Light Orchestra – 'It's a Livin' Thing'."

Chapter 52

AFTERWARDS

Lilly came back. Seven years after she disappeared, she came back. It was the fifteenth of November 1983. Gayle answered a knock on the door of her and Eddie's home in London to find Lilly standing there. At first Gayle had not known who she was – some woman selling something, she had supposed. The person on her doorstep had not looked like Lilly, not Lilly the way Gayle remembered her, fifteen going on sixteen. This was a twenty-three-year-old woman, heavily pregnant and with a bad perm. And then the stranger said Gayle's name and burst into tears and in that moment Gayle had known that a miracle was taking place and had held out her arms to her lost sister.

The baby was Luca's. Lilly had been with him almost the whole time since she ran away on the night of the Festival Queen Dance. She had never, she told Gayle, planned it that way; it had just sort of happened. And it probably wouldn't have happened at all if her sandal hadn't broken. She was almost home when that lace thing on her shoe snapped and she had to take it off. Then a long-distance lorry driver came along and stopped. He offered her a lift and so she took it. He told her he was headed for the ferry, on his way to England, and so Lilly got the idea, why not go with him? Just for a laugh, she said, and to teach Luca a lesson for being so unkind to her about winning the Festival Queen Competition. She knew he'd be going back to his hometown at the end of the summer so why not go there and wait for him? What an adventure it had seemed, what a laugh, and she even had her prize money, one hundred whole pounds tucked inside her shoulder bag. So that's what she did. Instead of going home she asked the driver to take her with him on the ferry. They were halfway to the ferry port when it crossed Lilly's mind that she might need a passport. The driver told her you didn't need a passport to travel between Ireland and England. He said there was a chance she might be asked for some sort of identification, but she would be unlucky if so. He went back and forth all the time and was hardly ever asked. Lilly was lucky. And then, once she was dropped off on the other side, it was easy. She made her way to Coldhope-on-Sea and checked into a bed and breakfast. For a while she lived off the money from her prize and just enjoyed herself. She had, she told Gayle, a great time. She even found the fair Luca's grandfather ran although she didn't dare go inside the fairground. She was too afraid the English police might be looking out for her, but it was, she said, a thrill just to stand at a distance looking at the big wheel and imagining Luca's face when he came back and found her waiting for him. And when her money had almost run out, she got a job working in a café on the seafront. That was a bit of pain, she said, but she got good tips and so she put up with it and waited for Luca.

He came back in the middle of August. At first he was

angry with her and he was different too, she said, different to the way she remembered him. Quieter and sort of mad with the world. He told her to go home and let her family and the police know she was safe but Lilly said no, it was too late for that now. She didn't want to go home, she didn't want to go back to school and do her stupid Leaving Cert. She was having an adventure, she liked being free and she didn't want it to end and, if Luca wouldn't let her stay with him, she'd go off on her own. She told him so and in the end she talked him round, because Luca loved her and she loved him and they wanted to be together. At first they managed to keep the fact that they were together a secret from Luca's grandfather but he found out somehow and he and Luca had a big row. Luca's grandfather thought Lilly was trouble and would only ever bring trouble to Luca too. He told Luca to get rid of her. So they decided to move away to a town in another part of England where Luca could get work with another fair. At first they went to Wales and stayed there for a while. When Luca heard about work in a fair in France, they decided to move there. They stayed in France for almost six years, moving around from town to town and fair to fair. At first Lilly loved it and found it exciting but over time she began to grow tired of the life. By the time she was twenty-two, she'd had enough and wanted to settle down in a proper house and live a normal life.

About the same time, Luca's grandfather sent a message to him that Lilly's father had come to Coldhope-on-Sea and was sniffing around the fair there. Someone had told him that Lilly had been seen in France with Luca and he wanted to know where Luca was now. Hearing this only made Lilly more unsettled and she and Luca had a huge row. And so she ran away again. It was to teach Luca another lesson, she told Gayle. It had worked well in 1976 so why not now? It was summertime, so she went to the coast and spent a couple of weeks there getting some sun and just enjoying herself. By the time she realised she was pregnant and went back to tell Luca, the fair had moved on and Luca with it. She tracked down the fair but Luca had moved on again, leaving no message for her. She had no idea what to do but, thinking he might have gone back to England, she decided to do the same.

As soon as she got back, she went to Luca's grandfather, but Ned claimed not to know where Luca was. He not only refused to take Lilly's word for it that the baby was Luca's, but also insulted her and pretty much told her to get lost. When Lilly said she had nowhere to go and almost no money, he told her that wasn't his problem. He said if she had nowhere else to go she should go home to Ireland. Upset, Lilly had run off, but just as she was leaving the fairground a girl came running after her. She said she was Luca's sister, Dawn, and she gave Lilly a piece of paper with a name and address written on it – Gayle's name and address which their father had left with Luca's grandfather as a contact in case he heard any news about Luca or Lilly. Dawn told Lilly that her grandfather had thrown it away but she had picked it up and kept it just in case.

And so, Lilly had gone to find Gayle.

At first, it had felt to Gayle like some sort of dream or a miracle: Lilly back, alive and safe and about to have a baby. She had wanted to ring home straightaway and let her parents know – but Lilly wouldn't hear of it. She wanted, she said, to do it in her own time, and in her own way. And she promised she would. Eddie, when Gayle told him this, was furious. He said it was cruel to leave Frank and Stella in ignorance for one more second, that it wasn't about what Lilly wanted anymore – she'd lost that right after what she'd done. Gayle had known he was right but she was terrified. She was afraid that if she went against her, Lilly might disappear again and they would never see her or the baby again. So she talked Eddie round and made him promise not to tell her parents until Lilly was ready. But she felt terrible about it, so much so that she stopped ringing them as much as usual. It felt so wrong to her, talking to them about ordinary things when all the time Lilly was in the next room. She tried to talk Lilly round but, each time she tried, Lilly just got so upset that Gayle let it be, trusting that in time Lilly would do the right thing.

Then Lilly refused to let Gayle take her to the hospital to have her pre-natal check-ups. Gayle wanted to register Lilly at the hospital where she herself worked but Lilly said she didn't want to be in the system. Why couldn't Gayle take care of her? She was a midwife after all, wasn't she? Gayle explained that she was still a trainee midwife but Lilly said that, as Gayle was a qualified nurse, that was just as good. When Gayle tried to force the issue Lilly got so distressed that Gayle, worried for Lilly's health as well as the baby's, gave in and let her have her own way again. Lilly didn't seem well to Gayle. She was sure her sister had not been taking care of herself. And she told herself that when the time came, she would take Lilly to the hospital to have the baby. She was certain Lilly would want that then too, but it didn't work out that way.

Lilly went into labour early and Gayle wasn't even in the house at the time. She had gone out to the shops to buy stuff for the baby and came back just in time to help deliver it. It was all very straightforward though – Lilly was fine and the baby was perfectly healthy. Gayle tried again to talk Lilly into going to the hospital but she refused, so Gayle gave in and cared for them both at home. But Gayle worried. Her sister didn't seem mentally stable – all these irrational notions didn't seem normal. And when, after the birth, Lilly became very quiet, more than quiet, Gayle worried that she might be suffering from post-natal depression. Then one day she found her holding the baby while in floods of tears. When Gayle asked what was wrong, Lilly said, "I want to go home. I want to go home and I want Mam."

And once she had made that decision, Lilly wanted to do it right away. Gayle did her best to calm her down and managed to talk her into waiting another week until the baby was stronger.

To keep Lilly happy, she booked the ferry. She wanted to ring her father and let him know they were coming, but Lilly wouldn't hear of it. She wanted to go back on her own terms, without anyone knowing about it. And once again, against her better judgement, Gayle let her have her own way. So what if Lilly was nervous about the whole thing? What mattered was that she was going home at last. Next to that, nothing else mattered. And she comforted herself with the thought of all the joy they were about to unleash on her mother and her father.

And so, without warning – no letter, no phone call – they caught the ferry back to Ireland. Lilly had a driver's license. When Gayle had tried to question her about it, Lilly said "Don't ask" so Gayle had not asked.

It was a very cold night in February, the 5th of February to be exact, when they knocked on the door of the house in Blackberry Lane. Their father had gone to the pub for a few pints and their mother had opened the door a crack and peered out. Gayle had been holding Lilly's baby and, at the expression in her mother's eyes, she had thought: she thinks it's mine.

Then Lilly stepped into the light and said, "Mam."

Their mother had known who she was straight away, not mistaking her as Gayle had for a stranger selling something. She had known it was Lilly and Lilly without another word had thrown herself into her mother's arms and started to cry. Gayle, watching them, had noticed that her mother did not react the way she had expected or imagined. Instead she was very quiet, and Gayle could see from her face that she was in shock. She had been expecting shock, but stupidly had thought it would be happy shock – that their mother would be so beside herself to have Lilly home again that nothing else would matter, that she'd be so joyful that everything else would take second place. And there was joy, and tears and disbelief and all the things Gayle had expected – but there was something else too, something she had not allowed for. There was anger.

It was alright to begin with. When the first shock was over, their mother did cry and said over and over again that it was like a miracle. She kept touching Lilly's hair – the perm had grown out and her natural hair looked as lovely as it did when she was fifteen.

But then Lilly tried to get her mother to notice the baby, to take her from Gayle and hold her. She said, "Mam, have you seen my baby? Look at my beautiful baby."

But her mother only had eyes for Lilly. She barely looked at the baby. And the baby must have sensed something in the room because she started to cry and she wouldn't stop. She just kept on and on crying at the top of her voice and Gayle said something to Eddie about trying the song he'd sung to her to calm her down on Christmas Eve. That was when Gayle noticed the expression on her mother's face: it was as if, she had thought, someone had just slapped her. She started asking questions, she wanted times and dates, she wanted to know everything that had happened. But it wasn't until she found out how long Lilly had been with Gayle and Eddie that Gayle realised how angry her mother really was.

Lilly didn't seem to notice anything – she just kept going on about the baby, asking Gayle to let their mother have a turn at holding her. But Gayle could see that their mother did not want to hold her. Instead she had got up and started moving around the room, fussing about the flowers. She kept going on about the early tulips, how she should have put them in the hall instead of on the table on the landing. Then she said something about how Granny's vase would look much better up there.

"Mam, leave it," Gayle had told her. "What does that matter at a time like this?"

But her mother ignored her and rushed off. Lilly followed her into the hall so Eddie and Gayle went too. Their mother was standing with Granny's vase in her hands; it was full of pink and white blossoms with long woody stems, so long they almost obscured her face. She was blathering on about them, about how she'd just swap the magnolia with the tulips, put the magnolia on the landing and the tulips in the hall where they'd get the light. She went up the stairs with the vase in her hands.

Gayle, distressed and with a terrible sense that everything was going wrong, had shouted at her: "*Never mind the flowers! Forget the blasted flowers!"*

Then Lilly said, "Yes, Mam, Gayle is right – forget the flowers. What do the flowers matter? Aren't you happy that I've come home?"

Their mother was on the landing. She had her back to them and had been just about to put the vase down on the table there. When Lilly spoke, it seemed to Gayle that their mother froze. Still with her back to them, she stood there like some sort of statue with the vase in her hands. Then Lilly slipped up the stairs behind her, fast and light on her feet, and stood on the step just below her mother.

Their mother turned around slowly, and Gayle saw the look of rage on her face before she heard the words she spoke.

"Don't you dare," she said. "Don't you dare come into my home after all these years and tell me what matters."

Her hands came down and the vase struck Lilly on the right side of her head. There was a terrible sickening thump and Gayle watched as Lilly rocked on her heels. Her hand shot out and Gayle thought she was going to grab the banister and save herself but she didn't. She fell in a sort of awful somersault. Afterwards, Eddie told Gayle that it wouldn't have made any difference. Even if Lilly had managed to clutch the banister, it wasn't the fall that killed her, it was the blow to the right temple. He knew right away that Lilly was dead although Gayle could not believe it, especially as there wasn't even any blood, just a mark on the side of her head. Her mother came down the stairs and Gayle later thought that she too knew that Lilly was dead because she just knelt down and lifted Lilly's head into her lap and she didn't try to wake Lilly up – she just held her.

That was when their father came home. Gayle could

remember hearing the key in the lock and how she had turned and stared at the door and waited for it to open. It took so long it was like slow motion. He must, she thought, have had a good few jars because he was stumbling a bit when he came in.

The baby stopped crying when she saw him and just stared at him. Her father saw Gayle first and he smiled and said something about her not telling them she was coming home. He said, "Jacqueline is away in Belfast for the weekend with some college thing – she'll be sorry to have missed you."

Then he spotted Eddie and Gayle thought: he still blames him for what happened to Lilly. It was so ridiculous that she almost laughed out loud. Then Eddie stood up from where he was kneeling and that was when her father saw Lilly, her head cradled in her mother's lap.

That was when her mother said, "She's come home, Frank. Lilly's come home."

Long afterwards, when she'd had nothing but time to process it, when every tiny detail of Gayle's story had been etched so deeply into her brain that it seemed almost a memory of her own, Jacqueline would remember that first telling of what happened the night Lilly died as one long unbroken narrative. Perhaps, she reasoned, it was because, as she listened to Gayle, in some mysterious way she had managed to split herself in two. There was the half of her, the self which knew instinctively, which had always known that this story could never end well. And that self wanted to rush ahead to the last page, to put herself out of her misery, to know the worst once and for all and be done with it.

But there was the other half too, which listened to every word her sister spoke, and it was this self that interjected, forcing Gayle to stop, to explain, to repeat, to clarify or justify. And it was this self who demanded to know why and when and how, who uttered the small cries of disbelief, of denial and finally of horror and grief and rage.

Jacqueline, who had been sitting down when Gayle began speaking, found herself, as her sister fell silent, standing looking out of the window. She had no memory of having moved.

Without turning she said, "How could all of this be kept from me? All this time, how could you do that to me? Why wasn't I told?"

She turned and faced her sister.

"There is no excuse, Jacqueline," said Gayle. "You should have been told, I know you should. But Dad said no. He said the only good thing out of that awful night was that you hadn't been there and he made us promise you would never know. You were only eighteen years old. He said it was too much, on top of all that had happened, to expect you to carry that secret too and it was better if you never knew."

Jacqueline spun round. "How could he believe that, how could he think it was better, living my life not knowing if my sister was alive or dead?"

"He just did," said Gayle.

"Then you should have made him see that he was wrong."

"We tried, we really did."

"We did," said Eddie. "I thought Frank was wrong too and I told him so that night. I always thought you should have been told, but he wouldn't have it. He said it was better if things went on as they were, rather than you finding out that Lilly was dead and it was your mother who killed her."

Gayle's hand went to her mouth. "Don't say that, Eddie, don't say *killed* – it was an accident. Mam didn't mean to hurt Lilly. Lilly fell, she just fell ..."

"It wasn't the fall that killed her," said Eddie. "It was the blow from the –"

"Oh, shut up, Eddie!" Gayle jumped to her feet. "Stop playing doctor!"

In some chamber of her mind Jacqueline registered it as the first time she had ever heard Gayle being unkind to him. She turned to Eddie.

"So you don't believe it was an accident?" she said.

Eddie shook his head. "It all happened so quickly ... I think your mother, the balance of her mind disturbed by an enormous shock –"

"*Did she mean to kill her?*" screamed Jacqueline.

"She meant to hit her," said Eddie quietly. "That's not the same as meaning to kill her."

"She didn't mean to kill her!" Gayle's voice was a wail. "Alright, she hit her, but only in a moment of anger. She never meant to kill her. I will never believe that – *never, never, never!* You don't know, Jacqueline. You weren't there and you'll probably never be able to see it this way but you are so lucky. It was the worst day of my life, of all our lives and you weren't there."

"*But I should have been told!*" Jacqueline screamed again. "*I had a right to know!*"

"Please, please, will you both stop shouting," said Eddie. "People will hear." He got up and walked to the door and stared at it as though he expected it to burst open, then he went back to his seat again. "Come on, Gayle," he said, "come and sit down and you too, Jacqueline. This isn't doing any good, all this shouting and yelling at each other."

Gayle went back to her seat but Jacqueline stayed where she was.

"And there was more to it than your right to know, Jacqueline," said Eddie. "Of course you had a right to know and of course you should have been told. No-one is saying anything else. But, right then, at the time it happened, your father made a decision, for right or wrong, that the less people who knew about it the better."

Jacqueline stared at him as the meaning of what he had said hit home. "You mean that I couldn't be relied on to keep quiet, don't you? That I couldn't be relied upon to go along with a cover-up?"

As neither Gayle nor Eddie spoke, Jacqueline, her legs suddenly feeling as though they might no longer support her, crossed the room quickly and sank into her chair.

"What did they do with her?" she said. "Where is she? Where's Lilly?"

Chapter 53

AFTERWARDS

Gayle looked at Eddie, her eyes stricken, all anger forgotten.

Eddie sat forward in his seat. "This is for me to tell. Gayle had no part in it. It was just your father and me." He entwined his fingers and dropped them between his knees. "There's no easy way to say this, Jacqueline, so I'm just going to say it. We took her out to sea – we got my grandfather's boat and we took her far out to sea ..." As Jacqueline made an inarticulate sound, he said plaintively, "He didn't know what else to do, and it had to be somewhere. I couldn't let Frank do it on his own so we did it together. And even then it almost killed him. He tried to make it right, he even said a prayer for Lilly and –"

Jacqueline stumbled for the door.

"Where are you going?" Gayle wailed.

Jacqueline felt her almost on her heels and stabbed her hands blindly behind her back. "Don't follow me, Gayle, just leave me alone. I need to be alone."

Before the door slammed behind her, she heard Eddie telling Gayle to let her go.

The garden was a blaze of sunshine, and everything silver on the bicycle shimmered as she approached. She yanked it toward her and used her sleeve to wipe the saddle, still damp from the rain. She told herself not to think. All that mattered was to put as much distance as possible between herself and those two people. If she'd had a car she would have been miles away already. She turned right outside the house and, climbing on, cycled in the opposite direction from the town. The saddle was too low and the handlebars needed adjusting. She had to lean forward more than was comfortable and her back would surely complain later. An image flashed before her eyes of Lilly's body lying in the hall of the house on Blackberry Lane and she wobbled and dismounted. Concentrate, she told herself, concentrate on the physical act of cycling. She got back up and forced herself to think only of her feet pushing against the pedals, the pull of the muscles in her calves and abdomen, her body strong and able for the task in hand. She almost lost her nerve as she approached the crest of the hill and saw the steep road unrolled before her, then she propelled herself forward and took her feet from the pedals. As she coasted down the hill, the wind roared in her ears, the hedges and the road beneath the wheels blurred. The sea, glimpsed from above, was a long band of dancing silver light. Halfway down the hill she opened her mouth and a sound issued from her, a long primeval roar of grief and helpless rage. The wind picked it up and whistled it back to her like a high desolate keening wail that did not end until the bicycle, running out of hill, came gradually and naturally to a standstill.

At the foot of the hill she turned left. She followed a narrow and rutted lane with a glimpse of the sea at its end.

On either side the hedges were bursting with enormous lush and creamy elderflower blossoms and spotted with yellow dog daisy buttons that winked in the sunlight as she passed. Jacqueline became aware of the sun on her head and arms and the tightness around her eyes where the tears had dried on her skin. As she cycled alongside the sea, the movement of the bicycle combined with the quality of the light on the water felt almost hypnotic. The thought came to her that this could be any road, any place – more than that, it could be any time, any year of her life, any day, any moment – it was as though she were cycling out of time.

They were sitting where she had left them, side by side on the sofa, no longer holding hands. A plate of sandwiches had replaced the biscuits and Eddie had one in his hands. He put it down quickly as Jacqueline came in and wiped at his lips.

Gayle, who had been slumped to one side in her seat, got up and came toward her. "Jacqueline, we've been so worried. Are you alright?"

Eddie said dryly, "I don't imagine she is, love."

"I'm fine," said Jacqueline.

"But where have you been – you haven't, you didn't ...?"

"Go to the nearest police station?" said Jacqueline. "No, I didn't and I haven't. For God's sake, Gayle, sit down – you look like crap."

Gayle sat down again. "What are you going to do, Jacqueline?"

"Do? Do about what? What can I possibly do that will change a single thing?"

"I understand that you must be shocked," said Gayle, "and angry and confused. I wouldn't blame you if you wanted to scream at me right now. And I'll understand if you can never forgive me."

"You understand nothing, Gayle," said Jacqueline. She thought about the sound that had issued involuntarily from her throat as she had coasted downhill on the bicycle, that scream of rage that the wind had turned to a keening wail. "Now, will you explain to me again why nobody told me?"

"We should have," said Gayle, "there's no excuse. I wanted to and I told Dad I was going to. And I came close to telling you so many times, that first year. And Mam wanted to tell you too. That day when she was dying, I think she was trying to tell you then. I know Dad thought she was, and in a way I really hoped she would."

"I thought she was asking *me* to tell the truth before it was too late," said Jacqueline.

"The truth about what?" said Gayle.

"About what I did that day, how I blackmailed Lilly, how it was my fault she went out at all that night." She came and sat down in the armchair opposite them. "But it was the other way around – Mam was trying to tell me what *she'd* done."

"She wanted to tell everyone," said Gayle, "but Dad made her see she couldn't."

"But after she was gone," said Jacqueline, "why didn't you tell me then?"

"Dad said it was too late to tell you then, that it would only steal your peace."

"My peace? What bloody peace? I haven't had a moment's peace since that summer."

"I know that," said Gayle, "but it wasn't that simple, Jacqueline. The longer we kept the secret, the harder it was to ever tell the truth. Because there wasn't just one lie

421

anymore, there was a whole bunch of lies. And I know this is going to sound crazy to you, Jacqueline, but as time went on I think I almost made myself believe that it had never happened, that she never had come back."

Jacqueline thought of something. "The anniversary," she said. "Every year you came home for it, every year we marked that day in July. And all the time everyone but me knew it was nothing, just another day. And every February the day that really counted just came and went and I had no idea of what it meant."

"I know and I'm so sorry!" Gayle began to sob and would not stop.

Eventually Eddie pulled her against his chest and held her there.

Jacqueline got up and went back to the window. "Tell me, Gayle," she said, "did you ever ask Lilly how she could do that to us, stay away so long and leave us in agony like that?"

"I did ask her, I did. I asked her how she could have left us for all those years not knowing if she was alive or dead. She just said she'd never intended it that way, that at first it had just seemed like a big adventure. And then she was having so much fun with Luca that she just couldn't bear to go back and be made to live like a child again. She thought about sending a postcard, just to let us know she was alive but she never got around to doing it. Then as time went on, it was just too hard to tell the truth, it had all gone too far. She said she thought about us a lot, Mam and Dad and me and you. She asked about you – 'Little Jacks' she called you."

Jacqueline leaned in and rested her forehead against the window glass. A thrush was pecking at the ground. Its speckled breast reminded her suddenly of Regina Quinn's blouse.

She said, "And what about her baby? I've been waiting for you to tell me, Gayle, or perhaps you think that's something I shouldn't know either? What happened to Lilly's baby?"

When she turned, Gayle had straightened up and was holding Eddie's hands once more.

"You're wrong, Jacqueline," said Gayle. "That, above all else, I've wanted to tell you a million times. Alison – Alison is Lilly's baby."

"Alison," Jacqueline repeated, "Alison is Lilly's baby." She wondered if she was still a little hysterical, if she would be a little hysterical for the rest of her life. "Of course she is. She has his eyes." She thought, I saw it but I didn't see it: Luca's smile, that blue-black hair. Alison is Luca's child. Lilly is dead but her child is alive and she is Alison. Alison whom she had known but never really known. Alison, not Gayle's at all, but Lilly's, a living part of Lilly. If she had known, if she had only known …

"We had to keep her," said Gayle. "She was Lilly's child. What else could we do?" It was not a question but a flat statement of fact.

"Lilly's child and you kept that from me," said Jacqueline, "Everyone knew it and I didn't."

"Everyone didn't know it," said Gayle. "Only the people who were there that night."

"What about Alison?" said Jacqueline. "Does she know it?"

Gayle shook her head. "How could we tell her? We couldn't, not without telling her everything and we couldn't do that. You must see that. Alison knows nothing – as far as she's concerned she's ours." The expression in her eyes darkened to what Jacqueline recognised as defiance. "She *is* ours."

"So how exactly did you make that work?" Jacqueline returned to her chair. She was surprised to discover an almost academic interest in the answer. "Isn't that sort of thing against the law or something?"

"I'll tell you how we made it work," Eddie said. "We broke the law and committed fraud and we lied and we kept on lying. That's how we made it work."

"We registered Alison as a home birth," said Gayle. "You have forty-two days to do that. And you know, technically that wasn't a lie, because Alison had actually been born in our house, so technically –"

"So technically you only lied about who her parents were," said Jacqueline. Even to her own ears she sounded bitter and Gayle flinched visibly.

"There was nothing else we could do," she said. "Except hand her over to the authorities, and we were never going to do that. Right from the beginning there was no doubt in our minds that we were going to do whatever it took to keep her. But even then we could never relax. I kept expecting a knock on the door. I kept expecting that someone would find out we'd falsified the records, or that Mam would say something to someone or that Luca would turn up. Of course, he didn't even know about the baby but Ned Early did – and in any case he could have come looking for Lilly. Poor Luca, I used to feel so guilty about him. I knew he didn't even know about the baby and Lilly did say they'd been fighting like cats and dogs the last two years or so. But still ..."

"Luca got married in June 1985," said Jacqueline. "I guess he gave up searching for her a lot sooner than I did."

"I'm sorry," said Gayle. "I know you must feel angry and hurt and –"

"Is that how I sound?" said Jacqueline. "Because I have no idea how I feel. But at least one thing makes sense now: just why it was all so odd about Alison."

"We had to make up that story about there being complications with the pregnancy," said Gayle. "I knew you thought there was something weird going on."

"I thought it was because of Eddie," said Jacqueline. "That you were afraid to let Mam and Dad know you were having a baby with him." She looked at Eddie. "It wasn't about you at all, it was never about you."

Eddie shook his head. "It was a bit," he said, "at first. Frank was never going to be happy about Gayle and me. And after what happened, after we did what we had to do that night, he could hardly bear to look at me. To be honest, I felt much the same way. And Stella, well ..." He looked at Gayle mournfully.

"And with Alison it was so difficult," said Gayle. "That first time I brought her home, no wonder you picked up on the atmosphere, Jacqueline. She was Lilly's child, all they had of her and they loved her. Dad needed to see her, he wanted her in the house, he wanted to see more of her. But it was too much for Mam. I don't think she could ever see Alison without being reminded of what she had done – not that she was ever likely to forget."

"That's why she left Dad and went to live up the road with Florence," said Jacqueline. "She couldn't stay in the house where she'd killed Lilly."

"It was an accident." Gayle's expression was suddenly mulish. "I will never believe it was anything but a terrible accident. And it would never have happened if I hadn't let myself be bullied by Lilly into turning up on the doorstep like that without any warning. And I can tell you this much, Dad never blamed Mam, not really. But you're right, Jacqueline, Mam always blamed herself. No matter how much I tried to make her see that what happened was an accident, the result of a moment of anger, she never could let herself off the hook. She said it was because of the anger that she blamed herself. She hadn't meant to kill Lilly, of course she hadn't, but she had wanted to hurt her, that was what she told me. She said that the moment she realised Lilly had been with Eddie and me all that time, had had the baby with us and spent Christmas, it made her feel so angry she could hardly breathe. Those months when Lilly was with us and didn't bother to let her and Dad know she was back and safe – Mam said it was those months more than all the years that had gone before that made her snap. It was the selfishness, she said, the thoughtlessness. She had wanted to shake Lilly, to slap her, and that was why she'd jumped up and started fussing with the flowers. That was why she could never forgive herself for that spur of the moment action with the vase on the stairs, because it had already been in her heart to strike Lilly. And that was why she wanted to turn herself in to the police and would have, if it hadn't been for Dad – and there was Alison of course. To stop her confessing he had to keep on reminding her of what that would do to Alison, what would happen to her if the truth ever came out. He said they might even have taken her away from us, and that Mam owed it to Lilly to make sure that would never happen. And so, Mam saw that and she kept quiet – not for herself but for Lilly and for Alison. But it ate at her from the inside."

"What will you do?" said Gayle again.

Eddie had left them alone and Dot had come in quietly with yet another fresh pot of tea and a plate, this time of cake. Bending down to transfer dishes from the tray to the table, Dot had fixed her gaze with firm intent on Jacqueline.

"Are you alright?" she said, her voice somehow managing to be both gentle and fierce at the same time.

And, meeting Dot's eyes Jacqueline saw in them unadulterated concern and it came to her: she really cares about me. If I asked her to run Gayle and Eddie from the house this minute, she would do it. A small shock of gratitude made her reach out and touch the back of Dot's hand.

"I'm okay, Dot, but thank you."

Now Jacqueline looked around her. In a thoughtless moment, she had called this place home. She had even admitted to herself that she liked the house, with its shabby but dignified senescence, that it did, in some odd way seem more like home than the house in Donegal. And now it was the place where she had finally heard and had to face the truth. Did that, she wondered, mean it was forever tainted with that tale of violence and secrets and hidden grief? She thought about Dot, endlessly supplying them with unwanted food, about her see-through hair and her sad smiles, her open-ended offer of hospitality and this most recent show of protectiveness.

"I'll probably just hang on here a bit," Jacqueline said to Gayle when Dot left. "I know that's not what you meant by 'What will you do?', but I quite literally mean that I'm not going to do anything." As Gayle buried her face in her hanky, Jacqueline added, "But I would like to see Alison soon, and her baby. For God's sake, when are they going to give the child a name? We can't keep on calling her Alison's baby for evermore."

Gayle looked up. "She wants to call her Lilly. She texted me about it earlier today. It was all her own idea, nobody said anything to her. But I told her I didn't know how you'd feel about it, and Alison said she would only do it if it was okay with us? What should I tell her, Jacqueline?"

"Tell her I think it's a lovely idea," said Jacqueline.

"You can tell her yourself," said Gayle, "when you see her. But, Jacqueline, you won't … you'd never say anything to Alison, would you? You'd never tell her the truth?"

Jacqueline looked at the strained, tired face of her sister, the fearful eyes watching her intently.

"As far as I'm concerned," she said, "the truth is that Lilly disappeared in 1976 and I never saw her again."

Chapter 54

NOW

"Where are you, Jacqueline?"

"I'm in the orchard."

"Are you alright? Is it done?"

"It's done, the *For Sale* sign is in the garden. I'm alright, Gayle, don't worry about me. How are you and how are Roy and Eddie?"

"Roy is fine, still surgically attached to his phone. And Eddie is great, completely obsessed with his first grandchild."

Lilly's grandchild, thought Jacqueline. "And Alison?"

"She's doing great, Jacqueline, she's wonderful with the baby. I don't think it's going to work out with the boyfriend, so she's on her own."

"She's not on her own," said Jacqueline. "She has you and Eddie and Roy and me."

"Thank you, Jacqueline. I'm not worried about her – she's a strong girl and she's always known her own mind. Just like …"

"Just like you," said Jacqueline. "And how is – how is Lilly?"

For a moment there was a silence on the line, then Gayle said, "I know, it's strange, isn't it, saying her name without …" Her voice trailed into silence.

"Without it making you want to weep," said Jacqueline.

"Something like that," said Gayle. "Oh Jacqueline, she's a peach, Lilly is an absolute peach. You won't believe how much she's changed since you saw her."

Jacqueline thought about the little creature with the crinkled face, impossibly tiny, impossibly pink – about the power she wielded, not just over hearts but the power to separate past from present.

She said, "I'd like to see her again soon, and Alison too, if that's okay. I'll be over again as soon as the house is sold."

"Of course it's okay, I can't wait," said Gayle. "Alison will be delighted too – she's awfully fond of you, Jacqueline. Are you still going back to Sea Holly Villa?"

"That's the plan."

"Has it something to do with the bird man?"

"Magpie?" Jacqueline hesitated. "I don't know…"

She glanced over her shoulder to where Magpie was standing waiting for her under the oldest apple tree.

"Maybe it has something to do with him, if he behaves himself, if he changes some of his ways like he says he will. But maybe it has to do with other people too …"

For some reason, Jimmy Small – she could never call him Schmalz – and his picnic came into her head, and she thought about the day the taxi had driven her away from Sea Holly Villa. They had stood in the doorway hand in hand, Dot and Jimmy, waving until the car passed beyond the gates. And looking back, Jacqueline had remembered something her mother used to say, when at the end of some

430

day-trip or outing, she, Lilly and Gayle started moaning that they did not want to go home. "Look back and you'll come back," she used to say.

"But what will you do there, Jacqueline?"

"I have no idea what I'll do there, Gayle. Try to get on with living, I suppose – one promise at a time."

When she hung up, Jacqueline, moving slowly under the trees toward Magpie, thought about her father. She thought about the despair that moved him the day he took up his hatchet and hacked away the branches. She knew in her heart that those trees had no memory of that despair nor of her and Lilly here that last day. She felt nothing but the lingering sadness that would never leave her. She hoped that they were somewhere, her father, her mother and Lilly. And the thought came to her, that if they were anywhere at all, it was probably right here with her now in the orchard. That if they knew anything now they knew everything and, that being the case, surely what needed healing had been healed, what needed forgetting had been forgotten and what needed forgiving had been forgiven.

The thought brought her peace and, as she reached Magpie, she was smiling.

Chapter 55

1976

Jacqueline is pretending to read, but all the time she is watching Lilly. Closer and closer she comes, until Jacqueline can see her toenails: they are painted and glitter in the sunlight like little bright-pink helmets. Lilly is wearing her new platform sandals – espadrilles, she calls them, not sandals. They have laces that criss-cross Lilly's brown legs, and the heels are chunky and high as two half-pounds of butter. Her dress is light blue and crinkly and it sways above Jacqueline's head and, when Lilly stoops, there is the scent of newly washed hair – lemons among the apple trees.

"Here, take it, you little sneak," says Lilly, "and you better not tell if you know what's good for you."

Jacqueline reaches up and takes the radio. It is still warm from the place under Lilly's arm, "I won't tell," she says.

"And don't you dare break it either."

"I won't break it, I'll take really good care of it." Jacqueline slides the silver aerial up as far as it will go.

"Right, well, make sure you do," says Lilly. "The coast

is clear now so I'm going. Daddy's gone to work and Mam's gone to Florence McNally's."

"Where's Gayle?" asks Jacqueline.

"How do I know where Gayle is? Now, do you know what you're supposed to say?"

Jacqueline closes her eyes and recites like a poem learned by heart, "Lilly had to go baby-sitting and they said they'll be late."

"No, that's wrong. You have to say that I'm baby-sitting for the Kellys."

"Why?"

"Because the Kellys are always late and I often stay over, that's why, and they haven't got a phone, so no one can check. Have you not paid attention to anything I told you?"

"I did, but I forgot. Why can't I just say that Sexy Sexton called for you?"

"Because he's a spiteful creep, that's why, and he told me the next time he sees Daddy he's going to tell him we broke up and why. And he's going to tell Daddy that he didn't take me to the dance tonight. So make sure you get it right, okay?"

"Okay," says Jacqueline. "Keep your hair on."

"You better not forget!" says Lilly.

"I won't forget," says Jacqueline.

She has her head bent over the radio and is busy twirling the silver dials. She is trying to find Radio Caroline and when she looks up again, Lilly has gone.

Her sister forever lost in her own story, and she has not even watched her go.

Finis

ALSO BY PUBLISHED BY

POOLBEG
CRIMS●N

THEY ALL FALL DOWN

CAT HOGAN

Fiction with an edge

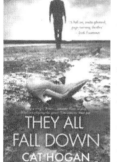

Ring-a-ring o' Roses . . . How far would you go?

Jen Harper likes to play it safe. She is settling into life on the outskirts of a sleepy fishing village with her little boy, Danny. Life by the sea – just how she wanted it.

When she meets Andy, she feels the time has come to put her baggage and the scars of the past behind her. Then she is introduced to Scott, Andy's best friend, and is stung by his obvious disdain for her. Why is Scott so protective of his best friend? What is the dark secret that threatens all of them?

In her attempt to find answers, Jen must confront her demons and push her relationships to their limits. By digging up the past, she puts Danny and herself in danger. Will she succeed in uncovering the truth before they all fall down?

Raw and energetic, They All Fall Down *is a fast-paced and addictive novel exploring the depths of flawed human nature, the thin line between love and obsession and the destructive nature of addiction.*

'A full on, multi-plotted, page-turning thriller' *– Irish Examiner*

ISBN 978-178199-8649

ALSO BY PUBLISHED BY

POOLBEG
CRIMS●N

THE OTHER SIDE OF THE WALL

ANDREA MARA

Fiction with an edge

When Sylvia looks out her bedroom window at night and sees a child face down in the pond next door, she races into her neighbour's garden. But the pond is empty, and no-one is answering the door.

Wondering if night feeds and sleep deprivation are getting to her, she hurriedly retreats. Besides, the fact that a local child has gone missing must be preying on her mind. Then, a week later, she hears the sound of a man crying through her bedroom wall.

The man living next door, Sam, has recently moved in. His wife and children are away for the summer and he joins them at weekends. Sylvia finds him friendly and helpful, yet she becomes increasingly uneasy about him.

Then Sylvia's little daughter wakes one night, screaming that there's a man in her room. This is followed by a series of bizarre disturbances in the house.

Sylvia's husband insists it's all in her mind, but she is certain it's not – there's something very wrong on the other side of the wall.

'A twisting tale of evil lurking behind a suburban hall door'
– *Sinéad Crowley, author of* One Bad Turn

ISBN 978-178199-8328

If you enjoyed this book from
Poolbeg why not visit our website:

www.poolbeg.com

and get another book delivered straight
to your home or to a friend's home.

All books despatched within 24 hours.

POOLBEG

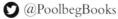
CRIMS●N

Why not join our mailing list at
www.poolbeg.com and get some
fantastic offers, competitions,
author interviews and social media exclusives.

f www.facebook.com/poolbeg
🐦 @PoolbegBooks

55328630R00250

Made in the USA
Middletown, DE
09 December 2017